CURSED LEGACY

HOUSE OF KANE BOOK ONE

Philip M Jones

Firesong Arts, LLC
P.O. Box 2164
Hillsboro, OR 97123

ISBN: 0-9998128-1-5
ISBN-13: 978-0-9998128-1-5

Published by Firesong Arts, LLC
Changing the World, One Word at a Time
https://www.firesongarts.com/
Editing by Sandra Johnson
Cover Illustration Copyright © 2018 by MatYan

I would like to dedicate the book to
my late mother, Dian Daisy Tanton Jones.

Special thank you to those who supported and inspired me in various ways on my journey to write this book: Kathy Empson, Anna Pedroso, Melinda Smith, Sarah Blake, Trish Garcia-Mulligan, Hollie Christiancy, Lizzy DesChane, Andrea Spinelli, Sandra Johnson, Jaye Kovach, Nathan Spinelli, Kim Brackett, Marvin Jones, Peggy Jones, Sommer Moon, Kerry Beckett, and Elyette Weinstein.

This list could easily be ten times as long...
I guess it's a good thing I've written more books.

PROLOGUE

Abigail Kane drove her car into the garage of an old beautifully restored Georgian Colonial home her parents had purchased when she was three years old. She arrived an hour later than expected. She had sent a text warning she would be late, but her mother hadn't responded. Abby knew her parents were home; their vehicles were both parked in the garage. It wasn't like her mom to ignore a text message.

She collected her purse and book bag before glancing at her phone one more time to see if a message came in. She feared her mother's silent treatment was a sign she was in trouble. Abby threw open the door. "Mom!" she yelled, hoping to end the guilt trip. Abby didn't mean to be late, losing track of time while hanging out with friends was an easy mistake for a girl who was almost seventeen.

Abby moved through the kitchen into the living room. "Dad?" she called out. She set her book bag on the foyer table next to a vase full of white lilies, pausing for a moment to enjoy the fragrance.

Where are they? Abby wondered. It was a beautiful spring day. Even the rain took a break to enjoy the sunshine; a rarity for Seattle. *Maybe they went for a walk,* she thought as she glanced at her phone. She checked the refrigerator door; no note.

She climbed the stairs to her room, when she reached the top she could see the door to her father's office slightly ajar at the end of the hallway. *He always kept this room locked,* she thought. It was where he kept all the important documents in a safe.

"Mom? Dad?" she called out again. No answer. Abby began walking down the long hallway towards the office. On the floor she could see red paint spilled on the carpet. *Mom's going to be pissed.* Coldness filled Abby as she approached.

That isn't paint…

Abby's heart began to pound in her chest a sickness filled her stomach. She started to tremble. "Mom? Dad?" her voice weak. There was no answer.

She took a deep breath and pushed the door open. Gently resting on the blood-stained carpet were two figures. Abby let out a scream. Hot tears ran down her cheeks before she fully realized what she was seeing.

She stared, frozen by the horror lying before her. It couldn't be true.

Abby blinked as though she could somehow erase what she saw. It didn't work. The two people she loved most in the world… her parents lay lifeless at her feet.

Abby approached her mother. She shook her softly. "Mom?" she said, her voice trembling. No response. "Mom!" Her father was wearing the same business suit he had worn earlier that day. It was charcoal grey; now it looked black as night. Glancing around frantically, Abby noticed for the first time something on the wall behind her father's desk.

She moved closer to get a better look at the strange symbol. It was a pentagram surrounding something in the center. *An eye?* Abby's heart began to race. It wasn't drawn on the wall, it was painted. In blood.

A sense of panic broke through the shock. Though she did not know the mark, she recognized the occult significance. Was this a warning? Or a message? She was sure this was no random act. Whoever had drawn the symbol had purposefully targeted two of the strongest witches in the Kane family. But… why?

Abby reached for the phone in her pocket as her tears broke through the shock again. It wasn't the police she called, she knew she should have, but she needed to do this first.

The phone rang once when a woman's voice answered. "Ms. Kane's office, how may I help you?"

Abby tried to steady her voice. "This is Abby, I need to speak with Vivian." She could barely speak. She walked over to the window as she waited to be connected. She could not bear the sight of her dead parents.

She stared out the window. It was a normal day. The neighbor mowed his lawn, a woman two houses down was gardening, and three kids rode their bikes up the street. Abby couldn't understand how life could be so normal on the other side of the window and so horrific where she stood.

"Abigail? Is something wrong?" her grandmother answered, her voice filled with worry.

"It's mom and dad. They're… dead," Abby said. She was growing numb.

"What?" Her grandmother's voice broke.

"You should come to the house, I have to call the police." Abby ended the call without waiting for her grandmother's response.

In a small corner of her brain, it occurred to Abby the person responsible for killing her parents might still be in the house. Even through her shock she realized if they were still here they could have already killed her if they had wanted. She hadn't entered the house quietly.

Abby walked past her dead parents. She couldn't stop staring. Memories rushed through her head… vacations and holidays, celebrations and birthdays. She began rocking trying to sooth herself but all she could do was play through the memories of her parents and how there would be no new ones.

This would be her last memory of them.

There was nothing left. Abby leaned against the door frame and slid to the floor, staring at the ruins of her childhood until her grandmother arrived.

The next few hours were a blur. At some point she heard Vivian screaming in horror as she ran into the room past Abby. The police had arrived, and she was ushered down the stairs. She still couldn't think. The scene upstairs in the study played in her mind, frozen like a still frame photo. They asked her a question. Blood. So much blood. The blanket around her shoulders slipped. *When did they put that on me?* she wondered before her thoughts were again consumed with blood. She answered questions, so many questions, but she couldn't remember what answers she gave. None of this could be real.

Her uncle Sebastian holding her as she stared into the distance. Her grandmother pacing and barking orders at the police. Only fragments of memories remained. She thought maybe she heard someone mention taking her to the hospital for shock, but she stayed at her grandmother's side. The flashing lights coming through the window, familiar faces from the neighborhood lined up behind the police tape surrounding her home, her uncle's arm around her shoulders; she was empty.

They were dead.

CHAPTER ONE

Abby sleepily walked into the small kitchenette of the hotel suite she was sharing with her Uncle. Sebastian Whitlock was a distinguished-looking gentleman in his mid-thirties; clean-cut with reddish brown hair and blue eyes. When Abby walked in, he was on his cell phone. *It sounds like he's on the phone with Rodger,* she thought. Sebastian gave her a welcoming smile as she took a seat across from him.

He was wearing a dark brown business suit and black tie. He looked nice, though Abby couldn't imagine why he would bother to dress for what amounted to the witch's version of witness protection. They had been hiding in hotel after hotel for nearly two months. There weren't a lot of people around the see his clothes.

"Uncle Rodger?" Abby asked Sebastian as he turned his phone off. He set it next to the newspaper, lost in thought. She could tell he missed his husband. *They haven't seen one another for over a month,* she thought. Abby had never been in a relationship, let alone married, but she wondered Sebastian being away from Rodger was anything like her missing home.

"He sends his best. He's still settling things at home. He wanted me to wish you a Happy Birthday!" Sebastian said, his weary smile didn't falter, but Abby was sure the celebratory tone in his voice was fake.

"Thanks, I hadn't realized that was today," Abby replied, sounding as empty as she felt.

Sebastian's smile melted away into a more solemn expression. "It's July sixteenth," he said. "You're seventeen now. One year away from being an adult. What do you want for your birthday?"

Abby felt dispassionate at the idea of being an adult. *How could it be any different?* Nothing seemed to stir her at all. She sighed and sat at the table, glancing at the food her uncle had ordered from room service without really looking at it. "Nobody can give me what I want for my birthday," Abby said, surprised by the bitterness in her own voice. "I just want to sleep."

"Good luck with that," Sebastian said with a knowing tone. Something about the way he said it made Abby think he meant more than just her insomnia.

"What do you mean?" Abby asked.

"Vivian and Fiona will be here shortly." Sebastian nodded. He was clearly trying to cheer her up. Abby gave him a pathetic smile for the effort. She appreciated that he tried. "Come on," he nudged. "At least have some toast and coffee."

Abby dutifully took a bite from the toast and poured herself a cup of coffee, which she nursed slowly. "How much time do I have before they get here?" she asked.

Fiona should be done with her dialysis in about an hour. I think they were planning to arrive shortly after," Sebastian said. "Just enough time for you to shower and make yourself presentable," he gently urged.

Abby knew he was kindly telling her she'd let herself go. It wasn't that she didn't know, Abby just didn't care anymore. How could she? She took another sip of coffee absentmindedly. There was no hoping it would help with the emotional hangover she'd lived with over the last two months. It hit her stomach just like everything else did, settling into a permanent knot in her middle. There would be no relief for her.

Sebastian stood and started making phone calls. It sounded like business. He'd been away from the office all this time and no doubt neglected his responsibilities. Abby felt guilty for keeping him away. She knew he was doing it for her benefit, but it wouldn't change the fact that they were dead. She tried to understand why they had been hiding away in this hotel, and many others, for over two months, while her parent's killer was still on the loose. She knew they all wanted to protect her, but why they thought he was planning to come after her, she had no idea. She wasn't anything special.

Abby strolled over to the large windows, situated fifty stories in the sky and peered out over Seattle and Elliott Bay. It was a breath-taking view. To her right, the Space Needle jetted into the sky, a distinctive monument in the Seattle skyline. To her left were the high-rises of the cities bustling business district. It had always been her home, and yet they were just images now; landmarks, not places. She didn't have a home anymore.

"I'm going to take a shower," Abby said between her uncle's phone calls.

"Good idea," Sebastian encouraged. As much as she hated to admit he was right, a hot shower always made her feel a bit better.

Abby disappeared into her bathroom and disrobed before working the shower knobs until she manipulated the temperature to just below scalding. She stepped in and let the water run over her head. The streaming water brought her into herself a bit and helped to wake her up somewhat. Her body was still alive, at least.

She quickly toweled off and dried her thick red hair, a process that always devoured a good portion of her day when and if she even bothered. Abby slipped into a light silk summer dress and let her hair hang loose. *They're lucky I've even bothered to clean up,* Abby thought as she went back into her bedroom.

She sat at her desk where her laptop had laid untouched for days. Abby opened the computer and waited a moment for it to power on. Her email inbox was filled with over four hundred messages from friends. When she went on her social media sites, the messages were just as overwhelming. She lethargically closed the computer and decided now wasn't the time to face the questions and condolences. She knew they meant well, but it was too much. She still couldn't face everything that happened. Each night was plagued with terrible dreams, and each day offered little relief from the horror of her new reality.

There was a polite knock. "They're here," Sebastian said through the door.

"I'll be out in a minute," Abby said as she gazed out the window wrapping herself in numbness. Now wasn't the time to let her grief get the better of her. *Better to not feel anything,* she thought. For now, apathy was her only ally against the pain, and she wore it like armor.

Abby stood and made her way into the living room. Standing in the middle of the brightly-colored hotel room was her grandmother, Vivian Kane. She was a woman whose aged beauty made her true age somewhat ambiguous, though Abby suspected she was well into her sixties if not older. Vivian wore a white dress suit with a strand of diamonds hovering over her silk blouse. Her alabaster white hair was styled up and full, making her look like a painting come to life. Aunt Fiona stood next to Abby's grandmother, a study in contrasts. She was far more reserved, wearing an understated black dress with a light summer jacket and three strands of pearls around her neck. Fiona's greying hair was pulled back into a tight bun, and still held remnants of its blond origins. Abby thought she looked rather severe and cold next to Vivian's glowing brightness.

Abby approached and gave her grandmother and great-aunt a polite hug. "Hello," was all she could bring herself to say.

"Hello darling," Vivian said before taking a seat on a long cream colored couch with dark blue throw pillows.

"It is nice seeing you again Abigail," Fiona said kindly before sitting next to her sister.

"Did you come to wish her a happy birthday?" Sebastian asked sitting next to Abby on the love seat.

Based on Vivian's initial reaction, Abby could tell her grandmother had forgotten. In truth Abby, didn't much care; she had forgotten, too. Vivian recovered from her absentmindedness with a smile. "Happy birthday darling," Vivian said. "We'll make all this up to you soon."

"Thank you," Abby said unable to think of anything better to say.

"Honestly Vivian, I thought that was why you were coming over," Sebastian said somewhat surprised.

"I'm afraid not," Vivian said looking to her sister.

"There's been a sighting," Fiona said, more to Sebastian than to Abby. "Cousin Gisela has seen one of the Thanos here in town."

"Thanos?" Abby questioned, it was the first time she felt curious about anything in months.

"The Thanos, have a long unpleasant history with the Kane side of your family," Sebastian explained looking at Vivian with suspicion. "Do you think they're responsible for Evan and Jessica?"

Abby winced slightly upon hearing her parent's names. It still seemed so unreal, and yet the nightmare hadn't ended. *So it must be real,* she reminded herself.

"We don't have proof," Fiona said.

"But we're certain," Vivian interjected impatiently.

"You know who killed them?" Abby asked her voice shaking.

"No, not exactly who, but we're getting close to finding out," Vivian offered a reassuring smile. "It's only a matter of time."

"What now?" Sebastian asked. "I want some payback."

"You needn't worry Sebastian," Vivian gave him a wicked smile. "Whoever killed your sister and my son will suffer like no other," her voice trailed off into a growl.

"What's important right now is keeping our family safe," Fiona reminded, gesturing towards Abby.

"Yes," Sebastian agreed.

"Until we get a handle on this situation, I'm going to send her away for her own good," Vivian glanced at Abby.

Abby followed the conversation, but was content to let them talk without her input.

"What do you mean send her away?" Sebastian asked with irritable suspicion.

"Believe me Sebastian, I have every confidence in you, however no one, not any one of us are safe here. They have been watching us, they know where we are and where we go," Vivian explained. "The murders occurred nearly an hour before Abigail arrived home. And at her own admission she was late. Am I correct?" she said, turning to Abby.

Abby thought for a moment. "Yes," she admitted, trying hard not to dwell on her memories of that day.

"If you had come home on time that afternoon…" Vivian trailed off, her voice strained. She stopped and visibly composed herself. Turning to face her granddaughter full on, she said, "You're all I have left Abigail. I can't lose you, too."

Abby could feel the pangs of grief encroaching on her thoughts. She swallowed her emotions and took a deep breath, invoking the strength to stay in control of the flood of tears threatening to break.

"Where should we go?" Sebastian asked.

"We aren't going anywhere, Sebastian," Vivian said, rebounding from the momentary break in her composure. "We have a rival coven to deal with. I'm sending Abigail to stay with a dear friend of mine who owes me a favor."

"Vivian, we should stick together as a family," Fiona protested. "My daughter, Margot is like a second mother to Abby, and Madison grew up with Abby, they are practically sisters. Abby should go into hiding with them."

"I agree with Fiona. We can't send Abby off with some stranger. She needs us. We need each other right now," Sebastian said.

"I don't want to cluster our family into one large group. If they are discovered, we stand to lose too many. If Abigail is their primary target, it would serve us well to keep her far out of their reach. If you don't expect this, neither will they." Vivian explained.

"I don't like this Vivian," Sebastian said. "She's my niece and I don't like the idea of shipping her away without any family around."

"It's not as if I'm eager to sequester her away from the rest of us," Vivian said raising her voice. "At the moment, I'm interested in making certain my granddaughter remains alive."

Abby noticed Aunt Fiona was watching her. "Abigail is seventeen today. She's by no means an adult but she certainly isn't a little girl anymore," Fiona observed. "Perhaps she should have a say in all of this."

Vivian looked at her sister with uncertainty and then looked to Abby. She didn't know how to digest all this new information. *Rival covens? Send me away? My parents...* "If these Thanos people are after me, I don't want to put anyone in danger," Abby said. "I don't think I could live with myself if anything happened to my cousins, Margot or Madison. They're the closest family I have left. Aside from you." She added weakly.

"It's settled then," Vivian said.

"Where are you sending her?" Sebastian insisted. Abby could see her uncle's cheeks and forehead turning red. *He's getting angry,* she noticed.

"To a very exclusive boarding school in Oxfordshire, called Armitage Hall," Vivian said. "A dear friend of mine, Valerie Grace, is the deputy headmistress. She is a highly competent witch and well equipped to provide Abigail with guidance and protection. Besides, it will only be for one year, where she can complete her education."

"Are you certain one year is enough?" Sebastian asked.

"I can hardly call myself a Kane if I cannot handle a single Thanos within a year." Vivian, sniffed in disdain. "Besides, I intend for us to have this matter dealt with in short order." She insisted.

Sebastian looked to Abby with uncertainty. "Abby, are you sure about this? You don't have to go, if you don't want to," he asked, looking for some reassurance.

Abby did her best to call up some semblance of confidence for her response. Instead she took a deep breath and nodded her head in agreement. The gesture did little to put her uncle at ease. "Very well," Sebastian said shaking his head in defeat.

Fiona stood. Abby noticed the bruises on the older woman's arms from her dialysis treatments. "I'll help you pack dear," she said softly, motioning towards the bedroom. *Aunt Fiona is so nice today.* Abby thought. She had always considered her great aunt to be cold and distant. Her helpful gesture seemed a bit strange.

"Right now? She has to go right now?" Sebastian let into Vivian.

Abby followed her great aunt into the bedroom. Fiona closed the door behind them, shutting out the argument brewing between Sebastian and Vivian. Abby could hear her grandmother and uncle arguing through the wall.

"Do you know Valerie Grace, the woman grandmother is shipping me off to stay with?" Abby asked.

"I met her once," Fiona said as she opened the luggage on the bed, as Abby began collecting her clothing from the drawers. "She seemed nice enough. I don't see any reason you wouldn't get along."

"What did grandmother do for her anyway? It seems like a pretty big favor," Abby asked curiously.

"I'm not certain, but I was under the impression Ms. Grace had a problem with an unfaithful lover. I suspect your grandmother helped her... deal with the problem," Fiona speculated as she folded several shirts and placed them neatly in the suit case.

"How do you suppose..." Abby started, curious in spite of herself.

"You know Vivian as well as I do," Fiona said cutting Abby off, absently. "There are few people in this world who can weave a curse as well as my sister."

"Oh," Abby said. She had heard stories, of course, but Abby was still so new to the world of spells and curses, it still seemed like fairy tales. Some curses were truly terrible, and the idea of using her magic to do anything horrible to another person made Abby sick. It was easy to forget her grandmother's reputation. She knew it was a talent that all the Kanes had, but in truth, it was a part of her family she didn't like thinking about very often.

The arguing in the next room stopped suddenly, and a suspicious silence settled upon the suite. Fiona listened carefully. Abby could feel a coldness moving through the air. Something was wrong.

Abby felt it just a moment before Fiona put up her hand to silence her, cutting off anything Abby might have said. The elder woman made her way to the door and cracked it open slightly. Abby came up from behind, and peered out over Fiona's head. She could see her grandmother and uncle standing in the living room, silently staring at the main entrance of the suite.

An eerie fog seeped in through the narrow gap beneath the door from the main hallway. There was a hint of green to the strange mist as it moved across the floor, crawling towards them. It was accompanied by a terrible smell, like rotting meat. Abby did her best to blind herself to the sickening stench.

Vivian shared a glance with Fiona who stepped quietly into the room. Abby followed her great aunt and watched the haze creeping over the marble tiles towards the single step into the sunken living room. She watched as the fog rolled onto the carpet like a waterfall. The smell became nearly unbearable.

Fiona stood next to Vivian as Abby approached Sebastian, taking her uncle's arm with uncertainty. Sebastian wrapped his arm protectively around Abby's shoulder. Her heart was pounding in her chest.

They're here for me, Abby thought. The last two months she never imagined she would care. She had fantasized a million times of facing death and accepting it with open arms. Now that death was literally at her doorstep, she found herself feeling afraid. Perhaps death wasn't as welcome as she had thought.

There was a brief pause and Fiona stepped forward and crossed her arms, making a strange symbol with her fingers. Fiona looked towards the ceiling and called out, "Manifestus Corporius!" she pointed her finger at the sickly green fog.

A thin beam of light came from the tip of Fiona's finger, pressing against the otherworldly mist. Abby could feel her heart leap into her throat as she watched the fog swirling and billowing into the form of a man. A face began to break through the green mist, coalescing into a man nearly six feet tall with dark olive skin and black curly hair. The last remnants of the fog evaporated around him.

His face was covered with a black bristly beard his eyes looked like hollow wells of darkness. He was dressed simply in black jeans and t-shirt, but there was a lingering menace to his appearance. There was a leather belt wrapped around his waist with a large knife holstered at his side. Abby was terrified. His soulless eyes bore into her as if they would devour her if she looked at them for too long.

"Hyperion Thanos," Vivian growled under her breath as the man took a physical form.

"You know him?" Sebastian asked as he postured himself, ready to cast a spell.

"We've met," Vivian said with disgust.

"Kane scum!" Hyperion yelled in heavily-accented English. He spit on the carpet at Vivian's feet. Sebastian pushed Abby behind him, putting himself between her and the Thanos witch.

With unprecedented speed Hyperion pulled the knife from the holster at his waist and held it in front of him. "Salisarius Begetum!" he yelled, the knife flung itself at Vivian. As it moved towards her it looked as though the knife shattered like glass and ricocheted away from Vivian falling to the floor in fractured pieces.

"You're going to have to do much better than that, Thanos," Vivian spat his name like a taunting curse, an imperious smile on her face. "I've seen all your family's tricks. Surely you've come up with something new by now."

The young man growled in frustration and looked over Vivian's shoulder at Abby. An evil grin crawled across his face.

"Vivian, we really shouldn't toy with him. The Thanos are dangerous," Fiona warned.

"He isn't the one who killed my son," Vivian said watching Hyperion carefully. "I can tell. Evan would have dealt with this one easily."

Hyperion reached up and pulled a leather band from around his wrist. It broke and a single glass bead fell to the floor. He then looked up and smiled. "The others are coming," he growled a menacing grin on his face.

Green mist began billowing into the room from the hallway once again. Both Vivian and Fiona began backing away.

"Get her out of here. I want her on a plane tonight!" Vivian barked.

Fiona began concentrating and twirling her hands together. "Invocitus Tempesta!" she yelled as she clapped her hands together. A strong wind flew through the hotel suite knocking over several potted plants and stirring loose paper into the air. A small tempest formed at Fiona's feat and moved towards the door pulling the green mist into the formidable twister.

"Grab your bag," Sebastian said. Abby didn't waste a moment and lunged towards her bedroom door. Just as she made it through, a blast of black energy slammed against the wall near her head. The wooden door sizzled where the black energy struck. She could hear ghostly moaning all around her, and another chill ran down her back.

Abby glanced back to see her grandmother making a hand gesture and pointing the palm of her hand at Hyperion Thanos. Flames erupted where he was standing. In a matter of seconds, he was little more than a pile of ash on the carpet.

Abby grabbed her phone and purse off the nightstand before collecting her luggage. As she turned to join her family she saw a ghostly figure standing in the doorway. There was a grey glow to the translucent man, standing there with sunken eyes and rotting teeth. He began approaching

Abby. She backed away until she stumbled and fell backwards onto her bed. The apparition pounded on top of her. Abby screamed. His ghostly hands wrapped around her throat. She couldn't feel his hands, but she still couldn't breathe. Within seconds Abby found herself fighting for air.

She tried to push him away, but her hands made no contact. It was as though he wasn't there. She fought for the air her lungs needed, but there was no breath. Ghostly figures swarmed over her, maniacally cheering her demise.

"Kill her… Kill her… Kill her…" Disembodied voices chanted in a chilling cacophony.

Abby's face burned. She was starting to feel faint. She knew, with certainty, this was it. She was going to die, just as her parents had. These last two months of insufferable grief would be for nothing, as she met the same fate as her parents. At least the pain would come to an end. At least she could sleep.

No! NO! Abby screamed in her head, unable to choke out the words. *I don't want to die. Please!* Suddenly the choking stopped. A rush of air filled her lungs. Abby inhaled between raking coughs, trying to come back from the brink of losing consciousness. She glanced up to see her grandmother standing in the doorway whispering some incantation under her breath. The apparitions were frenzied. They flew above her, crying out as though they were in pain. Abby knew Vivian was doing something to them, but she had no way to know what was happening. Everything was happening so fast. Her head was spinning.

As she watched, the spirits began to disappear as though they were evaporating. Vivian abruptly turned and fled back into the living room. Abby wasted no time. She collected her things and followed.

Sebastian stood near one of the large windows. Abby saw his lips move, but she didn't hear any words. As she watched, one of the windows buckled and turned to sand, crumbling to the floor. A burst of air came in from outside.

Fiona continued to concentrate, turning towards the missing window. The tempest in which she had captured the green mist began moving towards the gaping hole. Within moments she maneuvered it outside and released the spell. The tempest disappeared; the green fog hovering in the sky.

"It's about to move back in," Abby said as she noticed the green fog inching its way towards the open window.

"I don't' think so," Vivian growled. She repeated the spell her sister had used only moments before. "Manifestus Corporius!" Vivian said pointing her finger at the green cloud. A beam of light struck the fog, and the miasma began to take shape once more. This time, there were three different people manifesting within the mass of smoke. They became whole just where Fiona and Vivian had put them; fifty stories high, above Seattle's inner harbor. Their bodies dropped from the sky as gravity did its work.

Abby rushed to the window and looked down. She could barely see anything. Within moments she could tell there was a commotion on the street below.

"Take her now, get her out of town tonight. I'll make arrangements for her things to be sent ahead," Vivian said.

"We'll stay behind and make certain our tracks here are covered," Fiona reassured.

Abby rushed up to her grandmother and gave her a hug. "Be careful," she said and then gave her Grandaunt Fiona a hug. "Watch my grandmother for me."

"Of course, dear," Fiona cracked a reassuring smile.

"Come on Abby," Sebastian encouraged. "We'll be out of town on the next flight to anywhere but here."

"I'll call once arrangements have been made at the school," Vivian said giving Abby a peck on the cheek. "Thank you for being brave darling."

Abby fled through the door towards the elevator. "Now then," she heard Vivian's menacing growl, "lets clean up, shall we?"

CHAPTER TWO

Abby put her book away when the seat belt light turned on. She couldn't remember a thing she had read, but she knew if she appeared to be doing normal things people around her felt more comfortable. The passenger next to her hadn't said a word the entire nine-hour flight, which came as some relief to Abby, who was not interested in meaningless conversations. She stared at her reflection in the window. Her long red hair was pulled back in the same simple ponytail she had been wearing for the last four months. She saw rings under her eyes; the result of many sleepless nights. Her skin was almost translucent. For the first time in months, Abby really looked at herself. She felt like a ghost and was beginning to look like one.

The attack at the hotel felt like a dream; a continuation of a nightmare she had been living ever since coming home that day. She was beginning to feel like she was waking from a deep sleep after several all-nighters in a row. Sebastian told her things would work out, and her grandmother was working on solutions. All she could do was wait, and trust them. In the meantime, here she was, on a plane about to land in a foreign country to hide from a threat she barely thought could be real. Again.

She and Sebastian had flown all over the world, hopping from one remote hotel destination to another making sure the Thanos had lost their trail. For two months Abby woke, not knowing if today were the day those ghostly hands would find her throat once more. She shuddered, remembering how close she had come to death.

She shook off the phantasm. Now wasn't the time to dwell in the past.

The plane landed, and Abby collected her carry on. Her luggage had been sent ahead so she could travel lightly. She was grateful when the call came from Vivian, saying the arrangements had been made; Abby was tired of running. She thanked the staff as she got off the plane and made her way down the terminal to customs. It was four in the morning in London, and Abby imagined the woman her grandmother had arranged to pick her up would be displeased at having to wake so early, but it was the first flight they could get.

Much to Abby's relief, the line for immigration was incredibly short at this early hour. The man behind the counter only passively glanced at her passport. "How long are you staying?" he asked with disinterest.

"For the school term," she answered, her voice hoarse. She cleared her throat in case he asked more questions; instead he stamped her passport and waved her on. Abby continued down many long corridors

11

and hallways. She had heard that Heathrow Airport was immense, but the reality was more than she imagined. It was like the countless airports she had been through in the last few months, only larger. She fought the urge to compare it to Seatac; the thought of home was one she wanted to avoid just now.

She eventually found her way to the security checkpoint, where she was instructed to look for the deputy headmistress of her new school, a woman named Valerie Grace. She had a basic description, but not much else to go on.

As she passed security she saw a line of people holding up signs. There was a woman wearing a moleskin coat and an olive-green skirt holding a sign with "Abigail Kane" scrawled in a neat and steady hand. The woman was in her mid-fifties with strawberry blond hair cut in symmetrical lines at the shoulders and harsh bangs. She was a very serious looking woman with an outdated style. Valerie Grace was a woman clearly uninterested in the latest styles, and possessed an academic bearing. Abby could tell she would be a shrewd teacher. The thought was somewhat comforting. *I like to learn,* she thought, *maybe this won't be so bad.* Abby had a good feeling about the woman standing there with the sign.

Abby walked up to the woman and smiled extending her hand. "Ms. Grace? I'm Abigail Kane."

Ms. Grace allowed a warm smile, took Abby's hand, and shook it firmly. "Nice to meet you Miss Kane." She folded the sign and placed it in a large bag. "We already received your luggage and delivered it to your dormitory. How was your flight?" She motioned Abby to walk with her.

Abby followed struggling to keep up with Ms. Grace who set a fast and purposeful pace. "It was fine. I tried to sleep most of the way."

"Good. The term starts tomorrow, and I am certain you will want to be well rested for the first day." Abby struggled to keep up. "I don't know about your last school, Miss Kane, but Armitage Hall is one of the finest educational institutions in England. You are lucky a spot became available when it did."

"I'm a hard worker Ms. Grace, I've always enjoyed learning," Abby said trying to reassure her escort. She reminded herself that, while she attended school, Ms. Grace would be her guardian, and she should show her respect.

"I'm glad to hear it Miss Kane. I like your attitude. It will serve you well." She took a sharp turn towards a pair of glass doors. Abby nearly missed the turn, but caught up before Ms. Grace realized she had fallen behind. "Armitage Hall has been host to royalty, former prime ministers, and some of the greatest leaders our country has ever had. I wish to impress upon you the magnitude of privilege being afforded with this opportunity Miss Kane. There are students from some of the finest families in the Commonwealth unable to attend our school."

Abby had not realized she was going to such a distinguished institution. "Are there any other American's enrolled?"

"None," Ms. Grace answered. "You are not the first however. One of your senators attended for a year as an exchange student in the 1960's. Other than him, you are the only other American to attend. Your grandmother and I called in a number of favors for you to be accepted." Ms. Grace stopped and turned to look at Abby. "I hope you do not disappoint either of us, Miss Kane."

Abby shook her head, "I have no intention of doing so." She gave the woman a reassuring smile. She thought Ms. Grace looked a bit worried. The matronly woman continued walking. Abby followed her through the glass doors into a thoroughfare of cars and taxis. Ms. Grace continued on to a black Mercedes parked along the curb. As they approached, the driver circled the car, and opened the back door. They quickly stepped in and Abby noticed there was a thick glass partition between the driver and the passenger seat. The driver stepped in and pulled from the curb. The matronly educator ruffled through her large bag.

"I have a full academic schedule set up for you," Ms. Grace continued. "I was informed you are a talented violinist. I've arranged for you to meet with Professor Goodwin. He's a discriminating teacher and very selective about the students he's willing to work with. I recommend you practice regularly as he will not hesitate to eject you from his class if you do not meet standards."

Abby shifted in her seat doing her best to look alert and engaged despite the fatigue of travel.

"We will begin our private lessons once you are settled," Ms. Grace added.

"Private lessons?" Abby asked uncertain what she was referring to.

"Your lessons in magic," Ms. Grace responded. "Your grandmother was very explicit that your education in this matter should progress." Abby hadn't thought about her education in the occult arts for several months. "Considering your family's situation, I think it wise to follow her council."

Abby resented these secret traditions and clandestine lessons. They played no small part in her parent's death, and were the very reason she was so far from home now; even though she did not fully understand why or how. Her grandmother wanted her to learn to fight back, but Abby couldn't see the sense of it. Why even bother learning the things that would likely get her killed, too?

She noticed a softening in Ms. Grace's demeanor. "I'm very sorry for your loss," she said quietly into the still air of the car. "I will do my best to teach you how to protect yourself."

Abby couldn't think of anything to say. Whether Ms. Grace was reading her mind, or simply interpreting her body language, Abby was grateful. "Thank you, Ms. Grace." Everything was still too raw. It was difficult to hold back emotions. She looked out the window, and tried to still her thoughts.

The predawn night shrouded everything in darkness. The world seemed as hollow as Abby felt. "How many students are enrolled in the school?" Abby asked, attempting to pull herself away from despair.

"There are approximately eight hundred students in total. You will share a dorm room with two other girls; Sarah Chatterjee and Nina Carlisle. Both are exceptional students."

They traveled well beyond the bounds of London and into daylight. Nothing more was said, and Abby caught herself dozing on several occasions. Eventually, she surrendered to the fatigue, and allowed herself to slip into a shallow and restless sleep.

"Miss Kane, we have arrived," Valerie Grace stated, tapping her on the shoulder.

Abby opened her eyes. The car was parked in a courtyard surrounded by brick walls. A large stately manor stood looming in front of them with ivy growing over the façade; a relic of the past, built in the Tudor style. On either side of the main school were several smaller brick buildings of modern construction. The grounds were picturesque, as you would expect from a proper English boarding school. Stone pathways and beautifully manicured lawns stretched in every direction, surrounded by flower beds and perfectly maintained hedges. In many ways it reminded her of her private school back home, only this was much larger.

The driver came around and opened the door. Abby stepped out and shielded her eyes from the sun as she took in her new surroundings. She watched students go by wearing white shirts and dark green blazers with the school symbol embroidered on the lapel. The uniforms were not entirely imaginative or distinctive, but they weren't meant to be, that was the purpose. At least I don't have to worry about what I'm going to wear every day, she thought as she waited for Ms. Grace.

The chauffeur gathered Abby's carry-on bag and followed Ms. Grace, who assumed her, apparently typical, brisk pace towards the dormitories. Abby kept up despite feeling a bit groggy. She looked at her phone; 7:34 am. She felt fortunate the nap had given her a second wind.

"You will be staying in Plantagenet Hall. It's a girl's-only dormitory, no males are allowed in this building under any circumstances unless they are members of the faculty. The same goes for the boy's dormitory. Being found in the boy's dormitory may lead to immediate expulsion. Do you understand, Miss Kane?" the deputy headmistress's voice seemed almost scripted.

"I understand," she said. Several students passed by, engaged in what sounded like a discussion about music. Abby caught herself staring and quickly glanced away. *Everyone sounds so different,* she thought. She was no stranger to accents, but here she was the one who sounded out of place.

They entered Plantagenet Hall walking into a large common room where dozens of girls and young women were sitting on couches reading books, playing games, and engaged in lively conversations. They seemed friendly. Abby knew most of them had been students together since a young age. In many ways this made her feel like even more of an outsider. *It's only for a year,* she reminded herself. *I can get through a year.*

Abby followed Ms. Grace up an oak staircase that creaked with every step. They proceeded down a long hallway. Each door they passed was marked with a number. They stopped halfway down the hall, in front of door number seven. Ms. Grace knocked politely. Moments later, a young woman answered. She was short; no more than five feet tall, with a pretty, round face, soft features and deep brown eyes that matched the color of her hair. She had a friendly look about her, setting Abby at ease.

Before she could speak Ms. Grace pressed her way into the room. "Miss Carlisle, this is Abigail Kane, the new student I spoke to you about. Miss Kane, this is Nina Carlisle."

Abby stepped forward and offered her hand. Nina smiled warmly and returned the greeting. "It is very nice to meet you Abigail," Nina greeted politely.

"Thank you, it's nice to meet you too, Nina," Abby smiled in return.

On the far side of the room was another girl. She had dark skin, and Abby suspected she was of Arab or East Indian decent. The girl was pretty, with striking chestnut eyes. They watched as she set aside the book, and rose for introductions.

"Miss Chatterjee, I would like for you to meet your new roommate Abigail Kane. Miss Kane, this is Sarah Chatterjee." Ms. Grace seemed pressed upon, as though she had better things to do. Abby stepped forward and greeted Sarah.

The room was comfortably sized with three beds spaced apart so each girl had her own section. Sarah had decorated hers in bright colors with pictures, presumably of her family. Nina's area was covered with posters of celebrities and rock stars. The empty bed was obviously Abby's. There were several pieces of luggage already piled next to the boxes she'd sent ahead. No doubt selected for its ability to withstand the wear and tear of student life. Her space was barren of décor or character. There was no life in her corner of the room. It seemed oddly fitting.

15

"This is where I take my leave Miss Kane. I trust you girls will show her around and make her feel at home." Ms. Grace turned as though she were given marching orders and left.

The chauffeur placed Abby's carry-on next to her bed and followed. She turned to her new roommates and gave them an awkward smile.

When the door closed, Nina started beaming, her excitement startled Abby at first. "So, you're an American, we haven't had an American here before," she said, practically giddy.

"Calm down Nina. She's an American, not an alien." Sarah said apologetically.

"No need to apologize," Abby said warmly.

The two girls helped Abby unpack, chatting happily about life at Armitage Hall. Abby hadn't brought anything to personalize her space, she had spent too much time traveling lately to think about decorations or keepsakes.

She reached into her bag and pulled out a small frame. Her parents looked back at her, their happy smiles frozen in time. She choked back a gasp, and took a deep breath. She turned the picture over and quickly folded it into her clothing. She couldn't look at them. Not right now.

"Tell us about your old school. Was it like this?" Nina asked. Abby turned her attention to the pleasantries. Abby could tell Nina was a curious young woman, and it gave her something to focus on. She smiled.

"It was smaller than Armitage, and girls only," Abby explained as she carefully placed her violin case beneath her bed.

"Boyfriend?" Nina asked eagerly, barely giving Abby a chance to finish her sentence.

Abby couldn't' help but chuckle. "No," she admitted, somewhat embarrassed. She knew most girls her age typically had a boyfriend by now; at the very least been on a date. Abby could feel the blush in her cheeks.

Abby's hand brushed something as she pushed her violin under the bed. She grasped a small, hard object, and pulled it out. It was an ornate hairpin, with a stylized art deco butterfly on the clasp. It was quite pretty.

"What's this?" Abby asked.

"Oh," Nina said. "That... that was Emily's." There was a reserved tone in her voice as the other girl spoke. Abby was all too familiar with that sound these days, it was grief.

"Who- if it's okay for me to ask, who was Emily?" Abby asked cautiously. She didn't want to upset her roommates before she even got settled in.

For a moment, neither girl answered. Abby was quite sure she had stepped on a sensitive subject. She wished she hadn't found the hairpin.

"Emily was our roommate," Sarah said quietly. "Before you came."

"Oh." That didn't really answer anything, but the tension in the room was too thick, Abby couldn't bring herself to ask anymore.

16

Sarah silently took the hairpin from Abby and walked over to her desk.

"Do you play any other instruments besides the violin?" Nina asked, jumping back to her cheerful attitude. Although it felt more contrived than it had a moment before, there was something infectious about her bubbly personality, and Abby found herself smiling.

She could tell they could easily become fast friends, if Abby let herself. She needed to be careful. *I can't make friends here. I'm not staying long,* Abby reminded herself. *And I'm not sure what happened with Emily, but they seem sad enough without me butting in.*

"I can play the piano and cello, but not well," Abby responded, trying to lighten the mood as well. She got up and began placing several sweaters into her dresser drawer.

"Nina, you really shouldn't badger her," Sarah said affectionately. She placed a book mark in the large text book she had been reading and set it aside. Sarah glanced at the clock on the wall. "Nosh time."

Abby looked confused for a moment. "I'm hoping that means food?" Abby asked with a smile. Despite the shared language, the British vernacular would take some time. Sarah nodded, confirming Abby's assumption.

"Did you live in a dorm at your old school?" Nina continued her enthusiastic questioning. It was obvious she was excited and couldn't' help herself.

"No, Lancaster Prep was twenty miles from where I live in Seattle, so I drove to school every day. They had boarders, though. I just wasn't one of them." She answered as she tried on her school uniform. A wool-pleated skirt, knee high socks a white shirt with a dark green blazer. She felt like she was dressing up for Halloween. Her old school had a strict dress code rather than a uniform.

"Come on, I'll show you where we eat and then afterward I'll show you the tuck shop," Sarah said motioning her to follow her out the door.

CHAPTER THREE

There were dozens of students in the courtyard, boys and girls ranging in age from eight to eighteen having returned from holiday. Some of them noticed Abby and stared as she walked by. She never felt so self-conscious and out of place. She hated being the new girl. It was a little embarrassing. Abby smiled and tried to appear as friendly as possible.

Sarah guided Abby into Wellington Addition. It appeared to be an enormous cafeteria with row after row of tables. There were dozens of students sitting in small groups while others sat quietly alone, reading. At the back of the hall, a large table was covered with finger sandwiches, pastries, and various fruits, cheeses, and nuts. Sarah handed Abby a plate and started her way along the impressive spread picking her favorites. Abby followed her lead.

Sarah sat at a table in the far corner away from the other students. The corner suited Abby just fine. From here, she wasn't quite so bombarded by everyone's stares. Sarah seemed to enjoy being out of the way too.

"Are all the meals like this?" Abby asked.

"Once school is in session they serve us three meals a day. We can sit wherever we want but we have to eat at seven for breakfast, noon for dinner and six for supper. On the weekends and holidays it's much less formal and we see to it ourselves," Sarah answered.

Abby saw a group of students walk in. The two boys and two girls all around her age were each striking in their own way. It was hard not to look at them. They were all tall and athletic, with pretentious grace and undisputed good-looks. They were bathed in a wash of confidence that could only come from a lifetime of being told how perfect they are. Elegant and poised, it was clear that these four were the idols of Armitage Hall.

Abby had seen their type at her old school. She was never one to be impressed by popularity, but it was hard to look away. They were quite the picture.

"Are they in our year?" Abby asked. Sarah glanced at the group as they took a seat several tables away.

"Oh, yes. The blonde girl is Pru Morgan, her real name is Prunella but I wouldn't recommend you call her that. She's probably the most popular girl in school. At least she thinks she is because her family is old." She laughed, dryly. "The two guys with her are her boyfriend Rory Milton, and his best friend, Wyatt Simmons. They're both on the rowing team, so they get a lot of attention."

Sarah turned her attention back to her food. "The other girl is Pru's best friend. Her name is Cecily. She's nice... most of the time, but I would steer clear of the others."

Sarah's change in tone when speaking about Pru was palpable. Abby could tell she wasn't fond of her, and she had seen enough teen movies to guess why. Abby made a mental note not to get involved in school politics. It would only complicate things.

While she was examining the group, Nina arrived, grabbed some food, and started towards them. As she walked past the other students, Pru turned her attention to Nina with a wicked smile.

"Hey car-size," she said, her smile turning into a sarcastic grin. To her credit, Nina's steps barely faltered as she made her way to the table.

Abby wasn't certain if she should say anything. "Are you okay?" she couldn't help herself.

"Who me?" Nina asked trying to pretend she didn't notice what happened. Nina paused and let the ruse fall. She shook her head, looking at Abby. "Oh, I'm fine. Really. She's been calling me that since we were ten years old. I just thought she would have grown out of it by now." Abby looked concerned. Nina shrugged. "I'm okay, but watch out for her, Abby."

Abby looked at her quizzically. "What do you mean?"

"You're the new girl and, well, you're likely to get a lot of attention," Nina answered. "Pru doesn't like anyone else getting attention."

"She means from boys. You're very pretty; she'll likely see you as competition," Sarah added.

Abby had a difficult time thinking of herself as attractive. Sure, she was pretty, but while she felt she looked nice, it was hard for her to see the face staring back in the mirror as anything but normal. Granted she didn't have a lot of experience with the opposite sex, she doubted she was any competition for someone like Pru Morgan.

After everything that had been happening back home, her parents, her grandmother... being sent here was a huge change of pace, but there was no way she was ready to start dating.

"Well I can honestly say boys are the last thing on my mind right now." Abby pushed her plate away. "She doesn't have anything to worry about."

The two girls giggled. "I don't think that's going to matter to her." Sarah commented.

"Sarah's right," Nina agreed. "You'll likely get their attention whether you want it or not. You'll need to be careful. The boys around here don't need much in the way of encouragement, if you know what I mean."

"Wow, I'm really going to need your help on this one," Abby admitted, more concerned than amused. "I've only ever gone to an all-girls school. I don' really have a lot of experience with boys."

Nina giggled. "I'm afraid we won't be much help," she quipped.

"Afraid not, indeed," Sarah added. "We aren't exactly experienced in that field, either."

"Really?" Abby asked. "Surely you speak with boys all the time."

"We're not of interest to most of the boys here," Nina spoke up. "I'm not a twig," Nina motioned to her round figure.

"And I'm too… different," Sarah shrugged. "Besides which, my parents would completely lose it if I dated a boy," she added.

"Oh, come on, you girls are totally cute," Abby said encouragingly. "A co-ed school like this, where the boys outnumber the girls? You can't tell me you haven't had your fair share of attention."

Nina shook her head. "I've considered being a lesbian, but that hasn't really worked; I like boys too much," she laughed.

Abby shook her head, dismissively. "What about you Sarah? You're beautiful. You're telling me you haven't had a line of suitors?" Abby commented playfully.

Sarah looked down at the table, almost embarrassed, and added quietly. "I don't think I'm the right type for most of the boys around here."

"Type?" What do you mean by that?" Abby asked.

"Nothing," Sarah said. "Just that I'm not what the upper class are looking for in a daughter-in-law."

Abby laughed. "Sure, but we're talking about dating, not marriage."

"There is no difference when you're involved with an Aristocrat," Sarah said, seriously. "I don't fit into the picture on the mantle." Abby was shocked. She had heard of this sort of thing happening in Alabama and Georgia during the '50's, but she couldn't imagine that kind of prejudice here.

She leaned in close, and whispered, almost ashamed for mentioning it, "Is it because you're from India?"

She looked up at Abby, surprised. "Oh, no!" she giggled nervously. "My family is from India, but that's never been a problem." She said as though it was obvious.

"I'm sorry," Abby said. Now she felt incredibly silly. The foolish backwater American girl automatically assumed racism. *Stupid Abby,* she chided herself. "I guess I don't understand then." She admitted to Sarah.

Sarah looked like she was trying to find the words, "I…" she stopped.

"It's because her father is a self-made man," Nina spoke up. Abby looked at her, the question evident in her face. "Money," she added, pointedly.

"You mean that because her family hasn't been rich since Elizabethan times, she's… what? Lesser?" that made no sense to Abby. She knew about the classism that used to be prevalent in the Victorian era; it ran rampant in the US too, but the fact that such ignorance still existed was beyond reasoning. "Why would that matter to anyone here? This school isn't cheap. You still got in, so what's the problem?"

Nina shrugged. Sarah looked resigned. "It isn't about how much, it's about how old. New money just isn't as important as bloodlines," She explained.

Abby was silent, thinking. Bloodlines seemed to be very important in her world too. The power held by covens was a family trait, and most witches guarded that power with their lives. She knew all too-well what pain that kind of distinction could bring.

"Oh, it doesn't matter to some of them," Sarah added. "There's always Warren."

Nina giggled. "He doesn't exactly fit the mold either, Sarah." Before Abby could ask, Nina continued, "The students at this school come from some of the most powerful and influential families in England. We don't really fit into the status quo around here," Nina explained.

"There are students here who will inherit titles and fortunes that have existed for centuries. It comes with a number of expectations," Sarah added.

"Well, I understand that," Abby said. "Sometimes it feels like all my Grandmother wants is for me to learn the family business."

Sarah nodded. "Then you understand. I'm different and so is Nina. That's why we don't' always get along with the others."

"I don't think you need to worry, though, Abby," Nina said, misinterpreting the look on Abby's face. "Your family has money, yes? Being American isn't the same as being poor. No one will look down on you." That thought hadn't occurred to Abby. True, her family did come from money, and the Kane's had been around for generations upon generations. Many even emigrated from England, but none of that had ever mattered to her.

"I hope you don't get a bad impression of us, it's not like this everywhere. It's just this school. Armitage Hall takes great pride in aristocracy. Most of the important members of parliament were students here. Sometimes it gets a little out of hand, but most people are quite nice," Sarah added, her hushed tone indicated it was a topic not to be considered casual conversation.

"Just, not all of them," Nina added pointedly, glancing back at Pru.

The girls finished up their meal and placed their plates and utensils in a bin near the kitchen at the back of the dining hall. "Come on," Sarah said with a sweet smile. "I'll show you around the campus."

"I'll meet you back in the dorm," Nina said excusing herself politely. "I need to call my parents and let them know I've settled in."

"See you in a bit," Abby said as she and Sarah followed her out of the cafeteria.

Sarah set a lazy pace towards the main hall. It was a large structure built in the Tudor style. It was very old, the school obviously spared no expense to maintain such an old building. "This is the main hall," Sarah explained.

As they strolled around campus, with Sarah showing her where each of the buildings stood. Past the athletic field and various hidden nooks where benches provided a modicum of solitude for studies.

Abby was lost in her own thoughts as Sarah showed her around. The grass looked the same, the trees seemed no different, the beautiful campus had much in common to her old school back in Seattle. The buildings were older but aesthetically it all seemed the same. But Abby knew it wasn't the same. It was a different world though it bore many similarities, and differences were under the surface. Abby wondered what other things she would find that were different.

Nina and Sara were very kind. Abby could see herself becoming fast friends with both of them. She wondered if she should, but despite her reservations, Abby was already beginning to feel the loneliness breaking through her grief. *I have to be careful, I can't trust anybody here,* Abby thought, as Sarah showed her a quaint little stone bridge built over a swift brook. It was beautiful.

"Are you homesick?" Sarah asked cautiously.

Abby pulled herself from her thoughts and gave a brave smile. "Sorry," she said. She didn't want to explain what she was really thinking about. Abby knew she would have to lie and keep the truth from them. It was the only way to keep herself safe. To keep them safe. It felt awful, but Abby convinced herself it was for their own good. "A little," she said.

"It's alright," Sarah reassured kindly. "We all feel that way from time to time. We can head back. You're probably tired from your long trip and the time change."

"Thank you, Sarah," Abby said her gratitude genuine.

They made their way into the dorm. Abby glanced around. It was a strange thing to share her living space with two other girls. She had never shared a room with anyone else. As an only child, it would be an adjustment. Instead of losing herself in the difficulty of accepting more change, Abby took a deep breath and convinced herself she was going to make the best of it. After all, she was hopefully going to get two good friends out of the deal.

"How was the tour?" Nina asked gleefully from the desk beside her bed.

Abby sat at the edge of her own bed running her fingers over the soft feather down comforter. "It was lovely. Sarah was the perfect guide," She said giving her new friend a warm smile.

Abby sat on her bed, looking around the room. Her eyes glanced over the hairpin on Sarah's desk. "May I ask a question?" She asked tentatively.

"Of course." Nina turned in her chair giving Abby her full attention. Sarah leaned against the wall folding her arms.

"What is it?" Sarah asked.

"I know it might be a bad subject, but… What happened to Emily?" Abby asked.

Nina flinched as if startled. Sarah froze. Abby knew she had hit on something sensitive. No one moved or spoke for what felt like a full minute. Nina and Sarah looked at each other.

"I'm sorry. I didn't mean to pry," Abby apologized, placing her hand over her mouth. She felt bad. Whatever happened was obviously painful, and she wouldn't push. She was too familiar with not wanting to share certain feelings.

"It's alright, you weren't to know," Nina said, her voice tinged with sadness. "Emily disappeared four months ago. No one knows what happened to her."

Abby looked at her bed and choked back a gasp. Blood-soaked sheets covered a lifeless form, laying motionless on the bed. Abby blinked several times to get the image from her mind. This wasn't real. She knew it couldn't be. She could feel her heart racing and took a deep breath to calm herself. She had seen too much death, and it was making her mind wander into dark places. She wasn't going to lose her composure, not now, not in front of her new friends. "I'm sorry." *Too much death.* She thought.

"Don't be, we're all doing our best to move forward," Sarah said. "She was one of Pru's friends, but she was always very kind to us, to everyone for that matter."

Abby sensed their sadness. Her head was swimming with fatigue. "I think I'm going to take a nap, I think the jet lag is catching up to me. I hope you don't mind," Abby said. "I need to get used to the time change."

"It's not a bad idea at that," Sarah agreed. "We start classes tomorrow; you'll definitely want to be well rested."

"Absolutely. We can go hang out in the commons so you can get some rest," Nina offered. "It's no bother."

"Thanks, you two are the best," Abby said positioning her pillows. The door opened and closed quietly, as the girls left without another word. Abby stared at the ceiling for a few moments. She silently ran through everything she had seen and heard since landing at Heathrow only a few hours earlier.

As similar as she thought it would be, it was much more different than she had expected. Like any school there was always a Pru, some were nicer than others, but most were vipers waiting to strike at the first sign of weakness. She thought about Emily. Everyone grieves differently. She'd seen that clearly enough by traveling with her Uncle, but Pru and her friends seemed pretty blithe considering their friend went missing only a few months ago. Abby bristled. The way she had treated Nina was inexcusable. Abby didn't need that in her life.

She sighed. Luckily, it wasn't her problem. Ms. Grace had made it clear that Vivian wanted Abby focusing on her magical training while she was in England. She wished she didn't have to. It would be so much easier to forget that whole world existed. Forget about witches and curses. Forget about murders and grief. Forget everything and just…

She reached up and wiped away the tears that were forming. Now wasn't the time for that. "It's certainly been one hell of a day," She whispered to herself. It took only a few moments before Abby drifted into a deep and desperately needed sleep.

Abby turned over in bed and felt something next to her. She opened her eyes slowly allowing them to adjust to the darkness. There was something warm and wet on her hand. She looked down and saw crimson red.

Blood!

She looked to her side and saw a young woman laying next to her. Her blood soaked blond hair covered her face.

Abby recoiled and gasped in horror. *No! Not again!*

Abby startled herself awake. It was only a dream. Learning she was sleeping in a dead girl's bed had obviously gotten to her more than she realized. *She's not necessarily dead,* Abby thought. Taking a few breaths in and out to steady herself, Abby shook her head. *But after four months… could she still be alive?*

She sat up in her bed and realized it was dark outside. *How long have I been sleeping?* she wondered. She fumbled around for her phone, squinting as the bright LCD screen flashed the time. It was 4:00 am. She'd slept for over twelve hours. She hadn't even heard Nina and Sarah come in. Thank goodness they were kind enough to let her sleep.

I need some air. Abby quietly got out of bed and put on her running gear. No time like the present to check out the track she had seen. She pulled her hair back into a tight ponytail and silently left the dorm.

It was a muggy morning. The last tendrils of summer still lingered in the air. It would be gone in a couple of weeks and the bitter bite of autumn would begin taking over this northern portion of Oxford County.

She passed the beautifully manicured lawns in the main courtyard and walked past Wellington Addition, where the athletic field was located.

Though it was very early in the morning, night still lingered. There were only a few lights casting a glow over the courtyard as she made her way to the field.

The darkness gave Abby a brief pause. *It's fine. It's safe*, she convinced herself. It was a school after all. The Thanos didn't know where she was. Death seemed to be following her, but for the time being it wouldn't know to find her here. Reassured, she followed a path around the building and down a small hill over-looking the secondary athletic field.

The gym, with its state-of-the-art facilities was on the far side of the main campus, near the stadium, but Abby remembered from Sarah's tour that there was a smaller track, convenient to the dorms. She headed down the path pointed out to her earlier, until she saw it.

A small soccer field, or she supposed a football field by local terminology, was illuminated by a set of floodlights. The running track circled the field. It was just what she was looking for. She followed the concrete staircase past a set of bleachers and onto the turf. Abby took a few minutes to stretch and loosen up, enjoying her first real moment of quiet solitude since arriving. She liked her roommates well enough, but she knew they couldn't understand everything that was going on in her head. She certainly wasn't going to tell them about her parents. The less her fellow students knew about her reason for coming here, the better. She wasn't exactly in witness protection, but she intended to keep a low profile all the same. She remembered the looks on the endless parade of faces at her parent's funeral. She did *not* want that kind of pity from her classmates.

No. More than anything, this was her chance to regain a normal life. Abby just wanted to focus on her studies and graduate without causing a fuss. After that… she didn't have a plan for after. All she could do was keep her head down in this foreign country and hope her family could take care of things soon. She didn't want to be looking over her shoulder her whole life.

Abby finished stretching and took to the track. Running always seemed to help clear her mind. If she felt sad, she would run it away; if she felt angry, she would leave it behind. It was her favorite coping tool. No one could stop her from running.

She put her ear buds and cranked up the music. Abby got into position, like she was taught by her old track and field coach, and like an animal freed from a cage, launched herself into a brisk run.

Within minutes she lost herself in the music as adrenaline coursed through her body, giving her a head rush. At some point, she became aware of someone else on the track. She veered to an outer lane, trying to make sure whoever it was had room to pass her. Rounding a curve, she glanced behind, hoping to see them a bit better.

Her fellow runner was as a tall guy, well over six feet, wearing shorts and a plain hooded sweatshirt. His long legs gave him a large stride, but he continued to stay behind her. *He probably hasn't been running for long,* Abby thought. *He's still warming up.* She chastised herself for being oblivious to her surroundings, and sped up again. Her grandmother sent her away because she was in danger. However, remote the possibility of the Thanos knowing where she was, she should be taking this more seriously.

She glanced back again. The guy was moving faster now as if Abby's thoughts had spurred him into action. *Is he following me?* Abby considered her options and then shook herself. She was being unnecessarily paranoid. If this guy wanted to come after her, he likely would have done so when she wasn't paying attention. He was just out for a morning run, like she was.

Abby continued on with her steady pace. Her paranoia didn't quite let go of her, and she decided to remove the ear buds in order to hear when he was approaching. She found herself wanting to speed up, but refrained. She wasn't afraid of him. *I have no reason to be afraid.*

Before long, his stride brought him in line with her. Abby glanced over. Though his hood was up she could see just a student. She laughed silently at her foolishness. She set aside her worries, and looked at the boy, about her own age. He had short black hair and day's worth of stubble. He wore a man's face that still showed signs of the boy he had been. Not bad looking, Abby realized, but still just a student. She imagined a sea of broken hearts in his wake.

"Hi," Abby smiled as the boy passed by.

"Huhmm," The boy grunted in reply. He obviously wasn't friendly. *Not a morning person?* she wondered. Or, perhaps he was one of those aristocratic boys Sarah had warned her about. Her blood wasn't any bluer than her roommates. No matter, Abby didn't really want to get to know people who were like that anyway.

The young man's pace and stride set him to moving beyond Abby in a few short yards. She turned her thoughts back to her own run, and left him to his. Before she could focus on her stride he glanced back at her. She stumbled a half-step, and glanced back over at him. For just a moment, she thought she saw a red glow in his eyes. *It had to be a trick of the light,* she told herself, but her heart leapt and refused to sit still. Her mind tried to sort what she'd seen. *Ugh, Abby get a hold of yourself! A trick of the light, a missing girl, and now you're seeing monsters.*

She slowed her pace putting distance between them.

Abby couldn't shake the feeling of unease. She didn't want to alone with him now. Her grandmother had always encouraged her to trust her instincts, and despite everything, her brain was telling her couldn't be true, she thought perhaps this moment was an ideal time to heed that warning. Abby slowed to a stop, and left the track, quickly and quietly, following the path back to the dormitories.

When Abby reached the hilltop, she glanced back. The young man was still jogging, apparently unaware she had even left. Perhaps she was being silly, and her imagination had gotten the better of her. She shook her head, and tried to laugh it off, but regardless of her attempts at normalcy, she knew there was something about the boy that felt… different.

Abby could see the faint glow of daylight on the horizon, as she neared her dorm. In an hour, the school would be a hive of activity, buzzing from the first day of a new term. When she reached her room, she collected her uniform and travel bag. Nothing could be more normal than a shower and she needed to calm down.

Abby looked around the cafeteria and saw the hall was nearly full. There were a lot of younger students, which surprised her. She wondered what it must be like to be sent away at such a young age. Her curiosity was interrupted when a young man sneaked up behind Nina and threw his arms around her.

He was their age, meticulously groomed and debonair, though somewhat scrawny. He had dark brown, almost black hair and friendly features. Nina turned to see who was hugging her from behind. When she saw who it was, she squealed in excitement.

"Abby this is Warren Lampton," Nina introduced.

"It's nice to meet you Warren," Abby said shaking his hand.

"An American!" Warren said with surprise. "Welcome to Armitage Hall." He studied Abby with a discerning eye, for almost long enough to be rude. She was about to say something when he shook his head. "You're going to turn some heads at this school."

"Am I?' She asked, brows raised.

"Certainly. And not just because you're beautiful," He said with a wink.

Abby blushed slightly at the compliment. She never really thought of herself as beautiful, and this was her first time hearing it from someone less than five minutes after meeting them.

"Oh don't worry about Warren, Abby," Nina giggled as she nudged her friend. "He's a fancy boy."

Warren waggled his eyebrows at her. Abby had no illusions about what she meant, and giggled at the duo.

"You shouldn't speak for Warren like that, it's his thing to tell," Sarah chastised politely.

"It's okay Sarah, I haven't seen the inside of a closet since I was twelve," Warren said, amused.

"Whatever your preferences, it's nice to meet you," Abby said sincerely.

"Sounds like we have one of the open-minded ones," Warren laughed.

"Well I'm from Seattle, we're all crazy, coffee-drinking, tree-hugging, liberals out there. At least, that's' what they tell me," Abby added.

Warren laughed at that. "Lovely to know that geographic stereotypes aren't just limited to Westchester and Essex." With no more small talk than that, he joined them in breakfast, and was soon chatting like they were old friends.

Abby was pleased to learn Warren would be in two of her classes; Classical Literature and Advanced French. The only classes she wouldn't know at least one student would be Advanced Music Theory, Symphony and Political Science. *Not bad,* she thought, *I might be able to survive this after all.*

"So, what possessed you to enroll at Armitage Hall?" Warren asked. He didn't seem to mind prying. Fortunately, Abby had anticipated this question and ready with a rehearsed response.

"I've thought about doing a year of school abroad for a while now. My family has had some problems lately, so I decided this would be a good time," She explained. She silently congratulated herself. Insinuating there was a problem in the family was not untrue, and it was enough for people to paint their own picture. She relied on the fact that most people would be polite enough to not ask questions

"Well, none of us are strangers to familial problems," Warren said. "I think my mother quit keeping track of my father's infidelities after the second affair. Now she simply insists on his discretion, so he doesn't embarrass her. What whimsical freedom," He sighed dramatically.

"Warren's right Abby, we all have difficulties in our family in one form or another," Nina confessed. "If you ever want to talk about it we're here for you."

Abby was touched by Nina's sincere offer. "Thank you," she said, and happily let them change the subject.

As the conversation wandered on, Abby noticed a student sitting alone three tables away. It was the young man she encountered on the track. He was wearing his school uniform, and was still unshaven and unkempt. Despite that, she was again startled by how attractive he was. *No red glowing eyes, thank goodness.* She felt silly and slightly embarrassed at the thought. Abby caught herself staring at him.

When a lull came in the conversation, Abby nudged Sarah and pointed out the young man. "Who is that?" she whispered. Sarah looked and recoiled as though something dreadful had been pointed out to her.

"That's Edgar Kincaid." Sarah sounded like she was disgusted. Her voice was loud enough both Nina and Warren noticed.

"I ran into him on the track this morning," Abby explained.

"Oh? Did he speak to you?" Nina asked.

"We just said hello to one another," Abby responded. "He didn't seem particularly friendly," she added.

"You really should stay away from him Abby, he's bad news," Sarah stated. Her concern seemed genuine.

"I'm surprised to see he came back," Warren commented.

"Why?" Abby asked.

"After all the things that happened with Emily, the police, and everything. Her family still doesn't know what happened to her. It's just surprising," Warren stated as he stuffed a piece of toast in his mouth.

"Police? Emily?" Abby was confused. "Was he involved with her disappearance somehow?" She knew she was gossiping, but couldn't help but be curious, especially after her nightmare.

"She was Edgar's girlfriend," Nina explained. "They questioned him for days after she disappeared. Everyone thought he had something to do with it, but nothing was proven. Apparently, he even punched an officer at one point."

"I feel bad for her parents. They must be going out of their mind," Sarah added.

A pang of familiar grief settled in Abby's thoughts as she considered what Emily's parents might be going through and imagined she could relate on some level. She was beginning to connect the dots, and once again she realized perhaps her instincts earlier this morning were accurate.

The red glow in his eyes haunted her for the rest of the day.

CHAPTER FOUR

The first week flew by in a flurry of commotion and excitement. Abby was impressed with her professors. She was most of all impressed by Professor Goodwin, the music teacher who gave her a piece to practice. It was to be her audition to determine her place in the school's symphony. Abby was excited to have a real place to play. The violin was the only real solace left to her.

The first week Abby did her best to settle into her new classes. She found it wasn't very different from her old school, really. Homework was assigned in every class, and the expectations were high, but she was prepared for the workload. Her biggest challenge came in her calculus class.

Sitting right behind her in the lecture hall was Edgar Kincaid. Every day for a week he sat directly behind her. It felt like he was looming over her, like an enormous shadow. It was distracting. Even though they never exchanged a single word, being so near made it feel as though he was breathing down her neck.

On Friday Abby turned her head and he was staring down at her with an intense gaze. Their eyes locked for a brief profoundly uncomfortable moment. Abby could feel her heart racing, and then he glanced away, breaking the moment that lasted a mere fraction of a second. *Why is he staring at me? Is he looking for his next victim?* She took a moment to lock down her wayward thoughts. *Knock it off Abby, it's just rumors and hearsay. He's just a student, like me...* she told herself as she gathered her books and shoved them in her bag. Despite everything there was a part of Abby that suspected there was something different about him. How was something she couldn't place her finger on.

After classes Abby took the opportunity to practice her violin. After sitting so near to Edgar and his intense eyes, she needed to calm herself down. She made her way to one of the practice rooms Professor Goodwin had reserved for her, and began warming up with scales and finger exercises.

She pulled the sheet music from her folder and reviewed the notes. It was by Vivaldi, one of Abby's favorite composers. It was a piece she'd played before; Gloria in Excelsis Deo. It was not a particularly difficult piece; however, it was mostly a choral composition, which meant timing would be tricky. Abby was grateful for this test of her technical skill; it gave her something real to engulf herself in. It was a beautiful piece when all parts were present, and she intended to do it justice.

She set the violin to her shoulder, positioning her chin on the rest. The familiar weight was a great comfort to Abby who was still unsettled from the whirlwind culture-shock of the last two days. This, at least, she knew, and she gave herself over to it.

After completing practice, Abby made her way to the cafeteria where she found Sarah, Warren and Nina already eating supper.

The meal went quickly. The conversation was a series of joyful rambling about classes, gossip, and boys. Abby appreciated the easy atmosphere, and happily made small talk with the others.

After retiring to the dorms, the girls chatted for a few moments before focusing on their homework. Abby worked on her math and read a chapter for her World Economics course. She could feel herself getting tired. The jet lag still lingered, and the time change had her sleep cycle completely thrown off. Abby decided she would read "English Translations of Mimnermus" for her Classical Literature course in bed. With any luck, she would get most of it read before falling asleep. Based on her brief glance of the material, though, she had a feeling she wouldn't get very far.

Sleep came effortlessly.

Abby opened her eyes and found herself standing in the foyer of her home. She breathed deeply and took in the sweet fragrance of the freshly cut white lilies, sitting in a glass vase on the round table. Abby made her way up the stairs and to her room where she placed her book bag and purse.

"Mom?" she called out. There was no response. There was a strange thud coming from down the hallway. Abby stuck her head out and saw the doorway to her father's office slightly ajar. It was a peculiar thing to see. *He always locks the office*, she thought.

"Dad?" Abby called out. No answer. A sickly-familiar sensation began to form in the pit of Abby's stomach. The bitter taste of salt tears echoed on her lips. This had happened before. Abby began to step towards the office door. She reached out and pushed the door open. Before her hand reached its smooth wood veneer, it flung open abruptly. A dark faceless figure loomed at the doorway and before Abby could turn and run the figure reached out and grabbed her by the throat. She could feel herself being lifted from the ground and thrown into the room. She could feel a sharp pain in her head as she crashed against the wall. There was blood everywhere and two lumps on the floor in front of her. They were still dead.

"Mom? Dad?" she cried as she tried to stand.

Before she could come to her feet she could feel that dark figure grab a handful of hair and pull her up. Abby looked at the dark faceless figure. He looked like nothing more than a shadow, smelling of death and rot.

Abby whimpered. Her heart was pounding out of her chest. She tried to pull away, but his grip was too strong. She looked up and saw the shadow figure with a large knife in his free hand. He held it over her ready to plunge it deep into her skull at any moment. This time she would die with them.

Abby screamed when the knife came down.

"Abby," Nina said shaking her. Abby opened her eyes and realized she had broken out into a sweat. She was completely drenched and gasping for air.

"What's wrong?" Sarah asked. Her roommates were sitting on the edge of her bed, their faces covered in worry.

Abby sat up and caught her breath. She shook her head dismissively. "Sorry, it was just a bad dream," She said her voice still shaking.

"It didn't seem like a normal nightmare," Sarah observed still looking concerned.

"I'm sorry, I didn't wake you up did I?" Abby asked feeling terribly guilty. The last thing she wanted to do was have her problems bleed into the lives of her new friends. She was still shaking. She needed to find some fresh air.

"It's alright," Nina said. "Are you sure you're alright?"

Abby nodded catching her breath. She couldn't let the others see her fall apart. She wasn't going to drag them into this. "I'll be alright. I'm going to use the rest room and take a quick shower to relax," she said as calmly as possible. "I'll be alright. Please go back to sleep. I'll feel terrible if I'm responsible for ruining your rest."

"We're fine," Sarah reassured. "As long as you're certain you're alright."

"I am," Abby said. "I just need to relax and not think about it. Go back to sleep."

Abby glanced at her phone. It was two in the morning. *So much for a good night's rest,* she thought. She made her way to the bathroom, grateful that no one was awake at this time of night. She removed her pajamas and stepped into a warm stream of water. Every droplet felt cleansing as though it was washing away the remnants of her horrific dream. She let the water run over her skin letting the sensations sooth her troubled thoughts.

Being alone with only the sound of water raining down on her from the shower head, brought a wave of emotions. The dream had stirred her grief once again and Abby felt herself melt to the tile floor, tears uncontrollably flowed, lost in the water as it washed over her. Seeing her parents in the dream felt so real, as though she relived the whole thing over again, only this time the monster was there for her as well.

After what felt like hours, she pulled herself together, stepped out of the shower and dried off with a towel, wrapping it around her as she collected her discarded pajamas. With any luck both Nina and Sarah would be sound asleep, and wouldn't notice how long she was gone. Abby made her way back down the hallway of the dormitory towards her room.

Stepping into the room, movement caught her eye. She turned to look out the window. There was someone standing a few yards away, looking up at her dormitory. *Who could it be?* she wondered. For a moment she thought perhaps it was a faculty member out for a smoke, but they were just standing there, staring.

There was something familiar about the figure standing there. It was someone tall, with broad shoulders. He was little more than a silhouette breaking through the darkness. The figure shifted slightly, the light caught him briefly and there was a soft red glow reflecting from his eyes.

There faintly emerging from a shroud of darkness was a familiar face. Sharp features, with the faintest hint of scruff on his chin, with chilling red glowing eyes. The red fire in his eyes stared right at her. Abby stepped back, her heart racing. *Edgar Kincaid! It has to be... I can't be sure, but...* She only caught a faint glimpse of his face. It was the red glow in his eyes that quickened her heart and chilled her bones. *Who else could it be?*

She couldn't breathe. *Is Nina right? Did he kill Emily? He couldn't be human: not with eyes like that. Is he going after me next?* She stood still, as though moving would somehow alert him to her presence.

Her mind was consumed by the red glow staring up at her. The same questions repeated in her head. *Why me? Why now? Why him?* Like a desperate prayer to an unseen God who had long turned his sight away, she silently pleaded; please. *Make it stop.*

She watched him for a breathless eternity before he turned, and simply walked away.

Abby tried to slow her breathing. She knew most of what she had seen and thought was just panic telling her horror stories. It wasn't real. Her inner demons had followed her across the ocean and had no intention of letting her go.

She crawled into her bed and pulled the covers tightly around her, shivering with something unrelated to cold.

The long and sleepless night eventually gave way to dawn. Abby's nightmare kept repeating over and over in her mind. The shadow figure pursued her across the ocean, chasing her to Armitage Hall. A dark menacing presence, relentlessly seeking her; all the while it's eyes glowing a deep red. She knew Edgar couldn't be the man who killed her parents, but in the darkness of night, her imagination ran wild.

As the light slowly chased the shadows away, her thoughts turned to questions. What was he? Vivian had taught her everything she knew about their family and the mystical powers they possessed. Granted, it wasn't much, but over the years, she had learned a little about the magical world that lay hidden from the normal world. She had no doubt that Edgar wasn't part of the normal world. He may be walking around the school, attending classes, interacting with people, but he was different. Like her.

She wondered if he was a witch, too. She had never heard of a witch with glowing eyes, but she really didn't know as much as she would have liked. He could be something else. There were other things in this world, monsters in fact. She had only heard tales about Vampires and Werewolves and other creatures of the night. Was he one of those? He wasn't a Vampire; she had seen him in the daytime. Although, she could not be entirely certain, the myths surrounding Vampires were inconsistent. She wasn't sure if she could discuss something like this with Ms. Grace. She barely knew the woman. She couldn't talk to her Grandmother. A call home of this nature would have unpredictable results.

What about Emily? What had happened to her? What role did he play in her disappearance? Did he kill her? Her thoughts swam in circles as the dorm slowly sprang to life, preparing for the new day. She still didn't know what she would do, but without a plan, she knew the best thing to do would be set it aside for now. Abby needed to know what she was dealing with before she could do anything, and it was time for her to get serious about her own safety. Even if Edgar wasn't a threat, she knew all too well the dangers that were lurking in this world. She didn't want to get shipped off every time the family faced a potential threat.

Abby pulled out a sheet of paper and scribbled a brief note.

"Ms. Grace will see you now," The receptionist said from behind her sturdy desk.

"Thank you," Abby responded as she made her way into the office.

Ms. Grace was sitting behind an antique desk; the room clean and tidy. There was no art on the walls, no pictures on her desk, nor any other sign that she had a life outside of school. The only decoration was a series of neatly framed diplomas, certificates, and various honorifics she had accumulated over the course of her career.

Ms. Grace wore a dull green dress with a brown blazer, her hair held back in a tight bun. Abby thought she looked like the very image of a hardened schoolmarm, and shuddered. *She's not as severe as she looks,* Abby reminded herself.

She finished writing a note and motioned for Abby to have a seat.

"Good morning, Miss Kane. I received your message. Is there something I can do for you? Your note implied it was time sensitive."

"Thank you for seeing me Ms. Grace, I know you're busy," Abby began. "I was wondering if it would be possible for me to start my lessons with you early. Or, perhaps there is an occult library I could access."

Ms. Grace appeared to be considering Abby's request. Her eyes narrowed slightly, and it was apparent she was being studied. "Did something happen, Miss Kane?"

Abby was surprised; she was coming to learn the deputy headmistress was keenly observant, and had no problem cutting through diffusion. There was no use, but to be up front with her. Abby sighed.

"I feel helpless and unfocused, and I want to be ready to protect myself. I don't want to be sent half-way across the world every time my family has a problem," Abby explained. "I'm sorry. I apologize for my tone, but I don't like feeling as if I'm a liability. Studying sometimes makes me feel better, and if I can learn something that will help keep me safe, then I want to learn what you know."

There was a brief pause. "Very well," Ms. Grace replied in a monotone drawl. "Please report to my house, immediately after your evening meal. We will start our lessons tonight."

"Thank you, Ms. Grace." Abby responded, getting up from her seat.

"Miss Kane," the deputy headmistress said sharply. "I had hoped you would confide in me if there was something wrong. Your grandmother placed you here under my protection. I take my responsibilities very seriously."

"Thank you, Miss Grace, I will keep that in mind," Abby said, conflicted. "I'll see you this evening." Part of her wanted to confide in someone. She wanted to trust that her Grandmother's judge of character was a good one, and to accept Ms. Grace's offer, but she wasn't ready to trust a woman she barely knew with her suspicions, especially, knowing that they might prove unfounded.

She was certain Ms. Grace didn't completely buy her improvised excuse, which was probably a good thing. It meant her guardian had a keen ability to see through her clumsy attempts at subterfuge. Perhaps Ms. Grace already knew about Edgar Kincaid, and would lay Abby's fears to rest.

Classes that day seemed longer than usual. Abby felt confident she was able to contribute to the discussion in Classic Literature with meaningful comments, despite her poor study habits the night before. Professor Caldwell seemed convinced she was one of the few students who had completed the reading. He was upset at the rest of the class, and lectured them for ten minutes on the importance of doing their homework, then threatened them with a quiz, before releasing them for the day. It seemed it was school as usual, despite her growing unease.

In Calculus, Abby kept her back to Edgar and did her best to resist the urge to glance back. His presence pressed against her even though they never touched. By the end of class she could feel the anxiety pounding in her chest and fled the moment they were dismissed as though she were being chased.

She struggled through Music Theory and Symphony, where only her love of the material kept her focused. She was making casual friends with several students, but she was too distracted to be terribly chatty. Instead, she focused on her music, and let the time pass as it would.

Abby had always wanted to be a professional violinist but never allowed herself to hope too much. The family had certain expectations; in that she understood the denizens of this school better than even she realized. Being a witch didn't necessarily mean your life dreams would be fulfilled, unless of course those dreams were related to the family's secret talents. She wondered how Ms. Grace dealt with the delicate balance of witchcraft and work.

"What can you tell me about Ms. Grace?" Abby took the opportunity at lunch to broach the topic of her guardian with her roommates.

Sarah remained silent, and looked to the others as Nina made a face like something terribly smelly walked by. "That old trout?" Warren responded with distaste. "She's not the most popular faculty member, that's for certain." His tone softened slightly after his initial reaction.

"Is she really that bad?" Abby asked a bit concerned.

"She is the enemy of all things fun," Nina protested.

"Why do you ask?" Sarah inquired.

"She's my grandmother's friend and my guardian while I'm at school," she explained sheepishly, "but I don't really know anything about her."

"That old hag has a friend?" Warren quipped.

"Warren," Sarah warned. "Ms. Grace is a friend of Abby's family."

"She's mad as a coo-coo," Warren replied, undeterred by Sarah.

"You're just saying that because she's strict, and you've been called into her office for disciplinary infractions too many times," Sarah scolded. She turned back to Abby. "She's very reserved, and doesn't have a sense of humor to speak of. As a result, she tends to be unpopular with many of the students," Sarah explained.

"Something Sarah understands, too well," Nina teased her friend. "When she sees students having fun she shuts it down." In reply, Sarah threw her napkin in Nina's face, eliciting a laugh from the table.

Abby smiled at her. "I think you're fun, Sarah."

Nina clearly was not one of Ms. Grace's biggest fans. *Of course, it's entirely possible she deserves this reputation,* Abby thought. She had discerned for herself Valerie Grace was a stern and focused woman.

"How does your grandmother know her?" Sarah asked after a moment.

"Our families know each other, I never really thought to ask how." Abby didn't exactly lie. She took it at face value that the covens were connected, and never gave it much thought. She certainly couldn't tell her friends about the rumor that Ms. Grace had approached her grandmother to curse an unfaithful lover. Some secrets were better left unsaid.

"Oh Abby, you're not going to tell her what we said are you?" Nina seemed concerned.

"Of course not," Abby reassured her new friends. "I would never."

"I don't know what you're worried about. I would gladly say any of this to her face," Warren admitted with a smug grin.

"I think you have," Nina joked. Abby liked the playfulness shared between her new friends. She wanted to join in on the fun but she hesitated. Getting close to people worked counter to her survival, and she knew it. The fewer people she knew and associated with, the safer she was for now.

It would be easier if they weren't so nice to her.

"Seriously, we shouldn't be this disrespectful. She is, after all, Abby's guardian." Sarah's conservative upbringing was a bit of a blessing just now, and Abby smiled at her gratefully.

"It's alright, really. I just have to go to her place this evening, so I won't be in until later," Abby explained.

"Better you than me," Warren commented. "You have my sympathies."

"I think she's very intelligent," Sarah added in her defense.

A large figure entered the cafeteria, catching Abby's eye. It was Edgar. They locked eyes, and her breath caught for just a moment. No glow. She breathed a small sigh of relief, but could feel her heart racing. His gaze was still unsettling. Abruptly, he looked away. Abby watched him as she gathered some food on his plate and sat with his back to her on the far side of the cafeteria. *What is he? Why did he seem so focused on me?* she wondered. There was something different about him, she was sure of it. Abby thought she was going to lose her mind trying to figure out what it was. With Emily's disappearance, it seemed impossible to believe he wasn't, in some way, involved.

"Abby, you're okay, aren't you?" Nina asked, her concern was disarmingly direct.

Abby was abruptly pulled from her thoughts back into a moment of uncertainty. She could feel a crack in her composure. She wasn't sure how to control such things, but she tried not to go pale.

"Of course." She wasn't very convincing. "Why do you ask?"

"I didn't mean to pry, but I was worried." Nina hesitated, all signs of her usual excitement gone. "I did something I shouldn't have," she admitted.

Abby went silent, looking at the other girl.

Sarah was looking at Nina like a mother about to scold a child. "What did you do Nina?"

"I-I looked you up online… and." Any sign of Nina's abruptness was gone. She looked as if she had stepped on a landmine, and she knew it, but it was too late to take it back now. "I'm very sorry, I shouldn't have done that."

Abby could feel her stomach turn. She knew what Nina found, her parents murder had been all over the media. Her composure was beginning to crumble. There would be no concealing the truth from her classmates. The orphan had been unmasked.

"What's wrong?" Sarah insisted.

Abby should have known better than to try and keep it a secret. She had only delayed the inevitable pity that was bound to come from them knowing. These kinds of things were easily discovered by anyone who knew how to use a computer. *I should have used the alias Ms. Grace created for the school records,* she thought absently.

"I'm sorry, I shouldn't have said anything, I just felt bad. I didn't want you to feel like you had to keep it a secret from us." Nina added. Abby shook herself from her shock, and took a moment to regain her poise. Warren had a concerned look, the first time she had ever seen him being serious.

"It's alright, I understand," Abby said quietly. They were curious; the Internet was a natural place to go. She had Googled a few of her classmates at her old school for fun; why wouldn't they, out of concern?

"If there's anything I can do, or say..." Nina offered.

Abby shook her head, fighting back the tears she had worked so hard to drive away.

"Will someone let us in on this conversation?" Warren asked.

"My parents were murdered," Abby whispered.

Sarah let out a gasp. Warren retreated into his own thoughts. Abby could tell Nina felt terrible; her jovial demeanor overwhelmed by guilt.

"It... it was several months ago. I found them when I came home from school. It was all over the news. No doubt, Nina's search found several of those articles," she continued.

"I don't know what to say Abby," Warren said, his voice solemn.

"I'm okay. Really," She told them, as reassuringly as possible. "All things considered. My grandmother wanted to get me away from the media surrounding... the whole event." Abby struggled to piece the story together. There was much she left out. Her friends didn't need the gory details, and she couldn't tell them about the Thanos and the blood feud that caused their murder. She had intended to do her best to leave it all behind, but there was a certain amount of relief that came from not having to keep her grief, at least, a secret.

"Come on," Abby said breaking the heavy silence. "What better place to escape the media than one of the most populated cities in the world right?" she did her best to bring a little levity back to the table before she broke down crying.

An uncomfortable moment of silence passed before the four of them lapsed back into a casual conversation. It felt different. No one wanted to admit it, but the dynamic had changed, and grief was all too present during the remainder of lunch.

Abby left them with a wave, and went about her afternoon classes. Dredging up all the grief was too much. She couldn't let herself feel it now; she would be too wound up for the rest of the day. She found it difficult to focus, but she promised herself that she wouldn't make a big deal of it. So, a few people knew. Maybe that was okay. It wasn't a guarantee that they would pity her and treat her differently now. Right?

Abby kept to herself for the rest of the afternoon.

CHAPTER FIVE

Abby walked across campus toward her first evening lesson with Ms. Grace. She turned the corner of a large brick building, only to walk directly into a large wall of human flesh draped in a school uniform. Abby stumbled backwards, and nearly fell, but felt two strong hands grab her upper arms, pulling her upright. She dropped her book bag, spilling the contents on the concrete.

She gasped in horror. *He's got me!* Abby was about to let out a scream as she tried to pull away. His grasp was too strong. Her moment of terror melted away as she looked up at a face that did not belong to the young man who stood beneath her dorm window. Abby's heart was pounding in her chest as the adrenaline ran through her body. She took a deep breath.

"I'm sorry! I wasn't paying attention to where I was going," she said as she looked up at the face of an unfamiliar young man. She leaned down to pick up the contents of her bag, embarrassed by her own neglect.

The other student helped her gather her things and handed them to her. She looked over to see a young man she'd seen in her World Economics class. He had a curly mop of thick brown hair, which he obviously took great pains to control. He was arrestingly handsome, distinguished, and refined. She caught her breath. She wasn't sure which Prince or Lord she had just run down, but she was certain that with bearing like that, he must be royal. He had a brooding look; a trait which Abby assumed they taught to all the boys when they first come to Armitage Hall. There was a kind of perfection Abby had rarely seen before, in her limited exposure to young men. She had to remind herself to breathe in the moment their eyes locked.

"Are you alright, Miss Kane? I'm sorry I ran you over." His accent and deep voice were mesmerizing. It took Abby a moment to realize he knew who she was.

"I'm fine, thank you," she said unceremoniously shoving her things back in the bag. "I'm sorry. I don't think we've been introduced. I'm Abby Kane." She said offering a warm smile and extended her hand.

"I know," He said slyly, a rogue's smile lit upon his face. She had to remind herself to breathe again. He shook her hand and allowed her to hang for a moment. "I'm Benjamin Hodge, Ms. Grace sent me to make sure you made it to her place safely."

Abby didn't know whether to be flattered or annoyed by her guardian. "She wanted to save me from my clumsy self?" she tried to interject some humor.

"No, she believes you're not telling her certain things. And so, she asked me to keep an eye on you, until you see fit to share your burdens," Benjamin said, his sly smile playing on his full mouth. Abby tore her attention away from his lips, in order to hear what he actually said. *Ms. Grace confided something like this to a student?*

"Are you close with Ms. Grace?" Abby asked, only thinly hiding her concern.

"She's been teaching my sister and me private lessons for a few years," He responded as he motioned towards the path leading to Calder House. "She told us all about you." Abby wasn't sure she liked being talked about, but she needed to trust Ms. Grace's judgment.

Benjamin walked closely. Abby noticed how close he was; it was shockingly forward from someone she had literally met a minute ago. She liked the attention. She didn't want to like it, but she did.

The young man guided her down the path. Calder house was only a few yards from the main campus. It was a quaint cottage in the Tudor style, with a thatch roof and a beautiful garden. Benjamin quickly stepped forward as they approached and held the door open.

"Shouldn't we knock?" Abby asked.

"She wouldn't hear us. She's downstairs in her sanctum," Benjamin stated.

Abby paused a moment. *He knows?! He knows Ms. Grace is a witch?* "What?" Abby asked, her surprise escaping her.

He smiled devilishly, clearly enjoying her shock. "Well, as I said, Josephine and I have been learning from her for years. Are you not familiar with the Hodge family, Miss Kane? We are not so very different from your own," Benjamin said.

Abby's eyes widened at his admission. *He's a witch!* She hadn't met many other witches; her parents had seen to that. She had been raised cloistered in a life that was as normal as they could create. Sometimes, she appreciated the normalcy, but lately, she realized how little it had done to prepare her to face the world she was born into.

"I see," Abby said stepping over the threshold. The house was filled with antiques and Persian rugs over hardwood floors. There were piles of books everywhere, and mahogany tables with doilies. It was all very much as Abby had imagined it would be.

Benjamin followed her through the door. "This way, please," He said politely and guided her down a hallway to a wooden door. Abby spotted a symbol worked into the frame, barely noticeable unless one is trained to look for such things. It was a mark indicating a sanctum was beyond. Three interlinked circles with a pentagram in the center where the three circles meet. She had seen this symbol at her grandmother's house.

Her guide held the door for Abby, revealing a narrow stairwell. It was poorly lit, and Abby began descending the stairs cautiously. She hardly needed to make a fool of herself for a second time. She saw arcane markings etched into the wall, they were subtle, but Abby could see them. They were protective runes and wards. It would seem Ms. Grace had taken many precautions. Abby could feel the protective magic radiating around her as she descended the stairs.

The stairwell opened into a very large basement. There were bookshelves filled with old tomes, and portfolios no doubt containing ancient scrolls and parchments. A large desk covered in papers sat against the far side of the room, and several long tables covered in glass vials, small statues, and an astrolabe stood near the center. There was a small wooden box filled with soil in which various herbs were growing under a heat lamp.

It bore many similarities to the sanctum maintained by her grandmother. She noticed a set of overstuffed leather chairs near the fireplace on the north wall. On the floor were two pentagrams; both were mosaics consisting of various stones, each with their own special meaning.

Ms. Grace and a young woman Abby's age sat in leather chairs in deep conversation. Benjamin cleared his throat. The two women took notice and stood.

"Miss Kane, thank you for coming. I see Mr. Hodge found you," Ms. Grace said in her usual reserved tone.

"Yes, he was truly chivalrous. Thank you, Benjamin," Abby smiled as she moved into the sanctum.

"Hello, I'm Josephine." The young woman approached, extending her hand in greeting. She seemed quite friendly.

Abby shook her hand, excited to meet another person like herself. "A pleasure," she said, honestly.

Josephine was a pretty girl with long brown hair and big brown eyes, she had a wholesome look giving her a friendly appearance.

"I think you're in my Classic Literature course, right?" Abby asked.

"Yes, I believe so," Josephine answered. She seemed friendly enough. Abby knew she would be spending a great deal of time with her, so she was determined to be friends.

"As you can see there are several of us here at Armitage Hall," Ms. Grace stated as she walked over to one of the bookshelves. She pulled a particularly old looking volume from the shelf. "Have you met others of our kind? Other than your family, and the Hodge twins here, of course?"

"Twins?" Abby asked, surprised again. They did look a bit alike, and she felt foolish for not seeing the family resemblance sooner. Benjamin looked like he was trying not to laugh and Abby coughed to hide her embarrassment. "Only a couple," she said returning to the earlier question. "Not many. The

Westbrook coven has some connection with my family, since they are also in Seattle. I went to Lancaster Prep with one of their daughters, but that's pretty much it." She shrugged, hiding her discomfort. Being sheltered made her feel inadequate. She felt like a kid who was home schooled all her life before suddenly being thrown into a public school. Everyone in this room had years more experience with the occult than she did. She didn't want to show off her ignorance in front of them.

"Yes, well there are many covens spread across the globe as you know. Now that you are on the cusp of being an adult you are likely going to start meeting more of us," Ms. Grace stated, cradling the large book in her arms. "What are your specialties?"

"Specialties?" Abby seemed confused by the question.

Benjamin came round and stood next to his sister. Their resemblance was more apparent when they stood next to one another. *They look like book-ends,* Abby thought. "She means your magical talents. What are you particularly good at?" He clarified.

She mulled this over for a moment. "My grandmother believes I have good intuition, and sometimes I can sense things about other people, but I haven't mastered it yet. I suppose, I've always been fairly good with the elements, particularly water." Abby imagined Ms. Grace and the Hodge twins would find her completely lacking in talent. She never thought she was any good at witchcraft. Her grandmother was always harping on her to learn more. It had never been a problem before now. As a peripheral part of her life, it hadn't mattered. Her parents had made sure she focused on school.

Right now, she was wishing she had spent just a little more time listening to Vivian Kane; she wouldn't feel quite so humiliated by her lack of experience.

Ms. Grace held out her hand, a few moments later a spark of fire ignited in her palm. "Please do the same Miss Kane."

Abby put her hand out and concentrated for a moment, a small flame appeared. "I see you at least know the basics," Ms. Grace commented. She then placed a glass of water on a table. "Change this," she said.

Abby concentrated. She focused her attention on the glass of water as she found a place of stillness inside herself. She could feel the water as though it ran through her fingers as she extended her hand towards the glass. She imagined the sensation of cold and 'felt' the water inside the glass turning to ice. As though she had placed the very idea into the water, it began to solidify.

She held her concentration for a few moments, and then imagined the ice slowly turning back to water. Within seconds the ice melted back into its original form. Keeping her focus on the water in the glass, she then imagined the water turning into vapor. A fine mist began funneling out of the glass, coalescing into a small fog bank and obscuring the surface of the table. Abby smiled; at least she knew how to do this.

43

"Very good," Ms. Grace said. "Your grandmother taught you control well. Tell me what she taught you about alchemy."

The praise was short-lived. Abby released the energy and took a breath, turning her back to her mentor. "Not very much, a few simple things, like basic remedies and several toxins. Though, nothing too potent. My father was far better at Alchemy than grandmother. He was to teach me... but, that was before..."

Ms. Grace cleared her throat, keeping the conversation on track. "I think we will start with Alchemy then," She said. "As for your aptitude with intuition, I think this might help." She approached, handing Abby the large book she had been cradling in her arms. The title was "Insight Inward and Outward," which sounded utterly ridiculous to Abby. Still, she accepted the book graciously. "Mr. and Miss Hodge are both excellent students in the Alchemical arts. They will be helping you develop your mastery of this noble craft. Miss Hodge, in particular, has found many progressive uses for modern alchemy." Ms. Grace spoke of Josephine's talent like a proud parent.

Josephine looked amused. "She means my artwork. I use Alchemy to create paints and pigments," she explained.

Abby was impressed. "Can you do that too?" She asked Benjamin.

"She's the alchemist in the family." Benjamin replied, shaking his head. "I'm more for charms and glamours." *Of course, he is,* Abby thought wryly. She gave him a polite smile.

"Come," Ms. Grace said, waving Abby over to Josephine's side. "Let's begin."

Over the next few days, Abby did her best to focus on the methods and theory she was being taught. She came for lessons in the evenings after school, and learned all she could from Josephine.

She was surprised how much alchemy and cooking had in common. Each potion, reagent and elixir had what was essentially its own recipe. "Once you have mastered each recipe, you can begin to experiment and make the potions your own," Josephine told her. "Of course, you can't very well start creating your own until you fully understand the magical components of your ingredients. However, once you do, your imagination is the limit. It's really quite fascinating, don't you think?"

It was very subtle and a lot of work in a way she wasn't used to, but Alchemy seemed particularly useful. She could see that Josephine loved it. "It is interesting. Isn't this how most of our families survived a couple hundred years ago? By changing lead into gold?"

"Very good, Miss Kane. I see you have a basic understanding of our

44

history as well," Valerie Grace stated from her desk obviously listening in on the lesson. "Most of our families came to prominence through the judicious use of Alchemy. Primarily, the ability to turn lead into gold, and worthless crystals into precious gems." She stood from her desk and wandered over to the Alchemical lab they were using and carefully inspected the potion. Abby was concocting a simple elixir to aid in sleep. Ms. Grace nodded once and continued. "My ancestors were master jewelers. They sold their wares to European nobility. They were quite sought after, as a result the name still carries some influence." She looked at Abby. "A situation I trust you are somewhat familiar with."

Abby nodded absently. She knew her family was well off, but she doubted very much that the Kane's were respected or influential. Her father was just a businessman.

"I find a charm and wit works well for me," Benjamin stated with confidence, or perhaps arrogance, Abby wasn't certain which. She saw Josephine roll her eyes, and stifled a giggle.

"Yes, well your family was never assiduous in their studies of Alchemy. I made certain the two of you became at least basically proficient." Ms. Grace commented. Benjamin sighed and returned his attention to putting reagents away.

"Are there others like us here?" Abby asked cautiously.

"There are no other witches here. There are a few people who have small minor talents, most of them are completely unaware of the stunted gifts they possess," Ms. Grace answered her.

"I'm confused." Abby said. "If they have magical abilities, are they not witches, then?"

Ms. Grace shook her head. "Not as you understand it, Miss Kane. Those with talent and power come from families of witches; covens with a long history. Those that do not are simply sensitive to the energies we can manipulate. Many of them believe their subtle powers are simply a natural talent or skill. There is little reason to disabuse them of these beliefs." The older woman motioned to the book she had given Abby to read. "That book will help you learn how to discern people like ourselves from others. It will also help you gain the focus and discipline you need to learn how to identify other people who are different."

"Yes, but different *how*?" Abby asked again.

"This world is full of many powerful things, Abigail, surely your grandmother did not neglect to teach you this." Ms. Grace seemed a bit concerned.

"She did, but she didn't go into details," Abby admitted, once again resenting her sheltered life. She knew her parents meant well but these moments made her feel ignorant. A part of Abby felt guilty for even thinking such things about her parents.

"There are all manner of strange things in this world Miss Kane. You mustn't forget that." Valerie Grace began to pace in front of the fireplace. "All the things of fairy tale and myth were once real, and some are not unlike ourselves."

"So, there are werewolves and vampires among us?" Abby seemed skeptical having never encountered either. Even though her grandmother had told her about them she was given to exaggeration, and she didn't always trust some of the stories she was told.

"Indeed," Josephine said. A chill ran down her back.

"They aren't particularly common, but they exist none the less," Benjamin added. Abby was beginning to feel supremely left out of the loop.

"Are there any vampires here, in this school?" Abby asked, her thoughts turning to Edgar and his red glowing eyes.

"No," Ms. Grace stated flatly. "I have made certain of that."

Abby thought about all that she had seen since coming to Armitage Hall. She had already seen things she couldn't explain except through the occult. Maybe it wasn't a coincidence that she had started to dream about Emily's death after seeing Edgar's glowing eyes. She shivered involuntarily.

She looked around the room. *If I can't trust these people, then I'm already in danger,* she thought. Abby decided to break her silence. "What is Edgar Kincaid?"

Josephine let out an audible gasp as Ms. Grace stoicism broke, her eyes widened. "I'm sorry for bringing it up suddenly," Abby added quietly. "He's something different, though, isn't he? I mean I don't know what, but I can tell he isn't a normal human."

"We are not certain what he is, Abigail. I recommend you keep your distance until we know what we are dealing with. We know he isn't anything obvious, such as one of our kind. We have ruled out nearly anything in my library. I fear he is a mystery to us. At least for now." Ms. Grace stated as though she were ashamed of herself for not having an answer.

Abby was completely out of her league, if these three practiced witches didn't have the answers, how could she? "I encountered him on the track shortly after I arrived. I thought I saw his eyes glow red. Then a few nights ago, he was standing outside my building looking up at my window." Abby paused, but no one spoke, so she continued. "Apparently, he was dating Emily Wright, the girl who was in my dorm before I arrived." Abby confessed her suspicions, hoping her blunt honesty would solicit more information. Surely if they knew he wasn't human, maybe they could tell her something useful.

Josephine looked at Benjamin, who was lost in thought. Ms. Grace pursed her lips and made her way to a desk drawer. She shuffled through the contents until she found what she was looking for, a silver chain with a small locket. She approached Abby and carefully placed the delicate chain around her neck. "I want you to wear this amulet for the time being Miss Kane. It is a simple charm, but it may provide some protection."

"What is it? How will it help?" Abby asked inspecting the locket. It was made of silver and had a small symbol of a pentagram with smaller pentagrams at each of the five points. She opened the locket and saw a crystal inside scorched by a flame.

"It is a Windlow Amulet," Ms. Grace explained. "They are very rare and provide protection to the wearer when in danger. Agatha Windlow, crafted it two hundred years ago. She was a powerful witch who specialized in protective amulets and arcane wards. Of course, I will want it back when we are certain Mr. Kincaid is not a danger to you."

"May I?" Josephine asked motioning to the amulet. Abby nodded her approval and the twins moved in for a better look.

"How is this supposed to protect me? What could he possibly do?" Abby asked a little worried by the diligence behind Ms. Grace's concern.

"As I said, we are uncertain. However, we have our suspicions." Ms. Grace looked to Benjamin.

"I've been friends with Edgar for years, since we both arrived at Armitage Hall in year one," Benjamin began. "He has always been a good sort, friendly and popular," he stated as though he were talking about a time long ago. "Last year, he was dating Emily, as you said, and it was about four months ago when she went missing. Edgar changed. Not just a little, he was entirely a different person. No more charm. No more popularity. We have each seen the red glow in his eyes, though this doesn't happen often." The other two ladies nodded their confirmation. "It only seems to happen when he gets angry or irritated."

"We don't know what happened, but everything changed after Emily." Josephine added. "How it changed him remains a mystery."

"Wasn't Emily a friend of yours?" Ms. Grace asked Josephine.

"Yes," Josephine said slowly. "I knew her."

"Abigail, if anything happens you are to come to this house at once," Ms. Grace stated, her stoicism could not disguise her genuine concern. "This house has many protections which I personally designed and created. There is no safer place on campus. No matter what time of day or night, come here if there is trouble. Until we can discern what Mr. Kincaid truly is, I have no better way to protect you."

So much for coming to England for my own safety, Abby thought. *At least the threat here isn't personal like the vendetta with the Thanos coven. The fire might actually be better than the frying pan, in this case.*

"Don't be afraid to protect yourself. We can clean up any messes; you wouldn't be alone," Benjamin told her. "Besides we wouldn't want anything happening to you." She noticed his flirtations had returned, and smiled. It was a welcome bit of normalcy this evening.

Abby collected her book bag and threw it over her shoulder. "I should head back. I have to stay on top of my other classes." Abby thanked Ms. Grace for her hospitality and for the borrowed charm before heading toward the staircase.

"Abby wait," Benjamin called out putting the last of the reagents away. "I'll make sure you get back in one piece." Even though Abby didn't feel like she needed an escort, she liked having Benjamin around. She liked that he was a witch. It was a relief not to have to hide an entire part of her life and family from him.

Benjamin took Abby's bookbag and carried it for her. She wasn't used to the traditional chivalry he demonstrated. In truth Abby had mixed feelings about it. It was odd and uncomfortable, but she knew the gesture was out of politeness, and chose to take it that way.

"How are you adjusting to our little school?" Benjamin asked as they walked towards the dormitories. "You know, you fit in better than I thought."

"It's different from what I'm used to, but not necessarily in a bad way. What did you imagine I would be like?" Abby asked worried perhaps the English elite believed American's to be barbarians.

"It's just most American's I've met are boisterous and speak their minds freely," He answered honestly. "I'm sure you can imagine that would create quite a stir around here."

Abby stifled a laugh. "No. I'm not really like that. The United States is a big place. Where I'm from people are more reserved and private for the most part," Abby explained. "Besides, I went to a private school back home, with strict rules and a code of conduct not unlike the one here."

"That makes sense," Benjamin commented as they made their way into the courtyard. They were approaching Plantagenet Hall, a place Benjamin would not be allowed to enter.

"Thank you, for making sure I made it back safely," Abby said warmly as she retrieved her book bag.

"Before you go, I would like you to pick a date, ten years in the future," Benjamin said slyly.

Abby was confused by his rather strange request. "What for?"

"For our wedding, of course." He grinned. "After all, our families will likely expect us to marry our own kind. And as far as I know the Kane's have no disgraceful secrets in their past. An alliance would be natural. It makes perfect sense when you think about it." Benjamin made his argument as though it was the most practical and obvious path for their future.

Abby could not hide the slightly horrified look on her face. "What?"

Benjamin started laughing. "If only I had a mirror to show you the look on your face."

Abby flushed with embarrassment. Her lack of experience with boys had completely left her ill prepared for his dry sense of humor. She laughed as relief settled in. She mustered up her wit and attitude and playfully responded, "You're insufferable, Mr. Hodge." She then playfully retreated into the girl's dormitory, butterflies rolling in her stomach. She glanced back to see Benjamin Hodge sill watching her.

CHAPTER SIX

Abby convinced Nina to wake up early and go running with her. The plump girl only made it a quarter of the track before she slowed down to a brisk walk. Abby wanted desperately to jog ahead but didn't want to abandon her friend who was kind enough to join her.

"Are you going to the bonfire tonight?" Nina asked breathless.

"I haven't really given it much thought." Abby had forgotten about it. In truth, she had been too consumed with schoolwork, her extracurricular studies, and violin practice to think about the invitation.

"Warren says most of the popular students will be there." She sounded wistful. In the short time Abby had known her, she'd come to realize Nina was a kind-hearted girl whose feelings were as fragile as fine china.

"I don't think I'll go," Abby stated. The more she thought about it the less she wanted to attend. She didn't want to draw attention to herself, nor did she want to go where her friends were not welcome.

"Really? Why not? It seems like such a great opportunity." Nina seemed surprised.

"You're my friend Nina, granted I've barely known you for more than a month, but I know you're a good person and we'll be friends long after we both move on from Armitage Hall. I don't want to hang out with a crowd who wouldn't let someone as incredible as you hang out with them." Abby was sincere. She wasn't particularly fond of snobbery or elitism, of which this school had plenty.

Nina seemed surprised by her answer. "Really?" Abby could tell Nina was used to being left behind. She imagined that was why she and Warren were so close. Abby knew how it felt and how isolating it could be to be different.

"Of course," Abby added. "I'd rather spend the evening getting to know my new friends."

The two girls walked at a brisk pace. Nina eventually begged to stop and agreed to rest on the bleachers while Abby did a few laps around the field. She pushed herself to get the work-out she needed to clear her head.

She took ten minutes to herself to just run, and then Abby and Nina returned to the dormitory. She was starting to get used to the large communal showers. Being naked in front of dozens of other girls never seemed like something she would do, but everyone else seemed like it was perfectly natural. Another one of those cultural differences.

After her shower, Abby promised herself a little quiet time to try some of the meditation exercises Ms. Grace was teaching her. She settled herself in a secluded nook behind some hedges near the girl's dormitory. It was a quiet afternoon and there was still just enough warmth in the air to still be comfortable. She settled in and pulled the book Ms. Grace had loaned her. She rolled her eyes at the hokey title, and opened the cover to the first page.

She instantly realized she needed to handle the book with care. The old musty pages were brittle, and it would take very little to damage them. Abby didn't relish the idea of having to explain to Ms. Grace how she had inadvertently damaged one of the matron's precious books. It was clear her guardian placed great value in them.

"Close your eyes and empty your thoughts," the book instructed. It was only then she would supposedly be able to allow the essence of fate to move through her. The book read like a bad New Age meditation manual, and it took all of Abby's concentration not to put it away. She sighed and read a few more pages.

I might as well give one a try, she thought. Abby made herself as comfortable as she could on the bench and glanced around to make certain no one was around. She closed her eyes and placed her hands on her lap. *Think of nothing,* she reminded herself, pushing intrusive thoughts from her mind.

Abby sat in nothingness for what seemed an eternity. The only thing that came from the nothingness was more nothing… Abby opened her eyes and gave thought to giving up and trying another time, but something in her told her to keep going. She decided to give it another try.

Nothing…

There was a flash. It appeared in her mind for only a fraction of a second. She saw long light-colored hair floating beneath the water. She opened her eyes abruptly. Her heart was pounding in her chest. Abby honestly thought it would never work. She wasn't certain what the hair floating in the water meant; it didn't look familiar. It could have been her own hair, but it was hard to distinguish in the dark murky water. Still, she had done it!

Her success, however minor it might have been, put a smile on Abby's face. She had induced a vision. She couldn't wait to tell Ms. Grace of her success. She pushed the old book into her bag and threw it over her shoulder as she stood. For the first time, Abby felt like maybe there was something in the occult arts she might be good at.

She made her way up to the main courtyard towards the path that would lead her towards Ms. Grace's residence. Abby looked up to the sky. *It's probably going to be one of the last nice days before Fall,* she thought. The leaves along the path were beginning to turn. Already, a few lay on the lawns.

The path cut past the main building and turned a corner. Abby rounded the turn and stopped dead in her tracks. There, standing in front of her, was an enormous young man, Edgar Kincaid.

Abby reflexively stepped back. He had a wild look in his eye; she could see the red glow. She glanced around, but there was no aid to be found. She was alone.

"What are you?" Edgar questioned through gritted teeth. She stepped back again. He was over a foot taller than Abby and built of nothing but muscle. Abby couldn't breathe. His massive bulk filled Abby's vision; she knew she had nowhere to run.

Edgar lunged forward with speed that did not seem natural and grabbed Abby's wrist, painfully. She struggled fruitlessly to escape his crushing grip. The pain was so intense she struggled to breathe. "Let go!" she gasped, hoping someone might hear.

He pulled her close, his face covered in a look of fury, his eyes flashing bright red. "What are you?" he repeated, anger and frustration mingling in his menacing tone.

Abby fell to her knees. She feared her wrist was going to break. He did not seem the least bit worried. *The locket!* Using her free hand, she reached up and clenched the pendant hanging from her neck.

A faint glow surrounded her fist, and she could hear a faint sizzling sound. Edgar cried out in agony. His grip loosened just enough. She used his distraction to pull her wrist free. When she looked up, she saw Edgar was holding his hand. It was horribly burned.

Did the amulet do that? It must have. Abby's thoughts whirled as she came to her feet.

"*WHAT ARE YOU?*" Edgar roared. Anger roiled from every inch of his body. His eyes were bright red orbs of glowing energy.

She started, not by the sound, but by another sensation: the faint smell of sulfur. "Someone you should leave alone!" she said her voice trembling with fear. She turned and ran down the path towards Calder House. Her expeditious retreat didn't make her threat particularly forbidding, but wisdom dictated she remove herself. Clearly, he could sense she was different, but he didn't know what she was.

He doesn't know what I am? She filed the thought away to examine later. Pushing it from her mind, Abby ran as quickly as she could the rest of the way to Calder House.

Abby collapsed in an unceremonious heap on the floor, her heart and mind both running marathons. She could hear footsteps rushing up the stairs from the sanctum. She let her book bag drop to the floor as Benjamin, Josephine and Ms. Grace spilled into the living room where Abby was still panting and rubbing her wrist.

"What happened?" Benjamin asked. Ms. Grace came around the tall young man. With her glasses on the tip of her nose, she carefully looked Abby over before settling her eyes on Abby's wrist.

"I ran into Edgar, just now. I think he's gone," Abby said breathlessly.

Josephine glanced out the window. Ms. Grace approached and carefully took her hand, pulling back the thin sweater to expose her wrist. It was swollen and turning a sickly blackish blue. The stern woman let out a gasp.

"This could be broken." The reserved schoolmistress said, shocked. "What did he do to you? I insist you tell me." Abby was surprised by her guardian's tone.

"Bloody Hell!" Benjamin yelled as he noticed the hand print circling Abby's wrist. "I'm going to…"

"Do nothing!" Josephine interrupted, taking Benjamin's arm. "This is not the time," she snapped. His face was turning red. She turned to Abby with a concerned look on her face.

"I'm alright really." Abby tried to reassure them. She certainly didn't want anyone to get into a fight over this.

"Tell us what happened Abby, please." Ms. Grace softened, and guided her into the sanctum.

"Josephine, will you get some ice for this please?"

Josephine nodded, and dragged Benjamin into the kitchen with her.

Abby sat in an overstuffed leather chair, and stared into the fire.

Josephine came back a few moments later with a small bag of ice wrapped in a thick towel. She handed it to Abby who carefully applied it to her wrist. Abby noticed Benjamin return, somewhat more subdued than before.

"Thank you," she told Josephine, not just for the ice; Benjamin's raging temper wouldn't help matters right now. "I'll be okay, I don't think it's broken," Abby assured her attendants. She felt uncomfortable being the center of attention. She didn't like conflict or confrontation and feared things could easily escalate.

Abby told them the story. It seemed like it took ten minutes to explain what happened in a matter of seconds. "I found it rather unusual he didn't know what I was," Abby stated.

"How so?" Josephine asked.

"I… I've been reading a little about demons. Since our discussion the other day about other types of beings, I got curious," she answered, mildly embarrassed at having to admit her curiosity in something that for them, was so common as to be beneath mention.

The others looked surprised. "You think Edgar is a demon?" Benjamin asked.

Ms. Grace interjected, "Your curiosity is understandable, but why do you believe Mr. Kincaid to be a demon?"

Abby shrugged, embarrassed. "It seemed the likeliest option. The eyes. His temper... and just now, I thought I smelled sulfur when he attacked me." She was beginning to doubt her assumptions. Why did she even think that? If these three experienced witches hadn't considered it, why did she think she would have the answer?

"It is possible," Ms. Grace mused. "It's my understanding that there are certain types of demons which are particularly fond of collecting the souls of witches. Witches souls holding more power than a common mortal's soul," she explained.

"But, wouldn't a demon be able to identify exactly what I am then?" Abby asked.

Ms. Grace stood and paced in front of the fireplace. Abby could see the scuff marks on the floor indicating this was one of the deputy headmistress's favorite things to do when she was thinking.

"Perhaps we were mistaken in our assumptions," Ms. Grace said. Abby blinked, surprised to hear her mentor echoing the thought she had a moment before. "A demon could have influence here. But why didn't we see it sooner?"

"After the charm burned him, I could smell sulfur. Doesn't that imply he is demonic in nature?" Abby added.

"A demon should have had a stronger reaction to the charm," Ms. Grace answered.

"He's neither a demon nor possessed by one," Josephine added, "but it would seem there are demonic forces at work around him."

"It raises the question of whether he is in league with them or being manipulated by them," Ms. Grace said, still pacing. "Either way we should be cautious. I cannot easily expel him from school; his family is well-connected, politically. Besides he's a student and under my supervision. Until we have more facts I won't allow action to be taken."

Benjamin sat in the chair next to Abby. She didn't like how angry he still looked. She preferred the handsome flirtatious jokester she knew him to be. "Really I'm going to be fine." She said as an aside to him. "It's not broken, it's just a bruise." He gave her a forced smile and continued to brood in his chair. "Promise me you won't do anything, please." Abby was concerned, she didn't want Benjamin to go off and have a confrontation.

He hesitated for a few moments; obviously, he didn't want to make any promises. "Please Benjamin. Abby's right. We don't need any more problems right now," Josephine added.

"Josephine, I want you to make the poultice on page sixty-three of the Mystarium Arcanum Alchemicum. We'll place it on her wrist with some bandages. It should speed the healing process," Ms. Grace seemed distant and spoke as though she were only half there. She walked over to a bookcase and pulled a small book from the shelf and handed it to Benjamin. "I want you to prepare the warding salts on page two-hundred and fourteen. Make enough for the three of you; I've already erected the ward on this house. The three of you will need it for your dormitories."

She then pulled another book from a different bookshelf and retreated to her desk. "You should practice your exercises Miss Kane. You may need to know how to use those instincts sooner than planned," Ms. Grace said as she began committing pen to paper.

Abby remained in her chair and spent a few moments attempting to clear her mind and ignore the throbbing pain emanating from her wrist. It seemed futile at first, though she supposed working through this kind of distraction was a good lesson.

She stared into the fire, letting her thoughts drift.

Josephine appeared next to her, carrying a bowl full of foul-looking green goo. Abby curled her nose at the smell, but tried to ignore it. Without a word, she started applying the paste to Abby's wrist. It looked like guacamole and smelled like a horse stall before a good mucking out. Abby remained still, watching the other girl work. Her thoughts were a jumble. *Am I in shock?* she wondered. Her mind was jolted back to the pain in her wrist as Josephine started to wrap her injury in bandages.

"Don't take this off." Josephine stated as she finished wrapping Abby's wrist. "Come back tomorrow and I'll apply more poultice and fresh bandages." Abby nodded.

Ms. Grace produced three pieces of paper each inscribed with the same incantation, accompanied by a strange little symbol and handed each of them a copy. "This is a warding spell. The instructions are on the pages I have given you. Make certain when you inscribe the symbol on your doorway and windowpane you do so discretely. I do not want any of you sent to my office for defacing school property."

Benjamin handed Ms. Grace the salts he had prepared per the instructions. She took it to the Alchemical table and portioned it into three equal parts and brushed them into small bags. She then handed them out. "You will need these warding salts for the incantation. Make certain you follow the instructions to the letter."

"Thank you, Ms. Grace." Abby fumbled putting the items in her book bag, her bandaged wrist rendering her other hand useless.

"None of you do anything else without my approval," Ms. Grace added, her usual stern demeanor taking on a new tone of seriousness. "It is enough that you protect yourselves for now. Whatever demonic forces are at play here, we must act with caution. We cannot act until we know more about Edgar Kincaid."

CHAPTER SEVEN

Abby woke up to the alarm clock. It was refreshing to finally be on the same schedule as everyone else. It was Saturday morning, and for the first time since she started at Armitage Hall, her day was filled with fun and exciting things, rather than the dull drum of classes and perpetual study.

She got up and made her way to the bathroom. It was still early for a weekend, and the school was quiet. For the first time, Abby was able to shower in solitude and do her hair and makeup without having to compete for mirror space. It was heaven.

She returned to her room and began the process of picking what she would wear. Having to wear a uniform every day, it was a choice she rarely had to give much thought anymore.

Nina stirred behind her in the warm comfortable bed she so rarely liked to leave until late morning. Sarah was also just starting to wake up and untangling herself from her blankets.

"Good morning," Abby whispered.

"Good morning," Sarah responded quietly as she sat up in bed and found her slippers with wandering feet.

Abby pulled a periwinkle dress from her closet and presented it to Sarah. "What do you think? She asked in hushed tones.

"It's very nice," Sarah said allowing her eyes to focus. She stood and grabbed her bag of toiletries. "I'll be back in a couple minutes and we can grab something from the dining hall before we go into the village." Sarah was still groggy.

"Sounds good. Should I wake Nina?" She asked.

Sarah kicked Nina's bed on her way out. "Get up you lazy lay about." Nina stirred and mumbled something incoherent. Sarah shrugged. "I'd keep working at it. She'll be disappointed if we go without her." With that Sarah disappeared down the hall.

"Ni-na," Abby sang melodically as though she were coercing a child. She sat at the edge of Nina's bed. Abby walked her fingers up Nina's arm and neck onto her face where she playfully tweaked her nose. There was a slight stir. "Ni-na," Abby sang again. She could see a slight smile beginning to form on the edge of her friend's lips. "You, total faker!" Abby playfully accused and began tickling her friend's sides. Nina squirmed and squealed as Abby's relentless tickling continued. "Come on. You know we're going to leave soon. You need to get ready," Abby added.

Nina finally sat up. She gave Abby a dark look before grabbing her bag and making her way to the bathroom.

Abby took the time to put on her dress. It was one of her favorites. Her mother had picked it out on a shopping trip to San Francisco. It came from a little boutique where the owner designed and made all the clothing in her shop. Abby smiled as she remembered how much fun they had had that day. The designer had even done a fitting for her, so the dress would be tailored perfectly. She always felt classy in the dress, and a little bit sexy.

She carefully placed the delicate charm Ms. Grace had given her around her neck, and put on a pair of diamond-studded earrings her uncle Sebastian had given her for her sixteenth birthday. They were elegant solitaires; antique mine cut diamonds with a unique distinctive look. She had no idea where he'd gotten them, but they sparkled more in firelight and natural light than in the electric lights of modern times.

The thought of her family brought a familiar ache to her chest. She wondered if Sebastian was safe; if any of them were. She hadn't heard anything in a while. Had something else happened? She immediately pushed her thoughts aside; she wasn't ready to share her grief with the world. *Today is a holiday! No more gloomy thoughts!* she told herself. *I deserve to have a little fun.*

Though it was only an excursion into town for a sporting event, Abby wanted to look nice. She had noticed that many of the students took pride in dressing up when they got to wear something other than their uniform, or maybe it was another cultural difference, but as a result they typically wore their best clothing, and Abby wanted to be a part of that. It had been a long time since she cared about anything like her appearance, but in the last few weeks, she had found herself spending a little extra time making sure she looked her best.

It was only a coincidence that she had spent more time on her appearance since starting her specialized training. It had nothing whatsoever to do with meeting Benjamin Hodge. Today gave her an opportunity to express her own tastes and sense of style. That was all.

Satisfied she looked amazing, Abby sat and read from her book as she waited for her friends to return. They both returned, elegantly dressed for their day away from campus. Sarah wore a beautiful, yellow satin sari. The printed design was so elaborate, Abby's eyes couldn't follow the pattern. It was stunningly lovely.

Nina looked sophisticated in a pink fitted blazer with white and gold buttons, over a darker burgundy-colored blouse and a simple pencil skirt. It looked like a designer outfit, custom made to flatter her figure. They were a vision of complimentary contrasts.

"You both look so pretty." Abby said looking at her roommates. She was genuinely surprised how different they looked in regular clothing. They almost seemed like strangers.

"Well, you're a total knock out." Nina said giving Abby a looking over. "I love those earrings!" she said moving in for a closer look.

"Thank you." Abby tied one of the silk scarves her grandmother gave her for Christmas around her neck. She gave herself a final glance in the mirror. She fussed with her red hair until it flowed long and straight, ending in loose curls.

The three girls grabbed their purses and bags, making their way to the dining hall where they grabbed a quick bite to eat. Not in a hurry to wait, they started the short walk to the village.

"Please tell me there's a café or something in town." Abby pleaded as they strolled down the path.

"There is, and they have Italian coffees, too." Nina added. Being true-born Seattleite, Abby was a fan of strong Italian coffees. It had been nearly a month since she had smelled anything that resembled the coffee from home. Tea was great, but she only used it to stave away the horrible withdrawal from caffeine. It just wasn't the same.

The village was a quaint little town, consisting of a single main street lined with various shops and boutiques. At the end was a fancy looking hotel, no doubt for visiting parents and school alumni. There was a bustle along the avenue. Various students whose faces looked familiar, and even a few she knew by name added to the foot-traffic. A number of unfamiliar adults were present as well, who didn't appear to be garden-variety village dwellers. Abby imagined they were the parents of students competing in the sporting events.

"Did you girls think you could ditch me so easily?" A familiar voice said from behind them. Nina squealed and embraced Warren.

"Not at all." Abby said, giving Warren a warm smile. "I'm on a quest for some coffee!" she proclaimed, determined to indulge her craving. She needed something that would remind her of home.

"You Americans and your coffee…" Warren said, shaking his head. Abby playfully slugged him in the shoulder. "You're all so violent, too," he added with a smile.

Abby laughed. "That's right, Lord Lampton, you better watch it because I could totally take you," she bantered.

"Think so? I'm a dirty hair puller. I never fight fair." Warren quipped tying the girls up in laughter.

Abby playfully backed down. "No, not the hair! This took too long." Abby joked. "You got lucky this time."

"There's the café." Sarah pointed. It was a quaint little shop, with a menu of coffee, teas, and pastries. There were several small tables. Pictures of each graduating class from the school hanging on the walls. The owner had decorated the shop with porcelain tea sets and crocheted tea cozies. It was lovely.

Abby excitedly made her way to the counter and reviewed the menu. A nice middle-aged woman stood behind the counter with a blue apron and welcoming face. "What can I get you dear?"

Abby smiled. She was practically beaming with excitement. "I'll have a quad-shot sixteen-ounce mocha to go, please." She wanted a caffeine buzz and a quad always did the trick. The woman rang her up and Abby handed her the credit card her Grandmother had given her. She then turned to see an amused look on Nina and Warrens face. Sarah looked like a mother ready to scold a child.

"A quad?" Sarah questioned, tapping her foot.

Abby shrugged her shoulders and threw up her hands. "What can I say. I'm a complete addict." Her friends laughed and shook their heads.

A few moments later, Abby was in coffee heaven. She sat at the table with her friends who watched her consume the drink as though she had just discovered the meaning of life.

"You're hilarious Abby." Sarah stated as she laughed at Abby's delighted expressions.

Abby realized, this was the first moment in a very long time she felt content. It was as though she had shed the weight of grief for a few, blissful, hot beverage-induced, moments.

"Maybe I should switch to coffee," Nina laughed.

"Hello," A vaguely familiar voice interrupted. Abby looked up to see Pru and her friend, Cecily standing a few feet away. They were dressed to the hilt in their designer clothing and expensive hand bags, exactly as expected. Abby wasn't impressed. "You look positively fantastic Abby, I barely recognized you." Her backhanded compliment was weighted with her poor impression of kindness.

"Thank you Pru," Abby said in the same tone. "I love your Balenciaga handbag. Didn't I see that same one in Vogue... a couple years ago?"

Pru's false kindness melted away, leaving a challenge in her perfectly mascaraed eyes. She scoffed and retreated, clearly fuming. *Well, I didn't make any friends today.* Abby mentally shrugged.

Sarah, Nina and Warren giggled quietly, not wanting to invoke the attention of Pru who was only a few feet away, talking to Cecily in heated tones. "That was epic," Warren commented.

"She really doesn't like you Abby," Sarah said stifling, her laughter.

"I didn't realize you had claws," Nina said a smile on her face.

"I've been going to a girl's private school my entire life." Abby reminded them. "Sometimes you just have to defend yourself," she stated simply, and took another sip of coffee.

"I'm definitely switching to coffee!" Nina proclaimed.

The four friends strolled down the lane, making a few small purchases along the way. Abby picked up some chocolate sweets at one shop, Nina introduced Abby to the local tailor, explaining how they mostly do fittings and alterations. Abby was enjoying herself immensely. Her roommates were really fun people. *Maybe making friends wouldn't be the end of the world,* she thought, a soft simple smile playing on her face.

"The competition will start in about twenty minutes. We should start heading over to the pond so we can get good seats," Warren stated, looking at the time on his phone. Abby pulled out her own phone and sent Benjamin a good luck text.

"Who are you texting?" Nina questioned knowingly. She had a sly smile on her face.

"You know very well who," Abby said as her face turned red, and shoved her phone back into her purse.

"We should hurry," Sarah said. "The bleachers are going to fill quickly."

The four of them walked east of town where a parade of students, faculty members, and parents followed a path towards the water. The trail opened into a large clearing adjacent to an enormous pond.

Abby could see the markers in the water indicating the route. There were three sets of bleachers set up a great distance apart. There appeared to be seats located where the boats would launch, one at the center of the course, and one at the finish line.

"Mind if I join you?" Josephine approached, dressed in a tasteful brown dress matching the color of her eyes.

"Of course not," Abby responded. "You know my friends Sarah, Nina and Warren don't you?"

"I certainly do," Josephine waved politely.

"Where should we sit?" Sarah asked contemplating their options.

"I have no idea, I've never been to one of these before." Abby realized she had no clue which set of bleachers had the best view.

"Let's take the one at the end," Warren stated. "Then we can congratulate the team when we win."

"Sounds good," Nina agreed. The five of them walked through the grass towards the finishing line, where the bleachers were quickly filling with other spectators.

"If we sit near the top we can see farther," Josephine suggested.

"There are some seats over there." Warren pointed out a section at the top was still open. The group quickly climbed the stairs and claimed their seats.

"What schools are we playing against?" Abby inquired unfamiliar with the other schools in the competition.

"We're playing against two other schools, Lennox Academy and Winslow Prep," Sarah answered.

"We have a long-standing feud with Lennox Academy, but today, Winslow Prep is the school to beat," Nina added. The group continued to visit and chat casually as they waited for the starting pistol.

Abby noticed Josephine was keeping to herself. It's not that Abby knew her all that well, but Josephine did not seem to be her usual self with the others around. She had come to know the other girl as a kind and engaging young woman; studious, sure and passionate about alchemy. Perhaps a bit abstruse when discussing technical details of potions, which Abby did not understand, but Josephine was always kind to her. Today, she seemed distant and cold. The others didn't seem to notice, but Abby suspected they didn't know Josephine as well as she did. *Not that I really know her all that well,* she thought.

In the distance, the sound of a gun snapped Abby's attention away from her friend. A rising cheer could be heard from the starting line, and though they could see the thin vessels making their way across the pond it was difficult to tell if anyone was taking an early lead. Spectators were beginning to stand and wave the school flag. Abby and the others did the same. The boats were moving fast, Abby was having a difficult time distinguishing what boats belonged to each school. It wasn't until they approached the midpoint she was able to differentiate one school from the next. Armitage Hall was the dark green, Lennox Academy was a deep burgundy, and Winslow Prep was black. They were all so close it was impossible to tell who would win.

"Are they always this close?" Abby asked Josephine.

"Sometimes they are, but only when all the teams are strong competitors. This is actually a really good race," she said, casually waving her flag. Abby watched as they passed the middle row of bleachers. She could tell by the cheers in the distance Armitage Hall was likely in the lead. She could feel her heart beating faster with excitement.

"Don't do any magic," Josephine whispered in Abby's ear. "Benjamin likes to win fairly." The thought hadn't occurred to her. Abby wondered briefly if that was something other witches often did. She knew they used witchcraft to charm people and formulate advantageous business deals.

True, she still didn't know the culture around magic all that well. Was this kind of cheating common? Using it to win a school-sporting event seemed petty. She was glad Benjamin wouldn't approve.

The teams were reaching the final length of the course. It looked like Armitage Hall was ahead of Winslow Prep by half a boat length and a full boat length ahead of Lennox Academy.

"We're winning!" Sarah couldn't help herself. Abby was amused. It was nice to see a smile on her face; she felt it was something Sarah didn't do often enough. Warren and Nina were waving their flag wildly. Abby noticed Josephine was standing there, watching with a flag in her hand, but it didn't seem like she was really participating, it was as if she was going through the motions. *I guess this just isn't her thing?.She must only be here to support her brother,* Abby thought.

The boats were getting close enough Abby could see the young men rowing furiously. The lean racing shell cut through the water almost seamlessly as the crew used the oars to propel the watercraft to incredible speed.

It was clear Lennox Academy was lagging behind, but Winslow Prep was beginning to creep up towards Armitage Hall's boat. Abby could feel the nerves in her stomach as she watched the crew paddling the oars with synchronized strokes. They were close enough she could see the stern concentration on their faces as they powered through every stroke.

Abby could see Benjamin near the back in seventh position. She couldn't help but smile at the look of concentration on his face. Edgar sat just in front of him, in sixth position. She wasn't entirely certain what the placement meant but Warren had assured her when explaining the sport earlier, that these were important positions on the crew.

Nina was nearly biting her nails, and Sarah had a look of concern as Winslow Prep continued to close the gap. "Come on!" Warren yelled his hands balled into fists.

It looked like Winslow Prep and Armitage Hall were neck and neck, each stroke seemed to propel one boat in front of the other for a brief moment in a maddening exchange in who took the lead. Abby could feel the anxiousness growing as her body flushed with adrenaline. The finishing line was only a few yards away. It looked like Winslow Prep was about to win. Suddenly Armitage Hall rallied and crossed the line less than a yard ahead of Winslow Prep.

There was thunderous applause as the audience began cheering in a wild frenzy of excitement. Nina and Warren were jumping up and down while Sarah waved her flag frantically, beaming with joy. Abby felt herself get caught up in the moment. She glanced over at Josephine who was clapping, a bored look on her face.

"We won!" Nina yelled. She continued to jump up and down as though she were winding up to explode. Warren attempted to calm her down. Sarah was giddy, waving her flag and cheering with the crowd. Down in the water, the rowing team was celebrating, waving their paddles triumphantly, and all around them spectators were cheering.

The bleachers began to empty as the team congregated to receive their trophy and take pictures. Abby and her friends, along with other students, waited on the sideline for the athletes to finish their photo obligations near the boathouse.

"I'm heading back to school. I'll see you later," Josephine said.

"Is everything alright?" Abby asked before Josephine could escape.

"Quite alright. I'm not fond of crowds." She responded with a smile. Abby felt there was more to her discomfort, but it wasn't her place to pry. Instead she gave her a friendly smile and watched as Josephine disappeared into the crowd.

There was a great deal of excitement as the players mingled with students and visiting parents. Abby glanced around and discovered Nina and Sarah retreated to a table with several students, discussing the details of the sport. Abby had decided to join them, when she caught sight of Edgar Kincaid. She stopped dead in her tracks. He was wearing the rowing kit but had put on a jacket. He locked eyes with her. His face had the same irritated look as before, as though she was some disgusting monster. She didn't dare look away. She was absolutely terrified of Edgar, but she didn't want him to know that. He quickly disappeared in the crowd.

As soon as he was out of sight, Abby reminded herself to breathe. She continued her approach to the table and visited with the girls for a few minutes, but found it hard to concentrate on the conversation. She excused herself and went to check on Warren. Having a person like Edgar Kincaid around made Abby worry about the people she cared for.

She saw a line of tents where many of the athletes were changing, and followed the edge of the tent around back into an empty field. No one was out there. Abby sighed, knowing she was likely worried over nothing, and turned to head back. She stopped. Warren stood, arms wrapped around a tall oarsman. Abby hadn't seen such a heated embrace outside of television before, and seeing her friend making out with none other than Wyatt Simmons, one of Prunella Morgan's inner circle, was shocking, to say the least.

She blushed furiously, instantly realizing she shouldn't have seen this, and attempted to escape before they saw her. Her efforts to depart discretely failed. The two boys noticed her, and abruptly stepped apart from one another. Warren seemed pleased with himself, but Wyatt was obviously mortified.

"Please don't say anything," Wyatt said pleading with Abby.

"Why would I do that?" Abby questioned. She approached Warren and took his arm like a close friend. "Warren's my friend. There's nothing to be ashamed of," she said, as much to herself as to the two boys. "I'm only sorry I interrupted."

"Oh, he thinks there is," Warren added under his breath.

"Really?' Abby was surprised, her embarrassment faded. She was so used to being around gay people it hadn't occurred to her anyone would still hide it, not these days.

"I can't, my parents… I just can't." Wyatt fumbled with words and stormed off in a huff.

Abby stopped herself from trying to stop him. She wanted to help but knew it wasn't her place.

"Don't waste your time, I've been trying to convince him to get over it for nearly a year now," Warren said, irritated. It was obvious he could tell what she was thinking.

Abby waited a few moments and leaned her head on Warren's shoulder as he escorted her back to the crowd. "I'm sorry," Abby apologized.

"No harm done. I think you shook Wyatt up a little, but he'll get over it," Warren said.

"You've been seeing him for a year?" Abby asked, contemplating how difficult it would be to hide one's affections from the other students at a school where privacy was scarce.

"Yes, just over a year actually. If you can call what we have seeing each other." Warren seemed depressed.

"It won't always be like this," Abby tried to help.

"I know, but right now is the only time I have to deal with," He responded. "Sometimes it's hard waiting for things to get better." Abby hugged his arm affectionately.

"Aren't you a dish." Said a sweet masculine voice from her left. She released Warren and turned. Abby blushed deeply, seeing Benjamin, his eyes exploring her from head to toe. She was relieved to note he was wearing a jacket and sweatpants over his form-fitting rowing kit; she wasn't ready to face the full reality of him. Instead, she gave him a smile and threw her arms around him.

"Congratulations, Mr. Hodge," Abby said breaking the friendly hug. He didn't let go. Abby stiffened awkwardly, as he held her in his arms. She could feel her heart starting to speed as he pulled her tight to his body. Her breath quickened as she relaxed against him. He was surprisingly warm. When he released her he didn't let her go far, still holding her close. His hands stayed locked around her waist, and Abby found herself enjoying the unfamiliar sensation. She tried her best to relax into it. She knew how reserved she was, but standing with Benjamin this way felt good. *Perhaps I'm learning to loosen up…*

"You look really nice," He said. "In fact, you may very well be the most beautiful girl here." He said with his flirtatious grin. Abby blushed again, and started to mutter her thanks, but he kept talking. "There's always a victory party when we win these things. They're your standard piss parties, so I should probably bring a date. I would rather not be the only guy there without a partner," he said slyly.

"Oh? I guess we should try and find you a date," Abby responded playfully pretending to look around the crowd.

Benjamin laughed, and she smiled, looking up at his soft face. He locked eyes with Abby, and her heart stopped as she stared into his fathomless brown eyes. He kissed her. His lips were warm and soft, so much softer than she imagined.

It was her first real kiss. His hands on her waist held her upright, which was a relief since her knees had stopped working. He was sweeping her off her feet, and Abby could feel herself surrendering even further to his charms. She lost herself in the moment. When he pulled away Abby opened her eyes and instantly turned red, as she realized their kiss had drawn some attention.

Benjamin laughed at the expression on her face and wrapped his arm around her shoulder, escorting her through the crowd. Nina was bubbling with excitement. Abby tried not to notice; it would have embarrassed her more. Nina gave her a thumbs up and a wink. Warren shared a conspiratorial smile with her. Sarah looked surprised and worried at the same time.

"I'll see you guys later," Abby commented and waved as they weaved through the crowd.

"Are they your friends?" Benjamin asked.

"Yes, Nina and Sarah are my roommates and Warren is Nina's best friend. They've been great, especially when I arrived and didn't know anyone," Abby explained.

"I don't need to worry about this Warren, do I?" Benjamin asked with a smirk.

She laughed. "You mean to tell me, you've been going to this school for years and you didn't know Warren was totally, completely and hopelessly gay?"

Benjamin seemed amused. "Not really, I mean I've suspected it but never really knew. I haven't been in the loop these last few years," He responded. "Josephine and I spend most of our free time studying the craft. We've mostly lost touch with the other students."

"I could see how that might happen. Don't you have any friends though?" Abby thought it was sad the twins were so isolated from the other students, though, it did explain a few things about Josephine this afternoon.

"A couple, but no one close. You know how it is. You need to be careful around the populace. They can't know what we are," Benjamin said, his tone circumspect. "That's one of the things I really like about being around you, we don't have to hide anything, and we can be ourselves." Abby smiled. She recognized the appeal. She had thought about it herself in much the same way. Witchcraft had been a larger part of his life than it was for her, so it made sense that he grew up in further isolation.

The two of them finally broke through the crowd and followed the path back to the village. He let go of her shoulder and took her hand instead. *Another first*, Abby thought, gripping his hand back.

"I think you are the softest thing I've ever touched," Benjamin observed. His thumb stroked the back of her hand, sending tingles up her arm. Abby blushed.

"You're shameless Mr. Hodge," Abby quipped. She had never been particularly good at accepting compliments.

"I don't really want to go to that party," Benjamin declared, as though he was considering other options.

"Oh? You should celebrate your victory."

"I think I'd rather snog in the woods with a pretty girl." He gave her a wicked smile.

"What kind of girl do you think I am?" Abby laughed nervously. She was not entirely certain what the complete definition of snog was. She thought it meant making out, but her command of British slang was tenuous at best. *I guess I'm about to find out.* She grinned as Benjamin leaned in for another kiss.

CHAPTER EIGHT

Abby and Benjamin thought it best to keep their budding relationship a secret from Ms. Grace. They were both sure she would likely not approve, and Abby was convinced if their mentor found out she would inform her grandmother. The last thing Abby wanted was a surprise visit from Vivian Kane.

Abby headed through the crisp evening air towards Ms. Grace's cottage. The daylight was disappearing earlier and earlier; it was already dusk. Soon there would be no daylight after school hours. When Abby arrived, she gave Benjamin the same friendly greeting she gave the others. In return, he accentuated his greeting with a discrete wink, putting a smile on her face.

Abby made her way to the chair by the fireplace. She pulled out the book on meditation that Ms. Grace had her working from, and began to prepare her mind.

She slowly allowed the world to become a part of her awareness. With her eyes closed, she could sense the chairs around her, and then the room at large. She became aware of Josephine standing a few feet behind her, working with a mortar and pestle. She was grinding herbs and other reagents into a fine paste. She sensed the other girl's worry and concern, as though they radiated from her like a strange light. It was an odd sensation. She had never been able to sense other people's emotions with her powers, at least not intentionally.

She moved her consciousness to Benjamin. He seemed calm, a soft bemusement radiating from him that she had come to learn was his natural emotion, but there was more. Under that cool exterior was a sense of concern and, she wasn't certain but, perhaps a sense of regret and remorse. *I wonder what's bothering him,* Abby thought. She wasn't quite sure how to interpret what she was sensing, but she decided dwelling on it would be intrusive.

She left him to his thoughts, and switched her focus to Valerie Grace. There was a strong sense of duty accompanied by anxiety and determination. Abby could feel how tightly her teacher was wound. She stopped there, unwilling to probe any deeper. There were some secrets she wasn't sure she wanted the answer to.

She began pushing the environment out of her mind, focusing inward again and allowed herself to reenter consciousness. She opened her eyes.

A wave of fatigue coursed through her body. The book she was reading said dabbling in fate and using the Sight came with a toll. She couldn't disagree. It felt as if she had run a mile; her body besieged with feverish aches. It took a few minutes, but as she sat quietly reconnecting to her environment, she began to recover from the psychic whiplash of using the Sight.

"I did it," Abby proclaimed. A part of her had doubted it would work at all, afraid the exercise would be little more than hokey new-age drivel.

"What did you do?" Josephine asked.

"I performed the Empathy Meditation," She explained. "It allows me to reach out and be aware of the surface feelings of others. With practice, I can learn more perhaps even understand what people are thinking."

"You don't have to use it on me," Benjamin said. "I'll tell you anything you want." He gave her a wink.

"That's very impressive Abigail," Ms. Grace stated pulling her focus from the pages in front of her. "Your grandmother was right, you do have a special gift."

"Special?" Abby asked. "Can't any of us do this?"

"No, not at all, not everyone has a unique talent for magic. In fact, some of us wield these powers at a terrible price. You are one of the lucky few Miss Kane," Her teacher stated.

"I didn't realize," Abby responded. She had thought she was developing a skill with which she was simply deficient. Even if she wasn't as talented with magic in general, perhaps this could be the one thing through which she could excel.

"This may be something we can use to our advantage," Ms. Grace considered. "Don't you have Mr. Kincaid in one of your classes?"

"Yes," Abby responded. "Should I try this on him?"

"It might give us some insight into what he is, or at least what his motives are," Josephine added.

"Is it dangerous?" Benjamin asked with reservation.

"I doubt it will be. The power is subtle. Did any of you notice when she used the power on you a few minutes ago?" Ms. Grace pointed out. "It would, however, be wise to test things a bit further and give you a little more time to hone your skills."

Abby nodded. It made sense to practice before she used it for real.

"I think I want to attempt scrying next," Abby said. "I've been reading about it, and if I can do the Empathy Meditation, I think I'm ready."

"Very well, Miss Kane, you do seem to have an affinity for divination. What do you wish to use as your focus?" Ms. Grace inquired.

"Is this such a good idea?" Benjamin asked, concern evident in his voice. Both women ignored him.

"I was thinking, maybe water?" Abby continued. "I've always had a connection to the water. Besides I think crystal balls, and such are a little hokey."

"Hokey, indeed," Ms. Grace agreed. "Very well, there are plenty of saucers and bowls in the kitchen. Try to find one with a matte finish. You don't want the sheen from the plate to interfere with your vision. You are welcome to take whatever you need."

"According to the book, natural bodies of water work best," Abby stated.

"Very true. But we can't have you going out at night by yourself. Not with… things as they are," Ms. Grace seemed to be contemplating options.

"We can go with her," Benjamin stated a little too eagerly. "Safety in numbers, right?"

"Speak for yourself. I'm working on this new ointment that requires my near constant attention. I'm staying put," Josephine stated. "Why don't the two of you go," She added, almost as an afterthought. Abby wasn't certain if she was trying to give them some time alone, or if she really was more interested in her potions.

Ms. Grace seemed to consider things for a moment. "I suppose it would be alright. Just don't be late. I don't want anyone getting caught out of the dorms after dark."

"I don't think many people will be out this evening. It's getting too cold at night for casual strolls," Abby said. "But, we'll be careful, Ms. Grace. I promise." She added trying to reassure her guardian.

Abby put her coat back on, and Benjamin grabbed a thick wool pea coat draped over one of the leather chairs. The two climbed the stairs out of the basement and Abby quickly nabbed a dark brown bowl from the cupboard. "Shall we go to the pond or Moore brook?" Abby asked.

"Moore brook is closer," Benjamin stated as he fastened the buttons on his coat.

They walked out the door and Benjamin took her hand guiding her on a path into the wooded area. The path curved around a tree out of sight of the cottage. Benjamin swung Abby around and pushed her up against a tree trunk. He pressed his body against hers, grinning as if he'd won a prize.

He kissed her passionately and unexpectedly. "Hello, Miss Kane," He said playfully. Abby could feel his warm breath on her face. "I thought I would take a moment to give you the greeting I wanted to give you earlier."

Abby cupped his face with her hands, gazing into his beautiful brown eyes. She smiled and gave him a gentle kiss on the lips. He smiled his approval as he put his arms around her. They stood like that for a blissful moment, ignoring the world around them.

Benjamin slowly pulled away and threw an arm around her waist, before the two started down the path again. "Let's see how this works, then," Benjamin said as he guided her towards the brook.

They came upon a stone bridge offering a way to cross the raging stream, bloated from the rain earlier that day. It was familiar. Sarah had taken her this way when she first toured the campus. "Yes, this should work," Abby stated.

"What now?" Benjamin asked guiding her down to the edge of the water.

"I'm going to need to focus, so no distractions, Mr. Hodge," She chastised playfully. "I'll need to gaze into the water, I don't know for how long. I guess until something happens."

Abby began to pace the pebble-covered banks looking for a nice spot. The entire area was damp and muddy.

"Here. Let me help," Benjamin said. He stepped forward and found a spot right next to the water. He held out his right hand and closed his eyes in concentration. Abby watched waiting to see what he was doing. When he opened his eyes, there was a determined expression on his face as he moved his hand as though he were pushing something. Abby watched the water covering the small area begin to retreat back into the brisk little stream. The water moved over the small pebbles as though it were being called home, leaving an entire portion of the bank dry.

"Perfect." Abby was pleased with this thoughtfulness. She collected water from the brook in the bowl she brought with her and sat down folding her legs and placing the bowl in front of her. She gently placed her hands in her lap as she began the process of clearing her mind once more.

Her concentration was broken when she felt Benjamin sit directly behind her. He pressed his chest against her back and wrapped his arms around her waist, his legs spread on each side. She could feel the warmth of his body as he placed his chin on her shoulder. She resisted the urge to open her eyes to gaze at the ridiculously handsome boy behind her.

"I thought I said no distractions," Abby said playfully.

"I know," Benjamin stated in playful innocence. "That's why I'm going to keep you warm, so you aren't distracted by the cold."

"You think of everything don't you?" Abby laughed, and gave him a peck on the cheek, returning her focus to the task at hand. Abby gazed into the bowl and cleared her mind. She did as the book instructed, and allowed her vision to fall out of focus as she gazed into the water. She made several attempts with no success. She felt foolish. Maybe she shouldn't have pushed so fast. After a few minutes she was beginning to think it wasn't going to work.

She tried again. Nothing. *Patience, Abigail,* she told herself. "Patience is essential for the trained and untrained alike." She quoted. The book clearly stated persistence was necessary, and scrying was difficult. "One more time." She heard Benjamin chuckle softly behind her.

Abby closed her eyes and cleared her thoughts. When she opened them again, she allowed her eyes to become unfocused. She then looked down at her hands. The water inside the bowl began to shift, colors swirling and merging to reflect an image as though she were looking through a window submerged in water. Not sure it was working correctly, Abby forced herself to focus harder. Something began to take shape.

She could see a dark room, perhaps a basement. Josephine was there on the floor; she appeared to be injured and lay prone. She was trying to crawl away, but a large towering figure stepped in the way. He was carrying a large wooden stick, a paddle! He raised it above his head and Abby let out a choked breath. There was no mistake; red eyes glowed in the darkness as he swung the oar downward.

Abby was jolted back to consciousness as the paddle made contact with her friend's skull. "Edgar!" She gasped and leapt to her feet, knocking Benjamin on his back by surprise. She snapped back to herself and bolted back to Calder House. Abby was a practiced runner, but the tax from using the Sight, had worn on her, and her footing was tenuous. She tried to run and fight for air at the same time, and stumbled. Utterly exhausted, her body drained of every ounce of strength, Abby stumbled her way back to Calder House.

She could hear Benjamin calling her name, obviously confused and alarmed. She knew scrying was not an exact art. Her books told her it was capable of revealing the past, present and future. But what she had seen... She had to see with her own eyes it was not the present.

Abby flew through the front door and dashed down the stairs. There she saw Ms. Grace sitting by the fire, with a startled expression. At the table in the center of the room Josephine stood frozen with a beaker full of blue liquid and a confused look on her face.

"Thank God, Josephine. You're all right!" Abby rushed forward and gave her friend a hug. Josephine stood there bewildered.

Abby crumbled on the floor, relief sapping her of what little energy that remained. She felt faint, but managed to pick herself up with a little help from Ms. Grace.

"You saw something, didn't you?" Ms. Grace stated more than asked. "What did you see?" She guided Abby to one of the chairs and sat her down, allowing her to catch her breath.

Before Abby could speak, Benjamin burst into the room. "What the bloody hell just happened?" His voice was raised, and he was out of breath from running.

"Abby saw something in the water," Josephine said, as she put her experiment away.

"That much I figured out on my own," Benjamin barked. He leaned against the back of Abby's chair to catch his own breath.

71

"I saw… I saw Edgar Kincaid m-murder Josephine." Abby shuddered as she jumped to the crux of her vision.

Everyone was silent. Abby blinked. Was no one surprised? Ms. Grace seemed lost in thought and Abby noticed a brief but knowing exchange between Benjamin and his sister. Had they suspected this all along? Why was she the only one who seemed worried?

"Give us details Miss Kane, we must know everything," Ms. Grace stated. Her face dropped behind that implacable mask, her lips pursed; Abby had no way of knowing what she was thinking. Ms. Grace pulled a pen and notebook from her desk and prepared to take notes.

Abby took a breath and stilled her racing heart. Panic and shock wouldn't help now. She focused on the image from her vision, and did her best to explain everything from the damp chamber to the wooden paddle he used to bash Josephine's head in like a pumpkin. Abby struggled to remember any defining features in her vision. There were no windows to provide context as to the time of day or perhaps season.

"It sounds like the boathouse," Benjamin commented absently. Josephine looked at him, but had nothing to add.

"Is there anything else?" Ms. Grace persisted, clearly certain some detail was missing or overlooked. Abby reviewed the details again and again. There was little more to say. The room fell silent as the four of them pondered the meaning of Abby's vision. "I fear Mr. Kincaid is more dangerous than I had imagined," Ms. Grace said as she began to pace in front of the fireplace.

"That's an understatement." Benjamin seemed agitated.

Abby had an idea she was sure no one would like, but she thought it worth a chance. "I think I should try using the Sight on him." Abby suggested. "I mean, the meditation, from earlier. I don't think I should wait." They all looked at her, surprise and reluctance on all their faces. "I could find the key to this mystery, and prevent anything from happening to Josephine," she added.

"Or maybe you'll set into motion the events that will lead to the very thing you saw in the water." Benjamin's irritation made him a bit harsh. Abby could feel the sting in his words.

"What do you suggest then? We take him on?" Josephine asked dismissively.

"It's not a bad idea," Benjamin growled. Abby thought he looked like he was ready to tear someone's throat out. She placed her hand on his arm. He pulled away. He didn't want to be consoled, that much was clear.

Abby withdrew and realized this was a side of Benjamin she hadn't really seen before.

"No one is going to instigate a confrontation," Ms. Grace stated. "I think it's time I consulted my coven. There's obviously more going on here than I previously thought. I am going to have to contact your families as well. You are all in more danger than I feared."

Abby's heart leaped into her throat. Vivian Kane was certain to make an appearance. As much as she truly loved her grandmother, she was prone to the kind of melodrama Abby wanted most to avoid. "Ms. Grace, I don't think that would be a good idea. My grandmother is likely to pull me from the school," she said.

"Frankly, Ms. Kane, I'm not certain it would be an unwise decision all things considered." Ms. Grace continued to pace. "He's already hurt you once. None of this sits well with me."

Benjamin glanced at Abby, displeased with the course of the discussion. "Do you really think she would take you away?"

"My grandmother is many things, predictable is not one of them," Abby responded still breathless, the idea of her grandmother showing up was mortifying.

"I'm going to call her this evening. She has the final decision, Abigail. I'm very sorry. I sincerely hope she does not remove you from the school, but needs must." Ms. Grace climbed the stairs and disappeared into her private study, no doubt to call Vivian Kane.

CHAPTER NINE

Abby was anxious. The last two days she had done nothing but anticipate her grandmother's arrival. She wished Benjamin could be with her when she faced the matriarch of House Kane, but the less he had to do with her grandmother the better.

Ms. Grace sat quietly in a chair next to her as passengers flooded through the security checkpoint. Abby watched people coming and going, not thinking, just enjoying the endless parade of travelers. There was a commotion down the hall and Abby knew instantly her grandmother was involved.

"Get that filthy mongrel away from me!" A screeching cry came from the crowd. Abby recognized the voice at once. "Disgusting creatures indeed." Then she came into view. The lovely Vivian Kane, the head of their Coven; Abby's grandmother. She was a tall, lean woman with stark white hair. She looked like a grand dame of the stage; a fading Hollywood legend clinging to the last shred of her once great beauty. She was draped in a flowing white pantsuit accented by jewels, and a scarf adding a hint of color. She moved with the grace of a predator and slinked through the security checkpoint with more attitude than any one person should have the right to possess.

People all around were staring at her as she approached. "Oh! My precious dear, come give your grandmamma a hug and kiss," Vivian proclaimed dramatically. Abby cringed slightly. She dutifully stood and greeted her grandmother. Vivian held her at arm's length and took a long look. "Oh, my darling, you look tired. This is all my fault, I plucked you form one horror and unknowingly placed you in another." She pulled Abby into another long hug.

"I love you," Abby said sincerely. Any trace of exasperation at her grandmother's antics melted away with the embrace. She hadn't realized how much she missed her family. The last time she'd seen Vivian she had still been in a haze of grief.

Vivian made her way over to Ms. Grace. The two women were a study in contrasts. Vivian, with her beautiful white silk pant suit adorned with diamonds and jewels, with her over the top mannerisms and dramatic personality creating a presence that would not be ignored, was the antithesis of Valerie Grace with her plane brown dress and orthopedic shoes. Her reserved and unassuming presence made her a woman working almost desperately to pass unnoticed. Abby watched as they exchanged polite greetings.

"We have a car waiting outside," Ms. Grace stated in her passionless voice. Vivian took Abby's arm and followed the schoolmistress to the parked vehicle. The chauffeur opened the door and looked for luggage.

"Darling, I had it sent ahead," Vivian said in passing, waving a dismissive hand towards the driver as she stepped into the car. Ms. Grace and Abby followed, settling in for a ride. Abby noticed the window separating the driver from the back seat was already closed. I wonder if he's met her before, Abby laughed to herself.

"I don't suppose this quaint little car has any sherry? Or perhaps some brandy?" Vivian asked.

Abby watched as her grandmother looked for something that resembled a liquor cabinet.

"Grandmother, this is a school car," Abby stated, as though her grandmother understood such things, or at least should.

Vivian sat back with a whimsical, disgusted look. "That's no excuse, is it? If I'm to help you with this trifling problem, I would prefer a stiff drink." She stared out the window, pausing like the statue of a woman deep in thought, and sighed. "Well, if I am to be denied such simple luxuries, we might as well get on with it," Vivian stated. Abby just sighed and waited for the emotional tide to turn again.

"Abby has been practicing her divination skills, which I will add are developing quite nicely." Ms. Grace smiled sweetly. "She is showing proficiency in most aspects of the craft. There are a few still to be examined more closely. It won't be long before she's ready to start learning more advanced magic."

Vivian nodded, sagely. "I have plans in place for her education, but before I can allow her to come home, I need to deal with the Thanos coven. It is far too dangerous for one so young and untried." She placed a hand at her neck, as if it was hard for her to speak. "I fear for her safety so, you understand. She is all I have left of my poor son."

Abby watched the two women carry on as if she wasn't sitting there with them in the enclosed space of the car.

"I saw something grandmother," Abby said the seriousness of her words changed Vivian's expression. "It was something terrible."

"Yes,' Vivian said, "that is why I'm here, after all."

"Indeed," Ms. Grace said, addressing Vivian. "About the student I mentioned on the phone, there isn't much I can tell you. We know he's not human, not strictly so, anyway."

"What is the poor wretch? Surely not a true danger?" Vivian inquired intensely, obviously bored with the bland version Ms. Grace was delivering.

"We haven't figured it out yet," Abby helped. "What I saw, him murdering my friend, it was… awful." Abby swallowed hard, but continued. "I've even seen his eyes glow red. Do you know what he could be, Grandmother?"

Vivian appeared to contemplate a thought for a moment. "Not without more to go on. There could be something in your father's library, but your parents…" She paused. "Did you see anything about your parents in your vision?"

"No," Abby said, quickly wanting to move the topic away from her parents.

Vivian schooled her face into a mask of aloof, self-importance. "No matter. About the boy," She turned to Ms. Grace to continue her inquiries. "He sounds like a problem worth considering, but I don't really understand why I'm here."

Seeing her grandmother alone was too close to an unhealed wound. Abby couldn't bear to speak of her parents now. It was too hard to think of them and hold her grief in check, and from the brief moment of genuine emotions from Vivian, Abby knew it was the same for her. It was far too easy to forget that while Abby had lost a mother and father, Vivian Kane had lost a son and daughter. In the moment, she saw something in her grandmother she hadn't ever seen before; compassion, and loneliness.

"I do feel sorry for this friend of yours Abby, I do, but the affairs of the non-magical folk are hardly our concern, not when there is so much happening in our world," Vivian said.

Abby answered her with one bit of information she had been wanting to keep to herself. "Well, no, there are two other students at school who are witches. My friend in the vision, Josephine, is one of them. If Edgar isn't human, and he might be going to kill a witch, doesn't' that make it our problem?" She asked.

Vivian was silent for a few moments, Abby could tell she was letting herself soak in the information. "I suppose that might change things," she said.

"There's more." Ms. Grace interjected. "This boy has also injured your granddaughter."

Abby watched as Vivian went from contemplation to outrage inside of a single heartbeat. "What? What did he do to you?" she demanded.

"It wasn't bad, he bruised me was all. He grabbed my wrist and he injured me, but I'm fine now." Abby was trying to sooth her grandmother's outrage. "Really. I'm fine. See?" She held up her arm for inspection. She feared Vivian would demand the car turn around and take them back to the airport that very instant.

"How dare he put his hands on you! No granddaughter of mine should ever be handled with such disregard. Darling, why didn't you do something to him? Fight back? I did train you in basic defensive magics," Vivian pleaded.

"I… don't know." Abby said meekly. She felt as if she were in trouble.

"You're too soft-hearted, darling. You need to protect yourself. This is why I couldn't have you at home while we deal with our important matter." Vivian reached out to touch Abby's face, but dropped her hand just before it turned into an actual caress. Abby fought the urge to roll her eyes; even now Vivian's dramatics continued. How exhausting.

"It's okay, Grandmother. Ms. Grace gave me a protective charm. When I grabbed the charm, it burned him," Abby added, trying to demonstrate that Ms. Grace had done her job in protecting her.

Vivian brushed away a stray hair on Abby's forehead and studied her. For all her flamboyancy and penchant for dramatic flair, Abby knew Vivian Kane could see through people like glass. Her steely eyes pinned Abby to the seat of the car. "Darling, he scares you, and he should. We have no idea what we're dealing with," she said quietly then turned to Ms. Grace. "What do we know about this boy's family."

"Not very much I'm afraid. We know he was born in Alderley Edge, just outside Manchester. His mother is Nancy Kincaid, and there is no father listed on his birth certificate." The deputy headmistress stated as she rummaged through the large bag she took with her everywhere. "His grandparents, Noreen and Colin Kincaid, are prominent grocers in the Manchester area, however."

"How does the progeny of a grocer end up in a school like this?" Vivian demanded. "I thought this school was more discerning."

"I assure you they are Vivian." Ms. Grace seemed somewhat flustered. "They have more than enough influence to give their grandson the edge he needs in life."

"So, the boy comes from means?" Vivian clarified.

"Modest means by your standards to be sure, but means none the less. The political connections his grandfather has obtained will carry him far enough, I expect." Ms. Grace stated.

"Hmmm, well…" She trailed off in thought. "Is there really nothing about his father? You mentioned his eyes glowed. A demon perhaps? Or an efreet? What do you know about his mother?"

"We considered that, but he doesn't' appear to be a demon. He didn't know I was a witch." Abby interjected, then briefly explained their most recent encounter.

"Even his grandparents claim to know nothing of the father," Ms. Grace added. "His mother is not well; emotionally unstable. She's been hospitalized on multiple occasions for her outbursts. Mr. Kincaid was essentially raised by his grandparents," she mused aloud. "I did meet his mother once. She was a very strange woman."

"How do you mean, darling?" Vivian spoke up as the car breezed into the countryside.

"She was very religious. She wanted to know about the church facilities on campus, and in the village. She was dressed modestly, in a plane black dress, almost like a nun, and constantly clenched the crucifix around her neck. In truth I was happy to see her go when she did, but we haven't seen her since. I believe Edgar was only ten when she visited. That would have been seven years ago. We're at a loss, Vivian, that's why I called you," Ms. Grace continued. She paused, and almost as an afterthought, added, "Abby has offered to use the Sight on the boy."

Abby thought her grandmother looked displeased. "How good are you?" Vivian asked, looking directly in her eyes.

"I'm pretty good," Abby stated, mustering her confidence. "People don't seem to notice when I use the Sight on them, so I think it'll be safe." Abby was certain her grandmother could see every flaw and insecurity with those piercing eyes.

"I need to think about this, Abigail." Vivian said. "Is there really no hooch in this wretched thing?" Ms. Grace reached into her purse and pulled out a silver flask. Abby was shocked to see the prudish Valerie Grace in possession of a flask, never mind its contents. Vivian took a generous drink and handed it back to her.

The rest of the ride was uneventful. Abby's grandmother used the time to catch her up on family events. Vivian carefully avoided any discussion of the situation involving the hunt for her parent's murder, which made the whole conversation feel like a ridiculous waste of time. Abby hated small talk, especially when there were important things she wanted to know. Worse, Abby knew that a more private conversation, when it finally did happen, would be slim on details. All she could do was sit, wait, and listen to her Grandmother gossip.

When they arrived at school, Abby was relieved to see the courtyard was virtually empty. She didn't want her grandmother making a spectacle of herself in front of her fellow students. The three women stepped out of the car. "Go on ahead dear." Vivian waved Ms. Grace along. "We'll catch up in a few minutes. I want Abigail to show me her dormitory."

"Of course," Ms. Grace stated disappearing down the path.

"Do you want to see my room? My roommates might be there," Abby said.

"I'll be here for several days. I can meet them later," Vivian said, motioning for Abby to take a seat on one of the marble benches. There was a nervous feeling building in Abby's stomach. At times conversing with her grandmother was like traversing the sea in a storm, especially after she had had a few drinks.

Abby sat on the stone slab next to her grandmother who gazed upon the grounds passively taking in the cold chilly air. Several students walked by and politely smiled as they moved along the path.

"Tell me how you're really doing darling," Vivian said in a serious tone.

"I'm okay." Abby nodded, doing her best to reassure her grandmother. "I've made some friends here and I'm learning a lot."

Vivian looked at Abby studying her face Her grandmother smiled seemingly accepting of her well-being. "You have the Sight just as I thought," Vivian said, a sense of pride in her words.

"It would seem so," Abby said. "How did you know?"

"I've suspected it for some time," Vivian confessed. "It runs on your mother's side. The Whitlock's have a history of producing a witch every couple of generations gifted with the Sight. It's one of the reasons they are invaluable to the Kane Coven. You've always had a sense for people, and I saw the ability in you to anticipate outcomes that went far beyond the simple application of logic, my dear."

"I didn't realize," Abby said, thinking about what her grandmother said. It was true, but Abby always thought it was normal; something anyone could do. "I have to know," she said, finally getting the words out. "Is everyone back home really okay? Uncle Sebastian? Margot? Madison?"

Vivian nodded. "I assure you each and every one of them is absolutely fine my dear," Vivian said in her most reassuring tone. "We can talk about such matters later. Right now, you are my primary concern."

"I'm fine, really I am," Abby said, feeling even more nervous. She feared her grandmother would bring up her parents again. Her raw emotions were only barely under the surface and she was afraid her grandmother could easily expose them with a simple question.

The question lingered on Vivian's lips, Abby could see it, and the anticipation stirred the water in her eyes. It was as if Vivian could tell Abby was barely holding it together. In that moment Abby felt she and her grandmother stood on the precipice of an emotional well so deep there could be no bottom.

She couldn't afford to be vulnerable right now. *I don't need to know,* she convinced herself. *What if I can't pull myself back? I can't. Not now. Not with her,* she thought.

Vivian took a deep breath and looked away. It was obvious she was attempting to quell her own emotional reaction to seeing Abby. "Perhaps we should head back to Valerie's place," Vivian suggested.

Abby stood. A sense of relief set in. At the same time Abby could feel an enormous hole in herself and did her best to pretend it wasn't there.

She guided her grandmother to the trail that would lead them to Calder House. Abby noticed a slight frost coating the grass as they made their way into the trees. "I'll send you a nice winter coat when I return," Vivian said noticing it as well. "The winters here are much colder than back home."

Abby smiled. It was a rare occasion when she saw something that resembled a maternal instinct. "Thanks," Abby smiled hoping she would see more of this from her grandmother.

They approached the quaint cottage nestled in the woods surrounding the school campus. Abby showed her grandmother in and descended the stairs into the sanctum. She took a deep breath, steeling herself. Josephine and Benjamin would likely already be in the sanctum. She knew at some point during her grandmother's visit there would be an inevitable meeting. Though Abby and Benjamin decided to keep their relationship a secret from Vivian, Abby knew it was a gamble with poor odds. She feared any number of possible reactions her grandmother might have, none of which ended well to her imagination.

Ms. Grace was sitting in one of her leather chairs, both Benjamin and Josephine were reading books at different tables. They all quickly stopped what they were doing when Abby and Vivian entered.

Vivian glided into the room with some familiarity, as though she had been there many times before. For all Abby knew, she had been. The history between Vivian and Valerie Grace was still something of a mystery to her.

There was a heavy pause. "Well Abigail, are you going to introduce me to your friends or not?" Vivian's request felt like more of a demand, her genial manners shifted into an arctic front upon seeing Benjamin.

"Of course," Abby stuttered. She moved forward and started fidgeting with the hem of her school jacket. "This is Josephine and Benjamin Hodge," Abby said. Both offered warm greetings. Abby watched the exchange nervously.

"Benjamin and Josephine Hodge," Vivian said under her breath. She circled them like a predator circles their prey. "You must be related to Vincent Hodge, correct?"

"Yes, he was our great, great grandfather," Josephine answered evenly, meeting Vivian's gaze. Benjamin looked as uncomfortable as she felt. She wished she could go to him, but she knew that would make it worse.

"Surely you aren't old enough to know their great, great grandfather," Abby interjected with a tense chuckle.

"No, of course not, I only know of him by… reputation." Vivian said. Abby noted the slight pause in her grandmother's delivery with confusion, as Benjamin stiffened slightly. *What was that about?* She wondered.

Vivian's venomous smile began to soften as she looked at Abby. "I didn't come to discuss the history of the Hodge family. I'm here to discuss your future at this school," Vivian stated, her tone hard.

"I want to finish out the year," Abby stated, trying to sound as resolute as she could.

"Well you certainly aren't coming home, not with everything going on," Vivian retorted. "I'm not convinced, however that this is the best place for you in light of recent events."

Vivian was in full form, as though she were about to perform a poignant monologue from a Greek tragedy. "How can you help your friends? Use the Sight? I'm not convinced this will give them any more answers than they already have. Even if your gift happens to provide some insight into this mysterious Edgar Kincaid, what then? I love you dearly, Abigail, but you are not an experienced witch. Why, I don't think you've even cursed someone. I'm not sure you could bring yourself to harm another living person. What are you going to do when this boy attacks you? You don't have the right instincts, darling, and I fear if you were faced with danger, you won't have the edge you need to save yourself. It isn't in you." She paused for emphasis. "I don't say this to be cruel, Abigail. It is simply a truth we must face, my dear."

Abby struggled to hold her composure, she could feel hot tears welling in her eyes, but she held them at bay. "I don't intend to stay and fight, there are other things I can do. I want to help my friends in whatever way I can." Abby pleaded her case.

Vivian began to move toward the other two. She paused next to Benjamin, who carefully avoided making eye contact with the old woman. She looked him over from head to toe. "You are a beautiful thing, aren't you? And tall, too," Vivian said as though she had just discovered him hiding. "How long has this been going on?"

"What? What do you mean?" Benjamin said his handsome features contorted into feigned confusion.

"I wasn't speaking to you, Mr. Hodge, I was addressing my grand-daughter." Vivian's voice was chilling. "How long have you been seeing this boy?" Ms. Grace receded in her chair, clearly uncomfortable with the scene playing out. Abby remained resolutely silent. "Valerie, certainly you have some good scotch around this place, don't you?" she barked.

"Of course," Ms. Grace answered and took the opportunity to flee upstairs, no doubt to avoid the brewing confrontation.

"Do you think a stiff drink is going to solve our problems?" Abby was surprised she said it out loud.

Vivian had a wicked smile on her face. Abby could see Benjamin and Josephine were very uncomfortable. "No, my dear, the stiff drink is so I don't do anything supremely unwise."

Abby wasn't certain what that meant. Benjamin came around and stood next to Abby taking her hand. "We've been dating for over a month now." He said bravely; no doubt his attempt at chivalry, but the moment was so awkward, no one knew how to react.

"How precious." Vivian's words dripped with condescension. "I suppose the first young man you happen to meet who is also a witch has so much in common with you because he's just like you. Finally, someone to talk to who really understands who and what you are." Her grandmother's cynicism and mocking cut deeply.

"I'm not living out one of your many past relationships." Abby could feel the fight coming out in her. The part of herself she feared was in control.

Vivian's look became wild and menacing, and then suddenly, she softened.

Ms. Grace returned with an expensive looking bottle of dark golden-brown liquor. Without a word, she handed a glass holding a generous shot to Vivian.

Vivian took the drink, her eyes fixed on Abby as she downed the entire glass. She held it out for another shot. The challenge in the movement was evident to Abby, but she held her ground. Vivian smiled.

"Well there we have it," she said, seemingly proud of herself. "The girl has some fight in her after all. I had my doubts." She finished off another shot in short order.

Abby took a deep breath and looked at Benjamin who seemed terribly confused. "Here is what's going to happen my darlings," Vivian continued. "This decision will be yours, Abigail. You'll be eighteen in a few months. If you want to stay and help your friends, then I will allow it, but under one condition," Vivian said sternly.

"What is that?" Abby asked, She was worried what the conditions might be, but she was willing to agree to nearly anything if it meant she could stay.

Vivian downed her third shot of scotch before continuing. "We'll talk about it tomorrow, my dear. Just you and me." Vivian downed yet another shot of liquor. It's time for me to retire for the evening. I'm positively exhausted."

CHAPTER TEN

It was a quiet morning. The school day started little more than an hour ago, but while everyone else was in their classrooms, Abby stood in her own private lesson in Ms. Grace's sanctum. Vivian stood at the center of a pentagram created from a series of stones forming an unusual mosaic on the floor. Vivian reached over and adjusted Abby's fingering once more, correcting the arcane hex gesture she was trying to make with her right hand.

"That's better," Vivian said once she had contorted Abby's hand bringing the pinky and thumb together and sticking the remaining three fingers out.

"I can't believe you taught me that curse. You can't possible believe I'll ever use it," Abby stated, doing little to hide her anger. "I even had a nightmare about it last night."

"Darling, you need to protect yourself from the dangers that exist in this world," Vivian stated as she glanced at the books in Ms. Grace's personal library. It was obvious she was ignoring Abby's ire, which only pissed her off even more. "You know there are other things out there besides that vile Thanos family," Vivian warned.

There was a pause as Abby consciously stilled her frustration, and attempted to funnel the feeling into bravery. She had a question she wanted to ask her grandmother ever since she arrived. "Why did they… kill mom and dad?" Abby asked barely able to speak.

Vivian winced slightly. "Darling this is too much. I could not possibly burden you with these terrible things." Vivian poured herself a glass of scotch.

Abby looked at the clock, it was only 9:00 am. "Don't you think it's a little early for that?" Abby asked flatly. She was tired of being protected. The constant rules for her so-called well being were starting to feel patronizing, and her grandmother's drinking only made it worse.

Vivian glared at her. "Don't sass your grand-mamma, I've been through more than my fair share of loss. I need a little something to take the edge off. Besides darling, we're eight hours ahead here. Back home it's only one in the morning; the bars haven't even closed yet," she stated as she downed a generous shot. "Besides if you want me to tell you the truth, you're going to have to let me do it my way."

"Are you going to tell me, then, or not?" Abby asked, so angry and frustrated she didn't care anymore how aggravated her grandmother became.

"Well, aren't you in a little snit this morning." Vivian glared, taking another drink. Abby wanted to show her grandmother just what kind of mood she was really in, but thought better of the idea. Even the pleasant release of airing her feelings wasn't worth the fight it would cause.

"Please, I just want to understand… why my parents…" Abby couldn't finish the sentence. She didn't want to be vulnerable in front of her grandmother. Abby knew Vivian would somehow twist everything around and make it about herself. She needed this to be about her parents. Vivian was obviously pained by the look on Abby's face. She took another drink and put the cap back on the bottle.

"Fine," she said bitterly. "It's not like you can't find out for yourself if you wanted. I'm certain a detailed history of the vendetta between our two families is well documented in one of the books in this very room." Vivian waived her hands about in her dramatic fashion.

"The Kane and Thanos families have hated one another for generations," she continued. "It started back in the late seventeenth century. We were allies, once. As these things often go, a marriage was arranged to unite our two covens. Agreements were made and dowries were exchanged; some valuables, heirlooms, and the like. But most importantly, there was an exchange and lending of important artifacts related to the craft.

"Apparently, the marriage went sour. The details of why have long been forgotten, but with blood feuds, whys hardly matter after a generation or two. Our two families collapsed into a conflict that has been all-consuming." Vivian paused, clearly considering the bottle in front of her before continuing.

"For several years after the dissolution, the leaders of our covens attempted to reach an equitable division of assets, hoping to settle the claims over the resources and artifacts that were merged during the short alliance. They failed, of course, and at some point, someone decided to take matters into their own hands." Abby listened carefully as Vivian continued her story. It was rare to see her grandmother step out of her dramatics and speak seriously.

"No one really remembers who struck first. We say it was the Thanos family, and naturally they claim it was we who attacked them. In truth no one really cares anymore. For eight generations our families have fought, and there has been a great deal of blood spilled over so-called pride and honor."

Vivian stared into the empty space in front of her as she took a seat in one of the leather chairs near the fireplace, a fresh drink in her hand. Abby sat with her.

"Why so long?" Abby asked. "Why would everyone still be holding on to things that happened hundreds of years ago?"

"People don't always forget, and we took something they want back," Vivian stated.

"What?" Abby couldn't imagine anything worth centuries of bitter hatred and murderous revenge.

"Do you know what the Thanos coven is best known for, Abigail?" Vivian asked her, quietly. Abby shook her head.

"There have been many in the Thanos family who excelled in the practice of Necromancy. Death magic," she said at the question on Abby's face. "They accumulated artifacts and books from ancient Egypt on this subject. When the feud began, we made sure to retain many of these artifacts, so we could conceal them. Naturally, they have wanted them back all this time."

"Why don't we give them back?" Abby failed to see why people, her parents in particular, had to die to keep artifacts and books away from this other family all because of a centuries-old grudge.

"Necromancy is a terrible magic, my darling." Vivian stated taking another sip. "If you think the curses I taught you gave you nightmares, I'm quite certain that what you would find in my vault would leave you positively terrified."

Abby sat back into her chair, wondering if keeping these books and artifacts away from the Thanos family was worth the loss of her parents, and who knows how many others. She decided one day she would look at these items for herself, for now she could only trust her grandmother and her ancestors who seemed to agree.

"Why now? Why mom and dad?" she asked, feeling as though she had no more answers than before.

"Every couple of generations one of the Thanos family realizes their aptitude with Necromancy. They can only develop their gift so far before they cannot move forward without the books and artifacts we took from them. When this happens they typically start the conflict in an attempt to regain what they lost," Vivian stated.

"You think there's another Necromancer" Abby asked, her active imagination trying to conceive of how terrible death magic must be.

"I cannot say for certain, darling, however if history is true it would seem it may be the case," Vivian stated staring into the embers of a dying fire.

"What-" Abby started to ask another question but was interrupted.

"No more questions, darling," Vivian stated and finished off her scotch. "I cannot bear to speak of it a moment longer."

Abby wanted to ask about the symbol on the wall, but she could see she had exhausted her grandmother's patience on the subject. It was clearly not easy for her to speak of it, and evident the alcohol was starting to go to her head.

"It's just…" Abby hesitated but couldn't help herself. "We're going to be okay, right?" she asked, not knowing if the Thanos family and the necromancer would be successful in vanquishing her family. She was so far removed from everything she had no idea what was happening back home. There was still so much she didn't know. For the first time in her life, Abby wished she was truly a member of her family's coven, and not just the isolated daughter of Evan Kane.

Vivian stared into the glowing embers that suddenly burst into a raging fire under her watchful glare. Abby jumped, startled. "We will win," Vivian stated. Her voice was distant and emotionless. Abby had never seen her grandmother like this before, and she could feel the anger radiating from her body. Vivian seemed to snap out of a trance and looked at Abby, offering a weak smile. "You needn't worry about a thing my darling, your grand-mamma has everything under control. They won't know what hit them when I'm done." There was no exaggeration in her voice, nor any of the drama Abby was accustomed to. She had never seen her grandmother so serious in her entire life. Vivian's mood was strange and distant. There was a sinister tone to her words that made Abby profoundly uncomfortable.

Abby started to excuse herself. A hand grabbed her wrist. Vivian looked into Abby's eyes with a menacing glare. "You shouldn't speak of the curses I taught you. Not to anyone. Not Ms. Grace and certainly not to the Hodge twins, especially that boy you seem infatuated with." Her voice was cold and cutting. "A witch who betrays her coven… burns." Abby believed her grandmother would do just what she said. "Coven first, always and forever. Remember that." She added as she released Abby's wrist and gazed into the fire.

Abby wasted no time taking her leave. She had never shared an intense moment like that with her grandmother, before. She was used to drama and theatrics, seeing her so serious was unsettling. She didn't want to return to the dorms; she wouldn't have the privacy to reflect. Instead, she decided to go for a walk.

She came to Moore Brook where she experienced the terrible vision of Josephine being murdered. The stone bridge was overgrown with moss, and was a picturesque spot. She decided she would stay for a while and wrapped her coat tightly to keep warm.

The peace and solitude was a welcome change after the disturbing lessons and conversations with her grandmother of the last few days. Vivian would fly home tomorrow. It was difficult to think about home. She didn't know what it would be like to return to Seattle with her parents gone. She missed the familiarity of the streets and buildings. The coffee and cuisine. Familiar faces and fragrant flowers in the spring. She missed coming home to one of her parent's home cooked meals. She missed driving her car and her parent's rules. She missed the way everything was before she walked into her father's office last spring.

It was just starting to feel like she was building a life again. She was following her passion playing the violin. Then there was Benjamin, she really liked him and could see the possibility of more. The ruins of her old life were giving birth to new possibilities and opportunities she had only ever dreamed about. Months ago she would have never imagined anything could grow in her life or invoke passion for anything or anyone.

Abby started strolling back towards the dorms as she remembered happy times with her parents. She recalled on occasion when her mother made homemade caramel popcorn and they all stayed up until three in the morning watching funny movies and laughing together. The memory put a smile on her face and a tear in her eye.

She eventually made her way back to the dorms, and set her thoughts aside while she read and completed some of her assignments. Despite her best efforts to concentrate, Abby's thoughts were interrupted by memories of home and her parents. *Having grandmother here is bringing a lot up,* she thought.

Abby set her homework aside and made her way to the practice room with her violin. She tuned her instrument and thumbed through her sheet music. She was having a difficult time deciding what piece she would use to warm up with. She pulled a piece of sheet music from her folder and took a deep breath. Paganini's Caprice No. 4 in c minor. It had been one of her parent's favorite pieces.

She pulled the sheet music from her folder and placed it on the music stand. Abby held her instrument at the ready and placed the bow on the strings. She closed her eyes for a moment and breathed. Then she pulled the bow across the strings and created the melodic sounds of Paganini's classic concerto. No matter how she played this composition it always sounded sad. Today was no exception.

As Abby played the music written on the page, she felt the pain and sorrow move through her arm into the bow. It vibrated through the strings turning her emotions into sound. It was raw and unforgiving; Abby continued to play. She embraced the catharsis only music could give her. It was a release from her melancholy, and it provided relief as though she had quenched some desire she did not yet understand fully.

When she finished, she set her instrument aside and put her head in her hands. Abby rubbed the temples of her forehead and wondered how she could reconcile her grief with the hope that was beginning to return.

She took another deep breath and put her violin away. Her thoughts were too troublesome for practice. Instead, she decided she would get herself ready for dinner at the cottage later that evening. Ms. Grace was hosting a small supper for Vivian, Abby, and the Hodges. No amount of brooding would remove her social obligations.

Abby had spent the last six days learning how to cast the most horrible curses she could ever imagine. Now she was expected to make small-talk with the woman who had taught them to her; the only person who really understood her grief, and yet gave no succor.

She sighed and changed into a nice navy blue dress, determined to get through this.

Abby walked through the courtyard and onto the path leading into the small forest on the eastern part of the campus. The tall trees had lost all their leaves allowing the fading daylight to illuminate her path.

"You need an escort?" she heard Benjamin say behind her. She hadn't had much time to spend with him over the last week with her grandmother's hovering.

Abby turned and gave him a smile, "Sure," she stated waiting for him to catch up to her. He moved in for a kiss on the lips and Abby felt herself go rigid. She instinctively pulled back.

"What's wrong?" he asked, looking slightly hurt.

"I'm sorry," Abby said. She stopped and took his arm and gave him a kiss on the cheek. "I'm just so uptight with my grandmother around."

"Abby? You're not embarrassed by me, are you?" Benjamin asked with an uncertain look on his handsome face.

"What?" Abby was shocked he would even think such a thing. "Why on earth would I be embarrassed by you?"

"It's just you don't seem very comfortable with being affectionate when you're around your grandmother, even though she knows about us," Benjamin explained.

"Oh Benjamin, please, no, it's nothing like that, really," Abby tried to reassure him. She knew he could tell how tense she was, but she was having trouble explaining her apprehension. "I just don't want to antagonize her," she said.

"She really doesn't like me," Benjamin observed, taking Abby's hand. This time she let him.

"It's not personal. I don't think she'd like anyone I dated." Abby assured him, doing her best to loosen up. She felt bad for hurting his feelings. "I'm not embarrassed to date you at all. I can't believe you would think that."

Benjamin smiled and gave Abby a real kiss. Though she liked kissing Benjamin, Abby could feel a pang of guilt. "I believe you. I just wasn't sure."

She wanted to move forward with her life. Abby could feel the pull. For some reason, it was difficult to allow herself to accept that she would have to give up the past to do so. She wasn't certain she was ready to go that far. But there was Benjamin, pulling her along, and she wanted to go with him.

"I'm sorry I pulled away," Abby said. "I didn't mean to hurt your feelings."

"I get it," Benjamin stated. "I also know having your grandmother here is probably bringing up a lot of stuff for you. I just wanted to make sure it wasn't about us."

"I can assure you, nothing that's happened in the last week has been anything to do with us. My grandmother has gone out of her way to avoid bringing up the subject of you, which is really a good sign. You don't have anything to worry about."

Benjamin seemed relieved, almost as if he was afraid somehow her grandmother would try to poison their fledgling relationship. While she knew Vivian was not thrilled with the idea of their dating, but in truth she barely mentioned it beyond the first night. Abby was happy to let it lie.

"Here we are," Benjamin stated as they approached the house. They kissed for a few moments more before entering and assuming their dutiful roles.

Ms. Grace welcomed them and Abby took her place next to her grandmother. Benjamin quietly sat across from them. Josephine had backed out at the last minute due to a major art project deadline. But Abby suspected she simply didn't want to attend. She could hardly blame her; Vivian had done little to endear herself to either Josephine or Benjamin.

"I am not looking forward to the nine-hour flight home," Vivian stated as she politely cut her steak.

"How are Uncle Sebastian and Rodger doing?" Abby asked nervously, trying to keep the topics light. She feared any lull in the conversation would result in her grandmother hijacking the topics.

"Fine darling, everyone is doing well," Vivian assured. She seemed uninterested in talking about the health and well-being of the family. "Benjamin, Ms. Grace has sung your praises since I arrived," Vivian stated, Abby cringed slightly; she had hoped her grandmother would continue ignoring him.

"Thank you, Ms. Grace," Benjamin stated, looking uncomfortable. Abby feared he was being navigated into a trap.

"What are your plans for after you complete the school year? Oxford? Cambridge?" Vivian inquired. Her questions seemed nonchalant, however Abby knew this interrogation was just getting started.

"I was planning to travel for a while and then attended Oxford. I've been offered a spot on their rowing team if I keep up with practice during gap year," Benjamin answered politely.

"Very impressive. You really can't do any better than Oxford, darling." Vivian smiled. Abby noticed she'd already finished two glasses of wine and could only imagine how much she drank before dinner.

"Thank you, Mrs. Kane," Benjamin stated.

"I have fantastic news for my dear Abigail," Vivian stated, turning her attention to Abby. "I've had a private discussion with each of your teachers since I arrived." Abby was terrified at the thought. "Professor Goodwin says you are a truly gifted violinist. I know I haven't always been the most supportive of your little hobby. I've wanted you to focus more on your training in the arcane. However, he assures me you have something special. A gift for music, he called it." Vivian smiled, her pride seemed dubious.

"It is very kind of him to say," Abby said cautiously.

"Fortunately for you darling, one of my dear friends, Carlotta Alberti the famous Italian soprano, is currently on the board of admissions at Julliard. I've taken the liberty of speaking with her and arranged for you to attend next fall!" Vivian said. It was apparent she was very proud of herself.

"Julliard? In New York?" Abby stated, completely in shock. Of course, it was every musician's dream to be accepted into Julliard, but her mind wasn't able to grasp what her grandmother was telling her. *I know this has to be one of her tricks, but... Julliard!?* she thought.

"Yes darling, what other Julliard is there?" Vivian stated with a huge smile.

"But... but what about the matter with the Thanos?" Abby asked, her mind in a daze. "I thought it would be safer for me to be in hiding until this is all dealt with."

Vivian smiled. Abby realized too late that she had stepped solidly into the trap laid for her. She had opened the very can of worms her grandmother was hoping she would.

A satisfied glint settled in the old woman's eyes. Vivian leaned forward with her steak knife in hand as though it had become a weapon.

"I have something in the works." Vivian raised an eyebrow. Abby noticed both Ms. Grace and Benjamin enraptured by Vivian's statement. "I shall not speak of it further, but you can be assured, the Thanos *will* be dealt with by then," she added before cutting into her steak. Almost absently she added, "Julliard will be the opportunity of a life time."

Abby looked to Benjamin, she understood what was happening. Her grandmother was doing her best to orchestrate circumstances that would keep them apart. She knew her grandmother could care less about her musical interests, but she did seem to care about her relationship with Benjamin. At the same time Julliard was an opportunity like no other.

"It sounds like a wonderful opportunity," Ms. Grace congratulated. "Professor Goodwin has stated you are his best student."

"I'm surprised," Abby said, uncertain how else to react to her grandmother's august manipulations cleverly disguised as the chance of a lifetime. "Are you certain this conflict will be done by then?"

"Oh darling, leave all that to me," Vivian insisted pouring herself another glass of Malbec.

"Are you certain, Vivian?" Ms. Grace echoed Abby's statement. She sounded concerned, but also seemed to be choosing her words carefully.

Abby glanced at Benjamin who was silent, but she could tell he was curious.

"Oh, I have it in hand." She added. "There will be no obstacle in following your dreams, my dear. This is a fantastic opportunity for you, Abigail, and you would be a fool to pass it up, and you are no fool my darling. Don't you agree Mr. Hodge?"

Vivian's gaze was very pointed. A heavy silence fell, as Abby considered her grandmother.

"Of course," Benjamin smiled, though Abby could tell he was conflicted. "If this is your dream Abby, then you have to take it." He added looking at Abby his brown eyes were sincere, but sad. Vivian's smile widened.

"See darling, even your wonderful Mr. Hodge agrees with me." Vivian was supremely pleased with herself and filled her wine glass again. "You'll have everything in the world you want, darling."

"Thank you," was all Abby could think to say. She was certain there wasn't a single person in the room who was confused about what just happened.

There was a stone bench along the path back towards the dormitories. Abby pulled Benjamin over, taking a seat. She snuggled up to him as a fog bank started to move in from the south. "Benjamin, I'm not sure how I would be dealing with everything right now if it wasn't for you. My grandmother doesn't like us together for some reason, but I can guarantee you it won't keep me from dating whomever I want. There is a lot going on. I have a lot to consider, but I'm not going to give up my dreams for you, or anyone else for that matter. This is important to me. I'm going to tell you something even my grandmother doesn't know, or at least would never understand," she said.

Benjamin put his arm around her. "What's that?" He asked letting himself get comfortable. She could tell he was trying his best to prepare for bad news.

"I love the violin."

"That isn't a secret," he teased.

She continued on, ignoring him. "It's my dream to play in a symphony, and maybe even become a real concert violinist." Abby stated. "That's my dream, but Julliard was never a part of that dream."

"Abby," he said, seriously, "this is an opportunity that could lead you to your dream. Don't you want that?"

"I know it is, and I might take it, despite my grandmother's machinations." Abby stated. "But, there are some fine music schools here in England, too. Julliard isn't the only way to realize my dream." She paused, considering. "I guess what I'm saying is that despite my grandmother's insistence that everything has to be tied down right now, I want to keep my options open. I think I can do that without giving up my dream. Besides, I'm not one dimensional, I have more than one dream in life."

"Oh? What other dreams do you have?" Benjamin asked. A hint of his old playfulness crept back into his smile. Abby was relieved.

"Well you know one of mine. Tell me one of yours first," Abby insisted playfully.

"Me? I want a legacy," he said. A fire shone in his eyes Abby hadn't seen before. "I'm going to master the Craft, and one day, I will enchant an artifact whose power is unrivaled anywhere in the world. It will be my way of securing the Hodge coven," he stated. "I haven't decided what I'll make, but I think about it all the time, drafting ideas and researching the limitations of magic."

"That sounds very ambitious," she said. He sounded so sure. It made her smile to see such passion in him. "I see a future full of studying, and the need for a first-class sanctum." Abby laughed.

"Well, I wouldn't mind a collegiate rowing championship," Benjamin added more glibly. "What about you? Other than playing in the finest concert halls in the world, what do you want?"

She considered her answer, resisting the urge to feel sorry for herself. "It used to be so much clearer before everything happened a few months ago," Abby stated. "I... sometimes imagine settling down and having a family, but I don't know anymore."

"Why? You don't think you want to get married and have kids someday?" Benjamin inquired, he seemed surprised.

"Contrary to popular opinion, it's not the dream of every girl to grow up and be a mother," Abby said flatly, teasing him more. "I always thought it would be nice to find the right guy and start a little family. But..." she shrugged.

"But, now?" Benjamin asked.

"But after what happened with my parents, I'm not sure anymore. I just can't imagine bringing children into a world where terrible things can happen out of nowhere," Abby shared. It was difficult to think about what she wanted out of the future when so much of her life was still anchored in the past. Even her family's concerns are because of a generations-old blood debt. How could she possibly look forward?

"I know I may see things differently someday, but right now, that future just terrifies me." Benjamin squeezed her, and Abby could feel the emotions pressing against the emotional barrier she fought diligently to maintain. Seeing her grandmother and thinking about her future, one in which her parents would no longer be a part of, was too overwhelming. Despite her best efforts the tears began to flow, Abby buried her face in Benjamin's chest as she melted into an emotional puddle.

Benjamin held her. The emotional bloodletting was mercifully short, as Abby began to pull herself from the brink of despair. "Sorry," she said, wiping away the tears. It was a level of vulnerability she had rarely showed another human being.

"For what?" Benjamin asked. "You have nothing to be sorry about."

"I…" Abby began to speak and stopped herself. She shook her head and put on a brave smile. "I guess I still have a lot to work through."

"It's alright," Benjamin said. "I've never been through anything like you have. I can only imagine what it must be like. I don't think that what you've been through is something you, or anyone else, could simply put behind them."

"I'm glad you haven't, and I hope you never do," Abby said, easing back into the moment. She rallied, fighting against her instincts to bury her feelings and try to pretend everything was perfectly fine and normal.

They sat silently, there was comfort in his arms. She hadn't expected to find it there, not so soon. A few minutes passed, and Benjamin stood. He took Abby's hand and pulled her up. His handsome face beckoned her with a smile. He softly kissed her lips and played with the tip of her hair as he gazed down adoringly at her. "We're going to have to get back before lights out."

Abby looked at the time on her phone and realized he was right. She took his arm and started walking up the path towards the school dormitories. "If I'm lucky enough to be the guy you end up with, I'm going to try very hard to change your mind about having kids."

"Really?" Abby questioned with a smile. "Why is that?"

"I happen to believe we would have absolutely gorgeous children." Benjamin teased with a smug look on his face. His humor was a refreshing relief from the emotional cloud lingering in Abby's thoughts. Her laughter rang across the courtyard.

CHAPTER ELEVEN

"The car should be here in about ten minutes," Abby said standing in the doorway of Ms. Grace's guest room.

Vivian looked up from her luggage and gave Abby a quaint smile. "I'll have the chauffeur pick these up when he arrives," she commented as she secured the latch. "I'm glad you're here... alone," she said mysteriously. "I have something for you," she said reaching for her purse on the dresser. She pulled a small book from inside and handed it to Abby.

"The Picture of Dorian Gray," Abby read the title aloud. "What's this for?" she asked curiously.

"I want you to read it," Vivian said. "Only you aren't to tell anyone, especially the Hodges."

"Wh—"

"I've asked you to do so." Vivian said, holding up a hand to forestall Abby's question.

Abby raised an eyebrow. "It's just a book." She looked at her grandmother. "In fact, I think it's on the curriculum for some of the younger students."

"Not surprising," Vivian said imperiously. "Just read it darling. You said you would agree to my request for allowing you to stay. That book in your hands is my request."

There had to be some hidden agenda, some reason Vivian wanted her to read this book. "I read it years ago, when I was a freshman."

"It was rather good, don't you think?" Vivian asked. "Worth another read. It's relevance to your situation is far more poignant than you might think," she added mysteriously.

"I don't know what you're talking about," Abby insisted, her irritation more than showing.

"Read it," Vivian insisted abruptly. Her tone gave Abby a start. "And you are to swear not to speak of it. To anyone." *Why does she want me to read this book so much? It's just a book.*

"Abigail." Vivian said in a tone that made Abby wonder if she could hear her thoughts.

"Fine I swear." Abby shook her head and shoved the book in her bag. After that bit of awkwardness, she was eager to change the subject. "Can I come home for Christmas?"

"I'm afraid not darling," Vivian said slinging her purse over her shoulder. "We're all still in hiding, and it's best not to travel unless it's absolutely vital. Besides, you're well-hidden now. I don't want to take any more chances than necessary. Besides I won't be around for the holiday."

"What? Where will you be?" Abby asked.

Vivian raised an eyebrow as she put on her white leather traveling gloves. "Africa," she commented in passing. "Come along dear, we should head downstairs and let the chauffeur in when he arrives."

"Africa?" Abby repeated uncertain she heard correctly.

"I am working on a little something," Vivian said. "I'll spare you the details, however, it will most definitely put an end to this horrible Thanos problem, once and for all."

The idea of losing her grandmother flashed across her thoughts leaving her anxious. "Is it dangerous?" Abby asked.

"Not at all darling," Vivian said noticing the worry in Abby's eyes. She gently kissed Abby's forehead. Then, the older woman took her arm, guiding her into the hallway and down the stairs into the living room. "You needn't worry about me. I am quite able to take care of myself," she said with a reassuring smile.

There was a polite knock at the door and Abby quickly answered. An older gentleman stood at the door wearing a chauffeur's uniform.

"Wonderful, my luggage is upstairs. Be a darling, would you?" Vivian said dismissively and pulled Abby aside as the driver disappeared upstairs. "I spoke with Ms. Grace about your classmate…"

"Edgar Kincaid?" Abby found the name for Vivian.

"Yes, him," Vivian commented as though she had been interrupted. "I will be forwarding some books from my private library that may be of use in researching the… infernal influences that may be at work surrounding this situation." She paused as the chauffeur came down with the luggage. "Thank you darling. I'll be there in a minute," she said as the driver passed, on his way out to the car.

Abby waited for the man to pass out of hearing range. "What are you doing with books on the infernal?" she asked curiously.

"Darling, I maintain our coven's considerable library. Our family has been collecting books for centuries. It's not as though I collected these books myself. We don't all share Valerie's love of esoteric literature. Besides, I think you will learn that sometimes you purchase such things to hide them away, so they don't fall into the wrong hands."

Abby raised an eyebrow. "Who's to say who's hands are the right ones?" She asked rhetorically.

"It's a good question darling, and the only answer that matters at the moment is, the hands of our enemies… While I trust Valerie, you are to be certain those books are returned safely," Vivian said, her words weighted with warning.

"Are you suggesting Benjamin or Josephine would try to take them?" Abby asked uncertain what her grandmother was insinuating.

Vivian looked at Abby as though she was waiting for common sense to hit her over the head. "I'm suggesting you make certain those books make it back to my library," she said, clearly unwilling to explain herself. "Now darling, give me a hug. I don't want an emotional display in the courtyard for everyone to see," Vivian insisted pulling Abby into an embrace.

"That woman is terrifying," Benjamin said as he waved goodbye.

"Try growing up with her as your grandmother," Abby quipped, dryly. It had been a difficult week, Vivian saw to that. Abby was exhausted.

Abby and Benjamin headed back to the dining hall and found a vacant table where they could speak privately. "Tomorrow then?" Benjamin asked without preamble.

"That's the plan." Abby stated picking at her food, not feeling particularly hungry. "Now that she's tested my skills herself, my grandmother feels the Sight might actually be useful."

"Well as far as I'm concerned, you've been helpful from the beginning. If it wasn't for you, we wouldn't even know Josephine is in danger." Benjamin said as he ate every piece of protein in sight. He was preparing for another match, and the extra rowing practice meant extra portions.

Abby looked at her food, and pushed her plate away. Benjamin noticed she barely ate anything, "Are you nervous?"

"A little bit," Abby admitted.

"I'll be there," he said. "Ms. Grace made all the arrangements for me to come in and 'make up a class'," including the air quotes as he spoke. "Besides nothing is going to happen."

"I hope you're right." Abby wasn't convinced, but she was determined to help, regardless.

"By the way, what did your grandmother make you promise?" Benjamin asked. "I've worried about it all week. I was concerned she would demand you break up with me."

"At first I thought the same thing, but she didn't. I suspect the whole college thing was her attempt to cause trouble for us. She seems to have a plan for my life, but I don't know what it is. She made me promise to read a book. She was adamant that I swear not to tell anyone." She shrugged and shook her head. "That's all I should say, I don't want to completely break my word." Abby said solemnly. It was beginning to occur to Abby there was a surge of grief and homesickness lingering at the edges of her thoughts. No doubt the wreckage left in the emotional wake of her grandmother's visit.

"That doesn't sound so bad, I guess you got off easy." Benjamin sounded relieved. "Unless of course it's a really big book." Abby laughed at his quip. His sense of humor always put a smile on her face. Abby was relieved it helped her cut through some of the emotions her grandmother's visit stirred. "You seem a little down. Can I do anything?" he added.

Abby hesitated. "It's just having her here. It made me think of home... and my parents, a lot."

Benjamin seemed to immediately understand and placed his arm around her shoulder and pulled her closer in a tender moment of solace. They both glanced around to make certain a faculty member wasn't nearby to enforce the no touching rules. Abby was grateful. She buried her head in Benjamin's shoulder to keep the tears at bay.

"Why don't you take the rest of the day off," Benjamin suggested. "I'm certain Ms. Grace would understand."

After a few moments of pulling herself back together, Abby sat up and leaned forward. "Thanks, it's not a bad idea, but..." Abby stopped and took a deep breath. "I've cried more tears in the last couple months than I have my entire life before that combined. If I go back to my room and lay in bed all day, I'll probably have a melt-down."

"Is that really such a bad thing?" Benjamin asked.

"Not always. But right now, I think I want a distraction," Abby confessed as she watched the students come and go through the main door. She saw what appeared to be dozens of people her own age having a normal life, passing by without a care in the world. That was what she wanted. She wanted to feel normal again. She wanted to be in a world where the weight of her grief didn't coat every emotion in pain.

"Class can certainly give you something to focus on," Benjamin agreed. "And this business with Edgar."

"I think I could use all the distractions I can get right now." Abby mustered a smile, determined to stay on top of the emotional quicksand threatening to pull her under.

"I've got a pretty good distraction for you," Benjamin said with a sly smile.

"Oh, what is that?" Abby asked knowing full well she was stepping into his trap.

"The other day when I was approaching the table, you were in conversation with Nina and I overheard you call me something," Benjamin said with an enormous smile.

"Really?" Abby questioned as she searched for any memory of what she might have said. "I don't recollect calling you a name," she added, playfully confused.

"I seem to remember you uttering the word, 'Boyfriend,' in relation to, yours truly, of course," Benjamin accused playfully.

"I did?" Abby thought carefully. She could feel herself lighten as she bantered with Benjamin. "Are you certain you heard correctly?"

"Quite."

"Well, I don't know. It seems rather presumptuous of me," Abby said, wearing the first genuine smile she had in days. "I'm so sorry to worry you. I'll cease and desist immediately."

"Don't you dare," Benjamin said kissing her forehead. "I just wanted to point out that you said it first," he added with a chuckle.

"You suck," Abby laughed.

The next day Abby's nerves were on edge.

She walked into the mathematics lecture hall where Professor Langley stood at the bottom far end next to the chalk board, reviewing her notes for the lecture. Five rows of desks formed a half circle, elevated above the lectern like bleachers.

Edgar Kincaid was already seated in his usual place, directly behind Abby's spot. She glanced at her usual seat in the second row and saw Nina was there, riffling through her book bag. Abby made her way down the steps to the second row, making a point to ignore Edgar as she passed. She didn't want to alert him to the fact that anything was different about today. She sat stiffly in her chair and took a deep breath.

"Something wrong?" Nina asked.

Abby looked at her friend with uncertainty. Her thoughts were so preoccupied with what she was about to do that it took a moment for her friends question to register.

"I'm sorry. I'm a little distracted. I have a test coming up in the next class," Abby lied, adding a hint of guilt to her emotional burden.

A few seconds later Benjamin entered the room and made his way down to Professor Langley. He handed her a note and she nodded, giving Benjamin the okay to remain in class. She absently handed back the note, and Benjamin took a seat next to Abby.

"Why hello there," he said, trying to sound casual. Abby just smiled, glad he was there to back her up.

The lecture hall filled quickly. Abby glanced back to where Edgar was sitting. He sat with his head bowed, his typically angry and brooding look on his face. "I'll try in a minute," Abby whispered to Benjamin.

Professor Langley began her lecture on hyperbolic trigonometric functions. Abby was paying very little attention to the lesson, grateful her professor was not the kind of teacher who liked to put her students on the spot. Instead she turned her attention inward, preparing to engage in tangential stories rather than cotangents.

Abby waited a few minutes, wanting to be sure Professor Langley was well into her lecture before she started to use the Sight. When she was convinced the flow of education was well underway, she leaned back and began to allow her eyes to unfocus.

Abby cleared her thoughts and navigated her consciousness into a place of quiet and solitude. She allowed the professors voice to fade into the background, and worked on following the steps she learned in her meditation books. The florescent lights blurred into a dull glow. She could feel her mind pushing back the world of consciousness as a new sense began to emerge as though it had been submerged deeply into the ocean of Abby's thoughts.

The world began to come into focus again, spilling into Abby's mind through her other senses. She did not see it with her eyes or hear it with her ears, instead she could sense it with her mind. Her senses came to life in the moment, moving out from her own body into the room around her like a slow-moving mist.

She was aware of Benjamin next to her; she could feel his protectiveness and concern. She sensed his longing for her, and even a sense of peace at being beside her. It made her smile internally. She turned her attention away from him before she got too distracted, and focused on Nina. To her left, the other girl radiated kindness and warmth. It was endearing. She extended her senses further out until she could sense Professor Langley's passion for teaching, her love for her family, and the pride she held for teaching at the school. Abby continued to let her senses wash like a wave across the room. All around her she could sense the anxiety, ambivalence and disinterest of her fellow students.

Then she came to Edgar Kincaid. She hesitated for a moment, nearly losing the concentration she needed to continue. She feared what she might encounter. Would she see him brutally murder Emily? Would she see him murder another one of her friends? She took a deep breath, steeling herself. There was a whole set of reasons she agreed to do this, and she wouldn't back out now. As her senses descended upon Edgar Kincaid, she hit a wall of complex emotions just on the surface of his thoughts. Edgar was afraid, confused, and angry. He had little interest or passion about anything other than to understand himself. Abby could sense there was more, much more, below that. She focused harder, trying to break through his surface thoughts. The energy started to slowly flow into his mindspace, but didn't budge. She pressed harder still, concentrating, trying to see his inner self.

She felt very warm. The temperature in the room must have been rising. She began to sweat. Her Sight was engulfed in flames, and she couldn't catch her breath.

Through the flames she saw Edgar with a girl her own age. She had long blond hair, striking blue eyes, and porcelain white skin. It was Emily Wright. Abby recognized the girl from pictures Nina and Sarah had shown her. Edgar and Emily were laughing. They seemed so happy together. A sense of peace and joy flowed from the scene.

The vision began to change. She saw Edgar holding Emily in his arms ready to give her a kiss. She then began to melt, as though she were made of ice. He cried in agony, slamming his fists against the wall over and over until the brick began to crumble under his fists. Grief and sorrow overwhelmed her. It radiated from him like a beacon of hopelessness.

Without thinking, images of her parents, motionless on the floor appeared in her mind's eye. His pain triggered her own memories, and she could feel her own grief swelling, threatening to envelop her completely. Blood pooled at her feet, and it began to take over. The flames returned, and her vision was consumed, crumbling to ash.

She was in her father's office. The white carpet covered in blood. Her parents face down on the ground. The sun flooded the room in light, exposing the dark deed of faceless monsters. She sat on the floor between her parent's bodies. Slowly, with an intentional curiosity, she laid down beside them, mimicking the pose where she should have been. Where she would have been, if she died with them. Abby lay on the floor, staring into her mother's lifeless eyes.

She could hear voices calling her from outside. Benjamin, Professor Langley, Nina and then Ms. Grace. One by one, they called out to her, but she couldn't make out what they were saying. She just stayed there crying, her parents on either side. Where she should be.

Abby opened her eyes. It was dark. She paused for a moment and oriented herself to the world. Was she still in her meditative state? In some sort of waking dream? She sat up leaning on her elbows and looked around. She was in a hospital room with tubes attached to her arm. Abby could feel a slight panic building; she paused and steadied herself.

She carefully took a few deep breaths. *I'm in the hospital... Why?* She pressed the call button draped over the side of the hospital bed. In a matter of moments a nurse entered the room turning on a small lamp.

"Hello," she smiled sweetly. The middle-aged woman wore a standard nurse's uniform with a stethoscope around her neck. She glanced at a white board hanging above Abby's hospital bed. "You gave us a bit of a scare, Abigail."

"Abby, please call me Abby," she responded, her head pounding. "How long have I been here?" Her speech was off, obviously the effects of medication.

"About eight hours," the nurse said as she wrapped a blood pressure cuff around Abby's upper arm.

"What happened?" Abby asked. The disorientation was frustrating her.

"Apparently you blacked out in the middle of your class. You gave them quite a scare. When you didn't respond they called an ambulance. In fact, you have a number of friends sitting out in the waiting room," she commented. "One of them is a cute guy, I hope he's your boyfriend," she said teasingly as she changed the IV fluid.

"The tall one with the curly hair?" Abby asked trying to stay awake in the haze of drugs.

"That would be the one. The doctor will want to talk to you before you see any visitors. It shouldn't be long." The nurse recorded some numbers and left.

Abby could feel herself fading, fatigue and a strong pharmaceutical haze had her drifting off again, dozing.

She wasn't entirely certain how long it was before the doctor arrived, and his brief examination was a blurred event for which she was barely conscious. "Try to get some rest," he might have said to her. Abby nodded, and quickly faded away until morning.

The next day, Ms. Grace and Benjamin were waiting by the car when the nurse escorted Abby out of the hospital. She was exhausted and recovering from the haze of drugs. They helped her into the car and Benjamin sat next to her wrapping his arm around her shoulder, holding her close.

"What happened? We were worried sick." Ms. Grace commented. "The doctor said you had some kind of episode."

"Dissociative Episode," Benjamin corrected. Abby could tell he was irritated. "What did he do to you?"

"Nothing. It was my fault." Abby stared blankly forward, her voice little more than a raspy whisper.

"What do you mean this was your fault?" Ms. Grace demanded. "How can you blame yourself?"

"I was using the Sight," Abby started to explain. Her voice sounded like she hadn't used it in days. "I could only find surface emotions, so I pushed and tried to go deeper. He's suffered so much loss. It was a deep, profound loss, and it triggered my own grief. I... I wasn't prepared for it. It took me by surprise. I became lost in... everything." Benjamin pulled her tighter and kissed her on the head.

"What did you see?" Ms. Grace asked cautiously.

"There was so much confusion. I'm not certain I entirely understand what I saw," Abby confessed. She told Ms. Grace and Benjamin every detail she could remember about Edgar and Emily. She relived the memory of her melting in his arms, and stopped herself before she could fall back into her own memories again. "He genuinely mourns her," she added.

"Perhaps he has remorse for killing her," Benjamin suggested.

Abby looked at Benjamin with uncertainty. "Maybe," she said, *but there was no guilt,* she thought. Abby sat quietly in Benjamin's arms, combing through her thoughts for more details she had forgotten. "I don't think he knows what he is," she eventually said. "I got the impression he's confused about himself. Of course, I suppose that could mean any number of things, but I'm starting to wonder if he has any clue what's going on."

"You said it triggered your grief. How? What happened?" Benjamin asked cautiously.

Abby had planned to omit the portion of her vision with her parents. She didn't want to think about it. Her apprehension was evident based on the expressions of concern on her boyfriend and guardian's faces. "I saw my parent's dead, lying on the floor the way I f-found them that day... and myself, lying dead next to them." She shuddered, trying to purge her mind of the horrible image. She willed herself to mental control, hoping to draw out the emotional poison making her sick. *It wasn't real,* she reminded herself. *You're still alive.*

"Your grandmother told me about the day you found your parents," Ms. Grace said. Her voice was shaky. "I can't even imagine. I think we need to give you a little time off. The holiday break is coming. Perhaps it would be a good idea for you to start yours early."

"I don't need any special treatment, Ms. Grace." Abby protested. Her voice sounded pathetic.

"Nonsense." Benjamin stated. "You need to get yourself sorted out."

She looked at the two of them, so caring, both wanting so desperately to help her heal, and smiled weakly. *Yes,* she thought. *I'm still alive.*

CHAPTER TWELVE

The courtyard was filled with students going about their business. It felt good to be out of the dorm at last. By the third day of bed rest, Abby was exhausted of telling people just how fine she was. She wasn't going to break at the mere mention of anything stressful, and she was tired of having to prove it. Without asking permission, she put on her running gear and headed to the track.

She set the jogging app on her phone, put her ear buds in and hit play. It felt so good to be moving again. It had been weeks since she had any real time to run. As usual jogging helped to clear her mind, which she sorely needed. She took the time to set aside her own thoughts and sensations, and focus on what she had sensed from Edgar in that vision.

His grief was palpable. She remembered that all too-well. He treated it like an unwelcome guest that wouldn't leave. Fierce and combatant by nature; well that tracked with what she had seen in the few times they had met. Anger was by far the strongest emotion.

She dug deeper, trying to remember what she had realized coming home from the hospital. There was no guilt , but so much pointed to him being guilty. *How could he be innocent?* she thought. His reaction to Emily dissolving in the vision was very real. *It was honest, raw grief. Is it possible?...* she let the thought trail off. It would certainly explain why he felt angry and confused. The magnitude of his grief was undeniably genuine. He missed her, longed for her. "He couldn't have done it." She said out loud to no one.

She shook her head and refocused on her pacing. She used the pounding of her feet on the track as a metronome to her breath. Slowly she fell back into her rhythm, her thoughts never stopping their analysis.

She knew Edgar wasn't a demon. Ms. Grace was sure the Sight would have given a definite indication if he was, but even knowing that, demonic influences were still at work behind the emotions and images in the vision. The occasional hint of sulfur, the fire, and of course the glowing red eyes, all added up, but she just wasn't sure what it was. It was as if she was searching through the flames to grasp something just out of reach.

Abby finished her run early. She was still very tired from all the bed rest, and didn't want to overdo it. She walked back to the dorm and took a long hot shower, letting the water rinse away any stray thoughts and worries.

The winter break was coming up and Abby was grateful. She needed time away from the school for a bit. She mined her closet for something nice but comfortable and settled on a pair of designer jeans and a blue top with ribbon seams and crystal encrusted buttons. It was a bit fancy for lounging around at school, but she was tired of pajamas and school uniforms.

Abby grabbed her bag off the table, knocking something on the floor. She bent to retrieve the book now lying next to her foot, and glanced at its cover; The Picture of Dorian Gray. She was sure Vivian had her reasons for demanding that Abby turn her attentions to reading Oscar Wilde's classic novel, but she had no idea why her grandmother would extract a strict oath that it be kept a secret, especially from the Hodges and Ms. Grace. "More Kane family secrets," she said to herself. Vivian was a power unto herself. Abby shook her head and put the small book in her desk, silently promising her grandmother that she would get around to reading it once her mind was less occupied by the situation with Edgar Kincaid.

Abby grabbed her things and made her way to Calder house. Ms. Grace was no doubt still working in her office. It was after all the middle of the school day. Having permission to let herself in at any time, she made her way into the sanctum. She searched the impressive occult library for a book on the subject of occult history, hoping to find more details about the blood feud between her family and the Thanos. As she was glancing through the titles she saw a book about Demonic Hierarchies. She pulled the large text from the shelf and thumbed through some of the pages.

There were disturbing pictures of human sacrifice and demons fornicating with humans. Abby barely thumbed through the first couple chapters before she returned the book to the shelf. Something about seeing those images set her ill at ease. *What a loathsome book,* she thought. Demonology was something she was not eager to study and thought better of doing so without more guidance.

Taking a deep breath, Abby hoped her stomach would settle. The disturbing pictures were difficult to push aside. Eventually she found several books on witch history and settled on one that specifically dealt with the history of witchcraft in the British Isles. Abby knew enough about her family to know they originated in Yorkshire, England.

Abby settled into one of the leather chairs and started reading. It wasn't long before she found the first mention of the Kane coven. She learned more about her family history than she ever expected. "A long-established coven in Yorkshire originating sometime in the early eleventh century," she read. "They remained there until the War of the Roses."

It seems her family had support the Plantagenet line in the English civil war, while a group of covens in London, calling themselves the London Seven, supported the Tudor line. When the Plantagenet claimant fell, the

Kane's were driven out of England by the London Seven. *So, who are the London Seven?* she thought. *Could they have any connection to the Thanos?* Vivian kept telling her to stay out of it, but Abby couldn't help but be curious. The more she learned about her powers, the more she wanted to know about her family's Coven.

Her reading was interrupted by the sound of footsteps coming down the stairs. "Now, what are you doing in here?" a familiar voice said in a mock scolding tone.

Abby put a leather mark in her place, and cradled the book in her lap. She smiled up at Benjamin who approached her chair. With a quick glance to make certain Ms. Grace wasn't lurking in the corner, he grinned and leaned in for a kiss.

"I'm sick of my room," she sighed, unapologetic. "I had to get out and do something other than lay in bed." Abby watched as her boyfriend set his books on the table, removed his sports coat and loosened his tie. She stifled a giggle; he was the very image of an aristocrat at the end of a long day.

"Are you feeling well enough to be out and about?" Benjamin inquired as he took a seat next to her.

"If one more person asks me if I'm well enough to do anything I'll beat them to a bloody pulp," Abby growled, "and that includes you Mr. Hodge," she added playfully. Benjamin seemed convinced and started doing his homework as Abby continued reading.

A few minutes passed as Abby continued to read about the conflict between her family and the London Seven. Eventually she came to a list of the seven families that consisted of the alliance. She was surprised to see one of the family names was… Hodge. Abby looked up at Benjamin curiously.

"What's wrong?" Benjamin asked having noticed Abby's peculiar look.

"I don't think I can be your girlfriend," Abby stated.

"What do you mean?" Benjamin asked a hint of concern, uncertain if she was being serious.

"It says here your family is a member of the London Seven," Abby said.

Benjamin shook his head. "Not anymore. We were replaced by the Fox coven over a century ago," he explained. "What does that have to do with anything?" He asked curiously. Abby could tell there was a hint of concern.

She softened the moment with a smile. "I'm reading a history. Your family along with the others in the London Seven ran my family out of England nearly six centuries ago. We're practically enemies," She said with a playful smile.

Benjamin seemed somewhat relieved, and he forced a halfhearted chuckle at her humor. "The London Seven," Benjamin said, deep in thought. "We have our own complicated history with that group. Perhaps I'll tell you about it someday."

"I'm certain it's probably somewhere in this book," Abby said holding up the history book she found on the shelf.

"Be careful what you read. Not all those books are accurate. Sometimes they are written from a point of view that doesn't have all the facts, or intentionally attempts to portray themselves in a glorious heroic fashion when they were anything but," Benjamin said dismissively, a slight tone of disgust creeping into his voice. Abby could tell he was bothered by something, but couldn't bring herself to ask what.

"Well, don't worry. This book only goes up to the seventeenth century," Abby said.

She watched as Benjamin shifted back to his normal self, the playful mood restored. "What are you doing for the holidays?" he asked as he wrote out math problems effortlessly.

"I haven't really given it much thought," Abby admitted. "Home isn't really an option. I could always consider spending Christmas with my Uncle in San Francisco, but grandmother doesn't think it's a good idea for me to be traveling. Considering everything going on, she's probably right. I'll come up with something," she said not wanting to admit to Benjamin she would probably be staying in her room by herself.

"Would you consider spending the holiday with my family?" Benjamin asked as he continued with his homework.

"I wouldn't want to intrude," Abby stated, returning her attention to her book. Suddenly the book was pulled from her hands and she looked up to see Benjamin kneeling on the floor next to her. "Hey," she protested trying to nab her book back as he held it out of her reach.

"Your presence is never an intrusion," Benjamin said, planting a sudden kiss on her lips.

"What are your parents going to say if you bring some strange foreign girl home from school?" Abby asked playfully, stealing a kiss of her own.

"Not if. When," he said smiling, letting her recapture the book. He put his arms around her and fell backwards, pulling Abby on top of him. "I won't take no for an answer." He gave her a long kiss.

"Has any girl ever said no to you?" Abby whispered breathlessly. She relaxed against him, falling into the escalated kisses.

"No," he said with a spare breath.

Abby enjoyed the moment as the two lay on the floor kissing, allowing their bodies to tangle. She could feel herself flush with heat as her breath became heavy. She knew he would go as far as she let him, but she didn't want him to stop. She felt feverish with desire as his hands began to move from her breasts, and she could feel him hardening through his pants. This was a new kind of passion for Abby, and she allowed it to continue, even knowing if she didn't put on the breaks it would be nearly impossible to stop.

She didn't want to stop.

She broke the kiss, and pulled back. The two lay next to one another on the floor breathless. A few moments passed as the tension began to recede enough for clearer thoughts to prevail once again.

"When is your sister going to be here?" Abby asked as she sat up and straightened her blouse.

"She's not coming over tonight," Benjamin responded as he regained his breath. "She's going to be in the studio all evening working on her art project."

"Oh," Abby responded. "It's almost 4 o'clock, Ms. Grace will be here any minute."

"Nope," Benjamin stated, waiting for the excitement in his pants to die down. "She's going to the alumni function in the village this evening."

"What? You mean we didn't need to stop?" She asked playfully. He reached out and tickled her sides. He then leaned up against the chair and pulled Abby close. She snuggled, placing her head on his chest and wrapping her arms around his waist. She watched silently as he used his magic to rekindle the flames in the fireplace.

"You know, each time we do this we get closer and closer. It's not going to be much longer before it happens," Benjamin said, all joking aside.

"I know," Abby admitted. "I'm not sure I would have stopped this time if I knew Ms. Grace and Josephine weren't going to be here."

He paused, then asked cautiously. "Have you ever done it before?"

Abby shook her head no. "Have you?

"No," He admitted, somewhat reluctantly.

"Really?" Abby asked playfully. "Benjamin Hodge the Playboy of Armitage Hall, the most handsome man on campus hasn't conquered the entire sexually active female student body!"

Benjamin squeezed her. "I wasn't interested in any of them until I met you," he murmured.

"There are dozens of girls at this school prettier than me." Abby commented finding it hard to believe he wasn't interested.

"No, they were never really an option. You were raised differently, I think," Benjamin stated.

"What do you mean?" Abby was confused.

"I-we, Josephine and me, we were raised knowing we were different. We were taught we're something more than the others. I always knew I would only be with another person who was a witch. A woman I didn't have to hide myself from, or hope wouldn't run in horror as soon as I told her." Benjamin sounded lonely when he spoke. Abby could understand, but she had never felt separate from others, but perhaps it was her upbringing. She had been sheltered from the family crafts until she was older, and her parents had always kept her out of coven business. She had allowed herself to be friends with normal people; people who were not witches.

"Haven't you met other girls who are witches?" Abby asked.

"A couple, but none of them were like you," Benjamin sounded sincere. "We're like royalty, in a manner of speaking. We are at our best when we are with our own kind." Abby had never really thought about it that way. Her parents were both witches. The handful of other witches she knew in her family were with others of their kind. "What about you? Surely you couldn't have gone unnoticed for this long," Benjamin asked.

"My parents sent me to an all girl's school, remember? I barely even spoke to a boy I wasn't related to until I came here," Abby confessed.

"What now?" He asked, sincerely.

"I don't want to set a date or plan our first time," Abby admitted. "But we need to take precautions."

"Of course," Benjamin answered. "But you are ready?"

"I don't know," Abby answered honestly. "I think so, but I want to be prepared when the time comes. We came close and I don't want to have any mishaps. Can you imagine how my grandmother would react?" She knew the thought would kill the mood at least for a while.

Benjamin laughed and covered his eyes with his large hands. "Thank you for planting that image in my head."

Abby got up and collected the book she had been reading and stuffed it in her book bag. She grabbed her jacket from the coat rack next to the stairs and put it on.

"Where are you going?" Benjamin asked looking defeated.

"Somewhere you are not," Abby stated. She walked over to Benjamin and gave him a kiss on the cheek. "Until we sort out how we're going to play it safe, I think it's best we don't tempt fate."

"What? You don't want to bear my spawn?" Benjamin questioned pretending his feelings were hurt. His cute brown eyes were nearly impossible to resist.

"Ha!" Abby said. "I think I'll hit the snooze button on motherhood for a few more years, thank you." She started up the stairs.

"You don't really have to go. I'll behave, I promise," Benjamin pleaded as she ascended the staircase.

"It's not you I'm worried about," Abby said her final words as she disappeared, leaving her boyfriend with an enormous smile.

"That was the best shopping trip ever," Nina said while wrapping presents for the holiday.

Abby took a sip of hot cocoa as they shuffled through the mountains of gift bags and boxes piled in their dorm, from their epic shopping excursion.

"Anytime you want to meet up in London to go shopping you need only call." Abby smiled. It had been a pleasant afternoon.

"Your boyfriend will love what you got him." Sarah smiled as she cut some ribbon.

"I hope so," Abby said, feeling uncertain. Benjamin was the kind of guy who already had everything, which made gift shopping rather difficult.

"Are you off to spend the evening with him again?" Nina asked a big, knowing smile on her face.

Abby blushed slightly and headed for the door. "You know it," She quickly jaunted down the stairs and into the courtyard, a feeling of guilt following her.

She felt like she was lying to her roommates. It wasn't Benjamin who was forefront in her thoughts as she stepped into the brisk evening air. Perhaps it wasn't a betrayal in the classic sense, but if they knew how much time she spent thinking of Edgar Kincaid, it would be hard to explain.

He had been on her mind more than she cared to admit. The last several days had seen her mulling over all the possible theories about him, about his role in what happened to Emily, and about what he was. She definitely wasn't ready to talk to Nina and Sarah about their missing ex-roommate, but Abby decided it was time to present some of her theories about Edgar with her fellow witches.

She pressed down the path and entered Calder House placing her bag on the couch near the door. As she descended into the sanctum she could hear Benjamin and Josephine talking in angry tones. It sounded like they were arguing.

"What's wrong?" Abby asked as she reached the bottom step. She noticed Ms. Grace was nowhere in sight.

Benjamin looked at her as if they'd been caught committing a crime, and Josephine stoically turned her face away as Abby entered. Their expressions relaxed upon seeing her, though to Abby it seemed forced.

"It's nothing," Benjamin said, approaching and giving her a kiss on the cheek. "We're just arguing over what we're getting our parents for Christmas."

Abby knew a real argument from a stressful holiday gift when she heard one, but she didn't want to intrude on their privacy. If they wanted to keep it to themselves, that was their choice.

"Where's Ms. Grace?" she asked instead, and opened the box of books her grandmother had sent.

"She went to London for a conference. I don't think she's expected back until late tonight," Josephine said as she measured out reagents for a potion she was working on.

"I was hoping to bring this up while she was around, but I think I have some insight into our mysterious Mr. Kincaid." Abby said gesturing to the book she held. It was one of the books her grandmother had sent along after her visit.

"Really?" Josephine questioned, setting her experiment aside. She looked at Abby intently.

"What is it?" Benjamin asked, more cautious.

"I think I might know what he is," Abby said. "That is, I'm not sure, but I think he's a half breed," she added as she thumbed through the pages of the book she was holding. When she found the right page she pointed to the word.

Cambion.

"A cambion?" Benjamin seemed uncertain.

"It makes sense," Josephine said, half to herself. "I never considered that. There are demonic influences without any clear direct involvement of a demon. Coupled with his unnatural strength and eyes…" She trailed off in thought, looking pleased.

"Plus, there's his mother's unusual obsession with religion, and the occasional scent of sulfur, which the book says is a common element," Abby added in support of her working theory. "I can't be certain until I do more research, but it's the best thing I can come up with between the Sight and my interactions with him."

"We don't really know much about cambions," Benjamin said, looking to Josephine.

"Most intriguing," Josephine said as she moved to stand next to Benjamin. "They're very rare. I haven't heard of there being one in England in the last three-hundred years or so."

Benjamin shook his head. "Are you sure? All we have is this one book to go on."

"And what we've witnessed," Abby stated. "I'm thinking about approaching him. I don't think he knows what he is."

"No!" Both Josephine and Benjamin said in unison. Abby was startled by their outburst.

"No," Josephine added more calmly. "He's too dangerous. You saw it for yourself in the vision you had."

"She's right, Abby," Benjamin said. "He's already hurt you once. There's no telling what he's capable of."

"Abby please," Benjamin pleaded, "promise me you won't have anything to do with him."

The fear in Benjamin's eyes was clear. Abby could see their point, but still… "This could really help him," Abby countered softly.

Benjamin looked away, as if afraid to meet her eyes.

"If he is a cambion, then he's half demon, Abby. That makes him dangerous. Especially if we don't know what kind of demon he is," Josephine said. "We should be thinking of ways to get rid of him, not help him."

"Get rid of him?" Abby asked. The tone in Josephine's voice was concerning. "What do you mean get rid of him?"

"She means running him off," Benjamin explained. "Please, Abby promise me you won't go anywhere near that guy."

Benjamin's genuine concern was too much for Abby to resist. She nodded her agreement. Benjamin kissed her forehead, as if to settle an argument, and without another word the three of them went about their studies.

She was sure she wasn't wrong.

Edgar was surely going through an impossibly hard time. Did he even know what he was? She wanted to reach out to him and help him figure it out, but she had made a promise to Benjamin not to put herself in danger. She knew demons were beyond anything she knew how to deal with, and she knew she should be afraid of whatever Edgar was, but if Abby were in his position with powers that were starting to emerge and no idea what they were... For a brief moment she appreciated her grandmother more than she admitted. Her style of training was harsh, but at least Abby knew what she was.

She sighed. She wasn't going to reach any conclusions now, so she pushed it from her mind and decided she was going to enjoy the holiday. There was nothing to be done until they all returned from break anyway.

CHAPTER THIRTEEN

"Are you ready?" Benjamin's voice asked through the phone.

"Yes, I packed everything yesterday," Abby confirmed as she put her purse next to her luggage.

"Good, because we have a change in plans," Benjamin said. Abby fought down a moment of anxiety; she didn't particularly like surprises.

"Oh?"

"Yes!" Benjamin said. "The car is already here to pick us up. And here is the best part…" he paused, dragging out the suspense.

"You're a cruel man Mr. Hodge," Abby protested as he kept her hanging.

"My parents decided to come down and pick us up themselves. They are here right now waiting to meet you!" Abby nearly dropped her phone. "Hello? Abby? Are you there?"

She cleared her throat. "That's great!" She said, feigning excitement. "I'll be down in a couple of minutes."

"See you in a few ticks," Benjamin hung up.

Abby sat on the edge of the bed for a moment settling her nerves and giving herself a pep talk.

"Something wrong?" Sarah asked wrapping her robe around her waist.

"No… I mean yes… I mean no," Abby said feeling completely caught off guard.

"Stop for a minute," Sarah instructed as though she were one of the professors at the school. "What's wrong?"

Abby took a deep breath and looked at her friend who sat next to her on the edge of the bed. "Benjamin's parents are downstairs. It will be the first time I've met them. I'm so nervous I feel like I'm going to jump out of my own skin," she confessed.

Sarah smiled and wrapped her arm around Abby's shoulder. "I've known you for nearly four months now. You are one of the most likable people I know. They are going to love you," Sarah reassured.

"What if they don't?" Abby asked. Every insecurity she'd ever had seemed to have surfaced in the last few moments.

"Then they are a couple of tossers," Nina said from her bed, poking her head out from under the covers.

Abby and Sarah both laughed. "Good morning Nina," Abby said.

"Sarah's right. They are going to love you," Nina said, rolling out of bed. "Come on, the bathroom's going to be a complete madhouse by now."

"Nina's right. We need to get ready," Sarah said getting up and heading towards the door. "You can call me over the holiday if you need to," She added before excusing herself.

"Thanks," Abby called out. She got up and went over to the mirror to give herself a brief maintenance check. She decided to wear white slacks and a black blouse. She wore one of her signature scarves around her neck tucked in like an ascot. Abby purposefully wore her hair down the way Benjamin liked it, but now she hoped it didn't make her look too casual. She pulled out her long wool double-breasted coat, her grandmother sent her, and put it on, buttoning it up and fastening the belt around her waist. Finally, she put on some black leather fur lined gloves she had picked up in London. She decided it was a sophisticated look, something these old English families seemed to appreciate. She took a deep breath, collected her purse and luggage, and headed out of the room.

The courtyard was filled with students, parents and a long line of vehicles. It was a bustle of excitement as students met their families to travel home for an extended holiday. Abby looked around for a brief moment and saw Benjamin approaching with his parents.

Benjamin's father was a tall, middle-aged businessman, in a smart-looking suit. He stood as if he knew he was well-dressed and well-groomed. His mother was similarly a conservative woman in simple but tasteful attire, and her dark brown hair was pulled back in a tight bun. She was a pretty woman, and didn't need over stated clothing to accentuate her sharp features. Abby could instantly see the Hodge bloodline at work; both Benjamin and Josephine took after their mother.

"Hello," Benjamin said, brazenly giving Abby a peck on the cheek and taking her luggage. She stiffened slightly, uncertain of displaying affection so openly in front of his parents. "Abby this is my father, Asa Hodge, and my mother, Isobel."

She shook both their hands, smiling warmly. "It's nice to meet you Mr. and Mrs. Hodge." Abby was keenly aware of the shy and reserved part of her nature, and she wished she was more charming. She tried for a winning smile.

"It's very nice to meet you Miss Kane," Asa said, his voice warm and welcoming.

"We've heard so much about you, Abby. It feels like we already know you," Isobel said. She was a bit more withdrawn, but her welcome sounded genuine. Abby smiled again.

"I'll take your luggage to the car," Benjamin stated.

Together, they all piled in a large stretch Mercedes while the driver saw to their belongings. Mr. and Mrs. Hodge sat across from Josephine, Benjamin and Abby. "Abby, I understand you're from Seattle?" Isobel asked.

"Yes, born and raised," Abby said, smiling. Benjamin took her hand. Abby felt uncomfortable with his open affection, though his parents didn't seem to notice, or care.

"It's a lovely city. Asa and I have been there on several occasions, for business. Though, we were able to see some of the sites. We were particularly fond of the Volcano observatory. The mountains there certainly are majestic." Abby could tell that instead of interrogating her, Isobel was kindly trying to put her at ease.

"Yes, it is a beautiful place indeed," Asa interjected.

"I have always been fond of my hometown," Abby stated. "I practically grew up on the islands in my family's summer home near Friday Harbor."

"Is that the San Juan Islands? We haven't had occasion to visit them, but I've heard they're beautiful," Isobel added.

Abby nodded, but was cut off before she could respond further. "And, how is your grandmother?" Asa asked. Abby's heart froze for nearly half a second. She hadn't realized they knew her family, and of all people, Vivian Kane. She could only imagine the impression her grandmother had left. What must they think of her?

"If you know my grandmother, then you probably know she's unstoppable," Abby said lightly, trying to give no indication they struck a nerve. Mr. and Mrs. Hodge chuckled politely, offering Abby a great deal of relief. "I think she decided to spend this holiday on an African Safari. She's not one to stay home and do anything remotely traditional. But that's why I love her. My grandmother is a force of nature."

Isobel shifted slightly as though she was a bit uncomfortable. "We are of course, very sorry to hear about your parents." She expressed her sympathy.

"Mother!" Benjamin raised his voice, shocked.

Abby squeezed his hand tightly and gave him a comforting look. "It's alright, your mother was just being kind. Thank you, Mrs. Hodge. I fear your son is very protective. In truth, I don't think I'm the delicate flower he believes me to be." Isobel gave her son a look. Benjamin quickly calmed down and sat back.

"He gets the over protectiveness from his mother," Asa explained. "and his sense of humor from me."

"Ah, the joys of family," Josephine added sarcastically as she stared out the window.

"How far do you live from school?" Abby asked.

"Forty-five minutes if one's obeying all the traffic laws," Asa stated, checking his watch.

The conversation stayed light; Benjamin and Josephine talked about school, Benjamin spoke of the rowing team with all the pride it deserved, and Josephine mentioned her art in passing. There was little spoken of their academic studies, instead most of the conversation revolved around their studies in Ms. Grace's sanctum. There was no mention of Edgar Kincaid, even though Abby knew full well they had been spending much of their time discussing their mysterious classmate. Abby supposed this was just something they weren't ready to share with their parents. She could understand that; she was more comfortable with Vivian in the dark on that subject as well, at least until they knew more. Abby sat and listened to the light chatter with half an ear as she watched the countryside roll by.

The car drove along a large brick wall, eventually coming to an iron gate. The driver slowed down and paused a few moments as he entered a code at the security box. The gate slowly opened.

"Oh good, we're home," Josephine commented. The car started driving up a long private road, cutting through a densely-wooded area. Abby estimated the road through the estate went on for at least two kilometers before it opened onto the house.

The Hodge Family's ancestral home was a late eighteenth century manor with impeccably maintained lawns and a fountain in the center of the courtyard. There were several servants rushing about making ready for their arrival. Abby took note of the four men wearing black fatigues, carrying rifles, and walking large ferocious-looking dogs. She had never encountered such security measures. It was odd for her to think it was necessary for her friends to protect themselves this way. *Then again,* she thought, *if we had guards at the doors mom and dad might still be here...* She let the melancholy thought trail off, unwilling to follow it down that dark road. Instead, she steeled herself, and followed her hosts as they exited the car.

The group made their way into the house with little fanfare. The old Georgian-style manor was breath-taking. The solid stone walls and large windows instantly reminded her of Jane Austen and George Elliot, and she imagined it must have cost more than the worth of her home in Seattle to modernize. Most of the original fixtures were still intact, or incorporated in new ways. For Abby, it felt like stepping back in time.

Growing up in Seattle, she was accustomed to a balance of the old and new, even with so much taking on a modern tone, there were old Victorian and Colonial houses in the hills and on the island around the city proper. But 'old' took on an entirely new meaning here. Estates like this just didn't exist back home. Nothing had really prepared Abby for the vast dissonance at discovering how young Seattle was compared to West Midland Country.

"You have a lovely home, Mrs. Hodge," Abby commented breathlessly as she was escorted to her room. "Has it been in your family for long?"

"Actually, it's been in my husband's family since it was built in 1752," Isobel answered as she guided Abby up the stairs. "I grew up in my family home on the island of Jersey."

Abby fell silent again, taking in the architecture and artwork all around her, as she followed Isobel down a long hall lined with mahogany tables holding vases full of fresh flowers. The scent was a nice change from the stagnant environment of the dormitory, and Abby smiled at the homey touch.

Isobel opened a door and motioned for Abby to enter. "This is where you will be staying; we call it the Chinese room," she said warmly. The room was elegantly decorated in gold and red with a strong oriental theme.

"It's lovely. Thank you for having me, Mrs. Hodge," Abby said as she stepped into the room. She glanced around, familiarizing herself with the amenities, which included a private bathroom and a fireplace.

"You're very special. Benjamin has never brought anyone home before," Isobel smiled and looked at her watch. "I'll leave you to settle in, Miss Kane. I'm certain Benjamin will be along soon to show you around. Don't hesitate to ask the staff for anything you need."

"Thank you," Abby said as she looked at the bed and thought about how little sleep she got the night before. With the initial meeting behind her, relief was settling in.

Abby considered lying down but thought it wise to unpack first. After putting her clothes away and setting up her belongings in the bathroom, Abby laid on her bed and dozed for a few minutes. It wasn't long before she heard a polite knock on the door.

"Come in," Abby said, sitting up.

Benjamin came in and closed the door behind him a pleased look on his face. "Meeting the parents went very well I thought," Benjamin said, giving Abby a kiss and sitting next to her. "I could tell you were nervous. I don't know why, I can't imagine anyone wouldn't fall instantly in love with you." Abby couldn't help but smile as she blushed.

"They are very nice," Abby admitted. She was relieved to have the first meeting over with and two of the most difficult topics out of the way; her grandmother, and the death of her parents were things Abby preferred not to just drop into conversation.

"So, do you want to see the place or just stay here and snog for the rest of the day?" Benjamin asked in his usual sly manner that indicated he was only half joking.

Abby stood and took his hand a coy smile crept across her face. She gave him a sweet kiss on the lips. "I think you should show me around first." She knew it wasn't the response he was hoping for, but her smile was enough to convince him he would eventually get what he wanted. Benjamin got up, took her hand and started the grand tour of the Hodge family estate.

It was a beautiful place filled with history and family stories. He showed her the music room decorated in dark green with gold accents, where his grandmother used to teach him to play the piano.

"Are you any good?" Abby asked, watching his fingers trail absent-mindedly over the keys. She liked the idea of him at the piano, diligently following his grandmother's instruction as he learned the music.

"Not so much anymore. I never really kept it up. I regret it a little," Benjamin confessed. "Come on," he said, and led her out of the room.

They passed through the kitchen, where several staff members were working diligently to prepare supper. Abby couldn't help but notice the smell of roasting meat, as she watched the cooks prepare vegetables and bread for the meal.

"If you're ever hungry you can come here anytime and there's always something around to eat," Benjamin noted. As if to emphasize his point, he reached around a cook and snagged a fresh apple out of a basket on the table.

"I'll keep that in mind," Abby commented as he guided her through to the formal dining room. It was an enormous room with a table that looked twenty feet long. She imagined it could easily seat thirty people.

"Do your parents entertain a lot?" Abby asked, impressed by the size and grandeur as she gazed up at the three crystal chandeliers hanging from the ceiling above.

"Not as often as they used to when I was younger," Benjamin said. "Two hundred years ago the Ash Treaty was signed at this very table," he added.

"The Ash Treaty?" Abby asked, uncertain she had ever heard of such a thing.

"Yes, the War of Ash. You've never heard of it before?" Benjamin asked, looking somewhat surprised. Abby felt embarrassed. There were still so many things she was still learning. "It was one of the big wars between multiple covens. They called it the War of Ash, because, so many witches were burned at the stake during the war."

"It sounds terrible," Abby said. "It sounds like your family has been involved in many important things," she added, contemplating the many things that must have happened in a house this old.

"This way. There's something I've been wanting to show you since we arrived," Benjamin said excitedly. Taking her hand, he pulled her toward the main entry and out the front door. They followed a path around the main house to an old looking stone stable. It was a charming building with a thatch roof and cobblestone wall.

He guided her into the stables and brought her up to a large beautiful horse with a dark brown coat and white spot on his nose. "this is Charlemagne, my thoroughbred," he said.

"What a beautiful boy," Abby said, stroking the horses mane and giving him some affection.

"And this is Medea, Josephine's horse. She's a Mangalarga Marchador." Abby walked to the next stall. "She's lovely."

117

"Do you know how to ride?" Benjamin asked.

"I took lessons when I was younger. My cousin breeds horses back home," Abby shared as she continued to give the horses her affection. "Thank you for showing them to me. I can see that they're very special to you."

He looked thoughtful for a moment. "We'll go riding sometime over the holiday, but they aren't what I wanted to show you." Benjamin said as he beckoned her to continue to follow him. He grinned. "Follow me."

The two made their way into a different part of the main house, through a small entrance Abby wouldn't have seen if Benjamin hadn't been leading her. He guided Abby down a flight of stairs located near the back of the house, into an extensive wine cellar.

She made her way through a veritable catacomb of fine wines and barrels of liquor, awestruck at the grandeur. There was a chill in the air and Abby could smell the dusty damp stone and wood surrounding them. Some of the bottles looked ancient with labels that dated back well over a century. A thin layer of dust covered many of the bottles and Abby imagined some of the bottles were worth a fortune.

"Wow." She shook her head in amazement. "Your parents must throw some epic parties," she observed with a laugh. She imagined living in the remote countryside, and realized they must keep a large supply of everything.

"They've been known to throw some big parties," Benjamin commented. "Most of them are fairly dull if you ask me." He continued to make his way through the room, skirting barrels and wine racks.

"Where are you taking me? The dungeon?" Abby asked jokingly as they weaved through the dimly-lit room. Benjamin gave her a very serious look making her think for a moment perhaps he was actually going to take her to a dungeon. His serious look dissolved into a sweet smile and gave her a kiss. He then pulled her towards the very back of the basement.

"This is what I want to show you." Benjamin said. Abby looked around for the catch. All she could see were more wine racks filled with expensive and rare wines.

"I am impressed. It seems you have wine back here, too." She teased. Benjamin just smirked, and pulled on one of the racks. Like something out of a mystery novel, a secret passageway opened before them. Abby could see the sanctum markings on the edges of the wall.

Benjamin took both Abby's hands. "Miss Kane, will you please join me in my sanctum?" he asked, pulling her towards the chamber beyond.

It was a large room with a fireplace and a leather chair. There were several tables with the trappings she was more than familiar with. Near the door was a large, neatly kept desk. The wall to the right of the door was lined with bookshelves that were sparsely occupied.

"I don't have a very impressive library yet," Benjamin stated, "but it's a start."

"You're doing far better than me. I haven't even started one, let alone established a sanctum" Abby admitted, somewhat disappointed in herself.

"You don't have a sanctum back home?" he inquired.

"I was planning to make one. I never got around to it," Abby confessed.

"No, of course not," Benjamin said, sadly.

"Things are different in America," she said by way of an answer. "We don't usually have ancestral homes passed down from generation to generation. I probably won't create a permanent sanctum until I know where I plan to settle."

"Well I have some ideas about that," Benjamin said, standing behind her and putting his arms around her waist setting his chin on her shoulder.

"Oh really? What kind of ideas do you have Mr. Hodge?" Abby asked closing her eyes savoring the moment.

"You know, around here Mr. Hodge is my father," Benjamin murmured, kissing her on the nape of her neck.

Abby laughed and leaned into his touch, enjoying the warmth of his body. "Is that so?"

"Mhmn." His hands slowly wandered up her chest to play with the buttons on her coat. His fingers gently brushing against her breasts through the fine wool.

"Are you trying to get frisky with me?" Abby asked playfully.

"Always," he answered, unbuckling her overcoat. Abby smiled at the masterful way he unbuttoned the double-breasted garment without taking his lips from her neck. He slowly slid the coat from her shoulders, his hands igniting fires all along Abby's shoulders where he touched her. Her arms free, Abby spun abruptly, surprising Benjamin with a kiss.

They stood that way for a moment. Abby would happily have let it last forever, but soon his weren't the only hands that were wandering.

Abby was under no illusions. She was well aware of where this was headed, where things with Benjamin had been headed for months now. She gave herself over to the rush of adrenaline and the coursing sensations urging her onward.

Benjamin's kisses became more passionate, almost urgent. Abby could feel his hands unbuttoning her blouse as he pressed his body against her. She pulled the scarf form around her neck and discarded it on the floor. She then placed her hands on his chest. She could feel his muscles beneath the cashmere pullover.

She stepped back leaning against the cold stone wall to catch her breath. "Are you alright?" Benjamin asked breathlessly.

Abby nodded. He pressed her up against the wall and pulled her blouse back over her shoulders. The sensations running through her body were growing in intensity as his hands began to explore her bare skin.

Abby reached down and found the edges of his shirt and began pulling it up. Benjamin pulled it the rest of the way off and threw it to the ground, eagerly resuming where he had left off.

His muscular chest and abs were breathtaking to behold. He was an athlete with a defined and toned body to match. Abby did her best to take everything in with as many senses as she could. Breathing became even more difficult as he continued to kiss her. She could feel his heart pounding in his chest as he pressed himself against her. His hands wandered to her back where he began to unhook her bra. Abby could feel his excitement pressing against her thigh.

It's happening, she thought. "Hmmhm," she said. The excitement and physical sensations were beginning to eclipse what little anxiousness and apprehension that remained.

Abby wanted him, and she wanted to give herself to him. It wasn't how she imagined it would happen, on a cold stone floor in a sub-cellar, but what was happening felt right.

Her bra fell away and she could feel herself sliding down the wall. They continued to kiss as they slid to the unforgiving stone floor. They pulled away briefly and discarded their pants abandoning any care. The moment their pants were off their bodies united like two magnets clicking together.

Benjamin shifted, his hip sliding between her legs. He paused, breaking the kiss. It was clear he wanted desperately to continue, but was uncertain. Their eyes locked.

This was the moment to decide. She knew if she chose to, she could stop everything or make it happen. She allowed herself to gaze into his longing eyes. She could see his passion, his love for her. She could feel the heat of his breath on her face, and the flush of her skin under his. She took a deep breath, and nodded. In that moment, she knew she wanted him as badly as he wanted her. "Yes." She whispered her consent.

Benjamin needed no further encouragement, he pulled his discarded coat over and pulled out a box of condoms. He took one out and put the condom on. It didn't take long before his attention returned to Abby and resumed his love-making with a renewed sense of urgency.

The first time it hurt. She sort of expected that; she wasn't completely ignorant of what would happen, but, later, the second time was better. By the third time, it even started to feel nice. She was sure there would be a forth, but by then Abby was too sore to continue.

The two lay on the floor next to one another naked, catching their breath. They had barely spoken, yet Abby felt closer to him than if they'd just poured their hearts out all night long. She was exhausted and felt flushed. Her body had been through so much, she could feel aches and pains all over. Benjamin had not meant to hurt her; he had been gentle and tender, and she knew it wouldn't always be this way, but at the moment she felt like a rag doll. All her strength and vitality was drained. Her head swimming as feverish desire slowly receded, making room for the world to intrude. All she wanted to do was sleep.

"Are you alright?" Benjamin asked, rolling over and throwing an arm around her.

"I'll let you know when I can move again," Abby said. Her voice sounded like she just woke up.

"That was bloody brilliant," Benjamin said, wiping sweat off his forehead. He kissed her shoulder, tenderly.

Abby reached her hand out and blindly searched for her cell phone. "Holy sh…" She caught herself before finishing the phrase, but her expletive was noticed by her boyfriend.

He looked over. "What's wrong?"

Abby gathered her clothing. "It's almost five o'clock, we literally shagged the day away."

"What of it?" Benjamin seemed unconcerned.

Abby started putting on her underwear and fastened her bra. "Aren't your parents going to wonder where we've been?" Abby asked.

"Why would they? We're home," Benjamin gathered his clothing and pulled on his boxer briefs.

"What they must think…" Abby said as she buttoned her blouse. She wanted to make a good impression, but this was not the start to the visit that she had planned.

"I know exactly what they think," Benjamin said, pulling her into a hug. "They think we shagged the day away."

Abby looked at him, searching for any trace that he was teasing her. "What do you mean? They don't care?" she felt confused.

"Of course, they care. They just trust us," Benjamin said. He released her and pulled on his pants. "It's not like we're stupid kids. We're both seventeen," he added picking up condom wrappers and discarding them in the wastepaper basket.

"Really?" She asked. It was hard for her to imagine parents unconcerned with their seventeen-year-old son having sex in their home. Perhaps it was another one of the cultural differences between America and Europe.

Benjamin put on his t-shirt and pullover, walked over to Abby and gave her a kiss on the forehead. "Of course," he said. "Besides, you wouldn't know it by looking at them now, but they were quite the hippies at one time. Free love and everything. They're very cool with it. Besides, honestly,

I think they already believe we've been getting it off for months."

Abby was flushed. She was starting to realize her upbringing was far more conservative than she had imagined. "Just as long as your parents don't think I'm some Babylonian whore who corrupted their son," Abby retorted as she fiddled with her scarf. Her humor sounded forced, even to her, but he was gracious enough to let it stand.

Benjamin laughed, and pulled her into a tight hug. "I think they know me well enough to understand it was very much the other way around."

CHAPTER FOURTEEN

"Tomorrow is the big day," Benjamin said as the two of them lay in the over-sized bed in Abby's room.

"I know," Abby confessed. "It's been on my mind a lot."

"I could tell," Benjamin said.

"I'm sorry," Abby apologized. "I hope I haven't been a drag to be around. It's my first Christmas since my parents..." She caught herself getting choked up. A rush of feelings came so quickly and abruptly it was difficult to inhabit her own thoughts.

Benjamin reached out and pulled her into a tight hug. "I know," he whispered softly, just holding her closely.

Christmas had always been a time for family. It was a time to be around the people you love most in the world, and yet Abby was alone. There would be no more family Christmases. She would miss the hot cocoa her mother made in the morning before raiding their stockings above the fireplace, and their tradition of having Eggs Benedict after opening the presents. By mid-day cousin Margot and Madison would come over and spend the rest of the day together. Abby teared up thinking about how much she missed her parents, her family, her old life...

"It's okay," Benjamin whispered.

His soft caring words opened the floodgates. Abby buried her face in his chest as she allowed herself to release a torrent of tears. For the first time the pain felt bearable. Abby let herself move through the moment and began reconstructing her emotional fortitude. It was still hard. *It probably always will be,* she conceded to herself.

"Sorry." Abby instinctively apologized as she pulled herself together. "I know this isn't what you wanted to deal with this evening."

"I'm with you. I got what I wanted." Benjamin reassured her with a sweet smile. "It's your first Christmas without your parents and away from your family. I can't even begin to imagine how difficult it must be."

"For the most part, I'm handling it better than I thought," Abby confessed. "It comes in waves."

"You can talk about it anytime," Benjamin offered.

"Thanks," Abby said.

Benjamin lifted her chin bringing her eyes to his. "I mean it," he added.

Abby smiled. Even though she trusted Benjamin it was still difficult to be vulnerable. She didn't really know how to allow the raw emotions to break through her resolve. Having that kind of breakdown in front of someone screamed against every instinct she had. *Perhaps, I'm not so different from my grandmother,* she thought realizing her own way she didn't like letting people see her in a weakened state. She was quickly repulsed by her own insight and pushed it aside, unwilling to explore it any further.

"Thank you," "she said giving him a sweet kiss on the lips. "I'm not sure how I would be handling all of this if I was stuck at school in my room alone."

"I had a plan if you refused to join my family for the holiday," Benjamin said slyly.

Abby looked at him amused. "Oh? What plan is this?"

"I conspired with Nina. If you refused to join me she was going to kidnap you and drag you to stay with her family," Benjamin explained.

"She never mentioned anything," Abby said, trying to remember any mention of the holidays with the Carlisle family.

"She never had to. You quickly surrendered to my charms. I was planning to make it virtually impossible for you to say no," Benjamin said with a bright grin. "I'm glad you came." He added giving her a squeeze.

"Me too," Abby smiled. She felt safe there in his arms. For the first time in a while, Abby felt like maybe things really were going to get better.

Christmas morning came on Abby's sixth day at Hodge Manor. She woke up later than planned. Benjamin kept her up the night before fooling around. In fact, ever since they first had sex nearly a week before, they had done little else.

It became obvious to Abby that the Hodge family was very busy with their own personal interests. She hardly saw Asa and Josephine outside of meals, and Isobel checked in with her each morning to make certain she had everything she needed, but otherwise left her alone with Benjamin. Christmas morning was different however. A staff member delivered an itinerary for the day, before disappearing down the hallway.

"Seriously?" Abby muttered under her breath when she glanced down at the beautiful parchment with the day's scheduled activities. Morning tea, followed by the opening of presents, breakfast and later in the day there would be a formal dinner with guests arriving for cocktails an hour before.

She hadn't realized how formal and arranged everything had been. A stark contrast to the informal traditions of her own family. Fortunately, she was prepared, and had carefully picked out an evening dress for the occasion.

Abby set her itinerary on the dresser and looked at the clock. She only had about thirty minutes to present herself. She certainly didn't want to be late, so she quickly showered and put on a dark green skirt and a white silk blouse. She had already placed the presents under the tree save for one gift, which she planned to give Benjamin more privately.

She quickly peeked inside the drawer where she had placed it, to make sure it was still there. Satisfied it hadn't been moved, Abby checked her appearance in the mirror one last time, and made her way down to the living room.

She encountered Isobel in the hallway, no doubt on her way up to check in on her. Abby smiled warmly.

"How are you dear?" she greeted Abby with a peck on the cheek. "You look wonderful, do you need anything for the party this evening?"

"I think I have everything I need. Thank you for asking," Abby stated.

"Excellent," Isobel smiled. "I wanted to let you know several of your family members sent packages. I've taken the liberty of placing them under the tree."

"Thank you," Abby stated, surprised. "That was very thoughtful." She hadn't expected there to be anything for her from home.

The two women made their way down the stairs into the living room where Asa and Benjamin were already enjoying their tea. They both stood when the women entered the room.

"Good morning!" Benjamin greeted them cheerily, and gave Abby a chaste kiss on the cheek. Abby smiled.

Isobel made her way over to the shining silver tea service, which was laid out on a small table. "Abigail dear, we had the cook make you some coffee. Benjamin said you prefer it to tea," she stated, pouring Abby a cup.

"Thank you, how thoughtful," she said, eagerly accepting.

"Milk or sugar?" Benjamin asked offering from the tea service.

"Milk is for the weak," Abby joked, soliciting a polite chuckle from her hosts. "Where is Josephine?" Abby asked, remembering their strict schedule today.

Benjamin shrugged. "She'll be down in a minute."

Asa began sorting presents, as Abby and Benjamin took their seats on a small sofa near the tree, decorated in gold bulbs and white lights. Josephine joined them and poured herself a cup of tea before the presents were distributed.

"This one is for you dear," Asa commented placing a small present in his wife's lap.

Abby watched as the Hodge family engaged in their present sorting tradition. She watched as the matriarch of the small family glanced at the attached tag. "From my sister, Caroline," Isobel said. A staff member sat near the door with a note pad scribbling something down.

"What's going on?" Abby whispered into Benjamin's ear, referring to the staff member by the door.

He glanced over and smiled. "She's writing down what gifts were received and from whom so we can send thank you cards," Benjamin explained.

"I see," Abby said. This was a far more formal affair than any Christmas she had experienced. She watched as Isobel sat primly, opening her present slowly as though she were attempting to preserve the beautiful blue and gold wrapping paper. She gently set it aside once it was removed and opened a small box pulling out a gold charm of a pyramid.

"A gold charm of a pyramid," Isobel said, the staff member quickly scribbling on her note pad.

"Sounds like Caroline enjoyed her trip to Egypt earlier this year," Asa said, setting himself to rummaging through presents under the tree.

"We really should have let our guest start the tradition." Isobel politely scolded her husband giving Abby a sweet smile.

"You're quite right dear. My apologies," Asa said, pulling a rather large rectangular box from under the tree and passing it to Abby.

"It's quite alright," Abby said, uncertain how to else to respond. Such formality was lost on her and all she could do was hope not to make a fool of herself.

She looked down at the large present and wondered who it could be from. She hadn't expected much in the way of gifts. Abby found a small tag near the bow and read it aloud. "From Asa and Isobel Hodge," she was surprised to see her hosts had gotten her a gift. "Thank you," Abby said, somewhat speechless.

Abby mimicked the unwrapping process she saw Isobel employ, avoiding the barbaric ripping and tearing away of her past. Removing the wrapping paper, she uncovered a large garment box. She found the edges of the lid and lifted it carefully. She opened the tissue paper to reveal a classic English style-riding outfit.

"Josephine gave us an estimation on your size. Hopefully it fits properly. One of the maids is a talented seamstress who can do a fitting for you if you like," Isobel commented as Abby pulled the garment from the box.

"I don't' know what to say," Abby told them. "Thank you. How very thoughtful." She found she was repeating herself, but this was all so new to her. She was uncertain how much she should gush over their kindness. She was overwhelmed by their thoughtfulness, and was unsure how to show it.

Abby watched as each one of them opened their gifts. Each announcing who the gift was from then taking special care to unwrap each one. With each gift the servant by the door wrote down the details.

Benjamin seemed very pleased with the leather jacket and rowing gloves she had picked out for him. Each solicited a peck on the cheek. Even after nearly a week she still felt uncomfortable with displays of affection in front of his parents. Probably because she knew her parents would have disapproved. She quickly pushed aside the thought of her parents meeting her first boyfriend; it was a lovely dream that she knew would never come to pass. Now wasn't the time to indulge in painful fantasies.

Abby continued to open her presents. Josephine had gotten her a beautiful stationary set with Abby's initials engraved on the pen and embossed on the parchment. In return, she gifted Josephine with a silk scarf, having noticed how much she liked the one's she wore. Benjamin had gifted her with a new winter jogging outfit.

They were coming to the last few gifts under the tree. Asa pulled a very small square box wrapped in gold paper. "Abigail," he said passing the box down to Abby.

It was a tiny box. Abby regarded it with curiosity. It was small enough Abby thought perhaps it was a jewelry box. *Who would be getting me jewelry?* she wondered. Abby looked at the tag and read aloud, "Benjamin."

A sudden wave of apprehension flooded her thoughts. Her grandmother said to never accept jewelry from a man. "It's his way of marking his territory, darling." she would say. Well, Abby didn't really mind the gift; she and Benjamin were a couple, and she was not Vivian Kane. *Thank goodness,* she laughed to herself. She believed she was falling in love with Benjamin. A little jewelry was probably appropriate.

"Are you alright?" Benjamin asked. Abby quickly put on a smile.

"I'm fine." Abby answered. "I was just thinking about my grandmother." She started opening the package to find a small jewelry box marked Gerard & Co. "Benjamin you shouldn't have, this is so extravagant," Abby chastised. She was vaguely familiar with them being the company responsible for the maintenance of the royal jewels. She knew the Hodge's were more than wealthy, but this display of it embarrassed her.

"You haven't even opened it yet," Benjamin said, barely containing the excitement on his face.

Abby slowly and carefully opened the small box. Inside she found a platinum band with a large dark blue-purple stone with a small diamond on each side. It was a beautiful piece. "This is incredible, Benjamin. You really shouldn't have." Abby couldn't help but stare at the beautiful ring. "What kind of stone is this?"

"It's very rare," Benjamin said proudly, "just like you." Abby blushed. "It's a naturally occurring Tanzanite. You don't find them often. They are found only in the foothills of Mount Kilimanjaro. It changes color too."

Abby was speechless. She sat, staring at the beautiful ring, while her heart was melting away. Benjamin took her hand and placed the ring on her ring finger. It was stunning. The rest of the Hodges gathered around and took a closer look.

Several more gifts were handed out. Abby barely paid attention, she was so enamored with the beautiful stone resting on her finger. It was mesmerizing.

"It looks like the last one is for Abigail," Asa said, pulling Abby away from her ring.

"What?" she asked somewhat confused and quickly recovered. "Another one?"

"It appears to be the last gift under the tree," Isobel stated.

Abby accepted the package wrapped in brown shipping paper and secured with twine. She untied the binding and carefully removed the wrapping paper. Inside was an ornately carved box with a wax seal. On top was a small note.

"Please open this in private. Love, Vivian," Abby read aloud. She felt a flush of embarrassment. "I'm sorry. I can't imagine what my grandmother is being so secretive about."

"It is quite alright dear," Isobel reassured with a warm smile. "It's sealed. It must be very important."

"I'll open it later," Abby said setting it aside apprehensively. Her curiosity was peaked, but she didn't want her grandmother's theatrics to hold the Hodge family from moving forward with their traditions. She glanced over at the box sitting next to her on the floor. *What are you up to, grandmother?*

Abby could see the ice crystals coating every blade of grass as she began her stroll around the grounds. She had some time after breakfast, and decided that some fresh air was called for. The trees looked almost like ice sculptures. It was truly beautiful to see everything glisten beneath the sun.

Though the air was cold it was refreshing to have a few moments to gather her thoughts. If it wasn't for the strict schedule she was on she would have put on her new jogging outfit and gone on a proper run. Instead she set a brisk pace and decided to walk around a pond she heard about on the east side of the estate.

Abby took in deep breaths of fresh air, clearing her head. *So far, I've managed to hold it together,* she thought.

She wondered what her family was doing and what was happening with the Thanos. In a day or two she would hear from her grandmother with an update; no doubt edited to save her from worry. In truth, her grandmother's sparsely detailed reports only made her worry more. She knew things were being kept from her, but she had no idea what.

"Miss Kane, can we help you find something?" An unfamiliar voice startled her from her thoughts.

Abby turned to see two men wearing black wool uniforms, sporting riffles and restraining a large Rottweiler on a chain.

"No, I'm just out for a spot of air. Thank you," Abby said with a concerned smile. "I heard there was a pond on this part of the grounds," She added, feeling somewhat intimidated by two armed men and a dog that looked like it could devour her in a single gulp.

"Yes, mam. A few yards that way," one of the men stated, pointing her in the right direction.

"Thank you," Abby said before excusing herself. As she walked in the direction that was pointed out to her, she glanced back to see the men were standing there watching her. She felt ill at ease. Over the last few days she had been with Benjamin most of the time and the armed guards never approached. She imagined the Hodge family must take the security of their home very seriously. In addition to the personal safety of the family, Abby imagined the house likely contained many valuable treasures, some of the monetary kind, and many others more alighted to the arcane. After all there were rather large portions of the house she hadn't seen, and it was easy to assume they were off limits to her, even though no one had been so direct as to say so.

Abby found the pond. It was a large body of water. She could see how it would be rather nice on a hot summer day, and imagined Benjamin and Josephine swimming here as children. The idea of such a normal domestic scene made her smile.

She picked up her pace as she walked around the pond. She could feel the bite of cold beginning to seep through her clothing. The last thing Abby wanted was to fall ill, so she headed back towards the warmth of the house.

Abby came up to the back side of the house, and found a door that looked like it headed in toward the main hall. She had never entered that way before, but the cold was getting the best of her, and she wanted to get in out of the elements as soon as possible.

She stepped into darkness and closed the door behind her. Abby found instant relief from the bitter cold the moment she stepped back into the house. She allowed the warm air to fill her lungs while she searched for a light switch with her hands.

When the lights came on, Abby was standing in a long wide hallway. She had never been in this part of the house and wasn't entirely certain where she was. The hallway was decorated with a beautiful purple and gold wallpaper above the waist and a mahogany wood panel along the bottom half. The floor had an old hard wood finish, lined with beautifully handcrafted Persian rugs. Abby noticed there were old gas lights intermittently spaced along the wall no longer in use. Three crystal chandeliers hung from the ceiling lighting her way.

As she moved along the hallway, Abby noticed portraits hanging. Many of them looked quite old and she imagined they were likely Hodge ancestors, based on their attire and regal bearing. She noticed several places along the wall where it looked like portraits had once hung, but had recently been removed leaving a notable emptiness. The hanging fixtures were still in place. "I wonder why they were removed," she mused.

Nearly half way down the hallway to her left she came upon a door. There was a strange-looking lock on the door with arcane symbols surrounding the key hole. She leaned down for a better look. The small symbols glowed slightly a pale green. Abby had never seen anything like it before. Despite her curiosity, she wasn't about to touch it. For all she knew it was cursed against anyone who didn't have a key.

Abby was starting to get a sense she was in a part of the house she wasn't likely welcome. She quickly made her way down the hallway and stepped through the double doors closing them behind her.

"Did you see anything interesting?" a man's voice questioned. Abby nearly jumped out of her skin. She looked over to see Asa Hodge standing in a hallway she had only seen once before when she was given a tour of the manor house.

"I... I'm sorry! I just came in from the cold," Abby said. She could tell Benjamin's father looked displeased. "The back door was unlocked so I came in that way. I hope that was okay," she said. A mortified feeling moved through her, afraid she had ruined everything and given offense to people who had showed her nothing but kindness since she arrived.

"Of course, it's fine," a woman's voice came from the opposite direction giving Abby another start. She turned to see Isobel Hodge standing in her stately fashion with a quaint smile. Abby was certain Benjamin's parents shared a look between them and felt uncertain what it could mean. "Come along dear. I'll make certain you find your way back to your room," Isobel said, motioning for Abby to follow.

Without hesitation Abby followed Isobel down the hallway towards the main foyer. She couldn't help but feel like she had committed a major faux pas. If she had, Isobel was being kind enough to pretend nothing was the matter.

"I hope…" Abby began to say, unable to restrain her remorse.

"You are fine, dear," Isobel interrupted and walked her to the foot of the stairs. "If you need anything for the party this evening please let me know," she added checking her watch and excusing herself.

Abby sighed. She couldn't help but feel like she made a major misstep with Benjamin's parents. She didn't understand what she had seen but knew she shouldn't have been in that hallway. She was about to head up the stairway when she saw Josephine approaching.

"Is something wrong?" Josephine asked obviously seeing the remorse on Abby's face.

"I made a terrible mistake," Abby said.

"What?" Josephine asked somewhat concerned.

"I came in through the back door, and found a hallway I don't think I was supposed to see," she explained. "I wasn't trying to pry. I went outside for a walk and it was cold, so I came through the nearest door." She was nearly in tears over her blunder.

Josephine studied her for a long moment. Abby thought perhaps her friend was going to be mad at her. "I'm certain there isn't any harm done," Josephine said slowly, breaking her silence. "There isn't anything down there but a few old paintings and the entrance to A… my parent's sanctums," she said carefully.

Josephine was trying to put her at ease, but Abby didn't feel any better. "Are sure?" She asked her friend, hoping for more reassurance. She didn't want to feel unwelcome on the eve of the party later that evening.

"Don't worry about it. If you weren't supposed to be in that hallway, I'm certain it would have been locked," Josephine reasoned. Her friend seemed sincere, but there was something distant, and a bit cold in her tone. Abby sensed something was off about her initial reaction to the situation, but she hadn't the vaguest clue what it could be.

"You're probably right," Abby agreed, having no reason to distrust Josephine. "Thanks. I'm going to get ready for the party."

"Me too," Josephine said, joining Abby up the stairs. "I'll see you later," she added before disappearing down the hallway in the opposite direction.

Abby made her way to her room hoping Josephine was right. It was a rather strange exchange with Benjamin's family and hoped it would not sour the rest of her visit. She wondered if she should mention it to Benjamin, but thought perhaps she would wait until later that evening after the party. She wanted to put it behind her for now and focus on getting through meeting the rest of his family without stepping on any more toes.

Abby sat at the desk in her room, facing the package from Vivian. She still had no idea what could be inside, and she couldn't help the trepidation she felt at having to deal with Vivian's machinations again. *No time like the present,* she thought, and carefully traced the seal with her finger tip. The wooden box had extensive wood carvings of Celtic knot work masterfully done. She looked at the wax seal and saw the letter 'K' imprinted in the wax.

Abby removed a letter opener from the desk and used it to break the wax seal. She opened the lid and saw two envelopes. Both had her grandmother's writing on the cover. At the bottom, was a smaller black leather box. She placed the contents in front of her.

Abby opened the letter labeled "read this first":

> *Dear Abigail,*
>
> *I hope my letter and gifts find you well. I, too, could not bear to remain home and spend the holiday without your parents, and have taken a little trip to someplace less drizzling than Seattle. I will call you after the break and we can catch up. Inside the black leather box is my gift. It's an heirloom of great value and it's time to pass it on. I never had a daughter, and I am so happy to be able to give this to you, my granddaughter.*
>
> *You're an amazing young woman, Abigail. I don't know if I've ever said it before, but it is true. You will be eighteen in a couple months, however you are already a woman with more maturity and wisdom than people twice your age, and if you happen to be thinking of me as one of them, I cannot say I blame you. I was a terrible mother, I had your father because that's what a woman from my generation was supposed to do. Don't misunderstand, my dear, I loved your father deeply and I have never regretted having him; I simply know being a mother was never my calling in this life.*
>
> *All of this being said, my darling, the second envelop contains some legal and financial documentation. These are the second part of my gift to you. In it you will find legal documents from the Washington State District Court. Once you have signed them and send them back you will be granted full emancipation. You will become an adult in the eyes of the law. I know I can trust you to make*

decisions for yourself which you will be entitled to make in a few months anyway.

You will also find documents regarding your trust, which I believe you will find to be the more interesting of the documents. This includes your parent's assets as well as a little something extra from your uncle and myself. I recommend you speak to an attorney and financial advisor to help you manage your trust as soon as the opportunity presents itself.

You were always special my dear. You are intuitive, and possess a kind of bone wisdom that is so very rare. I expect great things from you Abigail.

I truly love you, my darling. It's time for you to be the woman you were born to be, though perhaps a little sooner than planned.

Yours truly,
Vivian Kane

Abby wiped the tears from her cheek. She put the letter aside and walked over to the armchair by the window.

Only a few months before, she was a naïve young woman so sheltered she didn't even know how little she knew. When she walked into that room with the sunlight coming in as though all was right in the world in a cruel irony and saw her parents lifeless on the floor, so much was taken away. Now everything was being given to her. Independence, money, a boyfriend and adulthood, everything she could want or need, everything she dreamed about growing up, and she would give it all back to be that little girl again.

Abby didn't know how long she sat there as the tears poured out. She stayed there for some time, even after the tears had stopped, just staring out the window at nothing. She felt like a porcelain doll broken into a million pieces, and no matter how carefully she glued the pieces back together everyone would always see the cracks.

Her grandmother had told her she was strong and wise, attributes she didn't feel. She was tired. Tired of feeling empty all the time. Tired of having to avoid thinking about her parents. Tired of grief. She wanted to be the adult Vivian seemed to think she could be.

Enough, she told herself. *Mom, Dad, I don't know if I am that woman, but I know I can be if I try.* She took a deep breath and smiled.

CHAPTER FIFTEEN

There was a knock at her door. She wasn't sure at what point she fell asleep, but she was grateful for the rest. She ran a hand over her hair to smooth the bedhead, and opened the door.

"I heard there is some party tonight." Benjamin said leaning against the door frame his eyebrows furrowed in his best attempt at being dashing. Abby thought his brooding look was among his best, and obliged his vanity.

"I heard a little something about a party." Abby played along.

"I also heard it was going to be pretty dull, so I thought I'd make an appearance and sneak out early," he added giving his sly suggestive grin she had grown familiar with over the last week.

"Really? I hope you don't let yourself get bored up here all alone," Abby said teasingly.

"Alone?" Benjamin pretended to be heart broken. "Well, maybe I could convince someone to join me?"

"Oh, you're going to have to try pretty hard to convince me. I have jewelry now. The bar has been raised," Abby said, jokingly as she gazed at her finger.

Benjamin came in and stood next to her. "The second I saw it I thought of you," he said tenderly, wrapping his arms around her.

"I don't know if I said it before, I was so surprised and shocked, but thank you," Abby said, resting her head on his chest.

"It was worth the look on your face" Benjamin said. "You looked a little worried at first."

Abby laughed. "Let's just say I haven't always had the best relationship role models and leave it at that."

Benjamin chuckled. "Am I in trouble?" He asked playfully.

"As far as I'm concerned, you're always in trouble," Abby responded, wrapping her arms around his waist.

"You're thinking about your family a lot today?" Benjamin asked his voice reverent on the subject.

"Yes," Abby admitted, feeling misty. She took a deep breath, grateful that she was all cried-out for the moment. She had already cried on his shoulder the night before. She didn't want to make a habit of such displays, despite his support thus far.

"We don't' have to do anything tonight, I just want to spend as much time with you as possible before we return to school and have to conform to the rules of conduct." He kissed the top of her head.

"I'd like that," Abby admitted. She felt safe in his arms. She felt protected and secure. She was losing any doubt she was falling in love with him. Not because of the gift, but because of the way his thoughtfulness felt so genuine.

With no other words, she simply kissed him again. He turned into it, deepening the kiss, and before long she found they were lying on the bed. She easily gave in to the kissing and playful laughter and wandering hands, but after a few minutes Abby put on the breaks.

"What is it?" Benjamin asked sounding worried.

Abby showed him the time on her phone. "I have to get ready for tonight," she said, tormenting him with her most alluring smile.

"Oh, it isn't right, leaving me hanging like this," Benjamin mockingly complained.

"From what I can tell there isn't anything hanging; everything is standing at attention," she teased him back. "Now shoo!"

Benjamin stood and covered his pants by pulling his jacket closed. He walked awkwardly to the door and turned before leaving. "You're going to pay for this later you know," he playfully threatened.

"We'll see about that. I have the ring, now I have all the power," she joked closing the door in his face.

"You're insufferable Miss Kane," Benjamin said through the door. Abby smiled and leaned against the wall. At that moment her thoughts on Benjamin Hodge seemed clearer. She more than cared for him; she was in love.

Smiling, she put on a bathrobe and started getting ready for the evening. Looking at the desk, she realized she hadn't opened her grandmother's other gift.

Abby slipped the ribbon off and opened the leather box. Inside was an intricately woven platinum cord with a diamond pendant. It was a large diamond, much larger than Abby had ever seen. It was not something she would typically find appealing. It's gaudy nature was much more akin to her grandmother's tastes.

There was a small note inside which read:

Darling, this is the Grimaldi Diamond. You should consider researching it when you have the time. It is one of the most precious gems our family has collected over the centuries. Please protect it with your life.

Abby wasn't sure what to think. *Great, a gaudy family heirloom,* she thought. It must have been important or Vivian wouldn't have taken the time to send it to her. Sometimes she wished her grandmother wasn't so cryptic, though. Abby didn't even try to understand the logic behind sending her something through a delivery service which she was supposed to protect with her life.

She checked the time, realizing she had spent far too long thinking about Kane family affairs. She set her grandmother's packages in the drawer, turning her attention to preparing for the Hodge family Christmas party.

She quickly put her hair up with the judicious use of hairpins and hair spray. A simple, yet elegant style. She had practiced this style on many occasions when she performed at concerts. The stylist who taught her how to do it called it a French Twist. Abby always felt very elegant with this style, and she hoped it would make her feel more like the adult she now legally was. With her hair set, she then started the lengthy process of makeup.

Satisfied with her face and hair, Abby pulled the dress she planned to wear from the hanger. It was a strapless cocktail dress made of cobalt blue silk, which she picked up and had tailored while she was in London. The color made her blue eyes explode in a way that made Abby feel particularly beautiful. It was form fitting, but not too tight, and she could move gracefully in it. It was modest, but beautiful. It suited Abby perfectly.

There was still nearly an hour before she was expected downstairs. She sat in a chair by the window, and spent a few minutes on-line checking social media and reading her email. Abby didn't post very often, and while she was in hiding, she thought it prudent not to even do that much. She could only read her friend's posts, and not reply. It was like watching her old life through a telescope.

She sent a Happy Christmas text to Nina, Sarah, Warren and several of her friends back home in Seattle, then set the phone aside. With little else to do, Abby sat at her desk and picked up the book her grandmother gave her.

The Picture of Dorian Gray was an easy read, and she was near the end when her phone gave her the alert she was expected downstairs. She marked her place and set the book down, grateful she hadn't had to think too hard for the last 40 minutes.

She jumped up and went to the closet door where a full-length mirror stood for a final look. Despite whatever else she was feeling today, she was excited for the party. She loved dressing up, and being around cultured and polite people. She looked at herself; hair was good, makeup good, the dress perfect, but it was missing something.

She wore her ring from this morning and the antique earrings she had carried with her form home, but her neck seemed like a barren wasteland in comparison. The charm Ms. Grace had loaned her was too informal and wouldn't be appropriate. She didn't have any other jewelry. Abby opened the black leather box Vivian had sent her again, and looked at the ostentatious diamond. She collected the large jewel and tried it on. It didn't look quite so gaudy once it was nestled in the hollow of her neck, though it was still a little more than Abby would choose for herself.

She pondered her reflection in the mirror for a moment and decided it would do. *It's better than nothing,* she thought, and headed to the party.

She descended the stair and noticed the staff bustling around preparing for the dinner party. Some paused and took notice of her; she took it as a good sign that she was turning heads. As she reached the bottom of the stairs she saw Benjamin in his tuxedo, he was playing with his phone completely distracted. He was so handsome; she paused to stare at him for a moment. His short brown curls were slicked back and controlled as usual. His eyes and brows were so expressive he barely needed to speak. He had large strong hands, muscular arms, and broad shoulders that almost seemed unreal. His years of rowing had stacked him perfectly. She wanted nothing more than to disappear upstairs with him, but duty would prevail, at least for a while.

"Good evening, Mr. Hodge," Abby purred, her tone voicing her approval of his appearance as she approached. He glanced up from his phone and froze. His eyes grew very wide, and his jaw hung open just enough that Abby was convinced he was teasing her. She smiled anyway, and took his arm.

His eyes followed her as though he had never seen her before. When he didn't drop the act, Abby started to wonder if she'd done something wrong. "What's the matter?" Abby asked quietly.

"I…" Benjamin stuttered.

"What's wrong? Did something happen?" A sense of panic washed over her. HE was never lost for words. She feared his parents had spoken to him about what had happened earlier in the day. She could feel a lump forming in her throat as her smile melted away.

It was as though he came out of a trance. "No," he said. He grinned like an idiot, his smile was like watching the sun come out from behind a cloud. "Nothing happened." He leaned over and kissed her cheek. "You took me by surprise, is all. I've never seen anyone, anything, so beautiful in my life."

Abby blushed and giggled slightly. "You're such a joker."

He grabbed her upper arms and looked her squarely in the eyes. "I'm not joking," he said his brown eyes serious. She could see how intense his feelings were. It both thrilled her and scared her for very different reasons. His face softened. "I actually don't think you realize how beautiful you really are."

Abby was taken off guard. She stood there for a moment thinking of what to say. 'Thank you' seemed so insufficient. "I… don't know what to say." He hugged her like he would never let go.

"You don't need to say anything." He spoke softly. "Now let's go in there and get this over with." She took his arm and the two of them made their way into the living room.

Mr. and Mrs. Hodge looked fantastic. Mr. Hodge was wearing a top hat and tails, which was something Abby had only ever seen in movies or at masquerade parties. He was standing with Mrs. Hodge who was wearing a dark green gown. Her diamond and emerald necklace and earrings complimented her style. She looked very glamorous. Abby didn't feel so strange wearing the diamond her grandmother had given her after seeing the fortune draped around Isobel's neck.

She spied Josephine, standing off to one side in a sea green dress that was very flattering. She was a pretty girl, but like Ms. Grace she didn't let herself be as beautiful as she could be. Abby had always thought Josephine was someone who preferred to stay in the background rather than be the center of attention. Perhaps, shy was the right word. Abby smiled. Josephine may come across as elitist from time to time, but Abby liked her.

Compliments were exchanged around the room as they took seats to enjoy cocktails and wine. The first guests to arrive were Mildred and Nigel Partridge. They were a round couple with pleasant faces and warm smiles. Mildred wore a floor length royal purple gown adorned with various peacock feathers at the waist and collar. She wore a grand necklace around her neck of amethysts and sapphires continuing the peacock feather motif. Nigel wore a full tuxedo with a purple tuxedo shirt that matched his wife's gown. Abby thought them the gaudiest thing she'd ever seen in public, and tried not to laugh.

"Good evening." Asa moved in, giving Mildred a familiar hug and shaking Nigel's hand. Isobel quickly followed her husband's lead.

Benjamin stepped forward taking Abby with him. She wore a polite smile for the introductions. "Welcome Aunt Mildred, Uncle Nigel," he said, giving both a warm hug. He then motioned to Mildred and her husband Nigel."

"It's very nice to meet the both of you," Abby said politely shaking their hands.

"Where are the twins?" Isobel asked politely.

"They are skiing in Switzerland this year," Nigel explained.

"You know how teenagers are with their friends," Mildred insinuated before the two of them made their way into the living room for cocktails.

"Not bad so far," Benjamin whispered with a wink.

Abby could tell she was a bit stiff from being nervous and took a deep breath to relax a little. Guests continued to arrive in small groups. Blake and Ester Hodge arrived with three children under the age of ten and a young woman who was introduced as their nanny. Then several other couples.

"And here are the last of them," Asa said as a young man entered with a well-trimmed beard and the familiar curly brown hair Abby had discerned was a common Hodge family trait. At his side was a young woman of Asian descent wearing a beautiful white silk dress.

Asa and Isobel greeted their guests warmly and followed them as they approached Benjamin. "Happy Holiday," the young man said, warmly greeting Benjamin with a hug.

"Happy Holiday," Benjamin returned the greeting. "I'd like you to meet my girlfriend Abigail Kane," he said pulling Abby forward. "This is my cousin Jacob Hodge and his wife Seiko."

"It's very nice to meet you," Abby said, greeting them both.

"A girlfriend… Finally," Jacob teased.

"We've all come to adore Abby. It feels like she's practically already a part of the family." Isobel said with a smile.

Abby could feel her heart leap into her throat. She hadn't expected to be so familiar with the Hodges as to be considered almost a part of the family. Though it wasn't an unwelcome shock, after the events earlier in the day, she was still surprised she hadn't been unceremoniously escorted out of the house. To be regarded so intimately was beyond a surprise. She smiled to hide her confusion and relief.

"I'm truly honored to be here," Abby managed to muster from her own muddled thoughts. She followed Benjamin and the other guests into the living room where cocktails flowed, and goblets of wine were freely passed around. Everyone seemed engaged in polite conversation while sipping their drinks.

Abby wandered around the room, meeting all of Benjamin's family. She noticed Mildred was staring at her. She quickly looked away when Abby saw her. *I wonder what that was about,* she thought. Abby moved along and engaged in light conversation.

Abby found herself caught in a conversation with two of Asa's cousins chatting happily about the Hodge family business. They were more than happy to tell her about their real estate and construction projects all over the world, but she noticed they seemed especially proud of the expanding business in Dubai.

"The Middle East," Abby said impressed. "I've always wanted to go there."

"We'll have to go during gap year," Benjamin suggested.

"What about your family? Kane Industries, isn't it?" Blake Hodge asked.

Abby was only vaguely aware of the family business, and had no ready answers to the questions that were sure to come. "Yes, my grandmother and uncle run the business," she said.

"How is their renewable energy initiative going?" Jacob asked.

Abby gulped. "Fine," she said having no idea what they were talking about. She realized she was going to have to take more of an interest in the family business, considering the sizable stake she inherited from her parent's estate.

"What kind of business does your family run?" Benjamin asked with new interest.

"They were timber barons back in the day. Now they've diversified into biotech and green technology" Abby explained exhausting the extent of her knowledge on the family business with two simple sentences. She felt a bit embarrassed and hid behind a friendly smile.

"I'd love to hear more about it sometime," Benjamin said. Abby felt some relief when another family member approached. With their arrival, the subject quickly changed to less intimidating topics.

When the time was right, Isobel Hodge declared dinner ready. The party moved into the formal dining room. The table was set with beautiful fine china, silver utensils, and gleaming crystal. Christmas roses so fragrant that Abby could smell them over the food wafting in from the kitchen adorned the centerpiece. Abby was seated to the left of Asa, across form aunt Mildred with Benjamin sitting next to her. Josephine sat at the far end of the table next to her mother. Abby thought it all looked like a postcard.

The food was exquisite. The table was laden with roast duck with various vegetables, rack of lamb with a creamy mint sauce, fine wines, delicious watercress soup, and a spinach salad with raspberries. It was a large and heavy meal, and Abby paced herself. The conversations continued as before, punctuated by clinking flatware as the guests enjoyed their meal.

Abby glanced across the table and noticed Mildred Partridge was still staring at her. They met eyes and Abby smiled feeling somewhat awkward. She was running through a list of topics for polite conversation, deciding which would be best for diffusing the tension when Mildred said, "Your grandmother is Vivian Kane?" Her tone was carefully polite, but there was a note of accusation that no one missed. The conversations at the table came to a dead stop.

"Yes," Abby answered politely.

"She gave you that necklace, didn't she?" It was more of a statement than a question.

"What's wrong?" Benjamin asked, looking at the necklace around Abby's neck, confused.

Mildred stood. "That," Mildred stated pointing to Abby's neck. "That is the Grimaldi Diamond!"

Gasps and shouts arose from every corner of the room. Next to her Benjamin looked confused and Josephine sat deadly still.

"Nonsense," Asa barked, "the Grimaldi diamond is a myth. Sit down Mildred."

"I swear *that* is the Grimaldi diamond!" Mildred didn't sit. "Did your grandmother give it to you, or not?" she demanded.

Abby didn't know what to do or say. She was cursing herself internally.

She wanted to cry, to run away, to defend herself, but she knew she should have researched the necklace before she wore it in public. She had no idea why anyone was so upset, but it was clearly the fault of this millstone around her neck. "I'll go upstairs and remove it at once," Abby stated, her head bowed like a scolded child.

"Wait, a minute, Aunt Mildred, what the bloody hell is the Grimaldi diamond?" Benjamin demanded, taking Abby's arm to keep her from leaving.

"That diamond holds a curse that consumed the power of the entire Grimaldi family. Somehow Justinius Kane, her ancestor," the emphasis was very clear, "created a curse that destroyed an entire lineage."

"He bound their power to that diamond," she continued into the silence. "Some believe the Kane family still holds the secrets of that vile curse. Now that I've seen this mythic diamond for myself, I'm convinced the story is true." Mildred sat down, dramatically. "Don't you see Asa? Vivian wanted us to see it."

"Excuse me." Abby pulled her arm from Benjamin and left the room as fast as she could. She couldn't stay. She ran up the stairs to her room, as the Hodge family erupted into a frenzy. She closed the door, solidly shutting out the quarrel downstairs.

Why didn't grandmother warn me about this? Abby was furious with herself. She had no business wearing the necklace when she had no clue what it was. Of course, her grandmother's note wasn't exactly helpful. Abby couldn't help but wonder if it was true. Did her grandmother plan this? Was she trying to rattle the Hodge family for some reason? Legendary diamonds, disastrous curses, mysterious books; what kind of game was her grandmother playing? And why did she keep using Abby this way?

She paced the floor, angry and embarrassed. When she realized she was still wearing the necklace she quickly removed it and put it back in the leather box. Abby felt like such a fool. She had caused offense to people who had shown her nothing but kindness. The Hodges had been so good to her, and she'd repaid them with insult.

Abby stood in front of the bathroom mirror pulling pins from her hair. "No," she told herself out loud, so she would hear it. "Vivian repaid them with insult. I just delivered the message."

She furiously wiped away the few stray tears she couldn't suppress. Her nerves were shot. The rich heavy meal in her stomach churned. She curled up on the bed, willing herself into oblivion. She was tired, angry, and so, so done with this day.

CHAPTER SIXTEEN

The next morning Abby awoke in Benjamin's arms. She couldn't remember him coming in the night before. He was still in his tuxedo, curled around her. She sat up, carefully trying not to disturb him. He began to stir.

No, no, no. She thought. *Please don't wake up.* She quickly retreated into the bathroom, mortified and still embarrassed about the night before.

She took a couple deep breaths, trying to calm herself.

"You can't hide in there all day you know," Benjamin said on the other side of the door.

"Yes, I can. You'd be surprised how stubborn I can be," Abby said.

"Probably not all that surprised," He said plainly. "Come on Abby." He knocked gently on the door. "You didn't do anything wrong. My aunt is just a suspicious old bat."

Abby opened the door a crack. "You're not mad?"

"I can't think of a single reason why I could possibly be mad at you," Benjamin said. Abby opened the door a little further.

"I don't want to cause a problem with you and your family, Benjamin," she said remorsefully.

"Please come out so we can talk," Benjamin pleaded.

"All right," she said, then hesitated, "but come back in a half hour, I'm a mess." She closed the door, firmly, and could hear a slight chuckle from the other side. She smiled. At least Benjamin didn't hate her. She took a quick shower, and got dressed.

While she waited for Benjamin to return, Abby hung her discarded dress from the night before. She started straitening up the desk and found the necklace resting where she had discarded it. She stared at the diamond for a few moments, wondering if the story Mildred Partridge had told them held any truth. There was still so much about her family that she didn't know.

As she put the box back in the desk drawer with the folded up letter her grandmother sent her, she noticed the second envelop still sat unopened. She pulled out the letter opener and sliced through the paper. Inside were several documents. One was the order of emancipation Vivian had mentioned. The decree itself was straightforward; just waiting for her signature and a stamp from a judge. She set it aside and looked at the other stack of papers.

It took her a moment to realize what she was looking at. The page was covered in numbers, codes, and the names of companies and various declarations of ownership. *These must be the trust documents and financial records she was talking about,* Abby realized.

She was looking at a long list of her family's holdings. The list was far longer than she had ever been led to believe. Abby did some rudimentary math in her head and realized there was more money than she had ever imagined; not just millions, there were hundreds of millions.

"Oh my God," she muttered under her breath, covering her mouth with shock. *Why didn't they ever tell me about this?* she wondered, staring at the figures on the page. She quit adding after a while and stared at the sheet blankly, her head swimming with unanswered questions.

She knew it was the kind of thing she would need to pay much closer attention to, but just then she felt a headache coming on. Between the remnants of her emotional hangover and her lack of quality sleep, she really didn't have the patience to deal with trying to figure it all out. She set the letter aside again to review later when her mind was clearer.

A run would be helpful. She wanted to feel the solid ground beneath her feet again. *Later,* she told herself. She moved to the window. It was bitter cold outside, with the low clouds there was a chance of snow in the forecast. *Definitely later.* She shivered at the thought of the cold. Then came a knock on the door. "Come in," Abby said politely. One of the maids entered with a silver tray.

"Mrs. Hodge said you might not be feeling well and asked me to bring you a tray," the maid explained, setting the silver service on the nightstand and excusing herself. Just as she was leaving Benjamin came in.

He had changed out of his tuxedo, and was instead wearing grey slacks and a black button down shirt. He also wore his leather wristband with the Celtic knot work, she noticed. Seeing it, Abby remembered she had forgotten to give him his other gift. She reminded herself to do it later, and turned her most apologetic smile on her boyfriend.

"Your mother sent up some food," Abby said gesturing towards the serving tray." She's very thoughtful," she added.

"She's like that," he said, closing the door behind him.

"So are you," Abby said, sitting in the window seat staring at the bitter cold. "I think it's going to snow."

There was a pause. Abby could feel Benjamin's large hands on her shoulders. "I know it got a little weird last night," he started, "but things don't need to be weird between us."

"I don't understand." Abby was pensive. "Why would she give me something like that and not explain what it was?"

"My father thinks it was meant to be a shot across our bow," Benjamin said.

"But why would she do that?" Abby was confused. "Why would she want to issue some stupid warning to your family? I thought we were allies?"

"We were kind of hoping you could tell us," Benjamin admitted. "We've never had any problems with the Kane family before. I thought maybe it was meant for me, that she was trying to warn me not to hurt you."

"That seems like an awfully big threat for what she sees as a youthful dalliance," Abby said dryly. "But who knows? With grandmother anything is possible." Abby stood and started pacing. "Everything she does is a calculated move. Every time she speaks she assesses how much damage she can do with as few words as possible. She sees us all as her pawns, and she maneuvers us as she sees fit."

Abby was fuming and tried to calm herself down. "Do you want to know what else she gave me besides that ridiculous Grimaldi Diamond?" Abby could feel her anger move to pain. She never felt comfortable with anger.

Benjamin gave her a curious look. "It isn't a Hodge Diamond is it?" he added jokingly. Abby retrieved the documents from the desk and handed them to him. "This is my emancipation decree. All I have to do is sign them and send them off and I'm officially an adult," Abby stated.

"Abby, that's great! I don't think she's playing you. She had you and your money under her guardianship before, now you're free of her. What good is a pawn you can't control?" he said.

"Oh, she'll try. I'm sure she's not done controlling me." Abby took a deep breath and exhaled slowly. "The rest is information on my trust. She recommended I seek legal and financial advice to manage it. I have no idea what anything on here means."

"Well one way or the other, you're free of her," Benjamin stated. "At least as free of her as you want to be."

"I now truly understand why my parents kept me from her for so long," Abby commented. "I don't understand how you can love someone so much and be upset with them at the same time."

"What do you mean they kept you from her?" Benjamin inquired.

"My parents and grandmother had a falling out when I was very young. I don't know the details, but I didn't see her again until I was twelve," Abby explained as she folded the documents and placed them in the desk drawer. She turned around and sat on the edge of the desk. "So, do you know any good barristers who are familiar with the American legal system?"

Benjamin chuckled. "I can think of a few. My father would probably be a better consultant on such matters." He stood and approached Abby. He seemed to notice something and hesitated. Abby looked down and saw nothing unusual. Benjamin's face turned red a look of anger consumed his handsome face. "Where did that come from?" he yelled. His sudden anger startled Abby.

"Where did what come from?" she questioned, completely confused and concerned by the look in his eyes.

Benjamin lunged forward and grabbed her book from the desk. It was the copy of The Picture of Dorian Gray that Vivian had given her. "What are you doing with this book?" he shouted. Abby stepped away. She had never seen him like this before. She backed away as far as she could.

"Why are you reading this book?" he demanded. Abby flinched.

"It was the book my grandmother gave me to read, the one she swore me to secrecy about," she said as she backed herself up against the wall.

"What did she tell you?" His eyes were wild, his brows furrowed, and his face was completely red. She could see his hands clench into fists He threw the book on the floor. "What did she tell you?"

Abby wanted to run, but he had her cornered. "N-Nothing," escaped her mouth. She stood paralyzed by fear and confusion. Benjamin punched the wall, threw open the door and stormed out.

She stood against the wall, completely frozen. She had no idea what happened or why, but her instincts were screaming at her to leave, and leave quickly. Abby closed and locked the door when she called a taxi. She put on warm winter clothing and packed her luggage, being sure of placing the necklace and the documents in her purse.

She noticed the book discarded on the floor. She picked it up and shoved it in her luggage. She was not about to leave the offending item where he would see it again. She would send for her things later, but she took the important things. If she left with only her purse, no one should be too suspicious.

She slipped out the door and down the stairs, offering the staff a story about taking a walk. They went about their business the moment they realized she didn't need anything, and Abby slipped into the brisk December air.

She made her way out the door and walked into the woods rather than down the road leading to the gate. She didn't want to look like she was leaving the estate.

She followed the forest trail for half a kilometer before looping back to the main driveway. It didn't take long before she reached the gate. Luckily, without all her luggage she was just small enough to fit between the bars, and slipped through.

There was a security camera near the security box and Abby quickly moved to the far side hoping no one noticed her. By the time she was through, the taxi was only a few minutes away. She anxiously waited, watching the driveway for any sign of security approaching. She did not want to be stopped just then. A quiet exit would be best.

When the taxi arrived, she hopped in anxiously. "Where to miss?" the driver asked as he pressed the button to start the fair. It was that moment Abby realized she had nowhere to go, no home, and no family nearby.

Abby thought for a moment. She glanced out the window and saw two armed guards in the distance approaching the gate. "Milestone, in Kensington," she said impulsively. She didn't want to go back to school. The Milestone hotel was where she stayed when her parents brought her to London several years ago. It was the only place she could think of.

Along the way Abby tried to make sense of what happened. The last two days were a flurry of wonderful, horrible and terrifying moments. Was she over reacting? She knew she shouldn't let her emotions run away with her, but she couldn't make sense what the book had to do with anything. Why would he get so upset over her reading that book? Was there some connection she was blithely ignoring? Something her grandmother had kept from her? She shivered. He was so angry. *I've never seen him like that before,* she thought. *Why? It was just a book!... wasn't it?* Abby shook herself. She couldn't understand how she had made such a disaster of the entire trip in so short a time.

All she knew was that she needed to get away. She needed to be somewhere she could be alone to think, and it was better for her hosts as well. She had done nothing but offend these kind people since she arrived. It was best if she just left.

The driver was moving at a high speed. Abby looked out the window and saw the countryside whizzing by. "Is there something wrong?" Abby asked.

"They're predicting a snow storm Miss. If you want to make it to London before it hits we need to make good time. Don't worry I'm an expert." The driver commented.

Abby took a deep breath and slouched down in her seat. Even her flight from Hodge Manor was to be fraught with danger, it would seem.

They were about an hour out of London when the snow started to fall. Abby glanced at her phone and saw five missed calls. She listened to the first one.

"Where the bloody hell are you?" the voice on the message growled. He was still mad. She didn't listen to the other four messages.

Her heart sank. She messed everything up. All she could see was his furious red face and his clenched fists. He could have killed her with his bare hands. *But why? I don't' understand! He'd been nothing but kind, patient, and a gentleman from the beginning.* She fought back tears again; she was not going to cry in the taxi.

The car slowed down to accommodate the increased traffic and the accumulation of snow. The taxi was moving at a crawl by the time they reached the city. It took a long time, but the driver eventually reached the hotel. Abby paid her fair in silence, and went inside.

146

At first, the staff seemed confused by her lack of luggage. Abby explained it was an unexpected trip for a sick friend. She offered her credit card, which the woman behind the counter declined. "No Miss Kane, your family has a corporate account with the hotel," she explained.

"How did you know I was a member of the family?" Abby asked.

"Your name and date of birth, as well as several other identifiers are listed on the account. The Hotel Manager is on his way to personally escort you to your room. Here is your room key," the woman was polite and accommodating.

A few moments later a distinguished looking gentleman in his mid-to-late-fifties approached wearing a nice charcoal-colored business suit. "Miss Kane, I'm Archibald Radcliffe, the manager of this establishment. I am pleased we can offer you our services once again. May I show you to your room?" He made a grand gesture towards the elevator. They took the lift up to the private suites. He swiped a key card through an electronic lock, and the elevator doors opened.

"Here we go Miss Kane." Archibald motioned for her to follow him down the hall. He came to a beautiful white door with gold gilded woodwork. He ran another key card and opened the door for her. Abby stepped in and found a beautiful suite that looked very much like the one she stayed in with her parents. In fact, she thought perhaps it was the very same, though it had been redecorated.

The room had a rococo décor with plush couches covered in pillows and gold fixtures throughout the suite. The bedroom was decorated in white and gold with an enormous bed that looked incredibly inviting. The bathroom maintained the aesthetic with modern fixtures hidden behind old world appeal. There was a small kitchenette and a study off to the side.

The windows had a beautiful view of the city and Abby could see the flakes falling, coating London in white. It was breathtaking.

"Thank you, Mr. Radcliffe." Abby stated when he finished pointing out the amenities.

"This was an unexpected trip?" Archibald asked. "Shall I have someone fetch some appropriate attire?"

"Yes, thank you," Abby was embarrassed by the fact she was dressed very casually for a hotel of this stature.

"Very good ma'am. I shall see to it right away." He nodded and opened the door to leave, and then hesitated. He turned and gave Abby a remorseful look. "I was very sorry to hear about your parents, Miss Kane." He quickly excused himself and closed the door behind him.

Abby stared at the closed door. *They know…* She realized her father must have come here on business quite frequently. *It makes sense. The European headquarters for Kane Industries are only a few blocks away,* she remembered.

She looked at her phone; three more missed calls and fourteen text messages. She scrolled through the messages. Most of them, unsurprisingly, were from Benjamin.

Benjamin: *Where are you?*

Benjamin: *Did you leave the estate?*

Benjamin: *Abby, answer your phone.*

She scrolled through them without answering. There was one from Benjamin's mother.

Isobel: *Are you OK, my dear?*
Benjamin told us you had left.

Abby ignored that one as well. She wasn't ready to deal with any of them, just yet. She was surprised to have text messages from Sarah, Nina and Warren. Apparently, Benjamin had contacted them to see if they knew where she had gone. Benjamin sent the last message fifteen minutes ago.

Benjamin: *I'm going out of my*
mind, please just tell me
you're alright.

Abby was conflicted, but she decided making him and the others worry was cruel. She first sent a text to Sarah, Nina and Warren.

Abby: *I'm fine, just a fight. I will call*
Benjamin later. It's OK.

Almost against her will, she punched in the letters for the text she would send her boyfriend.

Abby: *I'm alright. I just need*
to be alone.

Abby pushed send, and set her phone on the nightstand. She crawled into the plush bed, exhausted and ready for the world to disappear for a few hours. She faded in and out the entire evening. It was a restless sleep, filled with anxious dreams playing out every insecurity and fear swimming through her head. Around six the next morning, she gave up the pretense of sleep.

Abby needed to talk to someone, but who could she really talk to about any of this? She needed someone who knew her whole situation. Someone who understood her, believed in her, and would offer the kind of compassionate sounding board she needed. Someone... Someone she had spent two months traveling the world with while she came to terms with her parent's death.

He was eight hours behind in San Francisco, but Sebastian was fond of late nights, and it was only ten pm on the west coast. He would no doubt still be awake. She looked at her phone again, and pressed her speed dial.

It rang a few times before a welcome and familiar voice answered. "Hello? Abby?"

"Hi, Uncle Sebastian," she said trying to disguise the meltdown she was on the verge of having. "I didn't wake you, did I?"

"Of course not, you know me, I'm always up late," he responded, his voice tranquil. "Are you okay?"

Abby couldn't' stop herself. The details of the last few days spilled out of her, unfiltered. She explained everything; the dinner party, the Grimaldi Diamond, the book, and the terrifying response it solicited from her boyfriend. When she was finished, there was a heavy pause.

"Abby? I don't' know what Vivian's up to, but she shouldn't be using you like this. I can't believe she sent you that relic and didn't warn you about it."

Abby wiped away the tears that had sprung up during her recitation. "I wish I couldn't believe it," she said, morosely.

Sebastian chuckled, in a way that was more laconic than mirthful. "The book was a stroke of manipulative genius. Sometimes I admire that woman."

"What do you mean? What about the book? Why is she even doing all this?" Abby inquired more hurt than anything.

"I have no idea what she's up to, and to be completely honest we may never understand her motives. Vivian is a force unto herself. She always has been. As for the book," Sebastian sighed over the phone. "I'm afraid I know exactly what that's about."

"What? I don't understand what a book written over a hundred years ago has to do with anything," Abby admitted, her confusion giving way to frustration.

"The Hodge family had an ancestor named Vincent Hodge. Have you ever heard of him?"

Abby shook her head, then realized he couldn't see her. "No." She said into her phone. "Wait. I think grandmother mentioned him once, when she first met the twins. Who was he?"

"He was the inspiration for the character Dorian Gray." Sebastian explained.

"Well that doesn't seem particularly ominous," Abby confessed. "Victorian authors often based their characters on real people."

"There's a little more to it than that," he explained. "When the book was written, it was an instant scandal for the other Families. Vincent Hodge had discovered a secret to immortality, something other covens had been trying to uncover for centuries. Many witches knew the book was more than just fiction, and that it was about him. They wanted to learn his secrets, the ritual required terrible sacrifices, the kind that most of us would consider forbidden. Blood sacrifices, human blood, to be precise. Someone, perhaps more than one person had to die for the ritual to work. I don't really remember all the details, but it caused a great deal of problems for the Hodge family. They are still recovering from the ordeal."

"But, if he was immortal, wouldn't he still be around somewhere?" Abby asked.

"He never cast the spell. It was too theoretical, and the other covens banded together to stop him before he could enact the blood sacrifice. The secrets of that ritual were lost when he died. Thank goodness."

"So, grandmother gave me the book to read as, what? Some kind of warning? That the Hodges used to deal in blood magic?" Abby felt numb, she didn't know what to think.

"I guess," Sebastian responded. "Vivian is usually more direct but sometimes she uses subtlety if she thinks it will cause more damage in the long run."

"But why did she do this?" Abby asked. "Why didn't she just say something? What does she think they can do now? You said yourself that the secrets were lost…"

"I actually don't think you were the target Abby. Believe me, we've all been subjected to Vivian's games before. I don't think she's ever been particularly fond of the Hodge family, not for any reason other than their history that I'm aware of. I'm sure this wasn't personal."

"You don't think…" she said, "you don't think she gave me that book because she wants the spell for herself, do you?"

"Vivian, immortal. Now there is a truly terrifying thought. No," Sebastian said. "I think it's something else. Your grandmother would know full well that the Council wouldn't let the Hodges hold onto that ritual, and if she was after it, there would be better ways than tipping off the Hodges to her interest. I think this is much closer to home, and I wouldn't doubt that she finds your relationship with one of them inconvenient."

"What good is a pawn you can't control?" Abby muttered, remembering what Benjamin had said to her.

"What was that?" Sebastian asked.

"Nothing," Abby said. Taking a deep breath, she consciously righted herself. This line of thinking would get her nowhere.

Sebastian's voice was sympathetic. "I'm sorry she used you like this," he added. Her uncle was a good man. In this moment, Abby loved him more than anyone.

Abby wiped away a few tears from her cheek; relieved her uncle couldn't see her on the other side of the phone. "I'll be all right," Abby stated. She was bothered by how often she had to keep telling people that little phrase. She felt like she was turning into a broken record, and started to wonder if she really was all right.

"I can come out there, I have some time late next week. I could fly out and we can spend some time together. I know Rodger would love to see you," Sebastian stated.

"No really, I'm okay," Abby reassured her uncle. "This isn't the first-time grandmother has spun a web. Just wait until graduation to come out, then we'll have something fun to celebrate."

"Are you sure?" Sebastian questioned, obviously waiting to be convinced. Abby was sure. She didn't need him there coddling her. She could manage this mess on her own. "Absolutely," she affirmed. There was a brief pause.

"Abby, he didn't hurt you, did he?" Sebastian asked, she could tell he was worried.

"No," Abby reassured him. "Nothing like that. This was the first time I ever saw him this angry, and I admit, I was a little afraid of something like that happening, but he was never violent," she admitted.

"Well hopefully it was just a fluke. Just pay attention Abby. If that kind of thing happens more often, it's only a matter of time before someone gets hurt," Sebastian cautioned.

"I know, I still think he's a good man, I just think the last few days stretched all our patience to the limit," Abby explained.

"I sincerely hope you're right. You've had quite enough to deal with these last few months," her uncle stated. "You deserve a break. I'll tell you what, I'll take one for the team and try to keep your grandmother occupied for a while."

"Thank you," Abby responded. "Can I ask you something else? Something…" she hesitated to ask.

"Shoot."

"What's going on with the investigation?"

"You've been thinking about them a lot this Christmas, haven't you?"

"It… hasn't been easy," she said quietly. "Mom and dad were m-murdered. It's been over six months ago now, and no one will tell me anything. Please? Can you tell me what's happening?" Abby waited through a heavy pause.

"You're really sticking to the tough questions, aren't you?" Sebastian observed. Her uncle sighed. "I guess I should tell you what we know so far. We have proof that the Thanos family was responsible for the hit."

"Is everyone in the family alright?" Abby asked. "What kind of war is this?"

"We're fine, as you know your Grandmother is one of the most talented Hex Weavers in the Northern Hemisphere. I suspect her African Safari is a ruse to collect rare reagents for something she has planned for them. No doubt it will be something big. We've been hitting them hard on the financial front; Rodger and I set up a few dummy corporations and we've been attacking their assets. They won't be able to take much more. The Thanos are too heavily invested in their vineyards to develop a strong financial portfolio. I suspect in another month or two we'll be able to drive them out of their ancestral home. I'm hoping that one stings. Five-hundred years grows some very deep roots, especially for witches. It will force them to move their sanctums and regroup. That could set them back years, magically." Sebastian couldn't help but sound pleased. She knew he always enjoyed the financial matters of business, but listening to him discuss it was a welcome treat.

"It sounds like we're doing well." Abby said. *But my parents are still dead.* "But… do we know who killed them? Who actually did it?" she asked.

There was a long pause; it was painfully obvious it was the question he hoped she wouldn't ask. "Yes. I'm not sure I should tell you, Abby. I don't' want you doing anything rash."

"What could I do? I'm in hiding remember?" Abby said.

Sebastian paused again, deciding. "Atoro Thanos."

"Is he dead?" Abby asked.

"No, not yet," Sebastian admitted. "But it's only a matter of time."

"Thank you for talking to me about it," Abby said. "I was getting tired of people treating me like I am too fragile to handle all of this."

"I never thought you were too fragile, Abby. I just didn't want you to have to deal with anything more, at least right now," her uncle confided.

"I should let you go," Abby said. "I love you."

"Love you too," Sebastian said. "Take care of yourself, Abby."

She was avoiding the call to Benjamin. She didn't know what to say. All she knew is she wanted to be with him. There were too many feelings and emotions swimming around. Her mind and body couldn't take it any longer, she needed to fall apart; to scream and cry, and break things, but she couldn't. She wouldn't. Instead of breaking down, she simply went numb; a state which in the last six months had become natural to her.

Abby scrolled through the numbers in her phone until she came to his name and touched the call button. The phone didn't even finish the first ring before Benjamin answered. "Hello, Abby? Where are you?" There was a panicked tone to his voice.

"London," she said softly.

"Abby please let me come and get you," Benjamin pleaded. "I don't know what was wrong with me, I just, I felt like I was going to lose you."

"I know."

"What do you mean?" Benjamin asked, she could hear the hesitancy in his voice.

"My uncle told me about the connection between your family and the book," Abby confessed. "I don't care. Can we just... talk?" There was a long pause. "Benjamin? Are you still there?"

"Where in London are you?" Benjamin asked, Abby thought he sounded almost like he was crying.

"The Milestone," Abby answered. Her voice cracked.

"I'm on my way," Benjamin said and hung up the phone.

Abby crawled back in bed and cried herself to sleep.

CHAPTER SEVENTEEN

Her rest was interrupted by a knock. Abby got up and eagerly opened the door. Benjamin flew in closing the door behind him and pulled her in for a tight embrace. She melted into his arms. She was surprised by how quickly she forgot her fear and anger. All the fear, anxiety and embarrassment of the last few days all washed away with such a simple touch. He was here, all was forgiven.

"Please don't run away again," Benjamin whispered in her ear. He then cupped her face with his large hands. "Promise me," he insisted. She could see the fear and worry in his deep brown eyes. He needed her agreement.

"I didn't know what was happening, I've never seen you so angry before," Abby said. Benjamin pulled her back into an embrace. She rested her head on his chest, savoring the simple comfort of being held.

"I know," Benjamin said tenderly. "But that wasn't anger, Abby. I'm so, so sorry I scared you. My temper gets the better of me sometimes. I know it's not an excuse, but… please forgive me?" he murmured into her ear.

The two stood just holding one another. Abby didn't want it to end; she thought perhaps if this moment lasted for the rest of her life she would be happy.

Benjamin picked her up and took her to the bed. He started kissing her passionately. Abby stopped him. "We can't," she said reluctantly.

"Is there something wrong?" Benjamin asked his face just inches above her own, his adorable brows furrowed.

She looked up at him adoring his perfectly handsome face. "I left my pills in my luggage. I haven't taken them in two days," she answered, not wanting to stop any more than he did.

"I'm pretty certain we can find condoms in London," he said jokingly. "Maybe dinner too. I haven't eaten since Christmas, or slept for that matter."

"How about I order room service?" Abby suggested pulling the menu form the nightstand next to the bed. "What would you like?"

"I'll have whatever you're having," he said putting his jacket back on. He headed for the door.

"Are you leaving?" Abby pouted.

"Only for a minute, I think the hotel has a 24-hour drug store," Benjamin said as he disappeared out the door. Abby shook her head. *So single-minded.*

When he returned the two ate and talked. It was the first time they were really alone, without family looming nearby or social pressures. They talked for hours freely and intimately.

"You know we've never technically been on a date," Abby commented.

"Really?" Benjamin thought about it for a moment. "I guess by most people's definitions of a date you're right. I never really thought about it before. We're in London, we could go out tomorrow if you like."

"I'd like that… You look really tired Benjamin," Abby observed his wilting eyes and he didn't have his normal edge. "As much as it would be fun to fool around, how about we just go to bed?"

"Are you sure?" Benjamin seemed conflicted. Abby nodded.

"You get in bed, I'll turn out the lights and get ready. I won't be long." By the time she returned Benjamin was asleep. She got into the bed carefully trying not to disturb him. Within moments he snuggled up to her as though he instinctively knew she would be there. A shiver of joy ran down Abby's spine, releasing tension she thought she had already let go of. She felt elated and happy for the first time in days. She didn't care about ancient curses, death magic, manipulation games, or blood feuds. Right then she had everything she needed. Benjamin's arms were tight around her. She could smell him, feel him, hear him.

Everything would be alright.

"Are you certain you feel up to driving?" Abby asked as Benjamin put the last of their luggage into the back of his SUV. It had been a slow few days for them. They had done little more than stay cooped up in the hotel room. His hasty flight through the snowstorm to get to her the day after Christmas resulted in a nasty cold that lasted through New Years. Abby didn't mind that he was too sick to have their date because it meant they still got to be together, but that didn't mean she wanted him behind the wheel if he couldn't focus on driving safely.

"I feel much better. Besides I've always found a good drive relaxing," he reassured her. "I'm sorry I ruined our last couple days," he added giving her a quick kiss and opening the door for her.

"It wasn't your fault," Abby smiled and climbed into the passenger seat, buckling in for the long drive ahead. They pulled out into the busy streets of London and headed northwest towards Oxford.

"Just promise me if you get tired you'll pull over and let me drive," Abby said.

"Let you drive?" Benjamin questioned as though it were absurd. "My beautiful baby?" He added affectionately petting the dashboard.

Abby rolled her eyes and laughed, relieved his sense of humor had returned. It was a true sign he really was feeling better.

"I signed the emancipation paper work and sent it in yesterday," Abby told him.

"When does it become official?" Benjamin asked.

"Probably a couple weeks," she said as they crawled through the city traffic. "Knowing my grandmother, she's probably arranged to push everything through as quickly as possible. I think she must use charms to cut through bureaucratic red tape. I still wish I knew her motivations though. I turn eighteen in July, either way, so why go to all the trouble of cutting me loose six months early?"

"There's a lot of money and investments in your trust," Benjamin commented. "I glanced at the paper work you showed me. I would have thought she would want to stay in control of the money."

"Grandmother has more money than I could imagine. I'm certain I have a pittance compared to her," Abby said. "I doubt money is her primary motivator at the moment. She's very focused on the conflict with the Thanos. I suspect she feels she's giving me something she thinks I want. If there are strings attached I'm certain they will come to light soon enough."

"As a much older and wiser person, I recommend you don't look a gift horse in the mouth," Benjamin jested.

"Much older and wiser?" Abby laughed. "I'm really impressed by the quality of those three months you have on me," she added with a smile.

They made their way into the outskirts of the city where yards became bigger, houses less common and trees filled the open space with more frequency. Here, the snow was all but gone save for the occasional half melted snowman or a pile of plowed snow.

Abby sighed as she watched out the window, thinking about school. Even though they had only been out for a couple weeks it felt like months, so much had happened. A part of her was looking forward to returning to her regular routine; going to classes, studying with Ms. Grace, seeing her friends again. She had grown used to having roommates. Sarah and Nina were becoming good friends, and she adored Warren. She realized she had missed them these last two weeks.

"I've neglected my practice this last week," Abby commented realizing she would be rusty when she picked her violin back up. Professor Goodwin would notice her neglect upon hearing her play. He always had a good ear for those who didn't come to class well prepared.

"My parents said they would bring your things when they drop Josephine off at school." Benjamin explained. "It's probably already there in your room," he added gesturing at the time on the dashboard.

"I think I'm going to try and get some time in this evening," Abby said somewhat concerned.

"Why?" Benjamin asked. "I've heard you play. You're fantastic."

"Thank you, but you don't know Professor Goodwin. He will notice," Abby clarified. "He made it very clear we were to stay on top of our practice over the holiday. The winter concert is only a couple weeks away."

"I never realized your music teacher was such a task master," Benjamin commented.

"He isn't really," Abby explained. "He's very passionate and he expects a lot, but never more than we are capable of. I think he's a good teacher even when he pushes me to work harder. I've learned a lot from him."

"Do you have a solo in the winter concert?" Benjamin asked.

"No," Abby said. "No solos this time.'"

"I don't know why he wouldn't put you front and center," Benjamin said putting a smile on Abby's face.

"In some ways music can be like sports. You have to pay your dues," Abby explained.

"Well, I look forward to your concert. I'll be in the front row," Benjamin reassured. He took a deep breath, a regretful look on his face. "We're almost there. Back to the land of rules and regulations, where touching is off limits, and fraternization can result in immediate expulsion."

"Somehow I suspect we'll survive," Abby said with a grin. "We'll get away on the weekends. For now, that will have to do."

"This is going to be painful," Benjamin complained as he turned onto the driveway into the schools main parking lot.

"I think it will be fun!" Abby said enthusiastically with a coy smile.

"What do you mean?" Benjamin asked, confused as he pulled into a parking space.

"I can spend the whole week driving you wild," Abby said, her sweet smile turning wicked.

"You are a cheeky minx aren't you." Benjamin smiled. He released his seat belt so he could lean in for a kiss.

Abby kissed him back, and before long they were making out. It would be the last time for at least a week. Benjamin held her head and pressed his soft warm lips against her mouth. Abby could feel her heart racing.

There was an abrupt knock on the window. "You kids had better knock it off!" Professor McEwen shouted through the glass.

Benjamin and Abby quickly pulled themselves apart and did their best to look innocent. "Sorry Professor. It won't happen again," Benjamin waved.

The older gentleman gave them a stern look and quickly departed down a path towards the boy's dormitory. Abby could feel herself turning red as she straightened her shirt and pulled down the mirror from the sun shade to be certain her make up didn't smear.

"How do all the other bloody students get away with it?" Benjamin growled.

"I imagine the school parking lot isn't the greatest place for us to be snogging on campus," she said with a chuckle. "Besides, neither one of us are big rule breakers. We're obviously not very good at getting away with things."

Benjamin shrugged his shoulders. "You're probably right." They got out of the car and came around to the back to collect their luggage. "It's going to be nearly impossible to keep away from you, though," he said slamming the back of his SUV closed.

"We just have to be careful," Abby said. They started their way along the path towards the main courtyard.

"I guess." It was obvious he was trying to accept the challenges with trying to carry on the physical side of their relationship. The school didn't make it easy for them to be together on campus.

"It will make our time together on the weekend even more special," Abby offered, hoping to help him move into a state of acceptance. She was quickly learning Benjamin was the kind of guy who was used to getting his way.

He sighed and caught himself before he threw his arm around her shoulder as they walked. "You're right," he conceded.

"Of course, I am," Abby said playfully, "and if I were you, I'd get used to saying that a lot."

"You're a tease," Benjamin jested.

"That too," Abby agreed.

Abby made her way along the path to Calder House. She wanted to look on Ms. Grace after settling things in her room. Sarah and Nina hadn't returned yet and she wanted a chance to see her mentor. Abby realized she was growing rather fond of Ms. Grace and missed her while she was on holiday.

She knocked on the door and waited a few moments. There was no answer. She checked the latch and it wasn't locked. Ms. Grace was likely in her sanctum where she would be unlikely to hear a knock at the door. Abby pushed the door open and made her way past the parlor and through the living room to the stairwell leading into the sanctum.

"Ms. Grace?" Abby called down, attempting to not disturb her if she would rather not receive a visitor.

"Come down." Ms. Grace called out.

Abby descended the stairs and saw her mentor standing with a tea set in her hands. There was a rather large bottle of brandy on the tray that looked half empty. There was a foul smell permeating the sanctum, emanating from a greyish slush boiling over a burner at the Alchemy station. Abby resisted the urge to curl her nose.

"Abigail," Ms. Grace said warmly. She was less formal than usual, Abby noticed and wondered how much brandy she had already drank.

"Good evening, Ms. Grace," Abby greeted warmly. "I wanted to come say hello, now that I've returned."

"It is very nice to see you. I hope you had a nice holiday with the Hodge family," she said. Placing the tray on the end table next to one of the leather chairs by the fireplace. "Would you like some tea?"

"Yes, thank you," Abby said, coming around and taking a seat across from Ms. Grace. "It was a rather mixed experience."

"Oh?" Ms. Grace raised an eyebrow. "I'm more than willing to listen if you need to talk."

Abby gave Ms. Grace a somewhat censored version of what happened. She talked about her grandmother's gift, the Grimaldi diamond, and the book. Abby avoided only the details about her blossoming relationship with Benjamin.

"You kids have far more fun than I ever had at your age," Ms. Grace stated dryly, taking a sip of tea after pouring in a generous pour of brandy. She sat in the leather chair next to the fireplace.

"It was definitely an eventful break," Abby said.

"I had no idea you didn't already know about the Hodge family's spotted history," Ms. Grace said. "I would have thought Vivian would have told you."

Abby sighed. "Yes. Grandmother," she said bitterly. Ms. Grace seemed to notice her tone and raised an eyebrow. "She's apparently working on something big. I don't know what, but my uncle thinks it's some kind of curse related to the conflict."

"Your grandmother is perhaps the preeminent hex weaver of our time," Ms. Grace stated. "the Kane family has always been good with curses. I imagine were you to show any interest in that line of study you would excel. It seems to be in your blood, just as alchemy is in mine."

"Can we trade?" Abby jested, putting a rare smile on her mentor's face.

"If only it were so easy," Ms. Grace stated kindly. "You've come along nicely with your studies."

"I don't think you have to worry, Ms. Grace," Abby reassured. "I've learned a great deal, and more than a few things about our craft have sparked my interest."

"Mastering the Sight will take a great deal of work," Ms. Grace explained. "It is a truly rare gift. Unfortunately, I don't know any other witches who possess such a rare power."

"I had no idea it was so rare," Abby admitted. "Grandmother says it comes from the Whitlock side of my family."

"Yes, the Whitlock coven has a history of producing the occasional witch with the Sight. Unfortunately, as you know. You are one of the last of that line," Ms. Grace said regretfully.

"I know," Abby said. "My mother's family had died out for the most part. There's only my uncle Sebastian, aunt Wendy and I left now."

"Many Families have died off or faded for various reasons throughout the ages," Ms. Grace stated. "Some of those special gifts get passed on to other lines through marriage. Perhaps the Sight will carry on in the Kane line through your children." She smiled warmly.

"My children?" Abby chuckled. "It's a strange thing to think about."

"How I envy your age Miss Kane," Valerie said, her voice filled with regret. "You have so much in front of you. So many choices and opportunities lay in your path. You're a smart girl. Make sure, every once in a while, you choose happiness. Duty, honor and loyalty all have their place, but they also have their costs." The older woman spoke her wisdom with words coated in regret, once again making Abby wonder at her mentor's past.

"Can I ask you a question? It might be kind of personal," Abby asked. She watched as the older stoic woman raised an eyebrow and regarded her with uncertainty.

"You may ask," Ms. Grace stated, her tone gave no promise of an answer.

"How did you come to know my grandmother?" Abby wondered if the rumor she had heard was true.

Ms. Grace considered her words very carefully. The length of her silence made Abby feel as though she had overstepped a boundary. The older woman's stern look softened. "Your grandmother helped me with a situation for which I was poorly suited. I'm not a woman given to flights of fancy, and this was especially true when I was a young woman, not much older than yourself. Books were my joy. I couldn't' devour them fast enough. I was a studious girl with little experience with men," she explained.

"I met a man. A dashing fellow with perfect teeth and a smile that went on for miles," Ms. Grace continued. Abby could see an almost longing look in her expression. "I had no idea why a young handsome man like him would take the slightest interest in a bookish girl like myself," she continued. "I never was a great beauty. I do not see such things as a fault or shortcoming. My mind is the tool I rely upon. There is nothing to be lost in that," she added taking another sip.

"Did he break your heart?" Abby asked cautiously.

Ms. Grace smiled meekly. "In a manner of speaking. I learned things about him I could not reconcile with my conscience."

"I'm sorry, Ms. Grace," Abby said sincerely.

"Have you ever had a man break your heart Ms. Kane?" The older woman questioned, taking another sip of tea, staring into the flames as though it revealed the past to her.

"No," Abby confessed, shuddering at the thought. She could never imagine Benjamin would break her heart.

"At first, I thought I would go mad, as though I was becoming Bertha, to be locked away in Mr. Rochester's attic," Ms. Grace stated.

"Jane Eyre?" Abby asked, catching the literary reference.

"Very good, Ms. Kane." Valerie stated with a hint of a smile. "He was no country lord, however. He was a vampire," Abby gasped in shock. "I didn't know at first, you see. Despite my predilection for books and studying, it was never a topic I explored. I never imagined I would need to."

"Ms. Grace, I'm very sorry. I had no idea," Abby said, feeling bad about bringing up something so painful from the past.

"You needn't be," Ms. Grace stated. "I was responsible for getting myself in that situation and I got myself out," she said plainly.

Abby wondered what vampires were like. It was a curiosity she would save for another time. "If you got yourself out of the situation, what did you need my grandmother for?" Abby asked cautiously.

"To make sure he never bothered me again," Valerie said, the faintest hint of sorrow broke through her stoic demeanor. The older woman took another sip and broke her dower expression with a quaint smile. "Vivian laid a powerful prohibition curse on him. If he ever came near me again; the curse would take effect, which would almost certainly mean his death."

"I didn't know my grandmother could do that kind of thing," Abby said, thinking about the kind of power it must take to do something like that.

"You know Vivian Kane as your grandmother," Ms. Grace stated. "I know her as one of the most powerful witches alive. She is well known in our circles. You are going to find most witches know who she is. Some are fond of her, some are not. You should always be careful, Abby. Your grandmother's enemies may one day take notice of you."

Abby took a deep breath. "It would seem some of them already have," Abby said bitterly, a flash of her parent's dead on the floor intruded. She quickly pushed them away.

"Yes, I think you're right," Ms. Grace said kindly. "Now you must answer a question in kind Miss Kane."

Abby smiled. "I'm afraid I don't have many secrets," she said, somewhat amused by how tipsy Ms. Grace had become. Clearly, she was still on holiday.

"How long have you and Benjamin been courting?" Ms. Grace asked. Abby was again amused by her mentors antiquated terminology. She could see Ms. Grace was starting to get droopy eyes.

"How did you know?" Abby asked with a chuckle.

"You're terrible at intrigue Miss Kane," Valerie stated plainly.

"A couple months." Abby confessed.

"He's a nice young man. I've had the pleasure of teaching him since he first arrived. He couldn't have been more than eight years old. I've seen him grow from a young boy into a fine young man," Ms. Grace stated as she watched the flickering flames. There was a sense of pride when she spoke of Benjamin.

161

"I'm rather fond of him myself," Abby agreed, staring down at the ring he gave her Christmas morning.

"I only wish I had the chance to work with Josephine as long," Ms. Grace mumbled. "I do not understand that girl sometimes."

"What do you mean?" Abby asked. "Didn't Josephine arrive when Benjamin did?"

"No," Ms. Grace said her eyes barely open. "She came much later. Only the year before last. She went to some other school… in Winchester… if I recall."

That's odd. Why would they send the twins to two different schools? she thought. She conceded as how they probably had their reasons. She hoped someday to hear that story, but for now Abby turned her attention back to her mentor. As Abby looked over at Ms. Grace, she saw the older woman's eyes were closed, and a moment later she began to snore.

She got up and collected the tea cup from Ms. Grace's lap and placed it on the tray. Abby pulled a blanket from the back of the leather chair she had been sitting in and covered her teacher gently so as to not disturb her sleep. She then put a log on the fire to keep it going a few more hours. She then took the tray upstairs and left as quietly as she could.

It was dark out as Abby carefully traversed the path back towards the girl's dormitory. The courtyard was quiet with only the occasional lamp flooding the area in pale light. The moon was drowned out by clouds and a drizzle was starting to fall from the sky. "An English winter," she said to the sky. "Reminds me of home." She smiled at the thought.

Abby was nearly at the dormitory when she saw someone standing on the far side of the courtyard. *Benjamin,* she thought, putting a bright smile on her face. As her eyes adjusted she realized she wasn't looking at her boyfriend across the courtyard. The red glow in the eyes gave him away.

Edgar! A chill ran down her spine as she froze. *Is he watching me?* she wondered.

Edgar took a step forward and Abby flinched, her body flooded with adrenaline. When he took another step, she broke out into a run, not stopping to look back.

She burst into the dormitory and closed the door behind her. She leaned back against it, breathless. Slowly, Abby came around to a window to see if he was still following her. The courtyard was empty. Edgar had disappeared.

Abby sank to the floor, letting the fear wash through her. *This is not how I wanted to start the new school term,* she thought.

CHAPTER EIGHTEEN

The final note lingered in the air for a moment before the audience erupted in applause. Abby watched Professor Goodwin crack a rare smile as the winter concert came to a successful end. He was pleased. Abby felt elated. The rush of playing in front of an audience was exhilarating. She had forgotten how much she enjoyed the feeling of playing in front of a crowd and the satisfaction that came with performing.

Professor Goodwin took a bow and then stepped down from the podium and motioned to the students. The audience continued to clap as Abby and the rest of the students stood and took a bow.

She glanced into the audience and saw her friends standing in the front row. They all seemed so happy. It felt good to share this moment. Each responded exactly as Abby would expect from their personalities. Nina was practically jumping up and down, while Sarah was smiling and clapping her hands. Warren had a pleased grin on his face, which told Abby all she needed to know. Benjamin had a toothy grin as he clapped enthusiastically, while Josephine, next to him stood and clapped politely with a detached stare. She was so glad they decided to share this with her.

"Thank you all for coming," Professor Goodwin spoke into a microphone. "If you enjoyed the concert this evening, please be sure to attend our other performances as well. We will be performing at the Tulip Festival in late April. Thank you again," He waited a beat for the applause to die back down before stepping away from the microphone.

The curtains fell and Professor Goodwin dismissed the students with a wave. Abby collected the sheet music and was about to exit the stage when the professor approached.

"You better be careful Mr. Denis. Ms. Kane is poised to take your chair," the Professor mentioned as he walked by on his way off stage.

Gregory Denis, first chair first violin, gave Abby a smile. "If you think you're good enough, go for it," he said with confidence.

"I might," Abby said playfully.

She made her way off stage and back to the music room where she found her bag and instrument case. Abby gently set her violin in the case and loosened her bow before securing it inside.

"Don't forget the reception in the dining hall," Professor Goodwin called out with little interest. He gathered his things and quickly disappeared out the door.

Abby finished putting everything away and locked her violin case in her music locker. She exchanged a few accolades with several of the other music students and made her way into the hall towards the main gallery of the performance hall. She was glad to share in the elation of her fellow performers, but she wanted to see her friends.

The main gallery was a large open space lit by three large crystal chandeliers. The red carpet was a bit worn but it possessed the refinement of a proper performance hall, where the school orchestra performed twice a year on loan from the drama department.

The gallery was filled with unfamiliar faces. Family members no doubt come to hear their loved ones perform. Abby knew she would never find her parents in this crowd, but instinct made her look for them anyway. She caught herself quickly and pushed the thought aside.

"Abby!" Nina squealed. Abby quickly turned in the direction of Nina's voice. There she saw all her friends standing together waiting for her. Benjamin had a big grin on his face which melted her heart as she approached.

"Congratulations," they said as she greeted each one with a warm hug.

Benjamin's hug lasted a bit longer than the congratulatory embrace would typically last, and Abby gave him a sly grin. "You're terrible," she whispered playfully in his ear.

She then gave Josephine a brief and awkward hug. Abby could tell there was some kind of strangeness between them. It had been there since Christmas, but she wasn't sure where it came from. Although Josephine was polite and gracious, there was something mechanical, almost practiced, about her mannerisms. Abby again wondered if perhaps her accidental excursion through the hallway at Hodge Manor, and the dinner incident were both more egregious than she had been led to believe.

"Fine performance Ms. Kane," Valerie Grace stated as she approached. Abby couldn't help but notice Warren rolling his eyes as the deputy headmistress came forward. Ms. Grace narrowed her eyes at the young man briefly before turning her attention back to Abby. "I was particularly fond of Professor Goodwin's interpretation of Mussorgsky."

"Thank you, Ms. Grace," Abby said, beaming with pride. "It's a difficult piece and we've been working on it since the beginning of the school year."

"Hard work always pays off. Doesn't it, Miss Chatterjee?" Valerie asked, pointedly turning to Sarah, who was one of the best students in the school.

"Yes, Ms. Grace," Sarah said dutifully.

"Some students would do well to follow your exemplary study habits," Ms. Grace added, glancing at Warren pointedly. She then turned back to Abby and gave her a polite smile. "Have a nice evening dear. You truly were great this evening. I will see you tomorrow evening." She added and excused herself.

Abby noticed Warren fuming for a few moments. "What a…" he began.

"Let's go to the dining hall!" Nina said excitedly, no doubt an attempt to interrupt Warren's impending tirade about the totalitarianism of Ms. Grace. Nina grabbed Warren's arm and started pulling him towards the exit.

"I see Ms. Grace and your friend get along famously," Benjamin whispered in her ear. Abby smiled.

"They're the best of friends. Didn't you know?" she laughed.

"I'll see you in a few minutes," Sarah said, excusing herself.

"I think I'm going to call it a night," Josephine said dispassionately.

"Is everything okay?" Abby asked.

"Of course," Josephine said, with a sweet smile. "I didn't sleep well last night. It was a lovely performance." She excused herself and disappeared into the crowd.

Abby paused for a moment and then turned to Benjamin. "I think I've upset Josephine," she said.

"Why do you say that?" Benjamin asked.

"I don't know," Abby said with uncertainty. "Little things I guess. She seems more withdrawn than normal. Less engaged. Maybe everything that happened over the holiday changed things between us."

"What happened over the holiday really didn't have anything to do with her," Benjamin reasoned. "I really don't think there's anything personal going on. She's just preoccupied with her art projects. You know how moody artists can be."

Abby wondered if that was what was really going on. Benjamin had never lied to her before, but he may simply be trying to smooth things over. Abby still wasn't convinced, despite his reassurance, that his family wasn't upset over everything that happened. She took a deep breath and decided to trust her boyfriend.

"Shall we make an appearance at the reception?" Abby asked.

"I can think of some other things I'd rather do, but if you insist," Benjamin said with a wink and a wicked smile.

"I insist." Benjamin discretely took her hand and they began to weave through the crowd. When they came to the door, something dawned on Abby. She paused, soliciting an uncertain look from her boyfriend.

"Something wrong?" Benjamin asked.

"Yes, actually," Abby said. It had been three weeks since Christmas and Abby had forgotten the present she was going to give Benjamin in private. "I need to get something. I left it in my room," she said.

"What's so important it can't wait?" Benjamin asked curiously.

"The Christmas present I was going to give you in private. I forgot all about it when everything happened. I want to give it to you, tonight," Abby said with a big grin.

"You're just remembering now?" Benjamin teased.

Abby blushed with embarrassment. "Yes," she confessed. "Why don't you go to the reception and I'll join you in a couple minutes. It won't take long."

"If you insist," Benjamin smiled. Abby could feel the pull of a kiss, but they stopped themselves. There were far too many faculty around who might be willing to overlook the holding of hands, but certainly not a kiss.

"I'll see you in a few minutes," Abby reassured. Benjamin followed the crowd towards the dining hall while Abby made her way back to the girl's dormitory.

She rushed into her room and looked for the small wrapped gift in her dresser drawer. Abby took it and grabbed her purse off the bed while she was at it. She shoved the gift in her purse and threw it over her shoulder.

Abby allowed herself to catch her breath and realized she didn't need to be in such a hurry. It was difficult to run in a dignified fashion in the dress she was wearing anyway, she laughed at herself. She turned off the lights and headed down the stairs. The common room was virtually empty save for a few of the younger girls who waved as she passed by.

The night sky was clear, offering a winter chill that made Abby pull her coat tightly around her. She could see her breath in the air as she stepped into the courtyard. It was practically empty.

Abby could hear the click of her heals against the cement courtyard as she made her way back towards the dining hall. Then she heard the sound of another set of feet traveling across the courtyard a few feet away. She turned and froze.

"Edgar?" Abby questioned her eyes. The young man was only a few feet away. He towered over her by more than a foot. She could see his enormous muscles press against the jacket he was wearing. He was a truly intimidating presence and Abby could feel herself go cold. "What do you want?" She managed to choke out her question. She watched him closely, any sudden moves and she would run with everything she had.

"What did you do to Emily?" Edgar growled. She could see the red glow in his eyes.

"I never knew Emily," she said. Her voice was barely above a whisper.

Edgar stared at her as though he were in deep contemplation. He was watching her just as closely as she was watching him. Though he seemed outwardly calm, the glow in his eyes told a different story. "Why did you run away the other night, when I saw you here in the courtyard?" Edgar asked.

Abby considered her words carefully as she watched to make certain he didn't make any sudden moves. "Because the last time we spoke you nearly broke my wrist," she said, positioning herself to run.

Edgar had a peculiar expression on his face. She couldn't tell what he was thinking. For a moment it looked like remorse, but his expression quickly turned back to anger. His size alone made him look truly menacing, but coupled with his rage, Abby was terrified. If he got his hands on her, he could break her in half in a fraction of a second.

"I… I didn't mean to hurt you," Edgar said, his look softening slightly.

Abby was taken aback. There was a cautious curiosity growing in Abby's thoughts. She remembered the remorse she had seen from him with the Sight. She pushed the thought away, focusing on the conversation. "Then, why did you?" she asked.

There was a lengthy pause before Edgar answered, "I sometimes forget my strength," he said, putting his hands in his pockets. "What did you do to me?" he asked.

"I protected myself," Abby responded, keeping her guard up.

"With what?"

Abby gave careful consideration to how she would answer his question. She glanced around, there was no one nearby. "Magic."

Edgar stared at her with open curiosity. The red glow in his eyes seemed lessened. Abby new it was temporary, but for the moment it made her feel slightly better.

"Magic?"

Abby nodded.

"What are you? Some kind of witch?" Edgar asked dismissively.

Abby nodded.

Again he stared at her as though he was searching for the truth in her answer. He stepped forward. Abby stepped back. He stopped and held up his hands. "Sorry, I'm not going to hurt you," he said.

Abby watched him carefully as she weighed the chances of her escaping towards the dining hall before he could catch her. She didn't feel very confident she could pull it off, and certainly not in heels.

"What do you want from me?" Abby asked, her voice shaking.

Edgar looked at her with uncertainty. "I thought you had answers," He said.

"What kind of answers?" Abby asked doing her best to temper her curiosity. She didn't know what he meant. They were the ones trying to figure out what he was capable of. *Is it possible he doesn't know?* she wondered.

"I don't know what I was thinking," Edgar said, shaking his head. The red glow returned, noticeably brighter.

"Edgar?" Abby said cautiously.

The young man looked up at her with a glare. "What?" he said nearly growling.

Abby contemplated whether she would ask. After a few seconds, she mustered her bravery and went for it. "D…Do you know what you are?" she asked cautiously.

Edgar glared at her. His eyes burned like fire. She watched as his hands clenched into fists, and she could see his chest heaving. Abby instinctively took several steps away. It looked as if he was about to explode.

"Just who the hell do you think you are!?" Edgar roared.

Abby's eyes flew wide. She knew any moment now would be her last. Edgar would tear her apart.

"Abby!" A familiar voice called out. She turned and saw Benjamin rushing forward. She looked back towards Edgar. He was gone, as if he had vanished.

She could feel her whole-body trembling. Her knees were weak, and she could feel the nerves in her stomach churn.

Benjamin rushed forward and pulled Abby into an embrace. "What happened? Did he hurt you?" he asked, holding her at arm's length and looking her over.

"No, he didn't hurt me," she managed to say through chattering teeth.

"Come on. Lets get you to Ms. Grace's cottage. It's safe there." Benjamin put his arm around her and escorted her through the courtyard and down the wooded path.

Abby could feel the strength beginning to return as they neared Calder House. By the time they arrived she was starting to breathe normally again.

Abby had rarely felt so frightened in her life. Despite her fear, she realized it was a peculiar exchange. It certainly hadn't gone as she imagined. She was certain another encounter with Edgar Kincaid would involve dismemberment, or at the very least a broken limb.

She glanced over at Benjamin who was on the phone with someone. He hung up and stoked the fire. Abby had learned, Benjamin's silent brooding was an indication of how upset he was.

"He's lucky I didn't get there any sooner," Benjamin growled as he broke up a log with the fire poker, kneeling over the fireplace. The flickering flames cast a shadow over Benjamin's face. Abby knew Benjamin had a temper. It made her anxious seeing him this upset. She feared he would try and do something, and she couldn't bear thinking about something happening to him. She moved from the chair to the floor next to him and wrapped her arms around his waist, leaning her head against his shoulder. At first, he stiffened, and then he leaned into her and stroked her hair.

They held one another for several minutes until they heard footsteps coming down the stairs. Abby pulled away and sat in one of the leather chairs as Benjamin stood.

"Is everyone alright? Abigail?" Ms. Grace asked, her face covered in worry.

"I'm all right," Abby reassured her guardian. "Edgar just gave me a bit of a scare is all."

"He didn't hurt you?" Ms. Grace asked, sounding surprised.

"No. He never touched me," Abby said. "Strangely enough, he actually apologized for hurting me the last time we spoke."

Benjamin turned sharply and looked at her as if he couldn't believe what he just heard. "You actually spoke to him?" he questioned as though she had done something terribly wrong.

"Briefly," she admitted, uncertain she had done anything wrong. "What was I supposed to do?" Abby asked.

"Run," Benjamin said sharply.

"Mr. Hodge, I think level heads would serve us much better at the moment," Ms. Grace interjected.

"I'm going to kill him," Benjamin said with a certainty that sent chills down Abby's spine.

"Calm down Mr. Hodge!" Ms. Grace ordered. "I'll not have you putting yourself in danger when we aren't even certain what we're dealing with. You could get yourself killed. This foolishness will stop now!" she stated firmly. Abby was surprised by how authoritative Ms. Grace was in that moment.

Benjamin remained silent and began pacing near the staircase. Abby was afraid he was going to run up the stairs at any moment to go after Edgar. She tried to speak but she couldn't find any words. She was so confused and frightened. Nothing came to mind.

A moment later Josephine emerged from the stairwell. "What's going on?" she asked cautiously, obviously noticing the intense scene in front of her.

"Abigail had an encounter with Edgar Kincaid this evening," Ms. Grace stated. "Your brother seems determined to press for a confrontation."

Josephine approached Benjamin, putting her hands on his shoulders. She locked eyes with him before saying, "You know that isn't what you should do. Not now. We should wait until we know more."

She put her arms around him, and Benjamin pulled her into a hug. Josephine held Benjamin as one would a child, until he had calmed down. She glanced at Abby. There was a strange glint in her eye, that made Abby feel as though Josephine held her responsible for everything that was happening.

When Benjamin pulled away he looked only slightly better. His face was still red, and it was clear his temper was only slightly less volatile.

"Abigail, please tell us everything," Ms. Grace stated.

Abby sat in the leather chair and filled them in on every detail of her brief exchange with Edgar Kincaid. For now, at least, Abby omitted her thoughts on the matter, preferring to stick to the facts. She wasn't convinced Benjamin could stand to hear what she was thinking.

Between the remorse she had sensed from him when she used the Sight, and the fact he thought she had something to do with Emily's disappearance, she was more convinced than ever that Edgar Kincaid wasn't responsible for Emily's disappearance.

169

"He's probably trying to throw us off," Josephine said.

"What do you mean?" Abby asked.

"His question about Emily. He's probably trying to throw us off. You never even met Emily." Josephine sounded reasonable. "He did. Throwing suspicion onto your accusers is textbook psychopathy."

"It's possible," Ms. Grace said as she processed the new information.

"He was also probably trying to lull you into trusting him with that apology," Josephine added. "He's clearly dangerous. At best, if he doesn't' know his own strength, maybe he killed Emily by accident," she suggested.

It's possible, Abby had to concede, *but something still isn't adding up.* Her instincts were telling her there was still a lot more going on here that she didn't understand.

Abby looked over at Benjamin who was brooding in the corner. He seemed calmer, but the look on his face did little to put her mind at ease.

"It's not safe for her here," Benjamin broke his silence.

"How so?" Ms. Grace questioned.

"While the two of them are on campus together there is always the chance they could have another encounter. I think we need to remove her from campus." Benjamin explained.

"I can't just up and quit school," Abby protested. "Besides, during the school day he hasn't made any attempts to speak to me. There are too many people around."

Benjamin glanced at Josephine for a brief moment, and then turned to Ms. Grace. "I want to take her off campus. We can stay at my parents' home and commute for the remainder of the school year. Maybe we could even take our completion exams early."

Abby stood. Her own anger was beginning to emerge. She wasn't about to have her life be decided for her again. "I'm not going anywhere," she insisted, rising from the chair. Benjamin looked at her as though she had just slapped him across the face.

"What do you mean? You aren't safe in this place. My family and I can protect you in our home."

Abby shook her head. "If Edgar Kincaid wanted me dead, he would have killed me instead of trying to talk to me," She said. "There are things I don't understand, but I won't find the answers by running away. And.." she debated whether or not to continue, "and, I think he actually might need help."

Benjamin turned a brighter shade of red. She thought for certain he was going to break something. She glanced over at Josephine who stood with her arms folded. Abby wasn't certain, but she thought there was a slight curl at the edge of her lips. *Is she somehow amused by this?* Abby wondered shaking her head.

"I can't believe you're being so naïve!" Benjamin yelled. Abby flinched. It was a stab to the heart and she could feel the emotional blood dripping through her thoughts.

"Mr. Hodge, stop this instant!" Ms. Grace barked.

Abby stormed up the stairs and ran through the front door. Hot tears began running down her cheeks. They burned as if every tear carried the red hot fiery anger of Benjamin's words. She was only a few yards down the path when she slowed down and wiped away the tears. *Is it true?* Abby wondered. *Am I a stupid naïve little girl? Am I being ridiculous by wanting to give Edgar Kincaid the benefit of a doubt?* It didn't feel wrong, but everyone she knew was telling her she was a fool. Her thoughts rushed through her mind like race cars repetitiously going in circles around the same track.

"Abby! Wait up!" Josephine called out.

Abby turned and saw the young woman walking briskly to catch up. *Of all the people,* Abby thought, still convinced Josephine was upset with her.

"Ms. Grace and Benjamin asked me to make sure you made it back to the dormitory safely," Josephine explained as she approached.

"I'm fine. Really," Abby said. The curtness in her voice was a bit more than she had intended.

Josephine gave her a surprised look. "I know. I'm doing it because they asked me, not because you don't know how to take care of yourself. You are after all Vivian Kane's granddaughter."

Abby wheeled on her, frustrated past the point of civility. "Is that what this is about?"

"I don't' follow your meaning." Josephine said looking confused. "What is what about?"

"You have been acting different with me ever since the holiday," Abby explained. "We were friends, and now your distant and barely speak to me."

Josephine regarded Abby with uncertainty and folded her arms. There was a coldness to her gaze. Josephine sighed and looked away briefly. "My brother and I have always been close. Now you're dating him. It's a little weird for me," she said, sounding a bit nervous.

Abby considered her words carefully. It made sense. She couldn't help but feel like there was more to it, but she had no reason to disbelieve Josephine.

"I guess it could be weird to have a friend start dating your brother. I wouldn't know, since I don't have any siblings," Abby conceded.

"Look, I didn't mean for things to get weird between us," Josephine said. Abby thought she seemed a bit irritated but thought perhaps the night was too emotionally charged and she was taking things too personally. "I want to be your friend Abby."

171

Abby sighed and nodded.

"Me too," Abby agreed. The matter settled, the two girls began walking up the path together.

"So, you think Edgar Kincaid could be innocent?" Josephine asked.

"I don't know," Abby said. "Maybe I can try and find out one way or the other."

Josephine was silent for a moment, thinking. "Be careful Abby." She warned, a hard-edged concern in her voice, "Sometimes searching for the truth is dangerous. It could get you killed if you're not careful."

CHAPTER NINETEEN

"Congratulations," Sarah said as she sat with Abby for lunch at the far corner of the dining hall. "First chair is really impressive."

"Thanks," Abby smiled. The challenge process had been daunting, but Abby was glad she had done it, and not just because she had won. It felt good to be acknowledged for her hard work.

"Luckily, Gregory Denis took it well, but I won't be surprised if he tries to reclaim his seat before the end of the year." She said as they sat at the table alone. "There's Nina and Warren." Abby waived.

Their two friends approached with their trays and sat at the table. "Did you hear Abby's news?" Sarah asked excited.

"Yes, in Calculus," Nina smiled.

"Advanced French," Warren added. "Does this mean you'll be the Concert Mistress at your next performance?"

"Maybe," Abby said. "Gregory can challenge me in a month. If he wins he'll be Concert Master again."

"It will look really good on your transcripts," Sarah suggested.

"You're probably right," Abby conceded. Though she hadn't thought about it that way, it was true, universities would respond well to such achievements. She thought about her grandmother's offer to help get her into Julliard. It was the opportunity of a life time, she knew that, but Abby didn't want to make her way because her grandmother pulled strings to make it happen. Wherever she landed, she wanted to earn her place. This competition reminded Abby of how important that was to her.

"I think you have every right to be proud," Warren said. "You play really well and it's obvious how hard you've worked to become this good."

Abby smiled. Warren was always a bit stingy with compliments. "Thank you." She smiled.

"Are you still not speaking to Benjamin?" Nina asked her eyes were following something. Abby turned briefly to see she was watching Benjamin collecting food on his platter.

She could feel her heart flutter. They had barely spoken in the last week. Instead they were locked in a cold war. She hated it, but her feelings were still hurt and Benjamin was obviously still angry.

"We speak," Abby said invoking the cold demeanor she needed to protect herself. She could feel herself shutting down. Benjamin's words had cut deep. Abby wondered if she had taken it too seriously or if he simply hit too close to home with one of her big insecurities. Regardless she didn't know how to talk to him about it and he still seemed too angry.

Warren chuckled. "Clearly things are all back to normal, then," he said sarcastically.

"Have you told him about your recent achievement?" Nina asked.

Abby shook her head. "Leave her alone. Let them work it out." Sarah interjected obviously noticing how Abby had shut down. "It's none of our business anyway."

There was silence and Abby pushed her tray away and got up. "I need to hit the library before my next class," she said, eager to retreat before Benjamin joined the table, or worse sat somewhere else.

"Oh, come on Abby, we didn't mean to flutter the dovecotes," Warren pleaded.

"It's all right," Abby did her best to reassure, but she was certain she fooled no one. "I really do need to pick up a book I have on hold at the library before my next class." She quickly began to retreat, only to turn and come face to face with Benjamin.

"Hi," Benjamin said. His face was less red, and he didn't seem as irritated today as he had been.

"Hi," Abby said meekly. "Excuse me." She stepped around him to deposit her tray into the depository.

"Can we talk?" Benjamin asked.

Abby looked at him with uncertainty. She then glanced around the room filled with hundreds of students eating their lunch. "Maybe some other time, when we don't' have the whole school as an audience," she said.

"Tomorrow night?" Benjamin asked. "I have a thing, at the hotel in the village, with my father this evening. Something to do with the alumni foundation, but tomorrow?"

"I'll check my schedule," Abby said excusing herself. She quickly retreated from the dining hall. She didn't know why she was so cold and harsh to someone she loved so much, but she was scared. She never imagined words could be something to fear. In the hands of someone you love and care about, they were sharper than any knife.

A part of her didn't believe Benjamin had meant to hurt her feelings. But in his anger, he did. It was something she never wanted to feel again. Perhaps it would take some time to trust he wouldn't say something so condescending and hurtful.

After hitting the library to pick up a book, she headed back to her room and switched out the text books from her morning classes with the ones for her afternoon ones. She was about to leave for her next class when a wave of emotions settled over her. Abby sat on the edge of the bed and gave herself a moment to pull herself together before she completely lost her composure.

She could feel her love for Benjamin breaking through her anger and frustration. *It's time,* she thought. *I'm so tired of being angry. It's time to work things out.* She pulled out her phone and typed in a message.

> Abby: *Sorry about earlier. I'll*
> *be ready to talk*
> *tomorrow night.*

Abby sent the message to Benjamin and stood, just as she heard a knock at the door. She thought it strange to have someone coming by when classes were going to start in a few minutes. Abby opened the door and found Josephine waiting.

"Josephine? Is something wrong?" Abby asked.

"No not at all," Josephine said giving Abby a peculiar look. "I was wondering if I could ask you for some help."

"Of course," Abby said. "What do you need help with?"

"I'm working on a very complicated alchemical compound," she said glancing around to be certain no one would over hear them. "I could use a second pair of hands. Benjamin isn't going to be there."

"You aren't joining your father for the dinner this evening?" Abby asked.

"No, it's father and son night," Josephine's tone summarily dismissed their boyish antics. It clearly didn't involve her.

"I'm happy to help," Abby agreed.

"Thank you." Josephine smiled "I'll meet you here at… seven o'clock?"

"I'll be here," Abby confirmed.

It was a quarter to seven when Abby glanced at her phone. She closed the book on her desk and glanced over at Sarah who was reading one of her books on the floor, her feet on the bed. Nina was sitting at her own desk working out complicated math problems.

There was a soft knock at the door and Abby quickly collected her coat. "Who's here?" Sarah asked.

"I'm going to help Josephine with a project," Abby said, manufacturing an answer that wasn't a complete lie.

Sarah seemed satisfied with the answer and returned her attention to her book. Abby put on a warm smile and opened the door. "I'm ready," she said greeting Josephine.

"Great," the young woman smiled, waving politely to the other girls who took little notice of her.

Abby stepped into the hallway. "I'll be back in an hour or two," she commented before closing the door behind her.

The two young women made their way down the stairs and through the common room. It was a typical school night. Most of the girls were reading quietly or working on school work. A small group of younger girls sat in the corner of the commons playing a board game.

When Abby stepped into the fresh air she could feel the cold hit her face stinging the warmth from her cheeks.

"Brr," Abby said, pulling her coat tightly around her. There was a light wind that carried a bitter cold. They turned and made their way along the edge of the courtyard in the direction of the path that would take them to Calder House.

"What is this potion you're working on?" Abby asked curiously.

"An elixir that is supposed to clear cataracts," Josephine explained. "Benjamin and I have an older family member with cataracts in both eyes. They say she's beyond surgery and could potentially lose her sight completely. I'm hoping this potion will work."

"Oh," Abby said remorsefully. "Then I'm especially glad to help," she added.

The sky was clear, and the moon shined brightly above. It cast a hauntingly beautiful glow over the campus as Abby made her way to the far end of the courtyard. Several students were making their way form one building to another, but foot traffic was light this evening.

The two of them made their way down the path and approached the tree line just beyond the main building. There was a shuffling just beyond the trees. Abby stopped.

"Something wrong?" Josephine questioned curiously.

"I thought I heard something," Abby said. She waited a moment. There was nothing. She quickly dismissed her moment of paranoia. "Sorry, my mind is playing tricks on me," she said resuming their walk along the path.

They hadn't made it more than a few yards beyond the tree line when she heard what sounded like two shuffling sounds. "Is someone there?" she called out. Her intuition was screaming. Abby could feel her body filling with adrenaline.

"I heard something too," Josephine said, going alert and looking around at the edges of darkness closing in on them. "Probably just a couple students making out in the bushes," she commented when she saw nothing out of the ordinary.

Such things weren't unheard of among the students; she and Benjamin had been in a similar state in these very woods, more than once.

"I hope you're right," she said. They waited silently for a few moments, the effort was met with the distant muted sounds of the campus many yards away.

A shadow moved to Abby's right. There was a sound from behind her and Abby whirled around and saw a man shrouded in shadows step onto the path leading back to the courtyard. The dark figure stood silently, watching her.

A cold chill ran down Abby's spine. Whoever it was, he wasn't a student. She turned to look at Josephine. She was gone. Realizng the other girl must have run, Abby turned abruptly, ready to do the same. She lunged forward and felt herself slam into a tall man. His arms wrapped around her abruptly. He swung her around and slammed her onto the ground, knocking the wind out of her.

Abby gasped for breath. She recovered enough to try and crawl away. She only made it a few feet before the man was on her again. He grabbed a large handful of her hair and dragged her to her feet.

"Is Kane bitch, nai?" a man asked in very poor English.

"Vai," the man holding her by the hair said.

Is that... it's Greek! The Thanos! No! How did they find me? Abby screamed internally. She could feel herself starting to panic and fought to stay calm.

"Take her," the man in shadows said.

Abby twisted herself and kicked the man holding her hair in the knee as hard as she could. She heard a yelp of pain as he let go of her hair. She fell away to the ground and quickly got up. The other man came around and stood in her way. She turned to find the man she had kicked standing behind her.

"You come with us and we do no harm to you," the man said.

The pale moonlight cast a light on the men's faces. One looked to be in his forties, tall with a dark olive complexion and curly black hair. The other looked to be in his early twenties with a distinctive long scar over his right eye.

"I'm not going anywhere with you!" Abby yelled. Before they could react, she lunged to her left and dropped to the ground. They had expected her to make a run for it and overshot her position by a few feet. It was all Abby needed.

She turned to face them and held her hand up in a stop motion. "Ovius Lotravtus!" she shouted. A wave of force shot from her hand knocking both men onto their backs.

Abby didn't waist her moment. She stood and began running towards Calder House. She remembered what Ms. Grace said. "If you are in danger come to the house," the words still rang in the recesses of Abby's thoughts as she fled her attackers. *Where is Josephine?* she thought. *I hope she's safe!* She could hear footsteps behind her. She pressed herself as fast as she could; running blindly in the darkness along the path.

She glanced back to see the two men lumbering towards her. Abby was uncertain she would make it to the house before they caught up. She put every ounce of her fiber into running as fast as she could.

The world went into a blur for a brief moment, as something caught Abby's foot. She slammed into the ground, face first, a sharp pain shot through her body. Abby batted her eyes trying to make sense of everything.

When the daze began to lift, Abby realized she was laying on her back one of the men had his boot on her chest.

"This magissa is more trouble than is worth," the younger man said, looking down at her like an animal.

They must not be witches, she realized.

"We waste no more time," the older man said. "Kill her."

Abby felt her heart leap into her chest. The young man pulled a small knife from his belt. Abby screamed.

"Shut up!" the older man kicked her in the side, pinning her with his foot. Abby let out a pathetic whimper.

Abby stared up at the trees her mind swimming in panic and horror. She could see the young man getting ready to stab her in the chest with the knife. *Is this it? Is it over?* she thought as her fate came to an edge. Abby's eyes focused on the tree branches above her. She then imagined them swinging down and knocking the two men away.

It took a moment. Abby blinked and then sat up. It wasn't her imagination. The two men were lying several feet away groaning in pain. She stood, her body riddled in pain. She could feel blood running down from her forehead and quickly wiped it away.

She took several steps towards the house and felt dizzy. She was feeling a bit confused but knew she needed to get to the house for her own safety. Abby caught herself stumbling and held a tree.

There was shuffling behind her and she looked to see the two men beginning to rise. She managed to move to the next tree without falling, her knees wobbling, her footing uncertain.

Abby could see Calder House through the trees and called out for help. "Ms. Grace! Josephine!"

"Get her!" The older man said. But the two of them paused. They obviously had hesitations about attacking her again.

Abby leaned against a tree, wiping more blood from her forehead. The men approached cautiously and Abby readied herself. She turned to face them, and focused on the ground beneath their feet. The men continued to approach, the younger of the two brandishing his knife.

Abby continued to focus as best she could. Her head was pounding in agony. Leaves began to spin at their feat causing the men to stop in their tracks. Abby continued to concentrate, breathing heavily. She felt like she was going to pass out at any moment. She fought to keep her eyes open, to concentrate on her spell.

Several tree roots shot out from the ground twisting and wrapping themselves around the two men's ankles. The two of them fought against the roots, kicking at them and striking them with a knife. Abby forced herself to the next tree. The blood was dripping from her forehead. She could see out of only one eye, the other having swelled shut. Abby was beginning to feel woozy.

"Get out of here!" the older one yelled freeing himself from the roots. He gave Abby a glare and began running into the dense part of the woods.

The younger one struggled to free himself and eventually pulled his foot free. "House of Kane!" he cursed, spitting on the ground. He ran off into the darkness of the woods in the same direction as his partner.

Abby forced herself to the next tree. Her head was pounding. She reached out for the next tree and stumbled. She missed the tree and fell to the cold hard ground. Another set of aches jolted through her body.

She tried to get up, and stumbled onto her hands and knees. The house was only a few yards away.

Abby began crawling fighting to keep her eye open and focused on the door. Nearly every corner of her body was in agonizing pain. Every movement she made came at a price as her body protested against her efforts to reach the front door.

Abby's hands pulled her closer and closer to safety. Blood dripped from her forehead onto the path in front of her. She could feel her eye drooping, almost impossible to keep open. When she reached the first of three steps up to Ms. Grace's front door, she stopped to rest.

She called out, but she was uncertain her cry for help could be heard all the way down in the sanctum. "Somebody…"

Abby pulled herself up one step. Then the next. Abby was certain she would throw up and paused, not wanting to risk it. Her stomach settled and she crawled one last step.

Abby stared up at the latch willing herself to reach up and push the door open. She concentrated, willing herself to move further, but her body did not respond. As Abby strained to move her body failed her. She crumbled limp on the stone steps.

She could feel her shallow breathing as she lay against the freezing cold stone. She was fading. Abby blinked. *Am I going to die?* she wondered through the confusion. It was her last thought as the world faded into darkness.

CHAPTER TWENTY

Abby opened her eyes. Only one opened fully, the other managed only a thin crack. It was swollen shut. She glanced around and found herself in a small bedroom with floral wall paper and a slanted ceiling. There was a window to her left with the shades closed. It looked strangely familiar and then she realized, *this is Ms. Grace's guestroom.*

She looked down and saw Benjamin was holding her hand, his face covered in worry and frustration. She squeezed his hand and he looked up to see her awake, staring at him. She was relieved to see Benjamin's face soften the moment he realized she was awake. He leaned over and gave her a gentle kiss on the cheek. It was the only thing that didn't seem to hurt, Abby realized, as a rush of pain hit her all at once. She as unable to stifle a whimper.

"Josephine! I think they got Josephine!" she said doing her best to sit up. The pain paralyzed her and she fell back against the pillows.

"I'm fine," Josephine's voice came from the direction of the door. Abby glanced over and saw Josephine and Ms. Grace standing nearby.

A sense of relief washed over her upon seeing her friend was alright. She rubbed her head, offering no relief from the physical pain that screamed all over her body, none worse than her forehead. "What time is it?" she managed to force the words from her throat.

"About two-thirty in the morning," Benjamin answered.

"You gave us quite a scare," Ms. Grace stated. Despite her stoic tones, Abby could tell she was worried.

"Did Edgar do this?" Benjamin asked impatiently.

"No," she said as she trailed off into her own thoughts, doing the best she could to remember what happened. She was having a hard time sorting through her memories. Random flashes of blades and thick accents. She then turned to Josephine. "What happened to you? Are you alright?"

"I'm fine. Someone grabbed me and knocked me out. I didn't see anything until I woke up and found you on the doorstep," Josephine explained.

"Maybe we should let her rest," Ms. Grace suggested.

"I'm not leaving her side," Benjamin said harshly.

As she stared at Benjamin, her thoughts began to come together. She did her best to piece together what she could remember. "I was walking to the house with Josephine," Abby said. Everyone's attention turned back to her as she lay in bed wrapped tightly under the blankets. "There were two men in the forest along the path." She struggled to stay focused. The pain was so distracting, and her thoughts wanted to run away from her. "They attacked me." She took a deep breath, wincing as a sharp pain pulsed in her side.

"Who were they?" Benjamin asked, only barely containing his anger.

"They wanted me to come with them." Her words were slurred and forced. "They barely spoke English," she added closing her eyes for a moment as she spoke of her fragmented memories.

"Did she fall back to sleep?" Josephine asked after a few seconds.

Abby shook her head no and instantly regretted the effort. Pain seemed to be coming from every part of her body. "I think I heard them speaking Greek," she said weakly She felt like her head was going to split in two.

"Thanos!" Benjamin spit the name out like a curse word. "They'll pay for this Abby, I swear it!"

"No!" Abby cried squeezing his hand tightly. "No," she repeated weakly. "I don't want you going anywhere near them."

"Did you kill them?" Josephine asked.

"No. They got away," Abby said.

"I'll kill them myself," Benjamin growled through gritted teeth.

"Let's not make any decisions about what we're going to do this evening," Ms. Grace interjected. "Whoever the culprits are, they have likely taken their leave. Right now, what is important is nursing you back to health."

Benjamin looked at Abby as though she were so fragile his mere gaze would shatter her into a million pieces. He nodded his agreement, his anger seemed to soften slightly.

"I will collect some healing agents from the sanctum. They should ease the pain and hopefully help you sleep," Ms. Grace stated, excusing herself and stepping out.

Josephine moved closer and sat at the end of the bed "We've already treated most of the wounds," she said. "It shouldn't be more than a day or two before the worst of your injuries will heal."

"Thank you," Abby said. "Did they hurt you?"

"Just a bump on the head. I still have a lingering headache but I'm fine, compared to what you went through," Josephine explained.

"Thank you for not sending me to the hospital," she said looking over to Benjamin.

"Ms. Grace has a fine arsenal of healing reagents, so you were spared the trip," he smiled kissing her hand delicately.

"They know where I am," Abby said, feeling so weak and vulnerable she could feel a tear welling in her eye.

"It isn't safe for you anymore," Josephine stated the obvious. Benjamin glared at Josephine, it was obvious there was friction between the two of them.

"What's wrong?" Abby asked.

Benjamin's anger retreated when he turned his gaze back to Abby. "It's nothing. Josephine has been going on and on about how it's not safe for you here anymore for the last four hours. I've heard enough. She thinks you should leave," he said doing his best to contain his irritation.

"Just a few days ago, you were trying to get me to move, too," she said quietly.

"To our house, not out of the country!" he growled. Abby gave a start.

"She might not be wrong, though" Abby said meekly. "I have to think about what to do next. It clearly isn't safe for me here right now, and it would kill me if anything happened to you, or my friends just because I was here."

Benjamin looked stricken. "Abby, you can't! I'm not letting you lea—" he started.

Ms. Grace returned with a small wooden box full of bottles filled with ointments and tinctures. "Alright," she said walking around to the far side of the bed and pulling up a wooden chair. She put on her reading glasses and began sorting through the contents. "Where does it hurt the most, dear?" she asked in the closest thing to a motherly voice Abby had ever heard the older woman use.

"My forehead," Abby said.

"That is what I thought," She pulled out a small pink bottle and removed the cork from the top. She put it under her nose briefly and pulled it away with a repulsed look. "This is the one," she stated, quickly putting on a smile as though everything was going to be fine. She pulled out a dropper and dipped it into the pink bottle. "Open up," she said.

After Ms. Grace's repulsed look, Abby was uncertain, but complied. The older woman held the dropper over Abby's open mouth and let a single drop of greyish liquid fall onto her tongue.

The most repulsive taste Abby had ever experienced assaulted her taste buds. She nearly gagged and coughed painfully. It only took a few moments for the taste to go away and Abby took a deep breath of relief.

"It won't take long before you should feel some relief. Then I'll give you something for sleep," Ms. Grace said, returning the vial back into her small wooden box, and retrieved a light blue colored bottle. She then looked to Benjamin and gave him a kind smile. "We should let her sleep. She will recover soon enough."

"I'll sleep right here," Benjamin said. He clearly wasn't going to budge from his chair.

"Open wide," Ms. Grace said, returning her attention to Abby.

Abby regarded her with uncertainty. The last treatment was dreadful. She felt uncertain she could handle another tincture that tasted so dreadful.

"This one isn't as bad, I assure you," Ms. Grace prompted. It was that moment when Abby began to feel the pain in her head begin to dull. A wave of relief rushed through her mind as she felt only the faintest hint of discomfort. Abby opened her mouth and Ms. Grace leaned forward allowing a small drop of white liquid to fall onto Abby's tongue. "There now, that wasn't so bad was it?" she replaced the cork stopper and placed the bottle gingerly back into the box.

Abby paused for a moment in contemplation. There was only a dull sour taste with a hint of citrus. "No, not so bad," she agreed.

"The treatment should take effect in five to ten minutes," Ms. Grace explained.

"How did they find me?" Abby asked, her thoughts returning to the two men who had attacked her. She could still see their faces, the very thought quickened her heart.

"We aren't certain," Benjamin said.

"The Thanos family are witches," Ms. Grace reminded them, "There are many ways to employ occult powers to find people. Abby herself has a power that could be set to such purposes, with the right training."

"I thought you said my gift is rare." Abby said, already beginning to feel the pull of slumber.

"It is true, but there are other kinds of magic. The Thanos family are Necromancers. They commune with the dead. They use the spirits of those who have passed on as their servants, spies, even as weapons."

Abby remembered her last birthday at the hotel, when the Thanos attacked. She remembered being in her room with a deranged spirit choking her to death. It was a horrifying memory, one she had done well to suppress all this time.

"See? Running wouldn't do any good if they can find you again," Benjamin said glancing at Josephine. "Perhaps we should hole-up and be ready for them when they return."

"That doesn't seem wise," Josephine said. "Abby already said she wouldn't want to put any of us in the line of fire. We should respect her wishes."

"Why don't we allow ourselves to sleep on this," Ms. Grace stated. "We are unlikely to suffer another attack tonight, and it would be best if we considered the options when we are rested and at our best."

"They didn't bother to come after me themselves," Abby said.

"What do you mean?" Benjamin asked.

"They weren't witches," she said. "The men who attacked me. They called me a 'Maggisa.' It's the Greek word for witch. They were surprised when they realized and fled shortly after I started using magic against them."

"I wonder if they were awakened witch bounty hunters?" Ms. Grace speculated aloud.

"Once word returns to the Thanos that their minions failed to kill you, they may very well send one of their own," Josephine suggested.

"Wouldn't they assume she fled?" Benjamin said. "We could hide nearby, set a trap and take them out."

Abby could see the weighted pull of sleep quickly approaching. "I... I..." she said unable to finish her thought as it drifted away, and the waves of slumber pulled her under.

Abby slowly took each step cautiously down the stairs. Though she was feeling better her body was still recovering from the harsh beating she took in the attack. When she reached the bottom Ms. Grace quickly moved to help her take a seat at the kitchen table.

"You poor dear," Ms. Grace said sympathetically. "I can tell you are much better." It was clear she was trying to offer some hope.

"I do feel better. I'm still stiff from the swelling," Abby said with a big yawn.

"Are you hungry?" Ms. Grace asked, collecting a plate from her kitchen cupboard.

"I could eat," Abby said. Even though her stomach was rumbling the pain did little to awaken her appetite.

Moments later Ms. Grace placed a plate in front of Abby with a scrambled egg and a piece of toast. She looked at it with little interest but forced herself to smear marmalade on the toast and take a small bite.

"We should talk about what to do next," Ms. Grace stated taking a seat with a cup of tea. "Especially while Mr. Hodge is out."

"Where did he go?" Abby asked curiously.

"I insisted if he was going to sit by your side all day he at least speak to his professors this morning and get his assignments," Ms. Grace explained.

"I don't want to put anyone in danger." Abby said succinctly.

"That will be very difficult to do, Miss Kane," Valerie said taking a sip of her tea. "We've all become rather fond of you, especially Benjamin. I don't think he will leave your side, regardless of how much you might protest."

She's probably right, Abby thought. *I don't want to leave him, but I can't put him in danger. Josephine already got hurt because of me.*

"What would you do if you were in my situation?" Abby asked, looking for some guidance in the sea of indecision laboring her thoughts.

Ms. Grace regarded her with the same uncertainty Abby felt. "I don't envy your dilemma. There is no clear and certain solutions to your problem. If there was, it wouldn't be so hard for you to make a choice. You can go on the run, but it is likely they will find you again the same way they found you this time. You would be away from family, friends and resources. You would be potentially vulnerable if they were to find you flat footed again," She paused to take another sip of her tea. "If you stay, you can fortify yourself and cultivate the support of your friends and the resources at our disposal."

"Putting everyone in danger... for me..." Abby said trailing off into thoughts of seeing her friend's dead on the floor, just like her parents. She quickly blinked the imagery away. It was too much.

"There is no right choice here, Abigail," Ms. Grace stated. "The decision must be yours. If I were still your guardian, I would choose for you to stay where I could protect you. As it stands it is not my decision. You are an adult now."

"What about the school?" Abby asked. "I wouldn't want to invite an attack on the school where students could be hurt, or perhaps even worse." Abby thought about everyone she knew on campus; the teachers, students, her friends. None of them deserved to be caught in the crossfire. She couldn't bear the thought of anything happening to Sarah or Nina simply because they were unfortunate enough to be her roommates. She needed to get away from the school and find somewhere the Thanos would not immediately expect to find her.

"Is there something wrong?" Ms. Grace asked. "You went quiet, quite suddenly."

"Sorry," Abby shook her head and pulled herself back into the moment. "Something you said made me remember something."

"Oh?" Ms. Grace asked nursing her tea.

"You mentioned a safe house," Abby said. "What if I were to rent one of the small cottages just outside the village. If the Thanos return to the school they wouldn't find me there and they might assume I fled."

Ms. Grace raised an approving eyebrow. "I could certainly help you mystically fortify the house," she said, considering Abby's idea thoughtfully. "It would likely only buy you time. How much is uncertain, but… some."

"I only need to buy time until this conflict is over once and for all," Abby said.

"Your grandmother seems convinced this conflict will be over soon," Ms. Grace stated. "I realize Vivian Kane has a flare for the dramatics, but when it comes to such matters I would trust in her word."

"I hope you're right," Abby said.

"If this is what you are choosing to do, I will support you," Ms. Grace stated. "I will arrange for you to finish your course work from home. It wouldn't be hard to arrange for, after this recent injury of yours. If we are going to lead the Thanos to believe you've fled, it would be best if you were not seen around campus."

Abby could feel her heart sink. *I just became the concert mistress,* she thought, realizing she would have to give up something that meant a great deal to her. Abby could feel the waters of grief welling in her eyes. She batted them away and took a deep breath. *This is what I need to do,* she thought. *There's no more time to be a kid anymore. Grow up Abby.*

"You're right," Abby managed to mumble. She picked at her toast taking another bite.

"I'll start putting together some rituals we can use to protect your home. Keep in mind, nothing we can cast will stop them. It will only weaken and slow them. You will still need to be prepared," Ms. Grace said, excusing herself from the table and placing her teacup and saucer next to the sink, before heading down into her sanctum.

Abby forced herself to eat several more bites. She could feel the burden of trying to protect the people she loved, when she was the target of a murderous family of death witches. *Run, Abby. Leave them all behind. Do it for their own good. The only way you can keep Benjamin and the others safe is if you disappear.* She pushed the nagging thoughts aside and gently felt the swollen left side of her face.

She was startled when the front door swung open. Benjamin stepped through, looking surprised to see Abby sitting up at the table.

"You're already up and around?" Benjamin observed with uncertainty.

"Barely." Abby smiled weakly. "I feel a bit better."

Benjamin set his book bag down on one of the chairs and leaned down to give Abby a soft kiss on the head. "I'm glad you feel better. After last night, I never imagined you would be better so quickly."

"I think Ms. Grace used the good stuff," Abby commented. "I'm still tired."

"Do you want to go back to bed?" Benjamin asked as he took a seat next to her.

"No. I'm tired of sleeping too," she jested.

"A sense of humor. That's a good sign," Benjamin smiled. Abby was relieved to see he didn't seem angry anymore.

Abby stared down at the saucer and dry piece of toast. Her thoughts whirled like a storm. She did her best to pull the words she wanted to say from the chaos.

"What's wrong?" Benjamin asked, noticing her silence.

"I want to apologize," Abby said. "For being so cold and distant this last week," she added meekly.

Benjamin put his finger under Abby's chin and lifted her head, meeting her eyes. He leaned in and gave her a soft kiss on the lips. "I'm the one who should apologize. I was angry and frustrated. I said things I didn't mean."

"You meant them," Abby said. "You aren't wrong. I can be naïve sometimes. If it wasn't true, it wouldn't have bothered me so much when you said it. I just think there's enough evidence to suggest we might be wrong about Edgar."

"Right or wrong, it doesn't matter. He's the least of our worries at the moment. I won't let anything happen to you. I swear it."

Abby closed her eyes and shook her head no. "Benjamin please. I don't want you playing the hero. If the Thanos come around I want, you to run. I want you to get away as quickly as you can."

"Not without you," Benjamin said.

"This is what I was afraid of," Abby said under her breath. She searched for something she could say that would convince him, but she could see it in his eyes. He would not be dissuaded. *Even if I ran he'd come looking for me,* she thought.

Benjamin reached over and took her hand. "We're going to get through this together. Besides, this conflict with the Thanos, will be over soon."

Abby gave him an uncertain look and conceded. "Grandmother rarely fails to come through on her promises," she admitted.

"So, where are we moving to?" Benjamin asked eagerly.

Abby chuckled. "We haven't quite gotten that far into the plan yet. And I never actually said you were coming with me."

"Deal with it, love. I'm not going to leave you alone again," Benjamin said kissing her thoroughly.

Abby threw her book bag down on the bed and quickly switched out the books from her morning classes with the ones from her afternoon classes.

"Why are you in such a hurry?" Nina asked. "I can't imagine any class that exciting."

"It's music theory," Abby explained. "Professor Milliner is a stickler about being on time. Besides, he's annoyed with me for missing so much of his class before the holiday."

"Good luck," Sarah commented as Abby flew out the door to try and make it across campus in time.

She rushed down the stairs and through the commons bursting out into the courtyard. Students littered the yard, milling about and wandering towards their afternoon classes. Abby slowed down and carefully weaved her way through foot traffic.

Out of the corner of her eye, Abby saw something... someone... She paused and looked in the direction of the main building. There near the main entrance was a young woman her age. She had long blonde hair, pretty, with brown eyes. There was something familiar about her. The young woman made eye contact with Abby, a smile forming at the corner of her lips.

There was something haunting Abby's thoughts and she couldn't help but take a few steps towards the young woman. She hadn't taken more than a few steps when a wave of horror rippled through her body. *Emily!*

Abby's heart began pounding in her chest, as adrenaline coursed through her veins. She blinked several times testing her vision, hoping her imagination was getting the better of her. Every time her eyes opened Emily was still there.

"Emily," Abby whispered under her breath as students moved around her on their way to class. She took another step and Emily's smile melted away. She turned and looked behind her as if something or someone was coming after her. She then turned to face Abby. Emily's mouth moved as if she was trying to say something, but no sounds escaped her throat. There was a growing expression of urgency on her face as she continued saying something. Nothing but silence escaped her lips.

As Abby grew closer, Emily's expression evolved to panic. The formation of her lips gave the word form without sound.

Run!

Just as Abby realized what the apparition was trying to tell her, she saw Emily's skin begin to turn a sickly pale white. Emily dropped to her knees, the flesh on her face began to rot away before Abby's very eyes. Within seconds Emily was little more than a skeleton that collapsed onto the ground breaking apart into a million pieces.

Abby stood in horror, staring at the bones lying on the school courtyard. Students passed unnoticing. Only Abby saw the grizzly scene fate had shown her. *Why is she telling me to run? Why is she warning me? Is her killer nearby?* Abby looked around the courtyard looking for some familiar face, as though she would know the killer instantly if she saw them.

Then something caught Abby's eye. Two men emerged from the doors of the main building. One was tall and wearing a black suit he had black hair slicked back and wore a pair of sunglasses despite the overcast sky. The man next to him was slightly shorter and younger, wearing a baseball cap, a black shirt and blue jeans. The man in the business suit turned to the younger man and said something. He wasn't speaking English.

Neither man looked familiar and strangers were a rarity on campus. A terrible feeling came over Abby and she quickly turned away before they could take notice of her. Abby pulled the hood of her jacket over her head and started in the direction of the music hall.

It's time to get the hell out of here... she thought. *Why was Emily trying to warn me? What is her connection to me? If they were agents of the Thanos, what is their connection to Emily?... maybe a safe house doesn't sound like such a bad idea after all.*

CHAPTER TWENTY ONE

"It's really nice," Nina said looking around the empty living room. "Lots of space. From the outside, it didn't look as big."

It was a small house with two bedrooms, two bathrooms and a kitchen and dining room. It was quaint, painted in neutral tones. The cream-colored carpets matched the dull white walls and ceiling. It was a barren cottage of stone and wood, alluding to the promise of being a home. Abby loved everything about it.

"When are you going to get some furniture?" Warren asked.

"I have some coming this afternoon and the rest tomorrow," Abby said showing them the bathroom and then opening the door to reveal a stairwell. "Down here is a basement. It's quite large and the washing machine is down here," she explained, turning on the lights and escorting them into a large open area that spanned the entire floor space of the house.

Heavy beams supported the floors above and several pillars provided additional support. Small windows near the ceiling allowed a small filter of sunlight in from outside.

"What are you going to do with all this empty space?" Sarah asked.

"I haven't decided yet. I'm probably not going to be here long enough to bother, really," Abby couldn't tell them she was going to turn it into the beginnings of her sanctum. She still felt bad about telling them a lie. Perhaps it was because she had been telling so many of them since she decided to move out of the dorm.

Sarah approached Abby and gave her a gentle hug. "I'm sorry this happened to you," she said remorsefully. Her huge brown eyes melted Abby's heart. She felt like a horrible person for the cover story she gave them.

"To imagine, your parent's killer found you here of all places," Warren said shaking his head. *At least that part isn't a lie,* she thought.

"You must keep it quiet," Abby said. "They're so close to catching him we don't want the media to tip him off."

"To think, one of your father's business associates became so obsessed with you to do this!" Nina shook her head in horror. *That one is though,* she tucked her guilt away, reassuring herself once more that she would have told them the truth, if circumstances were different. *This is for their own good, Abby, you know that.*

"Are you sure this is safer than campus?" Sarah asked.

"I can't stay and put any of you at risk," Abby said. "This is safer for you. Besides if he's still around watching the campus he isn't going to see me. Hopefully he'll think I fled, and move on. Or, preferably they'll catch him."

189

"It's so creepy," Warren said, shivering.

"The local authorities are aware of what is going on and they plan to keep a close eye on me, until they catch him," Abby explained. The lie was getting so much deeper, she wondered if it wouldn't have been better to simply disappear. But she couldn't do that to them. Not after the same thing happened to Emily.

"Where is Benjamin?" Nina asked curiously.

"He's in Bristol with his father. He'll be back before dark," Abby reassured. She could tell they were worried about her being alone.

"We have to go,' Sarah said looking at the time on her phone. "We'll be by tomorrow to bring your homework. Ms. Grace has arranged for me to collect it every other day and bring it out to you."

"Thank you, Sarah. I couldn't have better friends," Abby said.

"Take care of that shiner," Warren teased, giving her a brief hug, before following Sarah up the stairs.

"Really Abby, if you need anything we're all glad to help," Nina told her while giving Abby a hug. She then excused herself and followed the others.

Abby strolled over to one of the windows that gave her a good view of the driveway. She watched as her friends piled into Warren's car and drove away. Abby waved, even though she knew they couldn't see her.

I'll miss seeing them every day, she thought. She looked around at her barren house. Her new home, for now at least.

No time like the present, Abby told herself. She then turned and made her way over to a wooden table next to the washer and dryer. There was a small wooden box sitting at the center. Abby opened the lid and pulled out several powders and dried herbs. Next, she pulled out a sheet of paper with a ritual written in Ms. Grace's steady hand.

"The Hearth Ritual," Abby read aloud. "Combining the ingredients below will create a fine powder. Sprinkle this along the bottom of every entrance into the house, including your windows. If someone enters your home with the intent to cause you direct physical harm, you will experience a tingling sensation along your spine."

Sounds useful, Abby thought as she reviewed the instructions more closely. She followed the instructions carefully, creating a small bowl of powder. Abby went through the entire house sprinkling the fine powder over every window seal and at every outside door.

"That was easy enough," Abby said to herself, putting away the remaining components of the Hearth Ritual. She glanced at the cardboard box on the floor next to the table. It held the components to several other rituals Ms. Grace had prepared for her. It brought a great deal of peace of mind to have someone looking out for her like Ms. Grace.

Abby went upstairs and worked on some school work for a while. It wasn't long before the delivery men brought her bed, dining room set, and a couch. Having at least three pieces of furniture in the house made it start to feel like it was coming together. *A real home,* she thought with a smile.

With the table, Abby had a new work space and pulled out a check from her purse. She placed it in an envelope and sealed it. She carefully addressed it to her new land lord and placed a stamp in the top right corner.

It's officially my place, Abby thought, looking around and taking in her new home. Even though she knew it was temporary, she couldn't help but fantasize about the conflict with the Thanos being over and staying in this quaint little cottage living a peaceful life. *Perhaps if things work out I'll keep it for a while, use it as my base of operations through gap year,* she thought.

She got up and headed out the front door up the driveway towards the postbox. She placed the envelope into the box and turned to return to her house. Abby froze in her spot. She blinked wondering if she trusted her eyes and there he was. Edgar Kincaid, jogging down the road in her direction. Abby was caught off guard and wasn't certain what to do. She then realized this road was frequently used by the track and field team for training. She had seen them using it before.

As he came closer he slowed down. Clearly, he intended to stop. Abby could feel her heart pounding in her chest. Despite having doubts that he was responsible for Emily's disappearance, Benjamin would be furious if Edgar knew where she was staying.

Edgar looked at her curiously and glanced at the house at the end of the driveway and back at her. "What are you doing out here?" He asked in his deep gruff voice.

"Nothing," Abby said. "Just checking in on a friend."

"You don't have to lie," Edgar said dismissively. Abby looked at him curiously. He knew she was lying. How did he…?

"How did you know I was different?" Abby asked curiously, trying to dismiss her lie. He obviously wasn't planning to attack her. She would no doubt already be dead if that was his intent. *Unless of course he enjoys playing with his targets,* Abby thought and quickly pushed it aside.

"You mean a witch?" He raised an eyebrow at her. "I didn't know that part, I could tell you were different the same way I could tell you just lied to me," Edgar said. "I can smell it"

Abby looked at him with uncertainty. "Smell it?" she asked making sure she heard him right. She wasn't sure if she should be horrified or intrigued.

"When people lie their scent changes," Edgar said gruffly.

"Have you been able to… smell, others like me?" Abby asked curiously.

"Yes," Edgar said letting his response linger for a moment. "The Hodge twins and the deputy headmistress have the same kind of scent."

He knows! Abby realized. She calmed her initial sense of panic, hoping he didn't notice. "What else can you do?" Abby asked cautiously. The last time they spoke their conversation ended with him getting so angry at her questions she thought for certain he was going to crush her with his bare hands This time seemed to be going better, but she hadn't forgotten the murderous look in his eyes.

"Why do you care?" Edgar demanded. He was obviously very suspicious of Abby, she could see it in his body language.

Abby shook her head and shrugged. "I know it isn't always easy being different," she said. She could tell he was considering her words carefully. *Hopefully he can smell the truth in my words as well as the lies,* she thought. "Have you figured out what you are yet?" she asked cautiously.

There was a glint of red in his eyes. Abby instinctively stepped back, uncertain how he would react. Then his look softened slightly, his effort to do so seemed intentional to Abby. "No," Edgar said his eyes narrowed in on Abby. "What do you know about it?" He dropped his voice into a low growl.

Abby took a deep breath and considered her words carefully. "I know when you get angry there's a momentary flash of red in your eyes. I know you're physically strong, and based on the answer to one of my previous questions, you have a keen sense of smell. You seem angry all the time. In fact, I'm not certain I've even seen you once when you didn't seem ready to tear something apart."

Edgar held her gaze as she spoke. Abby could tell he didn't know if he could trust her, and thought perhaps she had gone too far. For some reason, she couldn't help herself. "I think there's something going on which you don't understand. I don't know what you are. I don't know if I can find answers for you, but I'm willing to help you try."

The young man looked taken aback for a brief second and quickly recovered regarding her with uncertainty. "Why?" he asked. It was almost more an accusation than a question.

"Why, what?" Abby asked taking another step back.

"Why are you willing to help me?" Edgar asked, reigning in his abrupt manner.

"When I first came to this school, I heard about Emily. Most people seemed to think you had something to do with her disappearance. I'm not so certain," Abby confessed. She became nervous when she saw the red glow appear in his eyes.

"Why are you having doubts? No one else in this school seems to have any. As far as they're all concerned I killed her and dumped the body where no one would find her," Edgar growled. There was a bitter anger in his words. Abby imagined it wasn't easy for him at the school under the looming suspicions and so many unanswered questions.

"Will you get angry if I tell you the truth?" Abby asked cautiously.

Edgar considered her question for a moment. "Probably," he said. "But I promise not to do anything to you," he added with surprising sincerity.

Abby hesitated for a moment. "I used a power on you once," she admitted, and waited for his reaction. Edgar maintained a stone-cold glare. The red glow in his eyes persisted. "I can sometime sense people's emotions. When I used it on you I could feel your grief," she continued cautiously. Edgar stared at her blankly, the red glow in his eyes softened. "It doesn't seem like the kind of thing a murderer would feel."

Edgar raised an eyebrow. She had obviously intrigued him. "But you're still not convinced," he stated.

"I don't know what to think," Abby confessed.

"What if I did kill her?"

"Then I think you did it accidentally," Abby said flatly. She could tell Edgar was studying her closely.

"What happened to your face?" Edgar asked unexpectedly.

"I was attacked," Abby said, unwilling to elaborate further. He waited for more of an explanation, but Abby wasn't about to go into details. She could tell he was nearly impossible to lie to, and she wasn't about to tell him the truth of her attack.

He broke eye contact and regarded the road in front of him. "I'll think about your offer," Edgar said, and abruptly continued to jog along the road.

Abby waited for him to disappear around a turn in the main road before heading back into the house. Her heart was racing. She wasn't certain what to think. *He didn't attack me. Maybe he's lulling me into a false sense of trust around him, so I'll let my guard down. Maybe he's waiting to do the same thing to me as he did to Emily, but... No that's not it. He had nothing but remorse on his mind when I used the Sight on him,* Abby engaged in an internal battle. In truth, she still didn't know what to think of Edgar Kincaid.

She went back into the house and locked the door behind her. Abby knew a locked door would do little good against someone like Edgar Kincaid, or even against the Thanos, but the act offered some small feeling of security at least.

Abby regarded the pile of home work she had placed on her new dining room table. Though she had been looking forward to using her shiny new piece of furniture, Abby couldn't get her mind off of Edgar knowing where she lived, and the security measures sitting in the box downstairs.

Abby made her way downstairs and put the large cardboard box on the table. She began sifting through the various rituals Ms. Grace had put together for her, and set herself to preparing them.

As the delivery men departed, Benjamin put his arm around Abby and gave her a kiss on the forehead. "The injury on your forehead looks a lot better." He said giving her a smile.

"Are you going to stick around for a while?" Abby asked hopefully.

"I don't think I shall ever leave," Benjamin said picking up a box and taking it into the kitchen. "You might be stuck with me for good." He warned playfully.

"Don't you have school today?" Abby commented as she began unpacking a box of new cutlery.

Benjamin shook his head. "No, Ms. Grace arranged the same deal for me as she did for you. I will be working from here," Benjamin explained.

"Benjamin, are you sure?" Abby gasped. "Leaving school early isn't a casual thing. You have so many commitments. What about the rowing team? Have you really thought about this?" she asked, her words coming out a jumble of excitement and worry.

"Of course, I have. I'm not letting you out of my sight, Abby. Not until the matter between your family and the Thanos is settled."

"It could be a while." Abby said. "I don't want you putting your life on hold because of me," she said remorsefully. She felt guilty for the impact her problems were having on his life.

"Then… Are you breaking up with me?" Benjamin asked as he began putting away several pots and pans.

"No," Abby said blatantly.

"Good, then I'm here to help you through this," Benjamin said. "Besides even if you did break up with me, I'd stay anyway," he added playfully.

"So, I have no say in the matter?" Abby asked with a smile.

"Not really," Benjamin winked at her.

"When did our relationship take a turn into the 1950's?"

"I was going for the 19th century vibe, but if you prefer the 50's." Benjamin joked, stealing a kiss as he walked by with another box full of kitchen things. "Do you really need all this stuff?" he asked sorting through more pots and pans.

"I don't know," Abby confessed, looking at all the things she had purchased for the house and realizing she had gone a bit over board. "I was thinking I might keep this place for a little while. Use it as my base of operations during gap year."

"You're not going to Julliard?" Benjamin asked, surprised.

"No," Abby said decisively. She turned to finish putting a new set of knives into the wooden block. "I've given it some thought," she explained. "There's no certainty the conflict between my family and the Thanos will be resolved before September, and… I want to earn my place in school. Not have it handed to me because my grandmother knows the right people."

"Are you sure?" Benjamin asked. "It seems like an incredible opportunity."

"It is," Abby conceded. "But I can't. Not if I'm going to believe in myself."

"How do you mean?" Benjamin asked pausing.

"I need to see if I really have what it takes to make it on my own. If I got to Julliard because of Vivian I'm always going to question myself; wonder if I am good enough to be there or, if I got in because my grandmother made it happen. I put my application in for Oxford the same time you did. They have an excellent music department, one of the best in the world. I want to see if I get in on my own merit."

Benjamin approached with a coy smile. "You're amazing Abigail Kane," he whispered, pulling her close and giving her a soft kiss on the lips. Abby wrapped her arms around him and nestled her head against his chest.

"I'm entirely too neurotic and spend way too much time in my own head," Abby said, savoring their intimate moment.

"We should finish putting everything away, so we can…" Benjamin said. "Fool around?"

"We haven't done enough of that lately," Benjamin jested. "Are you feeling well enough? You're not still in pain?"

"It's been almost a week," Abby said feeling where the large gash used to be on her forehead. The bruises were almost all gone. "I'm fine," she reassured.

Benjamin pulled away after giving her another kiss and started sorting through another box. "Good, then maybe you'll start eating again."

"What do you mean?" Abby asked. She had noticed her clothes were feeling a bit loose.

"You haven't eaten much since the attack. Ms. Grace noticed too," Benjamin said.

It was true, Abby noticed as she reflected on the last few days. Her stomach had been upset since the attack and she was feeling anxious and jumpy. "I guess the stress of everything has gotten to me more than I realized," Abby conceded.

There was a knock on the front door. Abby felt her heart leap into her throat. *Calm down Abby you're fine,* she reassured herself. "I'll get it," Benjamin said, putting his box aside before answering the door.

Abby took the brief pause to remind herself, *You're safe here, Abby. That's the whole point. The Thanos haven't found you again.* She just hoped this new safe house would prove worth of the name .

CHAPTER TWENTY TWO

"Pardon the intrusion. We thought we would drop by for a moment," Ms. Grace said, entering with Josephine behind her ".I have something for you I wanted to drop off."

"Ms. Grace, Josephine. What a surprise," Abby said warmly greeting them both. "Welcome to our little place."

"I knew when we saw this place it would turn out to be nice and cozy," Ms. Grace stated, looking around at the furniture.

It had come together nicely, Abby thought. The light blue love seat across from the cream-colored couch framed the fireplace nicely in the living room. "I'm happy with it," Abby said. "I plan to get some artwork for the walls, but it's nice. I feel like I can be comfortable here."

Josephine looked out the kitchen window at the back yard. "You have a lovely view of the woods," she commented. "It's a nice little place. You could have an herb garden out back if you wanted to."

"I was thinking that very thing, just yesterday," Abby smiled.

"I brought you this," Ms. Grace stated gesturing to the large box in her hands. "I know you have developed a taste for it over the last few months."

"I have?" Abby questioned curiously accepting the box from Ms. Grace and opening it. Inside was a fine porcelain tea set. "This is lovely, Ms. Grace. Thank you very much," she said, placing it on the counter and giving her mentor a hug. "I really don't know how to thank you for everything you've done for me." She had not known Ms. Grace even a year and yet she already felt like the older woman was a part of her family.

"It's my pleasure. It is a rare thing to have a student, one can be so proud of. All three of you have truly reminded me how much I enjoy teaching," Ms. Grace stated. From the way she spoke Abby was certain there was something more.

"Is there something wrong?" Abby asked.

"No, nothing wrong," Ms. Grace reassured. "I've decided this will be my last year teaching at Armitage Hall."

"Aren't you a bit young to retire?" Benjamin asked.

Ms. Grace pursed her lips and gave Benjamin an amused look. "I will take that as a compliment, Mr. Hodge," she said, soliciting a polite chuckle. "I have other passions. I've decided to pursue one of them a bit more diligently."

"Is it a secret you are going to tell us?" Abby smiled.

Ms. Grace smiled breaking away from her usual stoic self. "As you know I have a great passion for books. I've decided I will put my efforts into brokering in rare arcane texts. It's a rather small, specialized market, but I feel I would do quite well. I already have an impressive library and I would like to help others build their own."

"It sounds absolutely perfect," Abby said, imagining Ms. Grace in an enormous library sorting through books. It seemed like the perfect fit.

"Will you be staying in the village?" Josephine asked.

"No, I would think such an endeavor would be better suited in London. Don't you think?" Ms. Grace stated.

"What made you decide to move on and do something else?" Abby asked.

"I've accomplished a great many things as a teacher. When I look ahead, there are few things left to accomplish here. I need something new and fresh. This is something which I assure you I have been thinking about for many years," Ms. Grace explained. "Watching the three of you follow your dreams gave me pause to think about my own."

"What about other students like us?" Benjamin asked. "Where will they go?"

"Students like the three of you are rare. Most families prefer training their own children these days. I'm afraid the tradition of fostering has rather gone out of style. I guess it shouldn't be much surprise. Covens have grown more insular over the last decade or two. Politics have become increasingly polarized, and people are less ready to trust their offspring to others. It's quite alright. It gives me a chance to focus on other things." Ms. Grace explained.

"We are the lucky ones, Ms. Grace," Abby said warmly.

"Thank you, dear," Valerie smiled. "I should move along. Do you want a ride back to the school, Josephine?"

"I'll stick around and help for a spell," the young woman said, glancing around at the boxes recently delivered from London department stores.

"That's very kind," Ms. Grace stated and began to excuse herself.

"I'll walk you out," Abby followed Ms. Grace through the front door. She glanced back to be certain Benjamin and Josephine stayed behind. They were opening boxes and chatting quietly to each other. Abby turned her attention to Ms. Grace. "I wanted a moment with you if I may," Abby said.

"Of course, Is there something wrong?" she asked, a concerned look on her face as they approached her dark green Fiat.

"No… at least I don't think so," Abby said.

"If you are trying to convince me, you have failed miserably," Ms. Grace stated plainly, pursing her lips.

"Sorry. I don't know who else to talk to about this," Abby glanced back at the house, making sure Benjamin wasn't coming out to look in on them. "I had another encounter with Edgar," she whispered.

Ms. Grace looked at her with uncertainty. "Where?"

"Here," Abby said. "I was putting something in the post box and he was jogging along the road. He stopped, and we spoke... briefly," she explained.

"I see. Does Benjamin know?" Ms. Grace asked.

"No, and I'd prefer to keep it that way for now." Abby shook her head. "I think he would lose it. He would go after Edgar for sure, and I don't want Benjamin putting himself in danger. I don't completely trust his temper," she confessed.

Ms. Grace nodded her head. "He does have a particularly short fuse. Especially where you and your safety are concerned. He must care for you very deeply."

"It feels like it" Abby smiled. "I don't think Edgar killed Emily. I can't be certain, but I have a feeling he isn't responsible."

"For Mr. Kincaid's sake, I hope you're right," Ms. Grace stated.

"He doesn't know what he is, but he's trying to figure it out. I don't know what I was thinking, but I offered to help him find some answers," Abby said. She watched as Ms. Grace's eyes widened for a moment.

"You are an inherently kind and goodhearted young woman," Ms. Grace observed. "It's natural to want to help those in need. Edgar is an anomaly. Have you considered he has powers he doesn't know how to control. He could have killed Miss Wright accidentally. He could do the same to you."

"I've thought of that," Abby conceded. "I don't know what to do. That's why I'm telling you this."

Ms. Grace sighed and put her hands on her hips. "Why don't I come by tomorrow while Mr. Hodge is preoccupied with his own school assignments? I'll bring several of the books your grandmother sent, and we shall see if we can't narrow things down a bit for Mr. Kincaid. We can stick to the demonic half-breed theory for now, and broaden our search from there if we need to."

"Thank you, Ms. Grace," Abby said giving her a warm hug, an act of intimacy the older woman still accepted with awkwardness.

"You should reconsider telling Mr. Hodge after things settle," Ms. Grace said, opening her car door and getting in. "If he finds out you're keeping a secret like this from him, it could be catastrophic for your relationship."

"I know you're right," Abby said. "I'll give him some time to cool down a little more and then I'll tell him."

"Have a nice evening." Ms. Grace closed her car door and backed out of the driveway.

Abby watched her friend pull away, and waved as she sped down the road back to the school before heading back in. As she stepped into the front room she was met with silence. Benjamin and Josephine stopped their conversation abruptly.

"Did you want some privacy?" Abby asked uncertain what to say.

"No," Josephine said. "We were just talking about gap year and where Benjamin is planning to take you in the middle of July." She smiled brightly.

"My birthday?" Abby asked excitedly. "You better not try and surprise me, Mr. Hodge. You know how I hate surprises." She could tell Benjamin wasn't in the same playful mood he was in earlier.

"You're going to love it," he reassured her quietly.

"I'm sure I will." Abby was still feeling like there was something else going on, but she thought better of pressing them. For all she knew it was Hodge coven business, a topic that was truly none of her concern.

"Are you going to call your grandmother and tell her about the attack?" Josephine asked as she put some new kitchen gadgets into the dishwasher for sterilization.

"No," Abby said. "I thought about it. Ms. Grace seemed to think it would be a good idea, but I'm not as certain. I can't always trust my grandmother to handle things with a reasonable perspective. She's capable of some drastic things, and I'm not certain she would respect my wishes if she felt I was acting against 'Kane interests,'" she added the last with air quotes, trying to mimic Vivian's trademark haughtiness.

"Do you think she will imprison you and hide you away?" Josephine jested.

"I wouldn't put it past her," Abby confessed in all seriousness. "Maybe if there's another attack I'll tell her, but for now I want to wait for a bit. Besides she hasn't answered the phone the last three times I've tried to call her."

"Whatever you decide, we are with you, Abby," Benjamin insisted.

There was a thought that occurred to Abby, one that concerned her the moment it dawned on her. "Benjamin? Your involvement with me isn't going to cause any problems between you and your coven, will it?"

"No," Benjamin said. Abby glanced at Josephine to see if she agreed. The other girl seemed suspiciously quiet. "I doubt Vivian Kane would win any popularity contests in our family, but that isn't about you. You aren't her."

"But if you risk your life for me and help defend me against the Thanos, aren't you potentially dragging your family into the conflict?" Abby asked unable to shake the doubts flooding her mind. "If you kill one of the Thanos, you would become a target. You could drag your entire family into a war, because of me."

"That's not going to happen," Benjamin insisted.

"How do you know?" Abby asked searching for some kind of reassurance.

"He doesn't," Josephine interjected harshly. "We have no connection to the Thanos, so we cannot guarantee they will leave us out of it," she said to him.

"Stop it. You're not helping!" Benjamin yelled at his sister.

"Sorry. I'll go then," Josephine said, getting up and heading for the front door.

"We should take you back to campus," Abby said.

"Don't worry about me. School is less than a mile away. I could use a good walk." Josephine collected her jacket.

Benjamin turned and threw his sister the keys to his car. "I'll walk in tomorrow and pick up my assignments. You should drive back."

"It's fine." Josephine's words were clipped. Abby wasn't sure if it was because of what she said, or if she was angry at Benjamin over something.

"Abby didn't have a vision in which Edgar Kincaid kills *me*. Take the bloody car," Benjamin said, trying to reign in his irritation.

Josephine sighed and surrendered. "Fine. See you in the morning. Abby, I'll catch up with you later." She excused herself.

Abby stood quietly. *He's risking too much for me. I can't let him do this,* Abby said to herself repeatedly.

"Stop," Benjamin said, softly catching her eyes. "I know what's going through your head. I told you, we're in this together."

Abby nodded her head. "I can't ask you to do this for me," she said. The fear she had for Benjamin was overwhelming.

"You didn't ask. I'm here because I want to be here. My family must accept that. If they decide to get involved in the conflict because of me then it's all the better for us."

"How can you say that?" Abby questioned, her emotions beginning to break through her resolve. She could feel a panic building in her stomach.

"Because if my family gets involved that means the Thanos fight a war on two fronts. They wouldn't stand a chance. Besides based on what my father told me the other day, rumor has it the Thanos are already considering suing for peace," Benjamin said.

Abby's eyes went wide at the news "Are you sure?" She asked, uncertain. She wanted to believe what he said was true, but this was the first she'd heard of it.

"It's rumor, but based on the beating your family has given them thus far, it must be true. Besides, me being around could be a deterrent. The Thanos might hesitate to make another run at you with me around. They would be foolish to take the risk of bringing another family into the conflict against them," he explained. "No one wants a war."

Abby's head was still swimming with uncertainty. She wanted to believe him. Benjamin had never lied to her before. His words were not without reason. She shook her head and leaned against the counter. Her nerves were completely unhinged, and she could feel her strength being sapped by the fear she was fighting to keep in check.

Benjamin stepped forward and leaned down, looking Abby in the eye while holding her shoulders in his large hands. "Promise me you aren't going to run away or try and do something drastic for my own good. I've come to know you well enough to know how you think Abby. Don't do that to me. Please," he pleaded.

Abby's heart melted. There was no defense against Benjamin's pleading. "Alright," she agreed reluctantly. Benjamin abruptly pulled her into another long embrace. He stroked her hair, one of his favorite things to do when they were together.

Despite Benjamin's comforting embrace, Abby still felt profoundly worried. The Thanos did not seem like people who would be easily deterred. She could see how witches with power over death would have little fear of it. The more she thought about the dark figure in her visions and the two men who attacked her she could feel an overwhelming sense of dread wash over her

"What's wrong? You're trembling." Benjamin looked down into her face.

Abby pulled away and leaned against the counter. She was having a hard time breathing.

"What's wrong?" Benjamin asked, the worry in his voice did little to settle her nerves. "Come on and sit down for a second."

He guided Abby over to the couch where she sat with her head down near her knees. Abby concentrated on her breathing imagining she was exhaling every fear that plagued her mind. It took a minute before her breathing started to return to normal.

Abby shook her head, leaning back on the couch and closing her eyes.

"You've been working yourself up a lot lately," Benjamin observed cautiously. "You haven't been yourself since the attack."

"I'm sorry," Abby said, she was shaking.

"You don't need to be sorry Abby. Considering what you've been through this last year, you're entitled to a break down from time to time," Benjamin said lightly. He was obviously trying to help her feel better.

She took another deep breath and let it out slowly. "I feel a bit better," she said shakily.

"Why don't' you take a sip of that potion Ms. Grace gave you. Get some sleep. There isn't that much left to do around here," Benjamin suggested. "I can finish up, and you could use the sleep."

"Do I look that terrible?" Abby questioned allowing herself a brief dalliance with vanity.

"No," Benjamin said. He got up and went into the kitchen to retrieve the small bottle filled with the same glowing pink substance Ms. Grace had given her a few days earlier. "I've been sleeping next to you the last few nights. I know how restless these nights have been for you since the attack," he added, offering Abby the small bottle.

She took it and screwed off the lid, before taking a tiny sip. "I can start sleeping on the couch if I'm keeping you awake," she offered.

"Not a chance," Benjamin smiled. He then headed back into the kitchen to return the potion. "You're my human heating pad." He laughed from the next room.

Abby chuckled. *It feels good to laugh about something,* she thought. "I'm glad to be useful for something," she called out, then stood. "I'm going to go lay down. It won't take long for the potion to kick in. The last time I barely made it to the bed."

"I'll look in on you later," Benjamin said, returning his attention to the boxes.

Abby started feeling groggy before she even made it up the stairs. She crawled into bed and pulled the warm soft comforter over her. Nestling her head on the pillow and let out a deep sigh. The draw of sleep was so strong Abby welcomed it without a fight.

Abby stepped out onto the back porch of her new house. It had been three weeks since they had moved in, and she was finally starting to feel comfortable in her new place. The anxiety was better, and sleep was beginning to become more peaceful. She sat at a small bistro table with her coffee and gazed out into the dense woods no more than a few yards from her back porch.

"It's nearly spring," Benjamin said, coming out the back door to join her. She looked over to see he was holding a small pile of mail in his hands.

"I know. Spring and Fall are my favorite times of the year," she commented with a contented sigh. "Is that really all our mail?"

"Yes," Benjamin said, placing it on the table as he took his seat. "Advertisements mostly." He sifted through the letters. His cheery demeanor melted away quite suddenly as he held a letter up for closer inspection.

"What's wrong?" Abby asked uncertain what could be so ominous about a piece of mail. Benjamin looked at the letter and then to Abby. He seemed angry. Benjamin slowly turned the letter around for Abby to see. It was clearly addressed to her with a normal postage stamp. The return address was from Edgar Kincaid.

"Why is he sending me a letter?" Abby asked, somewhat confused.

"My question exactly," Benjamin said handing the letter to Abby.

She held it in her hands for a moment and tore open the side, pulling out a hand-written note. Abby unfolded the note and saw it consisted of two words and his signature.

> *I accept.*
> *Edgar*

Abby swallowed the anxiousness swelling in her throat. She was going to have to tell Benjamin, there was no way around it now. She handed the note to Benjamin to read for himself. He eagerly snatched the paper and furrowed his brows in confusion.

"What's this supposed to mean? I accept? Abby what is he accepting?" Benjamin asked. She could tell he was getting more upset with every word, and she knew that when she answered him, he was likely going to lose his temper again.

She took a deep breath and steadied herself for the explosion. "My help," she answered honestly.

"Your help?" Benjamin questioned as though he was uncertain he heard her correctly. "Your help with what exactly?"

"I told him I would help him figure out what he is," Abby said as if she were ripping the deceit off like a Band-Aid.

"What? When?" Benjamin asked his voice raised.

"About three weeks ago," Abby said.

"Where did you see him? How does he know you live here?" Benjamin asked. His questions came at such a fast pace she was beginning to get flustered. "What would possess you to do this? You saw what he did to Josephine in your vision! Do you have some kind of death wish?"

Abby stared forward at the trees as Benjamin yelled at her. She knew there was no point in answering him while he was like this. His words began to fade into angry tones, mumbled incomprehensibly. She saw the budding leaves and the first hint of green returning to a world consumed by wintry death. She could feel the warmth from the sun on her face. She closed her eyes.

Then she felt someone take her hands. Abby opened her eyes. Benjamin was kneeling in front of her, holding both her hands. He didn't seem angry anymore, only worried. "I'm sorry I was yelling," he said. "Help me understand what's going on."

A tear ran down her cheek as she gazed into his eyes. A strange peace settled inside of her. It was peculiar and unfamiliar. "You're so angry all the time. I can't talk to you about things," she said almost serenely.

Benjamin seemed surprised. "Abby I don't' want that." He said looking away briefly as though he felt guilty. "There isn't anything I want more than for you to be safe."

The place of peace Abby inhabited began to evaporate as emotions crashed upon her emotional sanctuary. "Ms. Grace and I are going to help him," she explained. "Perhaps if he better understood what he is, we can deter him away from the events that took place in my vision."

"Or it could set into motion everything that will lead up to what you saw. Abby, he's dangerous," Benjamin persisted catching his raised voice. "I don't' know what to say anymore. The guy hurt you and now you want to help him? You are one of the kindest most compassionate people I've ever met, but this is too much. I can't go let you out of my sight without wondering if your safe." Benjamin stood. His increasing restlessness was obvious. "I can't sleep at night. It's already hard enough knowing the Thanos family is after you. I can't take this anymore, Abby!" He started to walk away.

"Benjamin!" She called after him.

"I just… need a moment," he said, and disappeared back into the house.

Abby sat frozen in her chair. She didn't know what Benjamin would do. Clearly, he was at some breaking point. It as a familiar place, she knew it well. Abby felt bad that Benjamin was so upset, but there was a part of her that felt relieved she wasn't hiding it from him anymore. She couldn't change who she was just because it was hard for him.

She stood and pulled her light jacket tightly around her. Abby maneuvered down the three steps from her back patio onto the grass. She needed to get away for a few minutes, too. She walked across her small lawn into the tree line.

Abby stepped into the woods. A few yards into the woods, she started to see patches of lingering fog; signs of a winter caught beneath the tree branches.

Something called out to her, drawing her deeper into the woods. Abby glanced back, but her house was no longer visible. She had gone much further than she realized.

Her vision began to blur. There was a strange flash. Something was happening, to her. Abby reached out and used the tree to hold her balance as her heart rate quickened. There was another flash, and an image came through; blood. She looked up and saw a gnarled old elm, its trunk stained with blood.

It's the Sight, she told herself. *What is it trying to show me?* She knelt and sat on the forest floor, leaning her back against a tree. She took several deep breaths and concentrated, pouring her focus into the Sight.

The forest began to take shape in her mind, as if a second forest visible only to her intuitive perception was laid over top of the physical forest she was in. Waves of images came at her in a flurry. Trees, bushes, birds and various wildlife flew through her mind as if she was running full-speed through the woods of her mind.

All at once, everything came to a sudden stop. She was sitting in the forest, in the middle of the night. The mood offered a pale light, barely enough to see by. It gave the forest an eerie feeling. She could hear rushed footsteps in the far distance. Then abruptly, the steps broke out into a run.

Abby looked in the distance and saw a young woman about her own age running towards her. As she came closer, Abby could see the panicked look on the girl's face. She was running from something, or someone. Abby thought the girl looked familiar, and tried to place where she'd seen her before.

Blonde hair fluttered behind the girl as she ran, a look of sheer terror in her blue eyes. Abby remembered the vision from when she'd first arrived, and the lifeless melting in Edgar's arms. *It's Emily!*

"Emily!" Abby shouted. She wasn't sure if she used her mind to scream the name, or her voice. The girl continued running as though Abby didn't exist. A second pair of footsteps approached through the trees, drawing nearer. Within seconds Abby could see a dark figure running after Emily.

Suddenly, a black crow swooped down, giving Abby a start. She looked up. There were hundreds of black birds perched in the trees surrounding her. Each one stared at her intently. Unsettled by their piercing black gaze, Abby turned to help Emily. She began running through the forest after the other girl, following the trail of the shadowy figure.

She could hear the young girl screaming for help somewhere in the distance. Abby could see the dark figure only a few yards ahead. She continued to run and nearly stumbled. Abby reached out a hand and caught herself, breaking her fall against one of the trees.

When she looked up, the dark figure was gone, and the forest had fallen silent. Abby looked around. There was nothing but darkness and a deafening silence.

In the far distance, she was certain she could see someone lying on the forest floor. "Emily?" Abby called out her voice shaking. The figure on the ground didn't move.

Abby came closer, and stopped a few yards away. As her eyes adjusted to the darkness, Abby could see Emily, wearing her school uniform lying on the ground covered in blood.

"Emily?" she whimpered.

A wave of horror moved through her like an emotional shock wave. Abby covered her mouth, stopping herself from screaming.

She turned to run away and made it only a few steps when the dark figure stepped out from behind a tree. Abby froze in horror. Before she could make out who the killer was, they reached out their hands and gouged Abby's eyes, pulling them from her sockets.

Abby let out a primal scream and dropped to her knees in pain. She covered the bloody pits vacant her eyes. The agony was unbearable. She crawled blindly until she came to what felt like a tree trunk, screaming the whole way. She knew it was useless. They were too strong, too powerful, and had already killed Emily. Abby just sat, waiting for her fate. Waiting for the dark figure to finish her off.

Moments passed, and nothing happened. Abby pulled her hands away and saw a shimmer of light. She opened her eyes. She was still in the forest. She looked down and saw her hands covered in blood. She felt her cheeks and they were covered in blood stained tears.

The pain was almost gone. Abby pulled her phone from her pocket and opened the camera app. She reversed the image, so she could look at herself. She was horrified by the image staring back at her. Abby's face was covered in blood, her eyes were completely bloodshot. Her vision had been too real, and her body was paying the price for her dabbling in fate.

She gave herself several moments to recover from the fatigue of having used her gift. Then, with a moment of gratitude that her eyes were still whole, she looked around at the forest surrounding her. Was this where Emily Wright had been murdered?

CHAPTER TWENTY THREE

Abby stood in the middle of the woods, surrounded by trees. She had no idea which way would take her home. The lingering backlash of her horrific vision made her head feel hazy as she tried to make sense of where she was. Nothing looked familiar.

I didn't need to see that, Abby thought. All she could see was Emily Wright laying on the forest floor, bludgeoned to death. It was too similar. Seeing such a macabre scene invoked the visceral memories of blood on the carpet and the smell of white lilies in the hall. Abby's thoughts were caught in a cycle of blood-stained horror that would never be unseen.

She did her best to push the disturbing images from her thoughts and turned her focus to the forest surrounding her. The trees loomed over her blotting out the sun leaving only a soft glow of daylight barely breaking through the shadowy darkness.

I'm stuck! Which way do I go? The forest all looked the same. *Don't freak out, Abby,* she told herself. *You know you can't be that far from home.* She looked up to the sky. It offered no bearing, the trees were far too thick.

There was a growing panic in Abby's stomach as she realized there were no trails to follow. She felt as though she was being consumed by a dark, dank forest. The images of Emily's dead body lying in the underbrush tainted her thoughts. Her heart quickened until she could feel her head throbbing, her cheeks flush with heat.

STOP! Abby screamed internally. She pinched herself and took several deep breaths to still the growing panic attack that threatened to eclipse her ability to think straight. She closed her eyes and concentrated for a few moments, stilling her screaming fears. Once her breathing returned to normal Abby opened her eyes.

I can't be lost, the forest isn't that big, she reminded herself. *I just need to pick a direction and walk until I reach the edge.* Then something occurred to her, *My phone!* She searched her pockets and pulled out her smartphone. She looked to see it had no reception, *I'm probably in a dead spot.*

She began walking and hoping her phone would pick up a signal. Abby traveled only a few yards when the first bar appeared. A sense of relief settled over her as she tapped her GPS alive to get her bearings. Abby gasped in surprise. She was nearly three-quarters of a mile from her house; she must have walked a great distance while she was in the Sight.

Shaken by the visions, and upset by this new development from her psychic gift, Abby slowly made her way home. When she finally arrived, she saw Benjamin's SUV was gone.

He must have decided to spend some time alone. The last thing she wanted to do was worry him even more. No doubt her blood shot eyes and blood-stained hands would be more than he could take right now.

Abby quickly made her way upstairs to the bathroom. She disrobed and took a hot shower, washing away the cold terror she had felt.

Emily's dead, she thought. It wasn't a surprise, but a part of Abby had hoped the young woman had simply run away for some unknown reason. It was a silly hope, but now she knew, there was no glimmer of hope to cling to.

Emily Wright had been murdered.

Abby's thoughts drifted to the dark shadow that had bludgeoned Emily to death, the shadow was human in form but there were no features, nothing to provide insight into her killer's identity. *How does Edgar fit in to this? If Edgar is a half-demon, what dark forces surround him that he may not even be aware of? Shadows and spirits are closely related. What if... what if the Thanos are somehow involved?*

Abby took another deep breath, letting the hot water sooth her anxieties. *Don't let yourself run wild,* she reminded trying to keep her imagination from running away with her. But that is easier said than done; the entire world felt like it was caving in.

The death witches hunting her down felt like a constant threat that loomed like a shadow over everything. Emily's death was haunting her, she clearly shared some strange connection to the girl who went missing last year, though she couldn't figure out what. Even Edgar Kincaid, with his glowing eyes and the possible demonic influences surrounding him, was still a mystery. It felt as though her life had taken a dark turn down a path she wasn't sure she wanted to follow. Ever since... that day she came home and found her parents.

Abby stepped out of the shower and dried herself off, taking a glance in the mirror. She looked terrible. She couldn't wash away the bloodshot eyes, and her face was sunken and hollow. She could see bones sticking out in places that didn't seem healthy. She sighed, realizing how much she had let herself go in the last couple weeks.

After getting dressed, Abby went down stairs and forced herself to eat a grapefruit and a hard-boiled egg. Her stomach protested every bite, but she forced herself to eat anyway. When she finished, she went over to her violin stand and picked up her instrument. She needed the calm that only music could bring her. She scanned several pieces and settled on a violin arrangement for Dido's Lament, by Henry Purcell, it somehow felt appropriate.

Abby put the violin under her chin and held the bow just above the strings. Gently pulling the bow, she created a beautifully sorrowful sound.

Abby played as though she were allowing the music to feel everything she couldn't bear to feel a moment longer. Her violin was the conduit, the sound of her relief. Playing gave her a spiritual catharsis, something she needed now more than anything. The music cried for her.

A polite knock on the door interrupted Abby's practice. She set her violin down and glanced at the time on her phone. Nine o'clock. *Ms. Grace was always precise in her timing,* she thought as she answered the door.

Ms. Grace's warm welcoming smile melted away immediately upon seeing Abby. "What on earth happened to your eyes?" she questioned, her voice weighted with concern.

"Come in and I'll tell you all about it," Abby offered. Ms. Grace stepped in carrying a pile of books in her arms. She set them on the dining room table and sat on the couch. She stared at Abby as if she thought she was going to crumble before her very eyes.

"By the way, Benjamin knows about what we've been doing for Edgar," Abby said as she took her seat.

Ms. Grace was beginning to return to her stoic self. Abby had come to learn it was the older woman's armor, when she was uncomfortable. "What did he do?"

"He got very angry and left. I don't know where he went. He found out this morning," Abby explained.

"Found out? You didn't tell him?" Ms. Grace asked.

"No. Edgar sent me a note through the post, accepting my offer to help," Abby explained. "Edgar obviously didn't want to knock on my front door and speak to me about it, which was probably wise, but since I'm not at school any longer, I didn't exactly leave him any other options."

"I take it Mr. Hodge intercepted this note." Ms. Grace deduced.

Abby nodded. "I'm not certain he'll ever trust me again."

"I was afraid of something like this," Ms. Grace stated somberly.

"The damage is done, I guess. I'll have to see what becomes of everything now that it's out in the open," Abby said, mournfully.

"I'm very sorry to hear of your situation," Ms. Grace offered kindly. "Shall I return another day?"

"No," Abby said. "I could use the distraction right now. I feel like we've been making some progress with our research on his situation."

"Yes… Now, what about your eyes? I'm certain that didn't happen due to tears," Ms. Grace observed, the concern still lingering in her expression.

"That is another thing entirely," Abby admitted. She took a deep breath and told Ms. Grace of the disturbing vision she had earlier that morning. "I can't get the images out of my head. They were horrifying."

Valerie Grace was silent for a long moment, processing all that Abby had told her. "It seems Ms. Wright is indeed dead," She finally said. "I'm afraid I have suspected it all along. She was a kind and thoughtful young girl. She would have never run off."

"I couldn't see who did it. I was about to make out who the murderer was, just before…" Abby waved vaguely in the direction of her face. "My body manifested some of my vision, it seems. When I came out of the vision, my eyes were like this." Abby sat, shivering with disgust and horror.

"I should have been more diligent in my instruction," Ms. Grace stated as if it were all her fault. "Channeling fate is very dangerous at times. I didn't realize what that really meant until now."

"I have a feeling it could have been worse." Abby shuddered to think how. "It isn't your fault Ms. Grace. I seem to have a knack for learning lessons the hard way."

"I'll see about finding more books on the subject of the Sight. It would behoove you to learn as much as you can from others who have shared your gift," Ms. Grace explained. "Had I known your gift would manifest so quickly I would have gathered them sooner."

"Thank you," Abby said. "I hope I don't' sound ungrateful, but thus far this hasn't felt like much of a gift."

"No, I would think not considering what you've seen," Ms. Grace agreed. "I suspect some of your predecessors would agree with your assessment." Her stiff demeanor softened for a moment. "Abigail, I know there are many dark things surrounding you right now. You must remember, life is full of great things, and many sad and terrifying things. You won't always live in the shadows. One day this will all be behind you."

"I know you're right." Abby conceded. "I'll get through this. If I've proven anything in the last year, it's that I'm a survivor. I'm looking forward to doing a little more of the living part. Survival sucks."

Ms. Grace wore an amused smile. "It does indeed, suck!" Ms. Grace stated in the most uptight humorous way. Abby couldn't help but laugh.

"I've never heard you swear before," Abby said.

"Is 'suck' considered a swear word? It seems relatively mild compared to any other expletives I might conjure," Ms. Grace said rather amused.

"It is," Abby assured, laughing in spite of herself.

"Well," Ms. Grace said, gesturing towards the stack of books. "Shall we get a start then?"

"Sounds good," Abby agreed. The two of them wandered over to the table, each taking a seat and starting with the books on top of the pile.

After nearly an hour of research Abby sat back in her chair and scribbled several notes on a notepad. "Between his physical strength, acute senses, the glowing red eyes and the infernal influences surrounding him, we can almost be certain he's a cambion," Abby stated.

Valerie Grace nearly let out a sigh, but stopped herself. "All our evidence is supporting our initial suspicions. The only way for us to be certain would be his cooperation in the investigation. Based on your brief interactions with him, he's been rather guarded. Most cambions have powers beyond what he has spoken of. He may have other powers that have manifested," Ms. Grace stated as she reviewed her notes.

"Yes, the pheromone thing," Abby said. "Influencing people through scent, it says," she added looking at a particular passage.

"It seems subtle. He may be unaware of this power, especially without some kind of guidance," Ms. Grace said.

"One of his parents is a demon then," Abby said.

"Considering the absence of a father, his mother's refusal to name one, and her particular brand of religious zealotry, things seem to be pointing to that conclusion, yes," Ms. Grace stated.

"Do you think it's time to approach him?" Abby asked hesitantly.

"I think there is little more we can discern on our own" Ms. Grace stated.

"Benjamin isn't going to like this."

"You did have a vision of Mr. Kincaid murdering his twin sister," Ms. Grace pointed out. "I doubt that is something he can simply ignore. Nor should we. That is why I recommend I be with you when we approach him with our findings. We can't be certain he's fully in control of himself," Ms. Grace stated. "He may still be responsible for Emily's death. We can't be certain what his nature drives him to do."

"It says here that cambions have many impulses, but because they possess a soul they have free will," Abby said.

"Yes," Ms. Grace stated. "Right now, he most likely doesn't understand the changes he is going through. He can be easily influenced and may not understand how to control his powers. Anything is possible at this stage."

"But what triggered the changes?" Abby asked searching through her notes. "Everyone said he was a relatively normal young man until last year, around the time Emily disappeared. What flipped the switch for him?"

Ms. Grace blushed. Abby looked at her curiously. She had never seen her mentor react in such a way. "Did you find something?" Abby asked.

Ms. Grace cleared her throat, "It would seem physical intimacy triggers the change. If nothing else a cambion is a creature of lust."

"Ah, so he and Emily had sex," Abby clarified, somewhat amused by her teacher's prudish nature on the topic.

"That would be my best guess," Ms. Grace stated, turning a brighter shade of pink.

Abby smiled and picked up the next book thumbing through the pages, looking for information on cambions they hadn't already found. This book and the next proved fruitless.

"Every book says the same thing," Abby said setting the book aside.

"It would seem we have exhausted the material your grandmother sent on the topic," Ms. Grace conceded as she scanned the last few pages of the book in front of her.

"How should we approach him?" Abby asked.

Ms. Grace remained silent, deep in thought. "Why don't I have him called into my office. We can speak with him there."

"I'd like to warn him first," Abby stated. "Even though he knows you're like me, he isn't thus far aware you've been helping me."

"Yes, fair warning would be wise. I don't imagine he would do well with surprises," Ms. Grace stated. "Perhaps you can write a note and let him know he will be meeting with both of us. Then he can decide what he wants to do."

"That sounds like a good idea," Abby said.

"I'll have it delivered to him this afternoon. Perhaps we can meet with him tomorrow towards the end of the day, say three o'clock," Ms. Grace suggested.

Abby pulled a piece of paper from her notepad and began writing a note.

> Edgar,
> Ms. Grace and I have been studying your situation. We
> may have answers but may need to know more before we
> can be certain. If you are still interested, please come to Ms.
> Grace's office at 3 o'clock tomorrow.
> Sincerely,
> Abby

She handed the note to Ms. Grace who gave it a cursory glance. "This looks fine," she said folding it and placing it in her large bag. "It's up to him to decide what he wants to do next."

"Edgar has proven to be unpredictable. He's as likely to be furious as he is to be grateful," Abby interjected.

"He's likely very scared. Who wouldn't be in his situation. All those changes happening suddenly and unexpectedly. I sincerely hope we can help the young man. Just as I hope he isn't responsible for killing Miss Wright."

Abby shuddered. "If he didn't kill her, it would mean someone else around here is a cold-blooded murderer." Her thoughts again returned to the dead girl's body discarded on the forest floor.

"Yes," Ms. Grace stated. "Perhaps. We shall have answers soon enough," she said, collecting her books and preparing herself to depart. "It would seem you came very close to discovering who the murderer was this morning. Be on guard, Abby."

"I know," Abby agreed. "I almost feel like someone is trying to keep me from the truth."

"Undoubtedly," Ms. Grace stated. "I would refrain from continued use of the Sight on the matter without supervision. Things seem to be escalating and we must be diligent in keeping you safe."

"I will do my best," Abby said. "It felt like it came to me this last time. I didn't seek it out. Like I was being drawn to something."

Ms. Grace raised an eyebrow. "Then you are already connected to this in some way," she stated. "All the more reason to exercise caution."

"A cambion?" Edgar inquired, sitting across from Ms. Grace in her rather spartan office. "A person that is the product of copulation between a human and a demon, typically an Incubus or Succubus." He read the sentence aloud from the book he had been handed.

Abby looked at him, trying to offer any words that might help. "I'm getting better with the Sight, but I don't think I'm good enough to confirm anything for you right now. This is our best educated guess."

Edgar seemed far less volatile than he had been the past few times Abby had encountered him. A fact for which she was very grateful. "So, I'm some kind of demon?" Edgar broke the long silence after having read several pages.

"Not precisely," Ms. Grace interjected. "You are only half demon, if our theory is correct."

Edgar reflected for a few moments. "That explains my mother's particular brand of insanity." He muttered, before looking up. "So, there are others like me?" He asked. He absently flipped through pages, looking for more information.

"I would assume so," Abby responded. "You said you can sense us, perhaps you can sense them as well." She added, hoping it sounded encouraging.

Abby reached into her book bag and grabbed a memory stick. Handing it to Edgar, she said, "You can have this. I took the liberty of scanning this book into a digital file, as well as a couple of others with information on cambions." He gave her a look of surprise, before gingerly reaching out and accepting the flash drive. "I'll be honest," she continued, "We haven't found very much on the subject that seems reputable or academic, but it's a start."

There was a heavy pause. Edgar looked up, and Abby could see pain in his eyes. "Why are you being so kind to me?" he asked, a flicker of anger broke through the pain with a flash of red in his eyes. "I'm a monster."

"You are not a monster Mr. Kincaid," Valerie stated vehemently. "Of that, I am quite sure."

"Ms. Grace is right. You're just different. Nothing I've read indicates your parentage has doomed you to some dark fate. You have to figure it out like the rest of us who are different."

Edgar seemed to calm down. It was clear to Abby, he hadn't anticipated acceptance. "You know, I was certain this was a trap. I came here to this meeting expecting you were going to do something to me," Edgar said.

"Like what?" Ms. Grace asked curiously.

Edgar shrugged. "Throw me in a dungeon, kill me, something."

"I can't imagine why we would do that," Abby stated slightly amused.

"It was just a sense I had. Obviously, I was wrong about witches," he said, clearly confused. Edgar returned his attention to the book in his hand. "Strength, acute sense, immunity to fire... that seems useful," he commented. "The ability to manipulate pheromones? What does that mean? I don't' think I can do that."

"Pheromones are chemical secretions released by all animals in various ways. These chemicals effect the behavior of other animals around them. In you, it seems to give you the ability to influence other people. Cambions typically use them to attract or seduce others, although they can be used for other purposes, I would assume." Ms. Grace explained, ever the instructor.

"It might take some practice to master, but maybe you already do it without realizing?" Abby suggested.

"How do you mean?" Edgar asked curiously.

"I've only interacted with you a few times," Abby explained. "but I don't' mind saying, until this meeting I've been absolutely terrified of you." She watched his reaction closely. "I'm thinking perhaps it's because you were uncertain about me and instinctively used them without even realizing," she suggested.

"This sort of power can be subtle," Ms. Grace interjected. "Perhaps with some focus and mindfulness, the effects will be more intentional, so to speak."

Edgar was obviously trying to take everything in. They had given him a great deal to work with. It was obvious everything weighed heavily on his thoughts.

"What can you do with the Sight?" Edgar asked.

Abby looked at him curiously. "It allows me to sense emotions and sometimes I can sense other things. Things that have happened, or might happen."

"Could you use it to find out what happened to Emily?" Edgar asked hopefully. Abby could see the pain in his eyes. *He doesn't know,* she thought, certain this time. *He didn't do it.* There was a sense of relief in her heart, but it was followed quickly by a black hole of uncertainty. They still didn't know who was guilty.

"I don't know," Abby admitted. "Sometimes I can't always control what I see. But, I could try. I've only recently learned I have the ability, and I have to admit I'm not all that good with it yet." She looked at Ms. Grace for support.

"But you'll try?" Edgar had only heard her offer. Abby hoped the rest of what she said had been understood.

"Yes, I'm willing to try," Abby said.

"It will likely help Miss Kane if you had something of Emily's. Something she could use as a focus. Something that had been important to her," Ms. Grace stated.

Edgar thought for a few moments. "I gave her a pendant for her birthday last year. She left it in her dorm when…" He stopped and swallowed back whatever he had been about to say before continuing. "Her parents returned it to me after she went missing."

"That should do," Abby said, remembering something she had read about the Sight and its uses with psychometry. In theory, she should be able to sense the history of an object by holding it.

Edgar's expression turned to that of irritation. "I don't have it here at the school. I left it in my room back home," he confessed. "I don't have any way to get it to you."

We have a holiday the week after next," Ms. Grace observed. "Why don't you bring it back with you and we can try then"

Edgar nodded his head It was clear he didn't want to wait that long, but had little choice.

"It's alright." Abby reassured. "It will give me more time to do some research on the best way to approach the situation with the Sight."

"You understand Mr. Kincaid that what, if anything, we discover may not be good news," Ms. Grace stated cautiously.

Edgar looked at the older woman with a flash of red in his eyes. "Other than her parents, there are few people who knew Emily better than I did," Edgar said. "She wasn't the type to disappear. She wouldn't do that to me, and she certainly wouldn't do that to her parents. I'm not an idiot. I know she's probably dead. She's been gone too long. I've spent the entirety of the last year doing my best to accept that. I just want to know who did it," he said, fury warring with frustration. "And why," he added softly.

"If Emily was murdered, I will personally work with you to deal with whatever monster would do such a thing to one of my students at this school," Ms. Grace stated.

"So, will I," Abby agreed. It felt weird keeping her knowledge to herself. Abby already knew that Emily was dead, but she and Ms. Grace agreed to not say anything until they learned more. Abby wasn't keen to disclose such information in a public place, considering her past interactions with Edgar. After seeing the rage, he still held on to, she didn't want to risk setting him off.

215

Edgar seemed relieved though, as if a weight had been lifted from his shoulders. He then looked at Abby curiously. "Why are you really helping me with this?" he asked. As Abby looked at him, a sense of calm came over her. It was strange considering how afraid she had been of him up until this very moment.

Abby considered how she was going to respond. She didn't want to tell him everything, but she knew she couldn't lie to him. "Because I know something about grief and not having answers," Abby said. "I know what it can do to you. I wouldn't wish it on anyone."

Edgar looked at her curiously. She hadn't lied, and she knew he could tell. "I've taken enough of your time," he said, standing. "I'll come back in a couple weeks, after the holiday."

"Come to my office when you return from break and we'll arrange a time," Ms. Grace stated.

Edgar was about to leave, and lingered at the door for a moment. He looked back briefly and said. "Thank you," before abruptly leaving.

Abby and Ms. Grace sat in silence for a few moments. "That went much better than I had imagined," Ms. Grace stated with a pleased look.

"Yes, it did," Abby said.

"Two weeks will be perfect; Benjamin and Josephine are spending the holiday with their father on a hunting trip. It's their birthday and plan to stay a couple extra days, which gives us time to work with Edgar."

"Very fortuitous." Ms. Grace stated. "Are things improving between you and Benjamin, then?"

"He came home yesterday and did his homework. He said he didn't want to talk about it and slept on the couch," Abby said with a sigh of frustration.

"Some time will perhaps help," Ms. Grace suggested. "Did he know about this meeting?"

"No, we barely spoke all evening," Abby explained. "Though, it wouldn't have stopped me, I think. My working with Edgar just isn't something we can come to an agreement on."

"Their trip will be the ideal opportunity then." Ms. Grace said.

Abby collected her purse. "Hopefully Benjamin will be ready to talk tonight. I don't think I can handle another evening of the silent treatment," she said.

"Abigail," Ms. Grace called after her. The younger girl halted, her mentor rarely called Abby by her full name.

"Is there something wrong?" Abby paused.

"I'm worried about you," The older woman said, looking at her over her reading glasses. "Please take care of yourself. I know you have been under a great deal of stress. You've lost a notable amount of weight since the attack, more than is healthy, I think."

Abby felt a wave of anxiousness move through her, settling in her stomach. She could feel herself getting nauseated. "I know," she confessed. "I force myself to eat something when I remember, but the stress has just been too much. I'm so distracted by everything I forget... a lot of things. Arguing with Benjamin isn't helping either."

"You need to keep your physical strength up. Your mind and body are so closely connected to one another," Ms. Grace stated. "I have an alchemical book with several remedies for stomach ailments. I'll see if I can find something that might help."

"Thank you, Ms. Grace," Abby said somewhat embarrassed. It was uncomfortable for others to notice, but she tried to remind herself it was spoken out of concern.

"Don't thank me," Ms. Grace stated. "Just take care of yourself."

"I will," Abby reassured.

Abby put away her clean dishes contemplating how well everything went earlier in the day. It was a stark contrast to how everything was going at home. She glanced at the time on her phone. It was past seven o'clock and Benjamin still hadn't come home.

It would seem like it's another round of the silent treatment, she thought as she dried her hands on the kitchen towel. She finished wrapping up the extra food that had been meant for him and placed it in the refrigerator.

Abby picked up her phone from her nightstand and considered texting him. She then opened her contact list and sent Josephine a text.

Abby: *Is Benjamin with you?*

A few moments passed by before a reply came.

Josephine: *Yes. Is everything okay?*

Abby: *I just wanted to make sure he was alright.*

Josephine: *I'll talk to him.*

Abby set her phone aside after plugging it into her charger.

Settling in on the couch, she caught herself dozing. She glanced at the phone and it was not even nine o'clock. *I've been so tired lately,* she thought. *Ms. Grace and Benjamin are right, I need to take better care of myself.* Giving in to their concerns ringing in her head, Abby reached over and turned off the light, before heading to her room. *Might as well call it an early night.*

217

An abrupt sound woke Abby from a deep sleep. She sat up, her heart pounding in her chest. *Another attack,* she thought scrambling to the far side of the bed, backing herself up against the wall. She could hardly breathe. Dread was pulsing through her heart, and she felt as though her lungs were incapable of filling with air.

Abby listened carefully over the deafening beat of her heart. There was silence. Had she imagined hearing something. *Was it a dream?* she thought as the prolonged silence continued.

A thin glow came from beneath her bedroom door. She watched it closely, expecting some mist to pour into her room like it had when the Thanos attacked them in Seattle last summer. Her eyes were transfixed, waiting for her fate to finally arrive. Abby could barely move, she felt paralyzed. A shadow moved across the doorway. Abby steadied herself, reaching for anything she could use as a weapon.

A digital chime resounded through the room. Abby nearly jumped out of her skin. It's my phone, she realized. Abby quietly crawled over to the night stand and collected her phone. She glanced at it briefly. It was Benjamin.

> Benjamin: *I'm staying in the dormitory tonight. I'll come home tomorrow. We need to talk.*

Abby didn't have time to respond. There was a shuffling noise from the kitchen. Abby dropped her phone, watching the door. She could hear footsteps approaching. Multiple footsteps. Hushed voices she couldn't make out.

Abby braced herself, ready to call down whatever magic she had on her would-be attackers.

"Abby?" Nina called out.

"Nina?" She questioned the door. "Nina is that you?" Her voice was shaking. *It's got to be a trick!*

"Can I come in?" Nina asked.

Abby sighed releasing as much tension as she could. *Calm down, Abby, they're not the bad guys,* she said to herself "Come in." Abby said pulling herself together.

The door opened a hand searched for the light switch. When the lights came on Abby was momentarily blinded. Her eyes quickly adjusted, and she could make out Nina and Sarah standing in her bedroom doorway.

"What are you doing here?" Abby asked confused. "How did you get in?"

"Benjamin came by earlier this evening and asked us to sneak out and stay with you tonight, so you wouldn't be alone," Sarah explained.

"He loaned us his key," Nina added showing Abby the key. "I think he's worried about you."

Abby buried her face in her hands. The relief flooded her mind beyond measure. She could feel the tears coming and she knew they would be impossible to stop.

"Oh, Abby," Sarah said, rushing forward and pulling her into an embrace. Nina quickly joined. They escorted her to the edge of the bed and sat on either side of her. Sarah held her arm and rested her head on Abby's shoulder while Nina rubbed her back.

"I don't think it's all that bad," Nina added. "Certainly, he doesn't mean to break up with you. He loves you!"

They don't realize what just almost happened. I could have killed them! For a brief moment, her anger welled up. *It's not their fault,* she reminded herself, willing her irritation away. *They didn't know.*

Abby shook her head. "I know he does," she said, answering Nina. "It's just a really emotional time right now. I'm such a mess."

"Everything considered, no one could blame you for having a little break down from time to time," Sarah comforted.

"You look tired," Nina observed.

"Why don't we turn in for the night? We obviously woke you," Sarah suggested.

"I promise not to be a blanket hog," Nina jested.

Abby smiled. *I have good friends,* she thought. Nina and Sarah escaped into the bathroom briefly before climbing into bed with her.

They turned out the lights and snuggled up under the blankets.

"I should have called Warren to join us," Nina said.

"I don't think we could fit another person in this bed. Even someone as scrawny as Warren." Sarah jested.

"What did Benjamin say?" Abby asked with hesitation.

"Not a lot," Nina commented.

"He says he's trying to work some things out. He didn't explain himself and I didn't feel it was any of my business to pry. He did ask us to come here tonight. He was worried about you and didn't want you to be alone," Sarah explained.

"We're here for you Abby. We'll always be here for you when you need us," Nina said sweetly.

"I feel really lucky having the two of you as friends," Abby said. A smile lit her face in the darkness as they chatted. *It feels good to be doing something that resembled normal,* Abby thought.

Abby wasn't certain how long they stayed up talking. Time felt like it didn't exist that night, gossiping away with two friends about everything imaginable until they all passed out.

219

Abby woke later than usual the next morning. She glanced at the time on her phone; ten thirty. The morning fog was still hovering, and was thick enough she couldn't even see the road at the end of the driveway. "Maybe the two of you should stick around a little longer," Abby suggested.

"Why?" Sarah asked as she finished putting away the last of their breakfast dishes.

"I have our stuff ready," Nina said, bringing in their overnight bags from the bathroom.

"The fog is pretty thick," Abby said answering Sarah's question. "Walking along the road could be dangerous."

Sarah came around and looked out the window. "It's pretty thick," she agreed.

"We could call a hackney," Nina suggested.

"A what?" Abby asked, confused.

"A cab driver," Sarah explained.

Nina pulled out her phone and opened an app. She tapped her screen several times and smiled.

"One will be here in twenty minutes," she smiled. "I love technology." She put her phone away.

"Did Benjamin mention when he would be coming home?" Nina asked.

Abby shook her head. "I was rather hoping that he had said something to you," she admitted.

"Oh, don't worry!" Sarah reassured her. "I'm sure he will be back before lunch."

Abby smiled at her friend's optimism. She wished she was as confident.

Abby sat and chatted with her friends absently until the cab arrived, then walked them outside. She gave each of them a quick hug, and then stood in the driveway and waved goodbye until they were up the road and disappeared into the fog.

Abby pulled her sweater closer around her shoulders and hurried in out of the cold to wait for Benjamin.

CHAPTER TWENTY FOUR

Abby sat on the couch with a book. Her mind was too preoccupied to retain anything. She glanced at her phone again; eleven-twenty. It had only been a little over thirty minutes since the girls had left. The time was passing maddeningly slow. *Maybe he isn't going to come back,* she thought.

She looked out the front window. The clouds were as thick as ever. Abby was beginning to wonder if it would ever burn off. She knew now why England was famous for its fog.

Reading was proving to be a futile activity. Abby abandoned the book, placing it on the coffee table. She needed something to do that would help her burn off nervous energy. She got up and went into the kitchen. She rummaged through the cupboards and found the cleaning supplies. She pulled on some rubber gloves and began giving her counter tops a thorough scrubbing.

It wasn't more than ten minutes later she could hear a familiar engine rumbling in the driveway. Abby always recognized the sound of Benjamin's SUV in the driveway. She felt herself flush with nervousness. They had a lot to work out and she knew she had things to take responsibility for. He wasn't without blame, she even felt a bit of anger herself, but she pushed it away. She always pushed the anger away.

Why? she wondered.

She removed the gloves and began putting away the supplies. She was just finishing up when she heard the front door open.

"Abby? Are you here?" Benjamin called out.

She stepped from the kitchen into the dining room. "I'm here," she said. Benjamin was wearing nice jeans and a dark green button down, and Abby's breath caught when she saw him. His curly brown hair was cut short and tamed. She couldn't help but make contact with his big brown eyes. *It's not fair for him to be so handsome when we're fighting.*

"Can we talk?" Benjamin asked. There was uncertainty in his voice.

Abby nodded and sat at the kitchen table. She could feel herself being guarded. Abby did her best to not completely shut down like the morning before last on the back patio.

"We would probably be more comfortable on the couch," he suggested.

"I'm comfortable here." Abby said, her words held more chill than she intended.

"Alright," Benjamin said taking a seat across from her. "I'm not sure where to begin."

Abby shrugged and shook her head. "Start wherever you need to."

Benjamin looked at her curiously, as though he were trying to understand something. "Are you all right?"

"That question is getting a bit old," Abby said, surprised by the bitterness in her own voice. "Why don't we skip to the crux of the problem here. You don't trust me to tell you the truth and I don't trust what you'll do with the truth. What do we do now?" Abby realized the anger had come out. She quickly took a breath and reigned it in. She glanced at Benjamin who seemed surprised.

"You've managed to summarize things well," Benjamin stated. She could tell he was doing his best to reign in his own anger. It was the best effort she had seen so far.

"You weren't the only one spending the last few days thinking about things. Thinking about us," Abby explained. "Despite hours upon hours of contemplation, I still don't know what to do?"

"Then let's focus on what we want," Benjamin said eagerly. "I want you. I want you more than anything else in the world. I don't want these problems or anything else to tear us apart. I'm in love with you, Abby." Benjamin said.

Abby caught herself feeling elated and terrified along with nearly every emotion that existed in between. She knew she felt it, but for some reason saying it was different. It made it more than just a feeling. Somehow it created something more.

"Abby say something," Benjamin said a worried look on his face.

"I... I..." Abby choked on her words. She couldn't speak.

Benjamin stood abruptly and came around the table so quickly Abby barely noticed. He pulled her up, pressed his body against her and began kissing her with such passion she could hardly breath. His touch, his lips awakened her body. He had learned how to make her body respond to his touch, his lips, his...

Abby pulled off her sweater as Benjamin unbuttoned his shirt and wrangled his pants off. She quickly discarded her own pants and returned to their kissing. Benjamin picked Abby up and carried her into the bedroom gently laying her down and positioning himself on top of her. Their kissing became deeper and urgent.

Abby could feel her body awaken. She wanted him, she wanted to be with him, to make love to him, to show him the love she held for him. There was a bliss here that words alone couldn't convey. Abby never wanted this moment to end.

When they were done, they held one another under the blankets. Abby felt safe and cared for in his arms. For some reason his arms fed a hunger of her body, heart and mind. She had given herself to him in every way she had to give, and though there was a vulnerability in doing so, there was a freedom to it she didn't yet understand.

"I don't like it when we fight," Abby said nestling her head on her boyfriend's shoulder.

"It probably won't be our last time, but I'm in favor of keeping it to a minimum," Benjamin jested putting a smile on Abby's face. She was relieved his sense of humor had returned.

"I've been so stressed lately," Abby confessed holding him close. "I'm glad we aren't quarreling anymore."

"Have you given any more thought to joining my family on the holiday weekend for my birthday stalking trip?" Benjamin asked playing with Abby's hair.

"Absolutely not," Abby responded with disgust.

Benjamin chuckled at her reaction. "Why not?"

"I'm not about to go shooting animals… or watching other people shoot animals. It's barbaric," Abby said.

Benjamin was obviously amused. "I thought all American's owned guns," he teased.

Abby tickled his side causing him to buckle over and restrain her hands. He moved in for a loving kiss. "We don't all have guns," she smiled and kissed him again. "Oh! And don't bring anything home with you either. I don't want one of those disturbing heads mounted on my walls." She shuddered.

"You're taking all the fun out of it," Benjamin playfully protested. "You really won't go?"

"You and I will have our own private birthday celebration after you get back. You should spend some time with your family. Once we start gap year you won't see much of them, anyway," Abby reasoned.

"I think you may very well know how to weasel your way out of anything." Benjamin smiled and stole another kiss.

Abby sat on the couch holding her cell phone in her hand, while Benjamin made dinner in the kitchen. She held her finger over the call icon and hesitated for a moment. She took a deep breath and tapped the screen. There was a ring, then another.

"Abigail, darling, are you well?" Vivian's voice came through the phone.

"Yes, I'm fine grandmother," Abby said. "Are you well?"

"Never better," Vivian said. Abby was certain she could hear the subtle clink of ice cubes in the background and wondered how many Vivian had already put back. "I'm nearly ready darling. Everything is in place, now. I'm waiting for the right concurrence of the constellations to occur. It shouldn't be more than another month. Perhaps two, if I find a better time."

"What are you planning?" Abby asked curiously, uncertain how forthcoming her grandmother would be.

"Bernard and I have created a curse. My brother wants to have a backup plan, but I'm certain it will end this war with a single application." Vivian said. *She sounds confident,* Abby thought. She didn't know her granduncle well, but she hoped his caution was unnecessary. More than anything Abby hoped her grandmother's confidence wasn't misplaced.

"What will it do?" Abby asked, knowing full well her grandmother was unlikely to tell her.

"Oh darling, I don't want you worrying about such things. These wars are terrible things and sometimes one must be willing to make difficult choices, in order for us to end things decisively. You understand, don't you darling?" Vivian asked as if she were innocent.

"I don't like where my imagination is going with this," Abby replied, unmoved by her grandmother's feigned innocence.

"This war will end, and the Thanos family will pay dearly for what they have done. This conflict has gone on for far too long. It is time for me to be certain it not only ends but never happens again," Vivian said changing her tone.

"It must be a very powerful curse," Abby said. "Is everyone alright? Margot? Madison?"

"Fine darling, everyone is just fine. If things go according to plan we'll all be back together by the end of Spring," Vivian said.

"I would like that," Abby confessed. She missed seeing her loved ones. "I would love to introduce Benjamin to the family," Abby added in an intentional effort to needle her grandmother. Abby wasn't certain why she felt compelled to do so, perhaps it was a lingering desire to retaliate for the chaos Vivian had sown during the Christmas holiday. There was a moment of silence on the other end.

"I'm certain some of them might even like the young man," Vivian said politely.

"Some of them…" Abby repeated.

"Well dear, he does come from a family with a poor reputation. The Hodges were expelled from the London Seven for their low character and reprehensible use of blood magic. Darling, such things are not easily overlooked," Vivian explained.

"You think I should hold something his ancestors did, over a hundred years ago, against him?" Abby whispered into the phone, hoping Benjamin couldn't hear the conversation from the next room. "I realize when you were younger the shock waves of that scandal were far more salacious, but I would venture to guess the Hodges have moved on, and it seems rather unbecoming to hold on to such things after all this time."

Vivian mockingly cut into Abby's tirade. "Oh, how he has hooked his tendrils into you," she said. "Please darling, please tell me you're at least using protection."

Abby turned a bright shade of red. "I'm not talking to you about this!" she said. The last thing in the world Abby wanted was to talk about sex with her grandmother.

"Darling you're destined for such greatness. I can feel it in my bones. Why would you mire yourself with mediocrity? I am certain, without doubt, you could do much better than a Hodge."

"I am not interested in relationship advice from you," Abby said looking over to see if Benjamin could hear.

"Darling I have so much experience in these matters," Vivian protested.

"You've had five husbands," Abby said.

"And I learned a great deal from every one of them," Vivian countered. "So, you can see, I have all the experience in the world."

"Well, I'm looking for one that will stick, so can we talk about something else please?" Abby asked unable to bear another moment speaking of relationships with Vivian Kane of all people.

"Of course, darling, anything, anything you want," Vivian said. The clink of ice cubes rattling in a glass filtered through the phone.

"I need to tell you something, and I don't want you going into your usual theatrics," Abby stated.

"I can't imagine what you mean, darling?" Vivian said, again feigning innocence.

"Yes, you do," Abby countered. "I'm serious. I need you to promise you aren't going to freak out or show up on my doorstep."

Vivian remained silent for a moment. "Darling, it's difficult to make such promises without knowing what you're talking about."

"Okay, just promise me you are going to let me handle things," Abby said. "I won't tell you until you promise."

"Fine darling, fine, I promise." Vivian said reluctantly.

"They found me," Abby said. "The Thanos found me."

"What!" Vivian screamed into the phone. There was a tirade of theatrics on the phone and even though Abby couldn't see her grandmother, she could visualize what was happening on the other end of the phone. She had seen the same display a dozen times before.

After a few moments of threats and curses, Abby could hear her grandmother calming down on the other end. "Are you hurt darling? Who was it? What did they do to you?"

"Two goons found me. They weren't witches, but they spoke Greek, so I'm certain they were hired by the Thanos," Abby said. "They roughed me up a bit but I ran them off."

"They hurt you?" Vivian asked. There was genuineness in her voice, and a rare note of concern.

"A little. But I'm fine. I've moved out of the dorm, and I'm finishing school from a small cottage I'm renting. We're hoping, if they are watching the school and they don't' see me there, they will think I've fled. Ms. Grace has been diligent in protecting me. My hideaway has a number of protective spells and wards. I should be safe here," Abby explained.

"My dearest, I feel I should come at once and hide you somewhere better. I was foolish to think they wouldn't find you eventually," Vivian said. Abby could hear her grandmother pouring herself another drink.

"Please don't," Abby said. "I'm fine. If you have a ritual in place and ready to end the war, then I should be fine. They sent goons to do their dirty work. Obviously, I'm not that important of a target anymore."

"How can you expect me to ignore this?" Vivian questioned. It was obvious she wanted to come, but Abby knew she could only cause more chaos in the long run.

"It isn't necessary," Abby insisted. "I'm not alone and I'm safe, at least as safe as anywhere else. You need to focus on whatever it is you have up your sleeve, especially if it will end this war. Then I won't have to worry about the Thanos anymore, and I can come home."

"Are you certain?" Vivian questioned, she was still not convinced.

"For now, I am," Abby reassured.

"If there is so much as another attack or anything remotely suspicious I insist you tell me at once. I will be there faster than you could imagine," Vivian said.

"If anything happens you'll be the first to know," Abby promised.

"I still don't like this," Vivian stated.

"Do you think your time is better served babysitting me or finishing your ritual?" Abby questioned dryly. "Besides, Ms. Grace and both Benjamin and Josephine have been very helpful. This place is the magical version of Fort Knox."

"Valerie is a highly skilled witch. I trust her abilities on this matter," Vivian said bluntly. "I will be contacting you soon. Once the ritual is ready I want you to come home. For a while at least."

"I will," Abby promised. "I'll probably bring Benjamin with me as well. I would appreciate it if you would make at least some small effort to be nice to him."

"Darling, I'm nothing but the epitome of charm and diplomacy," Vivian insisted.

"Only when you want to be. It shouldn't be that difficult. I know for a fact you can be very nice to people you utterly despise. I've seen it," Abby accused gently.

"I don't know what you could possibly be worried about," Vivian stated innocently. The clinking of ice filtered through the phone. "Speaking of which darling, I spoke recently with Carlotta Alberti. She's very excited about you attending Julliard. She's one of two faculty members who are like us. You will find her simply delightful, I'm sure."

"I'm not going to Julliard," Abby said bluntly. It was best to get it out in the open now.

"What?!" Vivian yelled into the phone. "Why on earth would you pass up on an opportunity like this? Abigail Kane! What has gotten into you?"

"I got into the Oxford Faculty of Music. No one pulled any strings to get me in. I earned it on my own accord. That is where I will be going to school," Abby stated plainly.

"Darling, please, I beg you not to throw away your future for that boy!" Vivian pleaded through the phone.

"You know, I think you're probably the first grandparent in history, ever to be upset that their grandchild got into one of the most prestigious universities in the world." Abby said, not bothering to hide her emotions. "I should get going. It's nearly dinner time here." She added.

"You mustn't do this!" Vivian shouted into the phone her words were becoming a touch slurred. "You can't give up your dreams for this boy!"

"Goodbye grandmother," Abby said. "Why don't we continue this conversation when you aren't drunk," Abby added ending the call. She took a deep breath and sighed.

"I can tell that didn't go well," Benjamin called out from the kitchen.

Abby got up and strolled over leaning against the counter. "How much of it did you overhear?"

"Bits and pieces. Enough to know she isn't particularly fond of me, to say the least," Benjamin said as he stirred something inside a large pot. "Should I be worried?" he asked.

"Definitely not," Abby smiled. "She was drunk when I called. There wasn't any possible way that phone call was going to end well."

"I didn't realize the Grand Dame of the Kane family was such a lush," Benjamin chuckled.

"She's been known to get... what do you call it? Snockered?" Abby said with a shrug.

Benjamin thought for a moment. "It works... Pissed, tossed, bladdered, tanked up and blotto, are all suitable as well," he jested.

"Thank you for the local slang tutorial," Abby smiled. "I'm starting to get it down."

Benjamin gave her a discriminating glance. "You're absolutely terrible. You butcher our language virtually every time you make an attempt to utilize our vernacular."

"I just used snockered right!" Abby playfully protested.

"You still use the word desert instead of pudding, nearly every day," Benjamin stated as though it were the final word on the matter. "It's unforgivable really."

"Unforgivable?" Abby laughed. "What about your improper use of the letter 's' instead of 'z' in words like 'socialize' or 'realize'? It's actually quite silly if you ask me," Abby teased.

"You have thrown down the gauntlet!" Benjamin said throwing the oven mitten in a mock gesture of outrage. He then stole a kiss.

It was such a relief to not be fighting. She needed these moments. There had been so few light-hearted moments in the last year, it almost felt like she was out of place. Like she wasn't meant to have them. Abby felt a bit like a rogue, stealing a bit of fun at a time when such things were hard to come by. *This is what I need,* she considered. *More laughter, more kisses,* she smiled warmly at Benjamin, *and him.*

"I'm relieved to see you're feeling better," Nina stated as she snuggled under a blanket in front of the television.

"Me too, I was very worried about you, Abby," Sarah said. She sat next to Warren on the couch and handed him a large bowl of popcorn.

"I'm happy you all came!" Abby said, feeling loved from being surrounded by her friends.

"There's really nothing better than being off campus for a movie night," Warren said excitedly. "Thanks for hosting, we haven't had many chances for all of us to hang out lately."

"I'm glad you came too," Benjamin said cuddling with Abby on the love seat. She appreciated Benjamin's efforts to lift her spirits by inviting her friends over. She gave him an approving smile.

"Normally, I would suggest a good horror movie but since your last couple of weeks have been fairly horrific, I would suggest a good romantic comedy, or melodrama," Warren stated as he flipped through viewing options on the screen.

"There's always a good action flick," Benjamin suggested.

"Hot guys running around and performing stunts sounds fantastic," Nina giggled.

"I'm fine with anything that doesn't involve copious amounts of blood," Sarah stated as she excused herself to use the restroom before the movie started.

Warren selected an action flick and got it ready, waiting for Sarah's return. "Are you ever going to come back to class?" he asked.

Abby looked at Benjamin briefly. "I'm not certain. I guess once they catch the guy, but until then we'll wait and see." Benjamin gave her a squeeze.

"You two are so cute together," Nina squealed.

"What about you, Warren?" Abby asked. "Did you invite anyone special over to join you this evening?"

"Ha!" Warren exclaimed. "I think my, so called, boyfriend has put extra locks on his closet. He's freaked out because the end of the school year is coming up and he doesn't know what he's going to do."

"I didn't know you had a boyfriend," Benjamin said. "Do I know him?"

"Uhh, well…" Warren started to say.

"I don't think the guy in question wants anyone to know," Abby responded quickly, not wanting Warren to feel uncomfortable.

"Oh, that's what you mean by extra locks on the closet," Benjamin stated finally catching on.

"Don't worry we'll get you caught up on the lingo," Warren winked, and laughed.

"So, what's this cinematic masterpiece we're about to watch?" Abby asked.

Nina read the brief description and offered her interpretation, "It's about four extremely hot guys trying to break out of prison without their shirts, apparently." She laughed soliciting similar responses from her friends.

"I think when I'm at university, I'll write a dissertation on the homo-eroticism of mainstream big budget action films," Warren stated as he laughed.

Their laughter was cut short by the crashing sound of glass in one of the back rooms followed by a blood-curdling scream from Sarah.

Everyone jumped to their feet. Benjamin and Abby ran to the bathroom and burst through the door. Sarah was standing against the wall, the window had been broken in and on the floor was a black raven twitching as it died. Abby grabbed Sarah and pulled her from the macabre scene as Benjamin looked out the window.

Another crashing sound upstairs startled everyone. The living room window shattered as the carcass of a black bird broke through the glass and died on the floor. Both Nina and Warren shrieked as they backed away avoiding the broken glass.

Windows throughout the house shattered as black birds crashed through, one after the other. Sickening thuds could be heard all over the house ravens crashed into the walls, their lifeless husks falling limply to the ground.

Sarah screamed. Abby tried to protect her, putting their backs to the wall. Abby could see Warren and Nina huddled in the corner of the living room. Benjamin shielded Abby and Sarah from the glass shards.

"Thanos," Abby whispered to Benjamin who looked worried. "They're here."

CHAPTER TWENTY FIVE

Abby could feel the panic growing in her heart but fought to keep it from taking over. If she lost control, she couldn't work her magic, and her friends needed her.

Everything stopped as an eerie silence settled upon the house. Everyone was still, as though moving would cause the horror to start again. Abby looked closely at the black birds. Dozens of lifeless corpses lay scattered around them. "Lost souls," Abby whispered.

"What?" Benjamin questioned as they looked at the carnage surrounding them.

"Raven's are said to be the embodiment of lost souls," Abby stated, detached from her own words. She then snapped out of her trance. "They sent a Necromancer," she added. Her eyes were wide as fear coursed through her body. Sarah was trembling in her arms, her hands covering her eyes. Abby handed Sarah off to Benjamin and ran into the living room.

"Abby no!" Benjamin yelled. He picked up the immobile Sarah, lifting her into his arms, and followed.

"What the bloody hell happened?" Warren asked, helping Nina to her feet.

Outside there was an eerie cackle. "Come out little one," A man's voice rang in accented English.

"Stay here," Benjamin said, placing Sarah down on the couch.

"This is my fight Benjamin, please," Abby insisted. "Stay with them." She looked at her friends who were terrified and confused.

"They're fine. You're not," he said flatly refusing her request.

"What's happening, Abby?" Nina asked, despondent with fear.

"Don't worry, we'll take care of this," Abby answered, she didn't have the time to explain.

"Please the three of you stay in here, I have to go out and face whoever is out there."

"Are you insane?" Warren questioned. "Something isn't right about all of this."

"Please," Abby pleaded again, as she opened the front door. She stepped out and Benjamin followed.

It was dark, and the air was filled with a thick fog. The patio light was virtually snuffed out by the dense fog. The air moved like tendrils floating in the water. Dozens more ravens lay scattered, lifeless around the perimeter of her house like a ghastly boundary line.

Abby took a step out the door, cautiously navigating the cement path, inching towards the driveway. She could feel her heart pounding in her chest. Every horror story about death magic and necromancy flooded her thoughts bringing unsolicited images of death and decay. She was trembling.

One step and then another. Each step was weighted with hesitation as she maneuvered around the corpses of dead black birds littering the ground. Abby stopped at the edge of the driveway and did her best to see through the fog.

Something unfamiliar was moving nearly ten feet away. As her eyes adjusted to the darkness she saw the fog floating around a dark figure. A man with olive skin and black hair neatly kept. He looked to be in his mid-thirties and wore a black suit that melted into the darkness of the night around him. Abby's eyes locked with his hollow black ones.

"It is time, Kane woman," the man stated, again in English so heavily accented it was difficult to understand.

"Leave now!" Benjamin yelled. His confidence was impressive, and Abby could tell he was using his powers to make himself seem taller and even more foreboding than he already was.

"Stay out of this Hodge!" The man spit after saying Benjamin's name.

Abby used this momentary distraction to use the Sight on the intruder. She did so only briefly and cautiously took in what she could. *This is not the man who killed my parents... He was once the apprentice of the man who did... This man's name is Greggori Thanos, and he is alone.* She closed the Sight and gave herself a moment.

"Greggori Thanos, you are not welcome here, and you shall not enter this house!" Abby yelled and raised her arms. A pale silver veil shrouded the home as she activated the ward. She could feel the fatigue beginning to set in at the unaccustomed use of her power. *I can't stop now,* she thought. *I can do this.*

The man looked at the protective ward shielding the house and smiled menacingly. "You know my name? Impressive, I did not know my reputation was so great!" He laughed, his pride and ego stroked.

"You are a fool, Greggori Thanos," Abby stated as she stepped forward. There was a strength she found inside, a sense of protectiveness over those she loved. "Leave now and never return or you will know... PAIN!" Abby said. Her voice carried her words with such conviction. She thought perhaps she saw a look of uncertainty flash across the Necromancer face.

He quickly recovered and regarded Abby with disdain. "I do not fear little girls," Greggori said as he raised his hands. As he did so, the hundreds of ravens lying dead on the ground came to life, their dead flesh

231

animated by terrible necromantic powers. They began flying around in a terrible flurry. There was a scream from inside the house and Abby looked back to see her three friends watch in horror from the broken window as birds began swarming around them.

The birds began swooping down. Abby could feel sharp claws rake across her cheek. She put her hands up, trying to protect her face. Benjamin dove to the ground and began muttering a spell that Abby couldn't quite hear. A tempest sprang up, pushing the birds away from them. The corpse-ravens started to avoid the mystical whirlwind as Benjamin continued to manipulate the wind.

Abby turned to face the Necromancer. Greggori wore a victorious smile as he smiled and opened his suit jacket to reveal three wicked-looking knives. "Slicinskofia!" Gregorri barked pointing his finger at Abby. All three knives shot towards Abby. She threw herself against the side of the house. Two of the knives flung by, embedding themselves into the front door.

There was a sharp pain in Abby's back. She winced as she reached back and found a large tear in her shirt. When she brought her hand back it was covered in blood.

"Fortinius Hempolos!" She shouted, pointing at a nearby garden hose. The rubber hose flung out and began coiling itself around Greggori's arms and legs.

She knew it wouldn't hold him for long and ran past him and down the driveway.

"Abby!" Benjamin called out. She ignored his plea. She needed to get Greggori away from her friends. She was his target, Abby knew he would follow. His hubris was too great to fail his mission.

She came to the end off the driveway and looked to the trees on the far side of the normally sleepy road. Abby glanced both ways and made a run for it. She nearly made it half way across the road when there was a blinding flash. Abby turned. Electrical energy crawled across the ground towards her like a snake of lightning. She attempted to dodge the strike, but the energy consumed her. Her whole body was riddled with pain.

Abby crumbled to the ground. She looked down at her arm. Small burns webbed across her flesh. She forced herself to crawl the rest of the way as a wicked laughter rang out into the darkness behind her. Abby looked back and saw Greggori Thanos slowly approaching. There was a cocky grin on his face. The kind that indicated he knew he had already won.

Despite the pain, Abby attempted to rally her strength. She couldn't take much more. "Katul Othoto!" she shouted, and snapped her finger. A spark shot from her finger towards Greggori Thanos growing into a large burst of flame.

"Xunsik Huul!" Greggori shouted, blowing air from his lips that extinguished the flames before they made contact. He laughed. "You are a silly little girl," he said through his laughter. "This is a waste of my talent," he added as he began to approach.

"Abby!" Benjamin shouted. She could tell he was somewhere on the driveway looking for her, but she couldn't see him.

"Oh," Greggori said with a grin. "Perhaps I shall kill the filthy Hodge in front of you, before I take you back to the family."

No! Abby screamed in her head. *I won't let you hurt him!* She raised her right arm and made a hex symbol with her hand, remembering the tiny corrections Vivian had drilled into her. "A-Vita Rend-Khol!" Abby spit the words from her mouth; a terrible curse she dreamed she would never have used. Greggori Thanos had forced her hand.

The necromancer stopped in his tracks. A look of panic spread across his face as he dropped the knife in his hand. Abby forced herself to watch as the exposed flesh on his arms, hands and face began to tear open. Seconds after opening, each wound grew black and began to fester. Abby cried out in horror as the curse she used took effect, but would not let herself look away. *I did this,* she thought. *This is what magic can do.* Greggori fell to his knees, screaming in pain. He lay on the pavement, convulsing as every sore on his body oozed a sickly puss. A few agonizingly long moments later, his body dropped to the ground. He didn't move.

Abby crawled over to the man she had cursed, staring at his motionless form. She silently began rocking. As she stared at him, her mind spun in circles, consumed by what she had done. She could hear footsteps approaching, and Abby looked up to see Benjamin stop dead in his tracks.

"What happened?" he looked down at Greggori who was covered in open wounds and pustules.

"Is still alive?" Abby asked, her voice a whisper.

Benjamin knelt next to the Greek man, and checked for signs of life. "Barely," Benjamin said. "What did you do?"

She didn't answer, though she heard his question, she was unable to formulate words. Abby couldn't take her eyes off the effects of the horrible curse she had used. The curse Vivian had taught her. Abby was scared of herself. She was scared of the pain and suffering she was able to inflict upon others. *This is what magic can do…*

Benjamin placed his hand on her knee. Abby jerked back into the present at his touch. She looked into his soft brown eyes, tears welling in her own.

"I'm sorry, I didn't mean to hurt anyone. I just wanted him to stop," she said, trying to make reason of the horrible situation.

"Abby…" Benjamin said, trying to console her. "You did what you had to do, you protected yourself and your friends." Abby looked up at her boyfriend. She didn't understand. She felt like a monster.

The fog was beginning to lift. Nina, Warren and Sarah approached from the driveway. They all looked pale. Their eyes were wide with uncertainty, fear and confusion. Abby could feel the regret swelling in her heart again. She never wanted her friends to see any of this. She wanted them to stay young and naïve, forever blind to the horrors the world was hiding from them.

"I… I don't understand what happened," Sarah said. Her sweet voice was a dagger in Abby's heart. Nina and Warren held each other as they looked at the dead birds all around them, and the man covered in grievous wounds lying in front of them.

"I'm sorry you saw all of this," Abby stated. She was trying to hold her tears back as she looked into their mortified faces. Benjamin had stepped away and was speaking into his phone. She wasn't certain who he was calling, but she spared a hope that it was his sister or Ms. Grace.

"What happened? What's going on?" Warren asked. His voice was shaky and uncertain.

"I don't know where to begin," Abby stated, as she held Sarah who was still trembling. Of all her friends Sarah was perhaps the most grounded, which of course made everything she saw all the more terrifying. Abby knew it must be a shock to all of them.

Benjamin came back shoving his phone in his pocket. "Ms. Grace and Josephine will be here in a couple of minutes; my parents and some members of my coven should be here within the hour. There's a lot to clean up here, but they can take care of it," he said, looking at the yard and the damage to the house. "Leave it to us, Abby."

"Why are your sister and Ms. Grace coming here?" Nina asked, wiping the tears from her cheeks.

"Coven?" Warren asked. "As in witches?"

"Yes," Abby responded cautiously. She could see the fear in their expressions. She didn't want to frighten them any further. "We have a lot to talk about." She looked to Benjamin for support.

"They've been awakened," Benjamin said. "You go ahead and take them in the house. I'll stay here until Ms. Grace and Josephine arrive."

"Ms. Grace is a witch too?" Warren asked. "I should have seen that coming from a mile away.'

"What do you mean by awakened?" Nina asked. "We weren't asleep."

"It means you are a non-witch who is now aware of our existence. 'Awakened to the truth', so to speak." Abby explained. "Please, let's go inside. I'll explain everything."

The four of them went into the house. Nina, Warren and Sarah sat on the couch. Instead of sitting Abby stood at the door and kept it wide open to make certain Benjamin was all right. She had never used the curse before and didn't know how long it would incapacitate someone for. She needed to be ready if Greggori regained consciousness.

Abby looked into the faces of her friends. Three blank faces stared back at her. They had just been irrevocably changed, simply by being near her. She took a deep breath and set her guilt aside; right now, she had to help them understand.

"Here's the thing," Abby began. "Witches are real. I know it sounds like fairy tales, but it's not. What you just saw was some of that magic at work."

They continued to stare at her, so Abby continued, "What I told you about my parent's killer being after me is true, but what I left out is that he is from a rival coven of witches, who want my whole family dead." She spent the next hour explaining her parent's murder, old family vendettas, the Thanos, and the true reason she came to Armitage Hall. Now that they had seen some of it for themselves, she was awakening them to the truth of a world they thought could only be fiction.

They just sat there, listening.

Just as she was finishing her story Ms. Grace and Josephine arrived. Abby stepped outside to speak with them.

"Abby!" Ms. Grace said. "What happened here? Are you alright?" She glanced around the yard at all the dead birds and broken windows, and frowned in worry. Josephine had a shocked look on her face and immediately approached Greggori who remained still on the ground. He hadn't moved from where he had fallen.

"Be careful," Benjamin stated, "I think he's still alive."

She shot him a look of surprise before she bent to examine him. Abby joined them, followed by the others. "I dare say he is still alive. He needs attention, or he'll be dead within the hour."

"I've never seen a curse like that before." Benjamin commented deep in thought.

"Neither have I," Josephine said, as she took a better look. "I'm impressed," she added.

Abby didn't feel proud, in fact she was afraid Benjamin and the others would look at her differently. Like a monster… The guilt ravaged Abby's thoughts as she gazed down at the man she had nearly killed, who could still die before the night was out, because of something she had done to him… *I may have killed him, I've never killed anyone before,* she thought and swallowed the swelling tears. *I don't' even like hunting.*

"His name is Greggori Thanos," Abby stated with more calm than she felt. Josephine looked at Abby quizzically.

"He told you his name?" Josephine asked. Abby thought she sensed the tiniest bit of mockery in the other girl's voice.

She shook her head, "I used the Sight and read his surface thoughts."

"You can do that?" Nina squeaked from behind Abby.

Ms. Grace let out a small noise, surprised three of the students from school were standing behind Abby.

"It… this curse," Abby said, ignoring Nina's question and waving in the direction of Greggori Thanos, "was something my grandmother taught me. I wish she hadn't." she confessed, hoping it would offer some relief from the grief and guilt overwhelming her.

"Don't be foolish," Josephine said pragmatically. "You would be dead now if she hadn't."

Abby shook her head, trying to keep the tears from spilling out. She wasn't ready to see the world the way Josephine did. How long would she have to practice magic before she was that cynical? For the first time she was grateful her parents had kept her from the craft for so long.

"Can we save him?" Abby asked.

"What?" Benjamin seemed surprised. "He tried to murder you, and you want to save him?"

"Abby, this man is dangerous. He knows too much," Josephine argued. "About you, where you live, even what you're capable of now. If he recovers he's going to come after you again, and be better prepared. For your own safety, Abby, he can't be allowed to go back."

Abby was devastated; she couldn't imagine how she could live with being responsible for his death. Even if he was her enemy he was still a human being. Her mind was swimming with thoughts and then it came to her. "My uncle," she said aloud, soliciting confused looks.

"Sebastian is in charge of gathering information on the Thanos for my Grandmother. He would want to interrogate Greggori for information. And, maybe we could use him to press his family for peace. Let my coven determine his fate." She looked at Ms. Grace, for support. "Please, I can't live with his blood on my hands," she added.

Ms. Grace nodded. "A wise decision. Be sure to call your uncle as soon as possible." She began dressing his injuries with an ointment she pulled from her enormous bag. Abby was grateful the older woman was always stocked with salves and potions.

"This is too much," Nina said as she looked around the carnage in the yard.

"I'll take her back inside," Warren said. "Sarah, come with us." He put his arm around Sarah and guided her into the house. She still hadn't said anything about all this, and Abby worried about her. *The shock must be too much for her,* she thought, grateful Warren was there.

Abby leaned against the house as she stared at the man on the ground. Ms. Grace continued to offer what assistance she could, and Josephine reluctantly started to help bandage the necromancer. Benjamin was pacing as he spoke into his phone again.

She looked at the night sky. The moon was beginning to break through the fog as it continued to disperse. Abby spent a few moments considering Greggori Thanos' dubious chances of survival. *It might be better to take care of this myself,* she thought, *in case Sebastian doesn't get here in time.*

There was only one way to do that though. She slid down the wall and sat with her knees to her chest. She attempted to clear her mind, readying herself to interrogate an unconscious witch. It took a few moments for her emotions to abate and her thoughts to still. Her guilt and remorse were intrusive, but she was eventually able to invoke her powers. Her eyes rolled back, and her consciousness awakened. It was an awareness familiar only to those who possess the Sight.

Abby carefully focused on Greggori Thanos. Though unconscious, his mind was still present. She could sense his confusion and disbelief. It was clear he thought his task here would be easy. He was prideful and self-important. His name was written in every thought and memory. His ego colored everything. *This man certainly thinks highly of himself,* she noted.

She pushed further and found his thoughts. He had been planning to take her prisoner. His intent was to hand her over to his coven, who would attempt to bargain her life for the books and artifacts the Kane family kept from them. If the family refused there was no question Greggori would kill her.

She pressed even deeper looking for more information that could help her family. Abby wasn't certain she had ever gone this deeply into anyone's mind before. This deep, the thoughts were unclear, more like shadows with form that required deciphering.

Abby settled in, concentrating on her Sight, allowing the power to lead her. Finally, thoughts and images of her and her family started to appear. She came to a set of thoughts about the war with the Kane family. She was no longer in Greggori's mind, but was watching a memory unfold as an outsider. She was there, and not there, watching a memory replay itself with Greggori's thought and emotions coloring the experience.

A man in his late thirties, perhaps in his early forties was speaking to Greggori. She couldn't hear the words, but she felt his disdain for the two thugs that were being hired to kidnap her. Behind the man giving orders, was a shadowed figure in the haze just behind him. Abby couldn't make out the face, but she sensed fear from Greggori. *Whoever the shadow was, Greggori is afraid of him,* Abby thought. *What is a necromancer afraid of?* She watched as the scene changed, and the two hit men returned, unsuccessful.

The distinguished-looking man turned his menacing grin towards Greggori, and Abby could sense the respect and endearment Greggori had for his man. Abby looked at him, as a name appeared in her head.

Atoro Thanos.

All at once she fought for breath. *It's him!* She realized.

She was looking into the face of the man who murdered her parents. His eyes were black soulless wells. Abby could feel herself drawn into them, and as she stared into the darkness she could see the strange symbol... a pentagram with an eye in the center. It was the same marking on the wall in her father's office.

Abby gasped for air, pulled from the Sight in her shock. Her body drained of all energy and strength, and she fell to the ground. Her head was pounding as though someone had bashed her skull against the concrete. She could hear people yelling her name, but couldn't distinguish any of the voices. Slowly the world came clear again, and she found herself being comforted by Benjamin as her body paid the price for the use of her power. Taxed beyond exhaustion, she sat still, unthinking. Slowly her breathing returned to normal and she could feel herself back in the moment.

"What did you see?" Benjamin asked when she was alert again.

Abby took a few breaths, "I saw him. I know who he is," she said her voice a sickly croak. "I saw the man who murdered my parents."

CHAPTER TWENTY SIX

Abby sat at the desk in her sanctuary reading a book, and doing her best to ignore the sound of workers upstairs replacing the windows. She spent much of the last two days using the Sight on Greggori and she was exhausted.

Benjamin came down stairs and placed a glass of water and a small saucer with several pills next to her. "Time for your daily dose," he said.

"Ugh," Abby said looking at the small pile of pills she had to take each day. She recognized three of them; one being her medication for anemia, one was her contraception pill and the other her daily multi-vitamin. There was a small thimble sized paper cup filled with a bluish liquid. "Benjamin? What's this for?"

Her boyfriend grabbed his own book and took a seat in a chair next to Abby's desk. He glanced over and smiled. "That's something I made for you. It's an elixir that should help with your stomach. Ms. Grace helped me with it. I'm hoping you'll eat a little more if your stomach isn't upset all the time."

"Thank you, that was very thoughtful," Abby said. "How is he?"

"I still can't believe you care what happens to that monster. He would have killed you," Benjamin said shaking his head, and then answering her question, "He's fine. My parents have him secured. I think your uncle has sent some people to collect him."

Abby finished taking her pills and washed them down. She was bothered that he was so close to danger because of her, not to mention her friends who were innocent to the world of witchcraft and the occult until they met her. Sarah was still having a hard time. She hadn't really spoken about it with either Abby or Nina, and Abby hoped the other girl would be okay soon. Nina and Warren were shaken, but their fear had given way to curiosity. Benjamin had been kind enough to indulge their questions over the last couple of days while Abby rested.

There was a buzz at the door.

I'll get it," Benjamin stated, jumping from his chair before Abby could respond. He had been particularly overprotective the last couple of days. She could tell he wanted to take care of her, though she was beginning to feel like she was being managed.

"Abby!" Benjamin called down to her from the top of the stairs. "You have guests."

Abby wasn't expecting anyone She set her book aside and made her way upstairs. She hadn't done much with herself, having thrown on a comfortable pair of jeans and a wool sweater. As she reached the front door, she was surprised to see two familiar faces. "Uncle Sebastian? Grandmother!" she said, questioning her own eyes.

Her uncle stood in the doorway smiling warmly, her grandmother right behind him. She rushed forward and gave them both a big hug. Abby did her best to hold back tears of joy as she spoke to them. "Why didn't you tell us you were coming?" Abby asked refusing to let go.

"Darling, nothing would have kept us away," Vivian said, stepping into the house. She glanced around the front room curling her nose slightly.

"I figured you'd tell me you were all right and not to bother, so I didn't give you a chance," Sebastian stated. "You are important to us, Abby. It isn't safe here for you anymore."

"You didn't have to do that." Abby muttered, pulling her uncle into the living room. Vivian was running her white glove along the banister seemingly impressed when she found her glove was still clean.

"Of course, we did, darling," Vivian said, looking out of place in the homey space Abby had made for herself. Vivian sat on the edge of a leather chair, still looking around the room as though she were being tainted by the cheap décor.

"I suppose you've met my boyfriend, Benjamin?" Abby asked her uncle. She loved Sebastian very much, and it meant a great deal to her both he and her grandmother came all the way to England.

"Of course, we met at the door," Sebastian stated. "It is very nice to meet you."

"Likewise," Benjamin stated, following them into the living room. "Mrs. Kane," Benjamin greeted Vivian politely with a slight bow of his head.

Vivian looked at him with a quaint smile. Her eyes burrowed into Benjamin so intensely that for a brief moment, Abby thought her grandmother was going to throw a curse at the young man.

"Benjamin Hodge," Vivian said politely, her disdain was weighted in every syllable. "I don't suppose you would mind letting us have a private conversation with Abigail. We have some important... private family business to discuss. I'm certain you understand," she spoke dismissively.

"Grandmother," Abby said giving Vivian a look.

"No, it's alright," Benjamin said. "I completely understand." He excused himself from the room and retreated to the basement.

"It wasn't necessary to be so rude, Vivian," Sebastian said.

"Rude? I don't know what you mean," Vivian said, putting on her most innocent smile. "I simply asked the young man for a few moments with my precious Abigail," she smiled sweetly. "We don't need a Hodge poking into our family's important matters."

Sebastian rolled his eyes and turned his attention back to Abby. He put his arms around her and pulled her close, kissing her on the head. "I missed you, Abby." His smile was warm. It was a taste of home that Abby hadn't realized was missing. It filled her heart and lifted her spirits more than anything else had in months.

"I missed you too," Abby said quietly, wiping tears from the corner of her eyes.

"We have some people taking care of the Necromancer you captured," Sebastian said without further preamble, "but I'm more than a little worried. This is the second attack since you've moved to England. You look pale and thin. What's been going on here?"

"I lost a lot of blood in the first attack, and I've been anemic ever since. It's been a drain on my energy. I've gained a little weight back, but I'm still working on it. My nerves have been making it hard to eat properly," Abby explained, as though she were a little girl who had done something wrong.

"Darling, where is your luggage? I'll help you pack," Vivian said, glancing down the hallway with uncertainty.

"Pack?" Abby questioned. "Where are we going?"

"Home," Sebastian stated.

"Is it safe there?" Abby asked with uncertainty.

"No more or less than anywhere else at this point," Sebastian suggested.

"What do you mean?" Abby asked.

"Thanks to you we have a major bargaining chip," Sebastian explained.

"Yes darling, those necromantic fiends want to enter negotiations for his return," Vivian added. "It appears this horrid Greggori person is important enough they won't risk losing him. They are unlikely to make another move while everything is so... uncertain."

"Is the war over then?" Abby asked.

"Not officially, but it would seem we're on the verge of coming to some kind of agreement." Sebastian suggested.

"That's great!" Abby said. Her excitement was quickly tempered when she thought about Benjamin, her friends, Ms. Grace... She had created a new life for herself here. Though she wanted more than anything to go home to Seattle to be with her family, she wasn't eager to abandon her friends or her life here either. Or Benjamin. Abby thought about all he means to her. He would no doubt come with her, but he wouldn't want to stay, at least not for long...

"Is there something wrong?" Sebastian asked. He could obviously tell Abby had lapsed deep into thought.

"No," Abby said. "I just didn't realize things would be happening so fast." She could feel her head spinning.

"Darling, this is wonderful news. We can all be a family again," Vivian urged, obviously trying to invoke some ember of excitement.

"I'm happy. Really, I am," Abby said unconvincingly.

"But?" Sebastian questioned.

"I want a chance to say goodbye to my friends here. School is almost over. I'd like to properly finish my courses," Abby explained.

"Darling you can come back and visit whenever you want," Vivian said dismissively.

Abby nodded her head. "I know," she confessed. "Isn't it safe enough for me to stay at least for another week or two?"

"What on earth are you talking about darling?" Vivian stood doing little to temper her outrage.

"Vivian please," Sebastian said, motioning for her to stop.

"She only wants to stay because of that boy," Vivian barked, folding her arms.

"Would you please stop calling him 'that boy'? He has a name," Abby said, irritated by Vivian's tantrum.

"Vivian, stop!" Sebastian shouted giving Vivian a look.

"Mr. Whitlock, I will not be silenced. Especially where my granddaughter is concerned," Vivian said imperiously, clutching the pearls dangling around her neck. "I am the matriarch of this coven and I am more than capable of deciding what is best."

"Yes, you are the matriarch, but you aren't our dictator," Sebastian countered. "It's perfectly reasonable that Abby would want to say goodbye to her friends. Her social life is not the issue here; her safety is."

"You think just because we have that horrid Greggori creature, they wouldn't make a move against us... against my darling granddaughter?" Vivian countered and turned to Abby. "Darling, please get your things ready. I'll have us on a flight this evening. Your friends will understand. You can see them again, soon."

Abby responded as calmly as she could. "You brought me here to hide, to protect me. We never knew how long I would be here. You just dropped me here without a word, and I started building a life for myself. For the first time since my old life was taken away from me, I have a home. I want to come home grandmother, and I will. There are few things I want more than to be with you and the rest of the family. Truly. But I am not going to abandon what I started here without saying goodbye. All I'm asking for is a couple weeks."

"But darling, the Thanos are cornered animals. There is no telling what they might do in their desperation," Vivian insisted. "We should leave at once. Bring that Bradly with you for all I care."

"His name is Benjamin, and you know it," Abby said rolling her eyes. "And none of this is about him."

"I think I have a solution," Sebastian interjected. Both Abby and Vivian turned their attention to the middle-aged man in his smart grey business suit.

"What, darling?" Vivian asked disapprovingly.

"Abby want's to, at the very least, wrap up the life she's built for herself here before returning home. Which is perfectly understandable," Sebastian nodded towards Abby. "Vivian, you are worried the Thanos family may come after her in a desperate act to gain leverage before our families enter into negotiations. A concern I share. We're all worried about you, Abby... especially your grandmother and me."

"That's right, darling. I only care about you, dear. You are the only thing I have left," Vivian pleaded, crocodile tears waiting in the wings, but never quite making an appearance.

Abby sighed. "What's your solution then?" she asked cautiously.

"You want two weeks to say goodbye and make arrangements to leave. I'll stay here with you," Sebastian stated.

"She would be much safer with her entire family surrounding her," Vivian protested.

"Really?" Abby said, beaming. She couldn't hide her excitement at the idea. "I would really love that! I would love to share with you the life I have here."

"Vivian, the chances of the Thanos attacking again in such a short time, when Abby has already proven herself against an older and much more experienced witch, seems unlikely," Sebastian explained. "I'm willing to remain and keep an eye out for any trouble."

Vivian sighed and rolled her eyes before glancing at the diamond studded watch on her wrist. Abby lightheartedly rushed her grandmother and gave her an enormous hug taking the old woman by surprise. "Darling, if I didn't know any better, I would accuse you of trying to choke me to death," Vivian said, as Abby pulled away.

"I would never," Abby said playfully. "I can't believe this is all over. I'll be able to put this all behind me."

"Remember, it isn't over yet. But, we are getting close," Sebastian warned. "Let's not let our guard down too much."

"I won't," Abby said. For the first time in a long time, it felt like things were going to get better. Hope had become an unfamiliar feeling' something Abby was determined to change.

"How did you ever convince your grandmother to go on a picnic?" Sebastian asked as they stepped through the tall grass.

"I didn't exactly explain to her that she would be traipsing through a field," Abby confessed with a wicked smile.

Abby glanced back to see Benjamin helping Vivian through the grass. She stifled a giggle as she watched her grandmother doing her best to traverse the uneven soft ground in her designer heals. Vivian begrudgingly accepted Benjamin's help and the look on her face was that of mild disgust poorly disguised with a polite grin.

"Darling are we almost there?" Vivian called out.

"Just a few more yards grandmother," Abby responded with an amused smile. She glanced over at her uncle and Ms. Grace who seemed equally amused.

The sky was clear and though there was a bit of a chill, it was a beautiful spring afternoon. Abby pulled her jacket closer in around her.

"Your boyfriend deserves a special commendation for helping your grandmother after the way she treated him," Sebastian commented.

"Benjamin has always been a polite and thoughtful young man," Ms. Grace stated proudly as though she were speaking of her own child.

"I warned him it will likely take her a long time to come around." Abby said as they passed the little brook that ran through campus. There was a grassy knoll ahead, with an incredible view of the English countryside. As they crested the small hill, Abby could see for at least a mile, green grassy fields with wild flowers. The landscape was occasionally broken by a small farm or a grove of trees. It was a magnificent view.

"I can see why you love this place so much," Sebastian said.

"It is one of my favorite places to come and think," Valerie said, placing the picnic basket on the ground.

Sebastian laid out the large blanket while Abby pulled several cushions out of the large bag she had carried. As the three of them sat, Vivian and Benjamin approached. Vivian was holding the young man's arm doing her best to maintain her poise. Once they arrived Vivian quickly took a seat on the blanket as though it were the most indignant thing she had ever had to endure.

"Thank you, Mr. Hodge," Vivian said dismissively.

"No problem at all Mrs. Kane," Benjamin said stiffly, and sat next to Abby. She gave him a sweet knowing smile.

"I understand you're returning to America tomorrow," Valerie stated.

"Yes, I'm working on a very important project. Time sensitive really," Vivian explained as she regarded the tea sandwiches with suspicion. "A rather impressive curse, to tell the truth. I'm afraid the details of which must remain… undisclosed for the time being."

"Of course, she isn't telling anyone in the family either," Sebastian added with a grin.

"Vivian does like her secrets," Valerie said affectionately.

"Wasn't your sister planning to join us?" Sebastian asked. "I only met her briefly."

"She has a large project she's working on in the art department," Benjamin explained. "She sends her regards and asks for your forgiveness. Being away this coming weekend has stolen much of the time she needs to complete the project. I'm afraid she's a bit preoccupied."

"It's perfectly understandable. I'm glad to hear no one ran her off," Sebastian said, pointedly giving Vivian a glance. Vivian raised an eyebrow and feigned innocence.

"Josephine has always been passionate about her art," Abby added.

"Yes, she's very talented for such a young artist. A true gift," Ms. Grace said. "I suspect we shall see her work in a gallery in a few short years."

"Josephine is a perfectionist," Benjamin explained. "She can be very single-minded, and she works hard. No doubt it will pay off for her someday."

"It's rather cold up here. Don't you think?" Vivian questioned obviously changing the subject. Her overt hint that she was done sitting on a blanket in the grass was not missed by anyone. Abby knew her grandmother was going to make the last twenty-four hours of her stay as uncomfortable as possible.

A week after Vivian was safely on a plane back to Seattle, it was time for another goodbye. "I'm going to miss you," Abby said, giving Benjamin another kiss. The car was out front, and his luggage packed. They stayed behind the closed door to the bedroom, giving Abby the more intimate moment she wanted before their parting.

"I'm going to miss you too," Benjamin said stealing another kiss wrapping his arms around her waist. "It's hard to imagine how long four days can feel when I'm not with you."

"Somehow, I think we'll both manage," Abby reassured him. "Besides after you get back we can finish packing and next weekend we'll be on a flight home."

"Is Seattle going to be home?" Benjamin asked.

Abby smiled. "It will always be home to me, I think. But maybe it won't be my only home," she added sweetly.

"Your grandmother gave me a smile before she left. I think it might even have been a little genuine," Benjamin said hopefully.

"It wasn't," Abby said flatly. "Give it some time. Just remember, what my grandmother thinks of you has no bearing on how I feel about you."

"I know," Benjamin said disappointed. "I hope the rest of your family isn't going to be so difficult to charm."

"They won't be. Sebastian is already fond of you, and I don't think any of the rest of my family would have any reason to dislike you," Abby reassured. "I can't imagine how they could. You're too adorable."

"Adorable!" Benjamin said clutching his heart with feigned pain. "Not stunning? Manly? Irresistible? God-like?"

"You stop," Abby smiled giving him another kiss. "I love you, Mr. Hodge," Abby said.

Benjamin had a surprised look on his face, his mouth opened wide with shock quickly melting away to a wide smile. "You finally said it."

"Said what?" Abby asked.

"That you love me. I've been waiting for ages to hear you utter those words," Benjamin said with a celebratory grin.

"I've said it dozens of times," Abby dismissed.

"Nope, you haven't," Benjamin insisted. "I've been waiting and listening carefully since you gave me such a hard time when I said it for the first time, weeks ago."

"You're being silly," Abby accused turning red. "How could I possibly go so long without saying it when I feel it every day."

Benjamin moved in for another long kiss. "I'm having second thoughts about going on this trip," he said devilishly. "I can think of some other things I'd rather do." He gave her a seductive smile.

Abby playfully pushed him away gently. "Sounds like fun, but there will be plenty of time for that when you return. You should spend some time with your family before we leave."

"It's times like this when I wish you were wrong," Benjamin said giving her another sweet kiss.

He broke away and collected his luggage. Abby got the door for him and they walked down the short hallway into the living room.

Josephine and Sebastian sat on the couch engaged in small talk. Josephine looked up as they approached. "You're worse than me," She accused, looking at Benjamin's bag. "I was ready over an hour ago."

"I got a later start," Benjamin said without explaining. "I'm ready now."

"I hope the two of you enjoy your trip," Sebastian said, standing as Josephine and Benjamin headed towards the door.

"Our family has been doing this for generations," Josephine explained. "It's never dull."

"Don't worry Abby. I won't bring anything back as you requested," Benjamin added humorously. It was obvious he was amused by her distaste for hunting.

"Thank you. Have a great time," Abby said as she watched Benjamin and Josephine deposit his luggage in the back of his SUV. She waved as they pulled away.

246

"He really cares about you," Sebastian observed as the car disappeared down the road.

Abby closed the door and took a seat on the couch with her uncle. "He says he loves me," Abby confessed.

Sebastian smiled. "I'm sure he does."

"You don't seem convinced," Abby observed.

"No, I'm just thinking about my first love. It was so intense. We fought all the time, and always had fun making up," Sebastian reminisced.

"I feel like there's a warning coming," Abby jested.

"Not a warning," Sebastian clarified. "A caution perhaps."

"Out with it then," Abby said, bracing herself.

"Benjamin seems like a very nice young man, and there isn't any doubt he cares about you."

"But…?" Abby lead.

"You know, Abby, first love rarely works out. Sure, there are exceptions. It's just statistically, the odds are never good. I just want to make sure you're prepared for every eventuality," Sebastian said.

"You and your statistics," Abby jested. "You're such a numbers person. It's why you're such a good businessman."

"I haven't done well for myself by ignoring numbers and odds," Sebastian agreed. "I don't want you to think I'm telling you it isn't going to work. I hope it does. I guess what I'm saying is protect your heart. You feel, and you love deeply. It is one of the greatest things about you. It also makes you incredibly vulnerable. All I'm saying is protect yourself."

"Is there something you are seeing that I'm not seeing?" Abby asked, wondering if her uncle was trying to warn her about something he'd observed. She trusted him, and she didn't think he was keeping things from her, but the idea that Sebastian was seeing some flaw in her relationship with Benjamin made her mind race with worry.

"Not at all," Sebastian said reassuringly. "Perhaps I shouldn't have mentioned it. I didn't intend to make you second guess your relationship with Benjamin. I just worry about you. You've been through so much." He sighed. "I guess I'm being over protective. I'll do my best to keep it in check."

"Don't you dare become another Vivian Kane," Abby jested.

Sebastian gave her a preposterous look. "Why ever not, darling? How could you not want a dozen Vivians pulling strings?" He jested in a decent imitation of her grandmother.

Abby made a face, and laughed at him. It felt good. Having her uncle stay with her made her feel like home. "Hopefully once you get to know Benjamin better you'll know what a good person he is," Abby said.

"I suspect I will."

CHAPTER TWENTY SEVEN

I'm going to miss this place, she thought as she began searching for the book she had been studying in preparation for using the Sight. *It feels like I just moved in.*

Tomorrow she would be meeting with Edgar and Ms. Grace and begin her investigation. She had precious little time as Benjamin would be back in a couple days and no doubt be displeased. She found the book in a pile on the counter, and pulled the large text form the stack. She settled on the couch with a cup of tea to wade through the various avenues she could use to set her power to good use.

An abrupt knock at the door startled her. Abby's heart leapt into her throat. She searched for the phone in her pocket and held it in her hand, ready to call her uncle at the first sign of trouble. She cautiously approached the front door and looked through the peephole. Standing on the other side of the door was Edgar Kincaid. Abby paused for a few moments, readying herself for whatever was to come. She took a deep breath and opened the door.

"Hello Edgar," Abby said warmly. "Is everything okay?"

"Sorry for showing up unannounced. I brought this to you," Edgar said holding out a necklace. It was a gold chain with a small heart charm attached. "I know we were supposed to meet tomorrow but I'm about to lose my mind. I was hoping you could try and see if you can learn something from it, like we talked about."

Abby felt uncertain. She stared at the charm for a brief moment. She understood how much pain he was in. What harm could it do? She gave him a welcoming smile. "Why don't you come in. I have some tea and we can give it a try," Abby said.

She paid close attention to the moment he passed the thresh hold, waiting to see how the wards would react. *There was nothing. He means me no harm; the hearth ritual would have taken effect if he had,* Abby realized. There was some small relief, despite her belief that Edgar never meant her any harm. "Have a seat," Abby said motioning to the couch. She sat next to him and motioned to the necklace. "May I?"

"Oh, yes," Edgar said handing the delicate piece to Abby. She could tell he was nervous. He wanted answers and Abby hoped she could give him some.

"I'm going to focus on this and see what kind of impressions I can pick up," Abby explained.

She held the necklace, cupped between both hands and sat on the edge of the couch. She began to clear her mind, searching for a balance between consciousness and detachment that left just enough room for fate to enter her mind. Like a trickle of water, a familiar sense began to fill the cleared space of her thoughts like sands filling an hour glass. As Abby's communion with Fate grew, she allowed her senses to gently reenter the world. Waves of images flooded through her thoughts and Abby waited for the maelstrom to settle, for fate to reveal what connections it maintained with the locket in her hands.

There were a few brief flashes of a young woman wearing a school uniform. *Emily...* She was laughing and sitting close to Edgar on a bench on the edge of the school courtyard. *They look so happy...* There was another flash.

Abby saw Emily getting out of bed in the middle off the night. Nina and Sarah were fast asleep in their beds. Abby watched as the young woman threw a warm bathrobe over her shoulders and stepped out into the hallway towards the bathroom. She hadn't made it more than a few steps when a shadowy figure emerged at the end of the hallway. Emily gave pause for a brief moment and then seemed to fall at ease. "What are you doing down here?" she asked. It was obviously someone she recognized.

The shadow figure remained silent. However, this silence was not the mere absence of sound. It was weighted with something more... something menacing. Emily seemed to pick up on the foul air between them and took a step back.

"What do you want? I told you I wouldn't tell anyone," Emily pleaded in whispers. There was a growing fear in her eyes as she backed away. The figure veiled in shadows remained still as though it were waiting for precisely the right moment to pounce.

Emily began breathing heavily. She turned and began running down the dark hallway towards the back stairs. Abby watched as the shadow figure gave chase. As it passed Abby it turned its head as though it could see her.

The shadow figure chased Emily down the hallway and Abby ran to keep up. She followed them down the stairs and out the door into the main courtyard. Abby could see Emily running towards the woods adjacent to campus. A sick feeling swelled in her stomach as she realized what was going to happen beyond the tree line. *I saw what happens there...* Then there was another flash.

Abby could feel her own connection to Emily and fate followed it like a current. She found herself in deep murky water. She could feel the cold seep through her clothing and chill her to her very core. Abby could see something in the distance, floating on the surface of the water. A round object, *a rock... a skull!* Abby recoiled in horror as she looked upon the final remains of Emily Wright.

Enough! Abby thought and attempted to pull herself from the Sight, but something was holding her there. She felt a menacing presence behind her, and Abby slowly turned to see what lurked behind her, what force was challenging her mastery of fate.

The dark shadow figure floated in the water watching her curiously. The figure was beginning to take more shape. It was more clearly a human form rather than a human like figure. There were eyes a nose and mouth. *It's getting clearer! I'm getting closer!* Abby realized. Then the water began to change suddenly from the deep grey-blue of natural water to a deep blood red.

The malignant presence began laughing, it was a maniacal laughter. It grew louder and louder. Abby covered her ears. She couldn't breathe. Something wasn't right. This wasn't how the Sight worked. Something, or someone, was interfering!

Abby dropped the necklace on the coffee table; the image too disturbing she managed to sever the connection despite resistance. *Emily...?* she thought. *Why are you doing this? What are you trying to show me?*

Edgar looked alarmed. "What's wrong?"

Abby took a deep breath and tried to center herself. She was weak and shaking. The tax from using her power so much in the last month stole her breath and sapped her strength. Her body was riddled with pain. She knew she couldn't keep going on this way, but she had to have answers. Edgar needed her to find answers. She'd seen enough of death to last her a lifetime, and she couldn't let this go unresolved.

"I'm sorry, Edgar. I'm certain... Emily is dead," Abby said barely above a whisper. It was a truth she had known, but she couldn't spare Edgar the truth any longer. She felt sick to her stomach.

Edgar stood and turned away. Abby could see he was fighting to stay in control. "What happened?" his voice broke with emotion.

Abby was unsettled by the images and impressions resonating in her thoughts. "I don't know for certain, but it wasn't an accident. Edgar, I'm certain someone is responsible."

"Why?" Edgar protested. "She didn't have any enemies; Emily was well liked by everyone. Who would want to kill her?"

"I have no idea," Abby stated. "They were only impressions, I didn't get any indication who, only that it was someone familiar to her." Abby could tell Edgar was struggling to accept the truth. "Maybe you should reconsider the tea, I can give you some whiskey with it if you like," she headed into the kitchen and put a new pot on to boil. She pulled the whiskey from the cupboard, Benjamin kept around for 'medicinal purposes' and placed it on the counter.

250

Abby noticed she had a message on her phone. She tapped the screen awake, and saw Benjamin sent a text checking up on her.

Benjamin: *How are you? You OK?*

Abby: *I'm fine. Doing some packing.*

She set her phone down and checked on the water. Within seconds she received another text. She glanced at it. Benjamin again. She tapped her phone.

Benjamin: *Where is Sebastian?*
Where is Ms. Grace? Who
is there with you?

Abby: *How did you know someone*
else was here with me?

Benjamin: *Josephine and I cast a*
protective ritual that
warns us when someone
new is at the house

Benjamin: *So, who is it?*

Abby could feel her heart sink. She couldn't lie to Benjamin. Abby had a brief panic and texted back. Edgar had obviously triggered their spell when he entered the house. It was unavoidable. She would have to tell Benjamin the truth and deal with the fall out when he returned.

Abby: *It's Edgar. I told him I would*
try and help him figure out
what happened to Emily.

There was a long pause. Abby held her breath. After a couple of minutes her phone dinged, another message. Abby glanced down at the screen.

Benjamin: *Stay there, I'm on my*
way home!

He's furious, Abby thought. *What am I going to do?* She was sure he would kill Edgar this time for sure. Abby was just trying to help, but their past fights did not leave her with any comfort about her boyfriend's state of mind.

Abby: *Please don't be angry. I'm*
only trying to help him. You
really don't need to come
home early.

She sent the text with shaking hands. Setting the phone aside, she pulled the kettle off the stove top and finished making the tea.

She left her phone on the counter and took the tray with the tea and whiskey into the living room where Edgar was sitting, his head in his hands. Despite the pose, he looked slightly better than when she'd left him. He was less pale, and the red glow was gone from his eyes. She set the tray on the coffee table and poured him a cup topping it off with a healthy shot of whiskey.

Edgar sat in deep contemplation as he sipped his tea. When he finished, Abby promptly poured him another cup. "What else did you see? Was there more?" he asked.

For a few moments, Abby contemplated how she would tell him the truth. There was really no good way to speak of the horrors in her vision. Abby did her best to describe what she saw and the impressions she had gotten from the vision.

"Can you try again?" Edgar asked. "We need more information. I can't rest until whoever did this pays," he growled, gripping the teacup so hard Abby was afraid it would break.

"It's very difficult, Edgar," Abby stated. "I haven't mastered this ability. I can try, but it takes a lot out of me. Please understand, I'm going to do my best, it's just that it may not be enough."

Edgar nodded his understanding. Abby reluctantly picked up the necklace and held it in her hands. Again, she pushed everything from her mind and entered a state of clarity. She repeated the process and focused solely on the necklace and Emily Wright.

Abby felt herself submerged in a large body of water. The bitter cold slammed against Abby as though she had been thrown into an ice-cold lake. Despite being under water, Abby could breath as though it was air. She looked up and saw a pale moon breaking through the surface offering the faintest glow beneath the water. Just above the surface Abby could see a dock nearby and a concrete slab near the edge of the water. She focused and recognized the rough wooden walls, and fading paint of the Armitage Hall crest.

"Come find me Abby," a disembodied voice whispered in her ear, garbled by water but the words were clear and chilling.

She turned. A corpse was floating in the water. Long tendrils of blonde hair floated in the currents in an eerie dance. The pale face of Emily wright floated mere inches away, her eyes closed. A feeling of dread came over Abby as Emily's face began to change. A subtle shift began to occur right in front of her eyes. Emily's blonde hair began to darken into a light red color. Her nose and lips began to narrow and take on a strangely familiar appearance.

Abby let out a scream as she saw her own dead face looking back at her. The water began turning dark as night as shadow descended upon her like a storm cloud.

Abby dropped the necklace, struggling to breath, as she abruptly cut off the Sight. Edgar stood alarmed as Abby's eyes rolled back in her head and she crumbled to the floor, hitting her head on the corner of the coffee table.

Edgar tried to catch her, but it was too late.

A few moments passed and Abby opened her eyes. Her guest was kneeling over her with his phone in hand.

"No!" she yelled. "I'm alright. Don't call anyone."

Edgar paused and saw Abby's eyes were open. He helped her onto the couch. "Really, I'll be alright," Abby reassured him. She could feel the warm trickle of blood run from a small gash just above her right eyebrow. Her head was throbbing as she attempted to catch her breath through the pain.

After a few moments, Abby tried to clear her mind and decipher what she saw, but the words kept echoing in her head. *Come find me, Abby.*

She had to help Emily.

"The boathouse," she gasped. "I think she's under the boathouse."

"I have to go out there," Edgar said, heading towards the door.

"Wait a minute," Abby said. "I'll get my coat and some flashlights. It's dark."

"You don't have to go," Edgar offered.

"You're not doing this alone. We don't really know what we're going to find," Abby said as she pulled her jacket on. Her head was throbbing, but she was steady on her feet. "Just take it slow. We'll find answers."

"It's a long walk," Edgar warned.

"I've walked it many times," Abby would not be dissuaded.

As the two made their way to the pond, Abby was thinking about what they were going to do. They were going to look for a body. In the last year, Abby had seen more death than she ever wanted to see.

Once we find the body, what then? Do we call the police? Will Edgar want me to use the Sight again to see if I can discern what happened? Who murdered Emily? The idea made Abby feel sick to her stomach. She'd already been subjected to terrible visions this evening, she wasn't eager to subject herself to more.

"Can you walk a little slower? I'm having a hard time keeping up," Abby was practically jogging. Even walking normally Edgar's stride made it difficult to keep up.

"Sorry," he said. "I'm anxious to find answers."

"I know," Abby acknowledged. "Even if we find her we may not find any answers."

"I know that," Edgar sounded slightly irritated. "I don't know what I'm going to do."

When they arrived at the pond, Abby could see the boathouse sat on the edge of a long dock, extending from the main doorway. "This is it!" Edgar said hurrying forward.

He rushed down the dock as Abby followed. The door was secured with a solid lock. Abby watched as Edgar took the lock in his hand and squeezed. It broke into a dozen little pieces in his hand.

"That's handy," Abby said, impressed with his strength. Her feeble attempt at humor did little to ease the growing anxiousness she felt.

The door to the boathouse creaked open; rowboats and paddles lined the walls. Her heart froze. She'd never been inside this boathouse before, but she was certain. This was the place in her first vision. Edgar was standing in almost the same spot where she had seen him bash in Josephine's skull.

Abby took a step back. She caught her breath, and tried to calm herself down. *It's okay, Abby. She isn't even here. Everything is fine.*

Edgar continued further into the boathouse. "Where do you think she is?" he asked.

Abby looked around. She was certain it was the location Emily had shown her less than an hour before. The old wooden walls were shabby and musty from years of water damage, and on the far wall from where they stood was an old faded crest of Armitage Hall.

"I think she's under the boathouse down there, under the water." Abby pointed into the dark recesses of the pond.

A feeling of pure dread washed over Abby. Scenes from her visions all washed together in front of her; crows, hair pins, corpses floating in the water, and so much blood. "Something isn't right," she whispered under her breath. She took another step back. "Something terrible is going to happen."

"What?" Edgar questioned turning to face Abby. She flashed her light in his direction and saw a girl, her age drenched in a tattered school uniform standing behind him. The girl walked through Edgar as though he wasn't there and stood at the edge of the boathouse pointing down.

A chill rattled Abby's bones. Cold sweat began dripping from her clammy forehead as waves of horror ravaged her limbs with each beat of her heart. Abby could feel her strength leave her. She sat abruptly to keep herself from falling. She pulled her knees into her chest and began rocking as her flashlight rolled away.

"What's wrong?" Edgar approached. "What happened?"

Abby shivered staring at the apparition. She pointed. "Emily's right there," her voice shaking barely audible.

"I don't see anything," Edgar said glancing back.

"She's under the boathouse." Abby blinked, hoping the vision in front of her would go away.

Edgar stood at the edge of the dock and dove into the pond. As he disappeared under the water the apparition fell through the floor, returning to the mortal remains to which she was bound.

Abby sat shivering as death visited her again. Her eyes were wide, and she was fighting the instinct to retreat into her own mind. Her breath came short. There wasn't enough air in the boat house. She felt the walls closing in, and knew she needed to calm down, but the panic was too strong.

A hand rose up from the water just in front of her. Abby jumped backward. The appendage placed a long, heavy stick on the dock, before disappearing back into the water. Abby's curiosity and instinct took over. She looked closer, and fought down the gorge as it rose in her throat. She was looking at a human femur bone.

The hand and head rose again from the water. Clearer now, she saw it was Edgar. He placed a largely intact pelvic bone on the wooden planks next to her, and dove again. Over and over he submerged and continued pulling bones from their watery grave. Abby just watched in horror. Finally, slowly, he climbed out of the water and placed a human skull on the dock between them.

Abby looked at the remains of Emily Wright, displayed like the grizzly crime scene they were. Edgar was sitting next to the macabre pile of bones his hands clenched in fists. She could hear him grunting in frustration as he fought to stay in control of himself. His face was red with rage, and she could see the grief tearing him apart.

Abby knew the moment he was having. She had been there. One year ago, she had been exactly where he is… the moment when all hope was lost, and the finality of death destroyed a piece of your soul forever.

Lights from outside lit up the interior of the boathouse. Abby turned towards the open door. In the distance she could see the lights of a vehicle approaching. *Benjamin?* she thought. *How would he know I'm here?*

Edgar stood alert. Abby felt so weak and drained. She crawled to the edge of the dock, and used one of the posts to pull herself to her feet. She stood that way, leaning on the pillion catching her breath while she waited.

Two car doors opened and shut. She saw Benjamin rush towards her in the darkness. A wave of relief washed over her. She knew she had told him not to, but she was glad they came. After a night of deathly visions and apparitions, Abby wanted nothing more than to hold her boyfriend. She began walking towards Benjamin each step a little less shaky, until she was running. She flew into his arms, barely containing her tears. She didn't care if he was angry, even furious, she needed his warmth just then.

"What the bloody hell happened here?" Benjamin demanded trying to calm Abby down.

Josephine stepped into view. Abby's heart sank. "Josephine! No!" she shouted. "You can't be here! You have to leave!"

"What?" Benjamin questioned. "Abby, calm down. What's happening?"

No! No! No! Abby screamed over and over in her mind. "My vision! Josephine... Edgar!" Benjamin looked confused, then scared as her words sunk in.

"We need to deal with this Benjamin," Josephine warned.

"But, Josephine-" Benjamin said, fear causing him to shake. "Something happened. Let me take care of Abby. Then we can... take care of this."

Benjamin escorted Abby to the car and put her in the passenger seat. "I'll be right back, we're going to see what's happened."

"No!" Abby panicked. "Something isn't right, Benjamin, don't let Josephine go in there!"

"Benjamin," Josephine barked. "This has gone too far. Fix this... Now!" There was a cold tone to Josephine's voice Abby had never heard before.

"I know," he murmured, looking at the boathouse.

"What do you mean?" Abby asked as she stood up. She was confused and shaking. "Benjamin please!"

Benjamin seemed distant and frustrated. "Abby," he said, barely able to speak her name. "I didn't want you to find out like this."

"It was only a matter of time Benjamin," Josephine interrupted. "She has the Sight. She would have figured it out sooner or later."

Abby looked at Josephine confused. "Wait. What are you saying?" Abby asked, she could feel an overwhelming dread lurking in her soul.

"Josephine, now is not the time," Benjamin argued. "I need to get her away from here."

"No! You will do as I say! There is too much at stake. You can't throw everything away, not now," Josephine insisted.

Abby looked at Benjamin, her lip quivered. Her body was shaking. "What is she talking about Benjamin?" Her voice rattled. Benjamin turned his head away; he couldn't look her in the eyes. Abby's heart started pounding.

"Tell her Benjamin," Josephine insisted her voice was mocking. "Tell your precious little Kane whelp all your family's secrets."

"It wasn't supposed to happen like this!" Benjamin yelled at Josephine. "I was supposed to have more time to bring her around."

"You were. And then we got sloppy. Deal with her, or I will." Josephine's eyes narrowed on Abby.

Abby choked on her own words. Her mouth tried to form them, but nothing came. Benjamin took her head in his hands and pulled her close.

Looking her in the eye. "I love you, Abigail Kane. You have to believe that," Benjamin said. "I have a way to keep you safe. From the Thanos, Edgar, everyone. Do you hear me, Abby? I can protect you."

Abby trembled, her mind running a mile a minute, the dread pulsating from her heart with every beat.

"Josephine can…" he said, excitement creeping into his voice. "It's the ritual. The one Vincent Hodge supposedly created over a century ago. The Picture of Dorian Gray, remember? She knows how to cast it!"

"But… how?" Abby asked looking from Benjamin to Josephine. "What are you talking about? What does that have to do with… with the boathouse?"

"It works, Abby! Do you understand? We can save you!" Benjamin pleaded.

Abby trembled a tear running down her cheek. She shook her head. "We can keep you safe," he continued. "You will always be safe from the Thanos, your Grandmother, from everything, and we can be together. Forever," Benjamin said. Tears streamed down his cheeks matching her own. His eyes were pleading, begging Abby to understand. "Abby, Please! She's willing to do a portrait for both of us."

"She…" Confusion overwhelmed Abby. What was he telling her? This made no sense! "But the Picture of Dorian Gray is just a novel!" she uttered her voice riddled with uncertainty.

"That stupid, fucking book!" Josephine snarled. "That ridiculous author knew nothing! Vincent was a fool. He couldn't incant his way through a basic ward. Though," she added thoughtfully, "Some of the book was right…" Josephine said raising an eyebrow. She began circling Abby like a predator circling its prey. "A portrait that ages instead of the witch. It was a magnificent spell; a thing of beauty." Her admiration and pride were palpable. Abby could feel her stomach turn. "It was the right plot, but he was wrong about the protagonist. Vincent Hodge could never have created a spell so masterful. If he had two hundred years to work it out, he would have failed." She laughed again, a maniacal edge to her voice. There was a wild look in her eye as she reveled in her private joke.

Abby's mind was racing. This was insane! What was she saying? That Vincent Hodge was… what? She knew the Hodge coven had secrets, and… and… blood magic. Her grandmother's words came back to her. Abby felt sick.

"Abby," Benjamin drew her attention back. "Do you understand? We can be together. You can be safe. Just let us cast the spell."

Safe? She could stop running from the Thanos. Her family could stop worrying about her. She would be free, she would be with Benjamin. He smiled warmly at her. "Come now, Benjamin, tell your lover the truth. We don't have time for dithering," Josephine warned.

Abby looked at him, confused. Benjamin looked down at their entwined hands. "There's one catch," Benjamin paused; a pained look in his eyes caused him to look away. "The… the ritual requires the life of a living person."

The ritual. The portrait. Josephine. Blood magic. Her blood turned to ice as the truth of what he was saying sunk in. "Emily," escaped Abby's lips as she shivered and stared into Benjamin's eyes. She was trying to absorb what he was telling her. "Is that why Emily is dead?" she asked. "Did she… did your sister…"

Josephine laughed again. "Sister? Ha! She still doesn't see it, does she? Are you sure this is the woman you want to spend eternity with, Benjamin? She seems a little slow." The cruelty in Josephine's voice made Abby want to hide. Something was very wrong. She wasn't the friend Abby had come to know in the last year.

"It's just one more person, and then we can be together forever," Benjamin stated still trying to comfort her. "Please Abby. We found something amazing."

Abby looked at him as though he were speaking a language she couldn't understand. "What?" she asked again, her brain in a fog of confusion.

"It's Edgar," Benjamin said. "Edgar is the key."

Josephine laughed again. "A cambion's blood has such unique powers. I should have seen it earlier."

She wanted to scream, but the Sight had taken too much from her. She was still in a daze, and this truth they were presenting, left her reeling. She tried to form words and nothing, but incoherent sounds escaped.

"I think she's going into shock," Benjamin said buckling her into the car seat as she sat stunned.

"We still need to deal with the demonspawn!" Josephine said motioning towards the boathouse.

"I'll be back Abby, in just a minute," Benjamin said trying to reassure her. Abby tried to shake her head no, but felt paralyzed. Josephine and Benjamin began approaching the boathouse and became little more than moving shadows in the night.

Abby fought internally to reconnect with herself. Her mind flooded with too many horrible thoughts to be present in her own body. She fought through the grief of her parent's death. She fought through the realization the man she loved was so removed from humanity he was beginning to lose his own. She fought through the tax her powers took from her body. She fought through her visions that paralyzed her with fear.

The world came into focus.

"Josephine…" she whispered. "Edgar! No, No, No!"

She unbuckled the seat belt and scrambled out of the car. She contemplated running for help, to contact the police, but she knew it would be futile. Benjamin and Josephine would manipulate them with their powers. If she was right about what Josephine was, she would only get more innocent people killed. At the promise of immortality, they would no doubt kill to maintain their freedom. And the secrets were too dear for them. They had to stop and cover their tracks. *Cover their tracks...* Abby thought. *Emily was Josephine's friend. Did she uncover the secret? Is that why they... they killed her?*

"No!" Abby said. She pulled herself from the car. She had to protect Edgar from whatever fate they had in store for him. Cambion or not, she needed to save him. She quickly made her way towards the boathouse. Abby knew what a witch could do. If they were going to kill him it wouldn't take long.

She flung the door open. Edgar was yelling at Josephine and Benjamin. Benjamin turned to Abby as she entered.

"Abby get back in the car!" Benjamin shouted. "I don't want you to see this."

Abby's anger gave her strength. "I thought you wanted me to kill for you. Maybe I should be here, so you can show me how." She flung her words like an accusation. Benjamin's eyes were full of regret.

"Stay out of this, witchling!" Josephine's icy gaze locked onto her.

"You're not going to get away with this," Edgar growled through his teeth like a wild animal. He was seething his chest barreled with each breath. His eyes were flaming orbs.

Josephine leaned in quietly, staring Edgar in the face. "I have gotten away with everything. You think I'm afraid of you?" she mocked. "I'm going to drain you of your blood and use it in a ritual. Then my protégé here and I will have nothing to fear, ever again."

Josephine raised her right hand towards the boats stacked against the wall and suddenly they flew by unseen forces towards Edgar knocking him to the ground.

"You're mad!" Abby shouted. "Josephine look at what you're doing!"

"You silly little girl, you have mistaken brilliance for madness. I'm not mad, I'm tired. Tired of living in the shadows and having my family keep my secrets. When I'm done here, the world will know the genius of the Hodge witches." Josephine said, a wild look filled her eyes.

"We will know what?" Abby questioned. She took a steadying breath, willing her courage to see her through this. "Know that you have been hiding behind the Hodge name since your secrets were first published? You're the one that created this spell, aren't you?"

Josephine smiled. "Clever little witch, finally figured that one out."

Edgar stared. "But that would make her…"

"Over a hundred years old? Yes," Josephine said with a satisfied smile. "I look pretty good for my age, though, don't I?" She offered a menacing grin. "Oh, I studied with the finest Necromancers in the world. It took me years to work out the proper incantations for that ritual. And who gets the credit? My lack-wit older brother."

"Vincent…" Abby allowed the name to spill from her lips.

Josephine glared at her. "Yes. Vincent. The heir to the Hodge coven, and therefore the only witch strong enough to create it. Bah! He was an idiot!" She looked at Benjamin, a fond expression touching her face. "With Benjamin's power at my side I will bring the Hodge coven back to its former glory." She turned to Abby. "Of course, he had hoped that you would join us. With your ability with the Sight emerging, I almost started to see the worth of it."

"It's not too late!" Benjamin said. "Abby, join us, and I can protect you. You'll be safe!"

Silence echoed through the boathouse. What could Abby say. Josephine was right, with her skill and experience along with Benjamin's power, and Abby's Sight they would be unstoppable. She looked at Edgar, the pile of bones lying at his feet. She was shaking all over. This was too much, too fast. She couldn't just let them kill Edgar.

Josephine broke the silence. "Enough! I'm done talking about this. Benjamin, kill him!"

CHAPTER TWENTY EIGHT

Benjamin took a step forward, drawing on his powers.

"No!" Abby pleaded.

"I don't think so," Edgar growled lunging forward tackling Benjamin to the ground before he could get a spell off. He lifted his fist ready to pummel Benjamin.

Josephine raised her hand and shouted, "Luvius Terronus!" Edgar was flung off Benjamin before he could strike and crashed against the side of the boathouse. Wood splintered and broke leaving an indention in the wall.

Edgar scrambled to his feet, miraculously unphased by the impact. His attention turned to Josephine. She again raised her hand ready to unleash a spell. Without thought or consideration, Abby rushed forward, made a fist with her right hand and pulled back. Josephine looked at her confused as Abby's fist made impact with Josephine's cheek. Her former friend crumbled to the ground and Abby bent over holding her fist in pain.

Josephine was clearly dazed, surprised by Abby's show of strength. "Abby get out of here!" Benjamin yelled, clearly worried Josephine would rise to exact her revenge.

"You treacherous little bitch!" Josephine roared as she pulled herself off the wooden floor.

Edgar lunged towards Josephine just as she came to her feet and grabbed her shirt in his fist. He threw her in the direction of Benjamin, who dodged. Josephine crashed against one of the dock pylons and slumped onto the wooden planks.

"Vinitori Totalis!" Benjamin yelled. Red crackling energy formed in his hand. He pointed at Edgar, the red energy shot like a bolt of lightning towards the enormous young man to Abby's right. She stepped in front of Edgar, her arms crossed in front of her as she did her best to deflect Benjamin's spell.

A sharp agonizing burning sensation radiated from Abby's left shoulder. Though her attempt to deflect the spell had an ablative affect, it was not strong enough to completely block Benjamin's magic. Abby let out an involuntary whimper as the pain radiated throughout her body. She fell to her knees, the pain sapping her of her strength.

"NO!" Benjamin cried out. He began to run forward but Edgar put himself between them, bringing Benjamin to a full halt. "Get out of the way!" he yelled.

Edgar cracked his knuckles and raised an eyebrow. He moved in a blur, his speed was so great that before Abby could make out what happened, Benjamin was flying through the air. He landed on his back, ten feet down the dock. He gasped for air, his face bloodied.

Abby pulled herself off the floor, doing her best to blind herself to the pain radiating from her shoulder. Suddenly, a force pushed her backward. She felt herself thrown into a stack of fiberglass racing crafts. Her body was screaming in agony as she crumbled to the ground. Catching her breath, Abby looked up to see Josephine standing over her. A menacing smile curled at the edge of the other girl's lips.

Josephine formed a hex symbol with the fingers of her left hand, "Aolon-!" Her spell was cut short as Edgar slammed into her knocking her against the wall. Josephine let out a moan as she leaned breathlessly against the wall.

Benjamin began crawling towards Abby, blood covering his face. Before he could reach her, Edgar reached down and offered Abby a hand up. She accepted, and he pulled her to her feet effortlessly.

"Get out of here," Edgar growled. "You don't want to be here for what's going to happen next."

"Let go of her!" Benjamin yelled coming to his feet. There was a wild look in his eye, his chest barreled, seething in fury. "Incantius Boninium!" he yelled.

Edgar flew against the wall, pinned by his wrists and ankles with mystical bindings. The young man fought against the magical energies holding him in place.

Josephine pulled herself from the floor, laughing maniacally. Any semblance of civility or sanity had taken leave from the woman, Abby once considered a friend. "It's over for you now," she said glaring at Edgar. She then turned to Abby, a murderous grin crept across her face. "We'll deal with you later," she added, before turning her attention back to Edgar.

Abby pulled herself from the ground and leaned against the wall, trying to catch her breath. The pain was nearly blinding. She whimpered as she pulled her coat off to reveal a terrible burn on her shoulder where Benjamin's spell struck her. She looked over to see Benjamin and Josephine positioning to finish Edgar off.

"I'll collect the knife and the receptacle I prepared for his blood," Josephine said and headed through the door.

Abby waited a moment for Josephine to leave. "Benjamin stop," she pleaded. "This isn't who you are. She wants you to become a monster just like she is!"

Benjamin winced. Abby could see the conflict in his eyes. Just then Edgar pulled his wrists free of the spell. A panic crept across Benjamin's face as he witnessed his spell being broken. The young lumbering man landed gracefully on his feet and glared at Benjamin. He reached out and shoved him aside and took off after Josephine.

Abby rushed to Benjamin's side. "Please stop," she pleaded.

Benjamin looked at her with uncertainty. He then scrambled to his feet and rushed out the door. Abby could feel her heart breaking with every step he took. She pulled herself up and gave chase.

Josephine was standing at the back of the SUV, when she noticed Edgar coming after her. She pulled a canister from her bag filled with a white powder resembling flour. She quickly took the top off and grabbed a handful. As Edgar came barreling towards her she blew the contents of her hand into his face. He stopped and batted his eyes for a moment and remained frozen as though he were petrified.

Benjamin caught up to Josephine and pulled a wicked looking knife from the trunk along with a strange looking copper bowl. It had what looked like Norse runes engraved around the lip. Josephine approached Edgar with the knife. He stood, unmoving. She watched carefully as though she didn't trust her own spell. She then slid the knife deep into Edgar's flesh. Benjamin rushed forward with the bowl and held it under the wound. Josephine then pulled the knife out and blood gushed into the bowl as Edgar stood helpless, frozen by some blasphemous spell.

Abby ran towards them, "Stafius Bombardus!" she yelled pointing her finger at Benjamin. The bowl flew out of Benjamin's hand and landed yards away disappearing in the tall grass.

"You've ruined our bloodletting, little bitch!" Josephine yelled, with fury in her eyes. She extended her hand and focused on the large SUV. Suddenly the enormous vehicle flew towards Abby.

She threw herself on the ground the vehicle flew over her and crashed mere feet away. Abby began to roll as the vehicle burst into flames.

"Abby!" she heard Benjamin yell.

"Stay away from me!" Abby screamed, halting Benjamin as he approached. She pulled herself up and saw Josephine standing behind Benjamin with an enormous grin on her face.

"It's time to quit playing games Benjamin," Josephine snarled. "She's a liability. Abby isn't going to come around. You chose poorly and it's time to fix this. I'll deal with the demonspawn and you deal with your little," she sneered, "mistake."

Abby looked at Benjamin as she stood trembling. Then she saw something out of the corner of her eye. Edgar managed to move his arm slightly. Then several of his fingers. Josephine could see her spell was breaking and reached for the canister she had set on the ground. Just as she opened the lid and took a handful of powder in her hand, Edgar's fist made contact with her face. Josephine flew six feet into the air and landed on the ground.

"No!" Benjamin yelled rushing towards his deranged mentor.

"Are you alright?" Edgar asked as he approached Abby. She nodded as she watched Benjamin pull Josephine to her feet.

"They're retreating back to the boathouse," Abby observed as they hobbled away.

"I'm going to finish this," Edgar said. After making certain Abby was alright, he gave pursuit just as Josephine and Benjamin retreated into the small structure.

Abby gave herself a moment to catch her breath. No matter how much air she took in it never seemed enough. Her heart was racing, and she did her best to keep herself from falling apart. Her thoughts were broken by the sounds of shouting inside the boathouse. Abby pushed herself, and even though her body had nothing more to give she ran towards the floating building. A sense of fear and dread filled her thoughts as she approached the doorway. As she entered Abby saw Edgar on the concrete floor.

Benjamin made a crushing motion with his fist and the fiberglass racing shells burst into a million splinters and shards of wood. He then raised his other hand and the splinters began flying around Edgar. The young man stood in the eye of a deadly cyclone.

Edgar was trapped. Abby moved towards the dock and gazed into the water. She raised her hands and clapped them together, then made a push away motion and started concentrating. The water beneath the dock began to recede, revealing the mulch and silt beneath. The water continued to move back until it reached the end of the dock. Abby then released her concentration. She turned and yelled, "Stop!" The other three turned towards Abby, their faces contorted into a look of surprise as a large wave raced towards the boathouse directly behind her.

The splinters of wood fell to the ground as Benjamin lost his concentration. Edgar lunged towards Josephine who was taken completely by surprise and bashed her against the wall. He then picked up a wooden paddle and Abby saw her vision come to pass as he brought the paddle down crushing Josephine's skull.

The wave consumed Abby, as she allowed herself to fall into the water. Benjamin clung to one of the rails used to stack the boats as Edgar pummeled Josephine with his fists. The water slammed into Benjamin, and forcefully pulled him from the railing and into the wave, overtaking the boathouse. Edgar and Josephine were swept up in the wave and as the water receded back into the pond, everyone was pulled into the deep murky waters by the tow.

Abby could hear Benjamin calling out from across the water. She crouched below the tall grass, deciding her next move. She couldn't stay. She knew it was too late to go back. Her heart was breaking as she put distance between herself and the pond. She ran as much as she could, making her way towards the house she once shared with Benjamin Hodge.

Get out, she thought. I need to get out of here. She grabbed her purse and collected what important documents she could from her office safe, including her passport. I need help, she thought. Uncle Sebastian! She reached for her phone to call her uncle and Ms. Grace. It dripped onto her floor as the water from the lake drained out of it.

Abby searched for the keys to her uncle's rental car, and found them lying on the counter. She grabbed them and rushed to the car in the driveway. Her hands were trembling so badly she could barely manage the door. She stopped for a moment and took a deep breath. She hopped in and drove as quickly as she could back to Calder House.

She set herself towards the school. Abby watched the road carefully. She couldn't be certain Benjamin might be watching the main roads looking for any sign of her. She pulled into the private drive her body shivering. Eventually she emerged into a small grove. There it was, Calder House. The home of Ms. Grace. Her mentor and her uncle were there. Safety!

Abby got out of the car and broke out into a run. She burst through the front door, collapsing into a wet heap on the floor.

"Abby?!" Sebastian asked, shock and worry tenting his voice. "What's going on?"

Abby looked at Ms. Grace, and stopped. Wait… she thought. What if she's part of this? Benjamin has been her apprentice for a long time… If Josephine could get to Benjamin, who was to say Ms. Grace wasn't a part of it too.

"Did you know?" Abby accused looking Ms. Grace in the eye. The middle-aged woman seemed confused and taken aback.

"What are you talking about?" Ms. Grace questioned. "Abby…?" The older woman was visibly confused.

"Did you know about Josephine? Do you know who Josephine really is?" Abby asked weakly, tears running down her face. Sebastian rushed towards her and sat her on the couch.

"You're injured," Sebastian observed pushing her long-wet hair aside for a better look.

Ms. Grace approached cautiously. "I don't understand," she said shaking her head. "Are you alright?" She looked concerned. Abby's suspicions were beginning to melt away, but she had to be certain.

"Did you know Josephine… murdered Emily?" Abby whimpered.

Ms. Grace recoiled in shock. "What is going on here?" Sebastian said trying to comfort Abby who trembled in his arms.

Ms. Grace shook her head. "It can't be… Josephine is a kind polite young woman… why would she kill Miss Wright?" Valerie questioned in shock as she sat cautiously in a chair. She was silent for a few moments and looked at Abby a tear breaking through the older woman's stoic resolve. "Are you certain?"

"She admitted it just before she tried to kill Edgar," Abby said, "and me." She watched as Ms. Grace buried her face in her hands. It was clear she was in shock. She didn't know, Abby realized. She was embarrassed by how relieved she was. The release of that weight being lifted, nearly brought her to tears. She liked Ms. Grace, and she had precious few allies right now.

"Where is Benjamin? Does he know what his sister did?" Sebastian asked cautiously as he looked over the terrible burn on Abby's shoulder.

Abby let out a horse laugh, that was anything but mirthful. "She's not his sister," she said bitterly.

"What?" Both of the others asked.

Abby looked at Sebastian. "She's… Josephine is the younger sister of Vincent Hodge. She's the one who created the spell."

"The portrait…" Ms. Grace began, her face contorting as the reality of the horror sank in.

"He knew." Abby said. "Benjamin, he helped her cover everything up." Abby whimpered as a new torrent of tears ran down her cheeks. Sebastian pulled her into his arms.

"Abby, it's alright. You're safe here with us."

Slowly the tears subsided, eventually giving way to deep sighs as she got her breathing under control.

"Tell us what happened." Sebastian urged.

Abby took a deep breath, and explained about Emily, and the visions she had been having since she moved into dorms last Fall. "They came back from their hunting trip early." She finished. "They were going to kill Edgar, but I guess I wasn't supposed to know that… yet." She fought down the bile that threatened to rise at the thought of Josephine's plan. "They wanted to use his demonic blood to make the spell stronger somehow."

"The blood of a cambion…" Ms. Grace whispered. "Of course. This is all my fault. Josephine knew nothing of cambions when she came here. I should have known she was far too interested in demonology…"

"It's not your fault, Ms. Grace. I'm the one who realized what Edgar was. When they came back for him… I tried to stop them. Edgar, he— he killed Josephine. Just like in my vision."

"Oh, Abby!" Sebastian wrapped his arms tighter around her as the torrent of tears began anew.

When they subsided again, Abby continued. "I fought them. I don't know what happened after I got away. They could all be dead." I might have killed Edgar and... and Benjamin, she thought.

Ms. Grace gasped looking away, biting her lip. "How could all of this happen right under my nose? I was so completely unaware of all of this. How can this be?" she questioned herself.

"They murdered to keep their secrets," Sebastian said. "They kept things hidden for years, centuries. There's no way either of you could have known."

Abby took a deep breath, wiping away the remaining tears. A heavy silence fell over the room as everyone did their best to reconcile themselves to the truth.

"We're getting you out of here tonight," Sebastian said.

"What about my things? My friends?" Abby questioned with uncertainty.

"They are just things Abby, they can be replaced. As for your friends..." Sebastian looked to Ms. Grace. "Valerie? Could we have Nina, Sarah and Warren brought here so Abby can say goodbye?"

"They should know... They should know the truth," Abby said. "Emily was their friend. And... they might be in danger if Benjamin thinks I told them."

Ms. Grace was still in shock. She stared at Abby for a brief moment and shook her head. "I will go and collect them while you pack. They will be safest here," she said as she stood and excused herself.

Abby sat in silence, she was still doing her best to pull herself from the daze of everything that had happened. Her world had been turned upside down. Again. From the embers of her old life she began building a new one, only to find it was crumbling all around her.

Am I cursed? Abby wondered. Is this what life is? One catastrophe after another? Am I destined to lose everything and everyone I care about? She could feel a cold chill setting in her bones as these and many other thoughts rattled around in her head.

She felt herself shutting down. The shock was seeping into her body, just as it had the night she had found her parents. Everything was changing again. Was she going to disappear again, too? What if she couldn't find her way back this time? Over the last year, she had learned how to open up; how to be happy again. She had good friends to help her. Nina and Sarah. Warren. Benjamin...

Sebastian pulled her close and held her. It was almost as if he could tell what was running through her mind. Abby could feel the treacherous emotional sea of thoughts beginning to quiet as she felt his loving arms around her. He looked her in the eye with a warm smile.

"Things aren't always going to be this difficult," Sebastian whispered, softly kissing her head. "We'll get through this together. That's what family does."

Abby sighed and made her way upstairs. She looked around the small room, and mechanically sort through the remains of her life. She collected her small overnight bag, and the small suitcase she had left here while she was packing up her house. This is it, everything I own now, Abby thought. Vivian would be shocked to see the state of my wardrobe, she thought sardonically. Her uncle was right, everything back at the house were just things. "Things can be replaced. I can do without everything I built here," Abby whispered under her breath.,"but can I leave the memories behind too?"

She sat on the bed and placed her head in her hands. She didn't think. She couldn't think. After everything that had happened that evening, she had no energy left for thought. She just sat there, until a gentle voice at the door said, "Abby?"

She looked up to see her uncle looking at her affectionately.

"I am not looking forward to grandmother's 'I told you so' comments," Abby confessed as she considered returning home. She didn't have anywhere else to stay. She certainly wasn't going back to her old home. Grandmother was all she had in Seattle. She didn't want to burden any of the other family members. "She's going to be almost impossible to live with. Maybe I have it coming. Maybe she was able to see something I couldn't. I can't believe it got this bad."

"Oh, Abby, don't do this to yourself. Your grandmother is a bitter old woman, a high functioning alcoholic, and a control freak. You are a grown woman now, Abby, you don't need to listen to her."

She sighed. "I know that, but…"

She could hear the front door open and several people enter, cutting off her thought. She made her way down the stairs and saw Nina, Sarah, and Warren wearing their night clothes and looking terribly worried. All three of them rushed to Abby pulling her into an embrace.

"What's the matter?" Nina asked.

"Those horrible people didn't come back, did they?" Sarah questioned, the fear in her eyes formed as tears.

"Ms. Grace wouldn't tell us what is happening just that there was something important to discuss," Warren explained.

"Have a seat," Abby said, motioning to the living room. Her three friends took a seat and Abby sat across from them. Ms. Grace and Sebastian stood on either side of Abby, lending their support. Abby began to tell them everything that happened that evening, from Edgar bringing her Emily's locket, to her visions, and Josephine finding them at the boathouse. When she got to Benjamin's involvement, she hesitated.

She wished it wasn't true, but it was too real to pretend otherwise. She told them what they found under the dock.

"Emily's dead?" Nina asked not wanting to believe, large tears welling in her eyes.

"Shouldn't we call the police?" Sarah asked, fighting back a series of emotions.

"No," Abby stated. "Benj— They would just use magic to manipulate them. It would only put innocent people in danger," Abby explained, feeling as frustrated as her friends.

"Is there nothing we can do?" Warren asked.

"I'm not certain yet," Abby confessed. She didn't want to think about that right now. She was still reconciling herself with the truth.

"I can't believe Josephine murdered Emily," Sarah said as though she was just catching up with the conversation. Abby moved over to the couch next to Sarah and held her for a while.

"She was a different person, Sarah. I swear, that was not the Josephine we knew. She was mad; completely crazy. There was something so sinister and angry about her." Abby shivered.

"I just don't know how she did it. Kept her secret so long," Nina added.

"She fooled us all," Warren agreed.

"Yes, she fooled us all," Ms. Grace agreed, her thoughts a million miles away.

"We should get going," Sebastian said as he stared at the screen on his phone. "There's a flight back to Seattle in a few hours."

"Seattle?" Warren questioned looking to Abby.

"You're leaving? Already?" Sarah asked.

"The sooner the better. It's not safe for me here anymore. Benjamin… he doesn't know what happened to me. It's better he doesn't learn the truth too soon." And I couldn't bear to face him if he did, she thought.

"Oh Abby, take care of yourself, please?" Sarah said, tears in her eyes.

Abby nodded, the emotions choked her voice. She took a deep breath. "It's time for me to go home, for a while, at least. I'm hoping the three of you will come and visit me in Seattle during gap year."

"You can count on it," Warren assured

The school car pulled up to the curb and the driver stepped out to retrieve the luggage from the trunk.

Abby glanced out the window at the enormous airport. She remembered the day, nine months before when she first arrived. Now she was back again, returning home. Abby felt as uncertain about the world today as the day she arrived.

"I'll get everything settled at the counter if you want a few minutes alone with Valerie," Sebastian said excusing himself from the car and disappearing behind the glass doors.

"I wish this had been a better experience for you," Ms. Grace said regretfully. Abby could tell she felt guilty. She was blaming herself for not knowing. We all are, she thought. Even Abby felt the pangs of guilt, as if she should have known.

"I don't know how I can ever trust myself again," Abby said her voice cracked with emotion. She quickly pulled herself together before she was swept away with another emotional wave. They never seemed to stop. "I fell in love with a murderer," she whispered.

Ms. Grace sighed. "You must not lose faith in yourself. He purposely hid things from us. We can't be expected to see through every intrigue and deceit people use against us. He was good at it, and so was Josephine. There are good people in this world, just like yourself. You must believe it. I know you do, you have some very nice people in your very own family."

"It's true," Abby confessed. "I guess it will take some time to reconcile what I know with how I feel."

"Yes," Ms. Grace stated. "I must do the same." Abby smiled at her friend. She saw a warmth and kindness to Ms. Grace she noticed for the first time beneath the stern and reserved woman she had come to know.

"Thank you, Ms. Grace," Abby said giving the older woman a hug. This time Valerie didn't stiffen, she could feel the genuine affection shared between them. "I don't' know how I would have survived this last year without your help."

Ms. Grace allowed a subtle smile. "You are kind to say so, Miss Kane."

Abby hesitated. "What is it?" the older woman asked.

"There is one thing that's been bothering me." Ms. Grace looked intrigued and nodded for her to go on. "I've been thinking about Josephine, and her powers. How long she's been around, and… How did the Thanos know where to find me?" she asked.

Silence was her only answer.

Maybe it's better if I don't know. Abby thought. I'm not sure I would want to know, anyway. As soon as I leave here, it won't matter anymore.

"Ms. Kane, some things can only cause more hurt to think about too hard. Perhaps it's best not to dwell on the occurrences of this past year."

Abby smiled, forcing back the tears she felt at her mentors words. She reached beneath her shirt at the neckline and pulled the charm necklace Ms. Grace had loaned to her earlier in the school year.

"You are an incredibly strong woman, Miss Kane. You've been through more in the last year than most people could even endure," Ms. Grace stated accepting her amulet back.

"I haven't felt very strong," Abby admitted. "In fact, I feel like I've been completely useless this entire year."

"Strength isn't always about doing the right thing or being a hero, Miss Kane. Sometimes it's about surviving the most terrible things in life and not giving up hope," Ms. Grace said, perhaps the most animated Abby had ever seen her. She chuckled at the notable change in the older woman's reserved demeanor.

Valerie stepped out of the car with Abby as they waited for Sebastian to return. "Will you come and visit me in Seattle some time?" Abby asked.

"I would be delighted," Valerie said.

Sebastian emerged from the airport with boarding passes in his hand. He approached and put his arm around Abby. "Alright, it's time to go."

Abby steeled herself. "I wish I knew where I was going to," She said. "I can't go home, and I definitely can't live with Vivian."

Sebastian chuckled, then looked thoughtful. "Why don't you stay with Rodger and me?" Sebastian suggested.

"Live in San Francisco?" She shook her head.

She told herself there were too many obstacles, but it was simple; Seattle was her home. She wanted to go home.

"Rodger and I bought a place on Bainbridge Island," Sebastian said. "We have been talking about it for a couple years. You know we've been considering adopting for a while. We also want to raise our kids around family. That's you," he added with a smile. "You are our family, you should be with us. I know it's what your mother would have wanted."

"I know you've mentioned it before. But… are you sure?" Abby asked cautiously. It was wonderful news, but she couldn't help but hold it cautiously. It felt like everything good was taken away.

"Of course, we were planning to move when this conflict is over, but it looks like you need us there now," Sebastian explained.

Abby couldn't help but smile. Sebastian had been her greatest support through everything that had happened in the last year. The idea that he and his husband would be moving near her home town was more than she could hope for. "I don't know what to say," Abby said with such relief. I won't be so alone after all.

"Say you'll come live with us, at least until you're ready to launch out on your own," Sebastian encouraged.

"Are you certain Rodger is alright with the idea?" Abby asked. The last thing she wanted was to cause strife.

"He thought of it before I did. He adores you Abby, almost as much as I do," Sebastian reassured her. Abby gave him a long and loving hug. "Come on, let's go home."

271

CHAPTER TWENTY NINE

Abby made her way down the stairs of her new home. The Seattle skyline framed Puget Sound from the enormous bay windows at the front of the house. Plush couches and chairs in dark browns and cream colored pillows filled the living room she passed through on her way into the kitchen.

A small round table sat in a small grove of windows with a view just as breathtaking as the one in the living room, only these windows overlooked trees. Uncle Rodger sat at the table reading his newspaper. He was a man in his early thirties with short blond hair and smart features. He wore a light grey business suit and a light blue tie. As Abby approached he set his newspaper aside and looked up at her with his stunning blue eyes and a bright smile.

"Good morning sleepy head," he said affectionately. "There's coffee and toast. Would you like something else?"

"No, I'm fine. The two of you have treated me like a queen this last week," she smiled. "Thank you for letting me stay with you. I'm not certain I could tolerate grandmother right now."

"You're welcome here," Rodger reassured affectionately as he passed the butter for the toast. "For as long as you like," he added.

"Where's Uncle Sebastian?" Abby asked as she poured herself a large cup of coffee.

"He's on the phone in his office. Sounds important whatever it is," Rodger said as he took a bite of his toast. "How did your phone call go in the middle of the night?"

"You heard? I'm sorry I didn't mean to disturb you," Abby apologized.

"You didn't disturb us. You know me, a night owl," Rodger smiled.

"It was my friend from England, Ms. Grace," Abby explained.

"Any updates on the fall out?" Rodger asked.

"Edgar Kincaid is alright. I'm not sure how, but I guess after everything that happened at the boathouse, he made his way to the train station and returned home," Abby said.

"And Benjamin?" Rodger asked cautiously.

Abby smiled weakly. It was still difficult to think about him. "The Hodge coven moved in and cleaned up the scene. Apparently, they swept away whatever evidence they could, and took Benjamin back with them. Ms. Grace hasn't heard a word from them since," she explained.

Rodger sighed and took a sip of his coffee. "I'm glad your friend is alright," he said. "If Benjamin knows what's good for him he'll leave you alone. One peep out of you and you could easily bring the wrath of many covens down on the Hodges," he said watching Abby's reaction closely.

Abby nodded, then sighed and took a large sip of coffee. "At least I'm managing to sleep better."

"How are the nightmares?" Rodger asked.

"Terrible," Abby admitted. "But they seemed to be less intense last night. I think they are getting better."

"It's going to take time. I know it sounds like such a cliché, but it really is true," Rodger said. "You're safe. That's what is important to remember. And you're surrounded with people who love you."

Abby sighed. "I know," she said. "It helps a lot being home. I wasn't certain what to expect when I came back, considering the circumstances around why I left. Now that I've been home a few days it makes everything that happened since I left, feel like a distant dream. I'm where I'm supposed to be."

"Yes, you are," Rodger agreed.

Sebastian entered the room with a dour look on his face. He was staring at the phone in his hand.

Something wrong?" Abby asked.

"I'm not certain," Sebastian said, taking a seat at the table and setting down his phone. "That was Vivian. She says the Thanos family is suing for peace. We're expected at a meeting of the Council of Overseers on Summer Solstice to settle terms."

Rodger seemed pleased. "Doesn't this mean it's over?" He sounded hopeful, however the look on Sebastian's face indicated to Abby there was something more.

"It could be," Sebastian said. "There is a hold on all hostilities until then."

"What else?" Abby asked. "There's something more isn't there?" she could see it in his expression.

"We've all been summoned. The entire coven," Sebastian said.

"What? Why?" Rodger asked, seemingly surprised by the response. "Usually the leaders meet with the council about things like this."

"Should we be worried?" Abby asked.

"I don't think so, but…" Sebastian didn't finish his sentence. He looked at Abby, a pained look on his face. "The entire Thanos coven will be there too," Sebastian added. "We'll be facing Atoro Thanos."

It was a sobering thought. She had only seen Atoro Thanos in the memories of Greggori. Soon the image would be flesh, and she would face the man himself. Abby sipped her coffee and watched as the light breeze stirred some rhododendron petals from a branch through the window.

"So, it's finally going to be over?" Abby asked, wondering if things would be different when justice was served, and she didn't have to hide for fear for her life.

"It sounds like it," Rodger said. "You won't be alone. We'll all face him together."

"I'm certain Vivian will demand his head on a platter," Sebastian said. He paused for a few moments. "I guess we should unpack some boxes. By the time we get completely settled in, we'll be off to Istanbul."

"Istanbul?" Abby questioned.

"That's where all of this is taking place," Sebastian explained.

"At the Hagia Sophia?" Rodger asked.

"The site where the Council of Overseers was formed nearly a thousand years ago," Sebastian confirmed.

"Sacred rituals in ancient places," Rodger mused. "The council is taking this matter very seriously, it seems."

"Good. It's time to end this pointless war."

Vivian Kane slinked into the large chamber filled with a gathering of witches from across the globe. She was wearing a white dress and dripping in jewels. Abby thought she was a bit overdone, but it was classic Vivian.

She followed her grandmother into the hall. Abby was dressed simply by comparison. Despite her grandmother's prompting, she refused to wear the Grimaldi diamond. Instead Abby wore a powder blue dress suit with a simple strand of pearls. She hoped her reserved presentation would perhaps temper her grandmother's gaudy flair.

Other members of the Kane Coven followed them into the large circular chamber. Abby was not as well acquainted with most of them outside the occasional familial visit. She wasn't entirely certain how she was related to all of them, but they made an impressive showing.

The chamber was immense, shaped like a bowl with a large circular center where three tables sat. Two were facing each other, while the third sat, elevated slightly above the others. The head table had seven witches seated in ostentatious chairs, and each draped in black robes with a symbol of their office at their throat.

One of the two lower tables was occupied by thirteen people, mostly men, with olive skin and black hair. Abby was hesitant to look too closely; she knew the man who killed her parents was among them. She would have to face him soon enough. The memory of his face was etched into her brain. The Sight made sure she couldn't forget him.

There was row after row of chairs circling the round platform. Each seat was occupied by unfamiliar faces watching as the Kane Coven made their way towards the empty table at the center. Abby could see people whispering and pointing, most of them were gesturing towards her grandmother who appeared to be savoring every moment as she walked imperiously towards the center.

As they came to their chairs Abby noticed an elderly woman with dark grey hair wearing white robes sitting at the center of the elevated table. She was surrounded by distinguished-looking representatives from some of the most respected witch families in the world. Abby took her seat and glanced at the opposite table. She saw him. Atoro Thanos! She focused on her breathing; she wasn't going to react. She wouldn't give him the satisfaction.

Abby felt a warm hand take her hand. She looked to her right and saw her grand-aunt, Fiona sitting to her right. The older reserved woman gave her a warm knowing smile. Despite her black funerary apparel, suggesting perpetual mourning, and her zealously reserved nature, her grandmother's sister was capable of incredible kindness. Abby returned the warm smile and appreciated the love and support offered with the simple gesture.

Her attention was drawn to the old woman in the white robes as she stood. "That's Cassandra Marsh, the Hierophant, a respectable witch from Boston," Vivian whispered in her ear. From what Abby could tell she was the leader of the Council of Overseers.

"I call to order this council to settle the dispute between the Thanos and the Kane Covens," Cassandra Marsh said, projecting her voice throughout the auditorium, motioning to both parties. "As we all know, the Thanos Coven is suing for peace. What are your terms?" The old woman looked to the Thanos Coven. Abby could see her grandmother smile wickedly, a part of her felt uneasy wondering what Vivian had up her sleeve.

An elderly man sitting near the center of the Thanos table stood. He was wearing a black suit and appeared to be in his eighties. Next to him was Atoro, who Abby noticed was staring directly at her. His eyes were black orbs as though they were hollow. His hair was long and slicked back with a goatee making him look like the devil himself. The old man stood, his hands on the table to steady his weary body. "We demand the return of our ancestral home, and the artifacts that were stolen form us!" he yelled in passable English.

"That's Cosimo Thanos," Vivian whispered. "He's only a figure head." Abby nodded and observed her grandmother who was obviously getting ready to perform.

The old woman turned and looked to Vivian. Abby could hear a slight rumble in the audience.

"Kane Coven, your response?"

Vivian Kane yawned, obviously unimpressed with Cosimo's display of dramatics. She stood as though it wasn't worth her time. "I really don't know why I bothered coming here today. It was a thirteen-hour flight, surely you could show some human decency and start this charade with your tail between your legs." Abby cringed, knowing her grandmother was only getting started. She could hear the audience rumble behind her.

"This is an outrage!" the Thanos patriarch yelled.

"Cosimo Thanos, it was you who came to sue for peace, and yet, you brought the Kane Coven demands?" Cassandra Marsh stated giving the Thanos patriarch a stern look. "If you wish to end this conflict you will need to make concessions, or by right the Kane family may continue to wage war against you," the elder woman stated as though she were scolding a child.

"Thank you, Mrs. Marsh, you are a wise woman indeed," Vivian stated, taking her seat once again.

"We offer no terms, other than to stop the conflict. We will accept our losses," Cosimo Thanos stated as he sat doing his best to salvage his dignity in the face of utter defeat."

Vivian reached out and took Abby's hand. Something was about to happen. Abby could feel it in her bones. "The war is over, my dear adversary. It was over weeks ago, you simply didn't know it," Vivian said, a wicked smile crawled across her face.

Silence echoed in the chamber, hidden below the ancient Hagia Sophia. It was as if the energy in the room were holding its breath.

"What do you mean," Cosimo demanded, slowly.

Abby watched as her grandmother stood still, watching Cosimo. Her audience was hooked, and like a seasoned performer, she kept all eyes on her. "Your extinction is now an undeniable certainty, my dear. I weaved a little curse... Well perhaps I will admit, it wasn't such a little curse after all," Vivian paused, allowing the tension to build. *She is in her element,* Abby thought. This was what her grandmother lived for.

"No Thanos will conceive or beget a child. Within a generation, you will no longer exist. I cursed your entire bloodline. This is the end of the Thanos Coven." The audience was in shock, as whispers and expressions of surprise spread across the room like a wave.

All thirteen members of the Thanos coven stood in outrage, slamming their fists on the table and yelling obscenities in Greek. Vivian sat down to watch the chaos and disorder her revelation created. Abby could tell it was the defining moment of her grandmother's life, she could see it in her eyes. She was savoring it like a fine wine, trying her best to look innocent when really her grandmother couldn't have been more pleased with herself.

The hall was abuzz with outrage, excitement and disbelief. "I call this chamber to order," Cassandra Marsh had to yell several times before the room became silenced. "This is disturbing news Mrs. Kane; will you lift the curse if concessions are made?"

The Thanos all leaned in, listening carefully as Vivian contemplated her options. "Perhaps," she said. The room fell completely silent. "I might… might consider lifting the curse if you meet my one single condition,' Abby could see Cosimo sink in his chair. She could tell he knew what was coming and he dreaded the ultimatum she was about to speak. "I want Atoro Thanos, the murderer of my son and daughter-in-law turned over to my coven for justice. This. Very. Moment."

The room erupted into sounds of shock and dismay. Sebastian took Abby's hand as the moment for justice was approaching. She could hear comments in the background and someone mentioning Atoro was Cosimo's only son.

"Order!" Cassandra Marsh yelled, "I'll have order!" The old woman appeared uncomfortable. Abby could tell the events transpiring had taken everyone off guard. "Cosimo Thanos, the Kane Coven has offered you the conditions of a truce, will you meet the terms?"

The elder patriarch turned to his coven and they spoke among themselves for a few moments. Atoro Thanos remained silent and stared at Abby, his eyes were unsettling, she couldn't help but notice the menacing grin on his face. He was a Necromancer, he had no fear of death.

Cosimo stood. His eyes were full of contained rage as he motioned to his son. Atoro stood and approached the center of the circle between the two tables. Atoro was even more menacing as he came closer. Cosimo joined him, and the two shared a few words. Atoro then turned and presented himself to Cassandra Marsh.

"Mrs. Kane are you satisfied this is Atoro Thanos?" the old witch in white asked officiously.

Vivian looked to Abby for confirmation. Abby nodded in the affirmative. "Yes, we are," Vivian said.

"Will you accept his surrender as fulfilling your stated conditions for a truce?" Cassandra Marsh asked, her imperious voice rang throughout the silent chamber.

Vivian paused allowing the tension to build; Abby was growing weary of the theatrics. "Yes… with one caveat," Vivian stood once again and started circling Atoro Thanos like a vulture. "The Kane Coven will not lift the curse on the Thanos." The audience quietly expressed their surprise as Cosimo slumped back in his chair.

"*However!* Each year on all hollows eve, when the shroud between our world and the next is at its weakest, we will perform a ritual that will suppress the curse for the coming year. Every year the Thanos Coven and their allies keep the peace, we will continue performing this ritual. If they break the truce, we will refrain and your fates will be sealed." Vivian spat the last words out as though they themselves were a curse.

Abby could see the pleasure in her grandmother's eyes. She had won. The victory felt hollow to Abby; her parents were still dead. It was a fact magic nor victory could change. All that was left was justice, and she supposed, revenge.

As the audience began to rumble with responses varying from outrage to admiration, Vivian sat in her chair and stared her ancient enemy in the eye.

"Miss Abigail Kane," Cassandra Marsh addressed Abby, who stood out of respect, not certain what to do. Her mind was racing a million miles a minute. Her nerves were on edge. "Please come forward."

Abby hesitantly approached the center, mere feet from the man who brutally murdered her parents.

"How do you wish to dispense justice upon Atoro Thanos?" The crowd rumbled as Abby realized the Council would place the sentencing of judgment in her hands. She looked to her grandmother who wore a pleased smile. *How did she orchestrate this?* she wondered.

Abby thought for a few brief moments. Even knowing the monster standing before her had killed her parents in the most brutal way possible, she had seen too much death. She knew firsthand how deep this cycle could go. She couldn't bring herself to kill him.

Abby turned and faced Atoro, and looked him squarely in the eye with every ounce of bravery she could rally. There were some places she didn't want to go, but she needed to see for herself. She turned her Sight on him, and looked at him in a way that few others could.

Abby allowed herself a brief moment to recover from the physical tax of using her Sight without preparation, and concentrated on evening her breath. She cleared her throat. He stared at her, emotionless. His eyes were empty, as though he were a soulless creature, and she fought to keep her resolve.

"You took two lives from us. Two people very much beloved by my family. They were more than just my parents. They were someone's children, siblings, cousins and friends. They never did a thing to you or your family. Their only crime was being the descendants of a bloodline you hate for reasons that predate the living memory of anyone in this room." Abby paused for a brief moment, holding on to her composure with every bit of strength she had.

The chamber was silent. Abby looked to the right of Atoro and saw a woman holding a child in the audience sitting directly behind the Thanos Coven. "Atoro Thanos... retrieve your son from the audience." Abby said her voice as cold as ice, she had to detach from herself to utter those words.

The Necromancer broke his steely glare, his face grimaced slightly. Abby knew his son was one of the few things he cared about in his world filled with death and decay.

"Justice is to be dispensed upon me! Not my son!" Atoro yelled through gritted teeth, his English barely discernible.

"So, it shall be. No harm will befall your son, I assure you," Abby stated remaining cold. It was the only way she would get through the ordeal. With great hesitation, Atoro approached the crowd and plucked the sleeping infant from his wife's arms. The woman was crying hysterically. Abby did her best to ignore the dramatic scene. She could feel herself shaking and concentrated on steadying herself. The murderer returned, his child in arm.

"Give him to me." Abby held out her arms. Atoro hesitated but complied.

"Now I take life from you." Abby said looking him in the eye.

She turned, slowly, tension building all around her. "Take solace in knowing your son will be cared for and deeply loved by our family. But know that he will never know your name or even that you exist." Abby held the infant in her arms and began walking away. She didn't return to the table, instead she began leaving the chamber. Abby glanced back and saw Atoro Thanos falling to his knees as Abby carried his son away.

Vivian stood; Abby could see the displeasure on her face. The audience erupted once again as cries from everywhere voiced every sentiment imaginable. Sebastian and Rodger quickly stood and followed their niece from the chamber as Cassandra Marsh tirelessly attempted to bring order back to the chamber.

Abby quickly exited and stepped into one of the antechambers allowing herself to have the panic attack she had been fighting off from the moment she entered the hall.

"Abby, I can't believe what just happened," Rodger said, sitting next to her trying to offer support.

"That wasn't what I expected," Sebastian stated, agreeing with his husband.

The sound of high heels on the stone floor approached swiftly. Fiona came around the corner. She had an uncertain look on her face. "What possessed you to do this?" Fiona asked, looking at the infant sleeping in Abby's arms, blithely unaware of the world around him.

Abby pulled herself together. "It was the only thing he cared about," she answered, starting to feel numb. "He's a necromancer, he has no fear of death. I wanted to punish him, and I wanted to save this child from being raised by that... monster."

"It's poetic enough, I suppose," Fiona said, raising an eyebrow.

"Abby what are you going to do with this child?" Rodger asked. Abby could tell he was concerned. Her justice had been impulsive, she had had no time to consider what she was doing.

"I certainly don't know what to do with him," Abby admitted, not knowing the first thing about infants or raising children.

"We'll take him," Sebastian stated looking to Rodger who nodded his head in agreement. "We've discussed adopting before, of course that is, if you don't want to raise him."

Abby smiled. "I can't imagine a better home for him," she said. "I turn eighteen in a month. I haven't even figured myself out, I couldn't possibly be responsible for this child." She looked down at the fragile boy wrapped in a blanket. She stood and handed the infant to Sebastian.

The moment was broken when Vivian burst into the room. It was more than apparent she was not pleased. "Well, I hope you're happy with yourself. The man who murdered your parents is alive and well."

"I don't know about well," Fiona said, giving Vivian a discerning look. "He did just lose his son."

Vivian glared at her sister and turned to Abby. "Your idea of justice is to hurt his feelings? He should be experiencing the slowest most painful death imaginable!"

"If that's what you wanted, you should have made certain the council called on you to dispense justice," Abby retorted with irritation.

"It was your opportunity, my darling, to rise to the occasion. I can't conceive of a good reason why you wouldn't have taken revenge upon the man who murdered your parents... my son," Vivian pleaded, motioning to each of them, "and your sister."

"I did the worst thing to him he could think of," Abby said. "He wasn't afraid of death. Living with this will stain his life just like losing my parents has stained mine. The Sight revealed his secrets to me, and now he will suffer. Death isn't always so terrible."

Vivian contemplated Abby's words, it was apparent she was softening to the idea, but only slightly. "What now darling?" Vivian questioned looking at the child with mild repulsion.

"Sebastian and Rodger have agreed to raise the child as their own," Abby stated. She could see her uncles already losing themselves in their role as parents.

"They'll be wonderful parents," Fiona added her support. Abby could tell she was trying to help ease Vivian's temper.

Abby took her first deep breath in months. She had no doubts about her decision. Sebastian and Rodger would make great parents, the Thanos threat was contained, and her parents, while not avenged, had received some measure of justice. She didn't know how long this peace would last, but she was grateful for the way things had played out.

Her thoughts strayed back to everything she'd been through in the last year. "Are you alright, Abigail?" Fiona asked, as Vivian fumed in the corner and Sebastian and Rodger cooed over their new son.

Abby looked to her elderly aunt, there was a kindness in her eyes. It was something the old woman rarely showed. Abby smiled reassuringly at her. "Yes, I'm fine. I was just thinking, there's still so little we know about the Sight and about what I can do with it. Despite everything, all my visions came true. Everything with Josephine, with Edgar and Emily, the Thanos…" she remembered all too-clearly the vile sensations of digging through Greggori's mind. "I would like to work with it more and grow my skills. I want to be prepared for whatever the future has in store for me."

She looked at her family gathered around her, and knew she was safe enough for now. "I just have a feeling that this isn't over yet."

COMING SOON
The exciting continuation of the House of Kane series.

CONVERSATIONS WITH THE DEAD

HOUSE OF KANE BOOK TWO

Philip M Jones

PUBLISHED BY FIRESONG ARTS
Changing the World, One Word at a Time
https://www.firesongarts.com/

PHILIP M JONES

Philip was born and raised in the Pacific Northwest, growing up in the shadow of Mt. St. Helens. He currently lives in Seattle, where he is a proud member of the LGBTQ community. In his free time he writes and sips tea and coffee while reading more than is typical of a 'normal' human being.

These books are a labor of love for him, and he hopes that you get as much enjoyment from reading them as he did from writing.

Look for House of Kane Book Two

CONVERSATIONS WITH THE DEAD
Coming soon!

Be sure to join Philip's Facebook page,
https://www.facebook.com/AuthorPhilipMJones/
for more information on upcoming books, release dates, and other fun things that Philip finds interesting.

Liked This Book?

Please leave a review!

Reviews help books gain the recognition they deserve. By leaving a review you are helping to ensure that many more books from this author can be written and published for you to enjoy!

Submit reviews to prteam@firesongarts.com
Or visit https://www.firesongarts.com/reviews

63615808R00163

Made in the USA
Middletown, DE
02 February 2018